"*Gordath Wood* is a strong first novel, full of real people, some very real horsemanship, and utterly convincing warcraft. It's a big story of overlapping worlds, with a plot as complex and twisting as the trails of Gordath Wood itself, a book as much for lovers of horses as lovers of fantasy."
—Toby Bishop, author of *Airs and Graces*

LOST

Lynn snaked the reins over Dungiven's neck and handed them to the man. She took half a step and realized what she had done.

"No!" she shouted.

It was too late. The man kicked Dungiven clumsily in the ribs. The horse threw up his head and trotted forward out of the clearing, the man bouncing in the saddle.

"Stop!" She lunged forward, but the man kicked again. The big horse bolted up the treacherous hillside, scrambling through leaves and rocks, sending an avalanche of debris down into the clearing. The horse made it safely to the top, and they disappeared over the top of the ridge until all she could hear was the sound of Dungiven crashing through the forest and her own sobs of rage . . .

Gordath Wood

Patrice Sarath

ACE BOOKS, NEW YORK

THE BERKLEY PUBLISHING GROUP
Published by the Penguin Group
Penguin Group (USA) Inc.
375 Hudson Street, New York, New York 10014, USA

Penguin Group (Canada), 90 Eglinton Avenue East, Suite 700, Toronto, Ontario M4P 2Y3, Canada
(a division of Pearson Penguin Canada Inc.)
Penguin Books Ltd., 80 Strand, London WC2R 0RL, England
Penguin Group Ireland, 25 St. Stephen's Green, Dublin 2, Ireland (a division of Penguin Books Ltd.)
Penguin Group (Australia), 250 Camberwell Road, Camberwell, Victoria 3124, Australia
(a division of Pearson Australia Group Pty. Ltd.)
Penguin Books India Pvt. Ltd., 11 Community Centre, Panchsheel Park, New Delhi—110 017, India
Penguin Group (NZ), 67 Apollo Drive, Rosedale, North Shore 0632, New Zealand
(a division of Pearson New Zealand Ltd.)
Penguin Books (South Africa) (Pty.) Ltd., 24 Sturdee Avenue, Rosebank, Johannesburg 2196,
South Africa

Penguin Books Ltd., Registered Offices: 80 Strand, London WC2R 0RL, England

This is a work of fiction. Names, characters, places, and incidents either are the product of the author's imagination or are used fictitiously, and any resemblance to actual persons, living or dead, business establishments, events, or locales is entirely coincidental. The publisher does not have any control over and does not assume any responsibility for author or third-party websites or their content.

GORDATH WOOD

An Ace Book / published by arrangement with the author

PRINTING HISTORY
Ace mass-market edition / July 2008

Copyright © 2008 by Patrice Sarath.
Cover art by Aleta Rafton.
Cover design by Annette Fiore DeFex.
Interior text design by Laura K. Corless.

ISBN: 978-0-441-01641-9

ACE
Ace Books are published by The Berkley Publishing Group,
a division of Penguin Group (USA) Inc.,
375 Hudson Street, New York, New York 10014.
ACE and the "A" design are trademarks belonging to Penguin Group (USA) Inc.

PRINTED IN THE UNITED STATES OF AMERICA

10 9 8 7 6 5 4 3 2 1

To Valerie
For the conversation, coffee, friendship, and laughs
This one's for you
1966–1993

Acknowledgments

For all that writing a book is a solitary endeavor, an author, especially a first-time author, has a lot of help. My thanks to my first readers of the Austin Slug Tribe and Cryptopolis, especially Sharon Casteel, Tom Konrad, Jane Hixon, Fred Stanton, Steve Wilson, Matthew Bey, and David Chang; also, Martin Owton, Gaie Sebold, and Lenora Rose Heikkinen. I also would like to thank Tom Van Dyke for information about modern weapons and gun laws, and for taking me out shooting—all errors on this subject are my own. Thanks to Ben Van Dyke and Kim and Aidan for your love and support. To my wonderful agent, Kae Tienstra, and my super editor, Susan Allison—thank you so much for your help and guidance. And finally, thanks to Cochise and Piper, Molly and Warlight, Windswept and Foxy, McKeever and Smokey, Reykur and Rauthsokkur, and all the other horses who were my first and best teachers.

One

At the Hunter's Chase van everyone gathered around Dungiven. The big gray horse fidgeted at the end of his reins, his black nostrils flaring and his tulip-shaped ears cocked with interest at the swirl of activity surrounding him. His saddle and bridle gleamed, and the dark blue yarn braided in his mane and tail set off the black and gray strands.

Lynn shrugged into her black jacket, all the while issuing commands.

"Gina, go find Mrs. Hunt at the owner's pavilion. Kate, is that the course map? Let me see—" Kate held it out, and Lynn scanned it while she drew on her boots. Nothing Dungiven couldn't handle, but she hadn't had time to walk the course. Dungiven's regular rider had just been carried out in the ambulance after a fall in another class. Nothing serious, a broken collarbone and a cracked rib, but it meant Hunter's Chase would have to scratch its entry in the Classic.

Not if I can help it, Lynn thought. She felt an unearthly quiver of excitement in her belly. Someone handed her a hairnet and bobby pins, and she stuck her dark hair up haphazardly and crammed her helmet on top, buckling the chin strap. Kate pinned the stock under her chin.

Dungiven snorted as if to laugh at Lynn's pretensions. Lynn was good, but she was Hunter's Chase's manager. She hadn't ridden a professional show-jumping course in years. The butterflies multiplied. *Stop that,* she scolded herself. "Time?" she said, and Kate turned her wrist to see her watch.

"Five minutes," Kate said. "Hold your chin up; I don't want to stick you." Lynn obeyed, Kate's knuckles brushing her throat.

Gina came running up awkwardly in her long boots.

"She says to scratch," she called out. "She doesn't want you to ride him—" She faltered to a halt. Lynn felt color flood her cheeks.

Because she doesn't think I'm good enough.

Kate's fingers stilled. Everyone looked at Gina, then at Lynn. Lynn opened her mouth and found she couldn't think of anything to say.

"Oh," she said finally. "Okay. Well. That's probably for the best." She stepped back and began undoing from the top down. She took off her hard hat and pulled off the hairnet and the bobby pins, letting her hair fall down to her shoulders. No one met her eyes; somehow that made it hurt worse, that they knew how keenly she felt the disappointment. "All right, strip him and get him ready for the van. He's done for the day."

Lynn went around to the cab of the big twelve-horse van and sat down on the running board to take off her boots. It was peaceful there. The late afternoon sun was warm against her face, and the loudspeaker was muted. She could feel muffled hoofbeats through the soles of her boots and let her heartbeat find its own cadence. The headache that had been threatening all afternoon throbbed with the same pulse. Lynn sighed and closed her eyes for a moment. She should have known Mrs. Hunt wouldn't let her ride.

When she opened them again, she squinted against the sun that gleamed off row after row of vans and trailers in the rough pasture. The outskirts of Gordath Wood inched forward into the grassy space, sending forth saplings and underbrush, but this close to cleared land the woods were sparse, unthreatening. Here and there the foliage gleamed red, heralding an early fall, though it was still only September. Gordath Wood always turned earlier than the rest of the woods in Westchester County, though. One of the strange forest's quirks, she thought.

As if to emphasize its eerie reputation, a swirl of movement deep in the wood caught her eye. For a moment the trees swayed amid their still brothers, and a handful of birds shot into the sky. Thunder rolled at the edge of her hearing, and she could have sworn that the van shook. The movement subsided, and Lynn shrugged, pulling at her boot.

Another noise interrupted her: Joe, the van driver. He leaned against the side of the van, arms folded across his T-shirt, his brown eyes quizzical.

"What?" she said in the face of his lengthening scrutiny.

"What did she say?"

She shrugged. "Nothing. Just to scratch."

Joe kept looking at her.

"What!" she snapped.

He said, "It's just—I ain't seen you that happy about horse shows for a long time." She laughed and shook her head, but the sound held very little humor.

"Yeah, well," she said, and tugged at her long black boot. "Look where it got me." He came over and knelt down in front of her, taking the boot by the heel and the ankle. He pulled it off with a smooth tug.

"Last I heard, it was still allowed," he said. He handed her the boot and held her gaze.

She knew that if she let him be kind to her, she would start to cry. She made a disparaging noise. "Thanks. I'll keep it in mind." She tugged at her other boot.

He stood, and she pretended to be absorbed in her struggle with her boot, all the while aware of him waiting and then walking away. When he was gone, she stopped pulling. The boots were smudged from fingerprints. If she had been allowed to ride out, Kate would have taken a rag and wiped down her boots once she was in the saddle. She and Dungiven would have gleamed in the late-afternoon sun like bright black and silver coins. Lynn sat for a moment longer on the running board, seeing the course in her mind's eye.

The parking lot was almost empty when the Hunter's Chase van was fully loaded. The last horse in was Dungiven, wrapped in a white shipping blanket with blue piping, the HC logo fluttering on the bottom corner. Lynn nodded at Gina, and the girl clucked to him and led him up the ramp.

Just then it felt as if the ground slid out from beneath her feet. Lynn caught herself against the trailer. Dungiven threw up his head. "What was that?" she said.

With a rising rumble that came straight out of the woods, the ground rolled violently. Horses whinnied, and the trailers and trucks swayed and shuddered. Lynn fell hard on her butt.

Dungiven scrambled backward off the unsteady ramp in a tangle of legs and blankets, lost his balance, and went down. Lynn's involuntary cry was lost in the bone-shaking tremor. Finally, finally, the quake tapered off and died.

Lynn scrambled to her feet and fell to one knee beside the big horse, fear seizing her heart. Dungiven stayed down, breathing hard, snorting with every breath. Joe squatted next to her. "Is he okay?"

"Don't know," Lynn said, her voice taut. She pointed with her chin. "Get behind his haunches and push."

At first Dungiven resisted, thrashing his head, and then finally he scrambled to his feet, his shipping gear askew. Lynn reached up and straightened his head bumper, looking him over. No scrapes, nothing but grass clinging to his shipping blanket.

"Whoa," she said under her breath. She handed the lead rope to Kate, who looked shocked and pale. Everyone was doing the same thing they were: checking on horses, making sure the expensive animals were okay. "Here. Trot him out for me. Gina, check on the horses in the van; make sure no one is down."

Kate trotted the big horse down a ways and back, his gait true and strong. Lynn's heart slowed. He looked undamaged.

Gina jumped out of the back of the van. "They're all okay, but a little tense," she reported. "I handed out carrots."

"Thanks," Lynn said. She still felt shaky. An earthquake in Westchester County? She didn't know that was even possible. "Okay, let's try this again."

She took the lead rope and began walking the horse up the ramp. Dungiven took a few steps and then in one move reversed direction and scrambled backward as if the earth were sliding under his feet again. Lynn was dragged along for several heart-stopping seconds before she found her footing again.

Out of the corner of her eye she saw Joe catch him on the other side of the halter and help bring the horse to a stop. They stared at each other; he looked pale under his tan. Lynn's pulse hammered in her head.

"Think it's the earthquake?" Joe said. He nodded at the van. "After all, he was right there when it happened."

"It must have been," Lynn said. "Let's give him a moment, then try again."

They waited in the quiet evening. Lynn breathed soft and slow, letting Dungiven pick up on her calm. After a moment, she nodded to Joe. She clucked to the big horse. He planted his forefeet, and then, when she insisted with firm hands and body language, Dungiven rose into the air on his hind legs. When he landed, his thudding hooves just missed her boots.

This time Joe stayed prudently back. "You okay?" he called.

"Think so," Lynn said with a tight little voice. She looked at the horse. "Your price tag just went down. You know that, don't you?"

Dungiven snorted, cocking his ears over her shoulder. She turned and saw Mrs. Hunt. Lynn took a deep breath and waited for her employer.

Mrs. Hunt was no horsewoman, but when she came to watch her horses win, she played the part. Today she wore a black hacking jacket and boots, a lovely chignon holding her dark brown hair in place. A gold pin nestled in the folds of the snow-white stock at her throat, and her breeches fit like a second skin. Her outfit was immaculate; *she* hadn't spent the day around sweaty horses, dusty rings, greasy hamburgers, and sticky lemonade.

"Is he all right?"

"Doesn't seem to be harmed, but I think Dr. Cotter should check him out. Are you all right?" Lynn added.

"I rely on you to make sure the horses are safe and sound, Lynn. Please see to it nothing like this happens again."

As if the earthquake was her fault. Lynn paused until she got herself under control.

Mrs. Hunt stood and waited, her lips pursed. Howard Fleming, owner of the Pennington Stables show grounds, came up behind them, putting his wide hands possessively on Mrs. Hunt's shoulders. A heavyset man in a ginger houndstooth jacket, his reddened face and bulbous nose rose from his collar as if they had misplaced his neck.

"You can always leave him here, Kathy," he joked. "I've been meaning to get my hands on that stud of yours for a year now. I'll just throw him in with a couple of my mares." He leered.

With no hint of annoyance on her face, Mrs. Hunt freed herself from his intrusive grip.

"That is quite kind of you, Howard," she said. "I'm sure Lynn will be able to bring him home."

Fleming frowned.

Lynn tried to look absorbed in straightening the horse's shipping blanket.

"Let me get one of my grooms to take care of this," he urged. He smiled at Lynn. "We'll have him taken care of in no time, Liz. A stallion is no horse for a girl to handle."

Lynn kept from rolling her eyes with pure effort.

"Thank you, again," Mrs. Hunt said firmly. "I'm sure we will manage just fine."

"The thing is," Lynn said, turning to Mrs. Hunt and wishing Fleming were somewhere else, "we need to get the rest of the horses home. They've been waiting on the van, and I don't like them being cooped up and stressed like that." She took a deep breath. "I could ride him home."

"What? That horse is worth a fortune! You can't be seriously thinking to *ride* him!" exploded Fleming.

"Lynn, it's light out here, but it's way dark already in the woods," said Gina. "I mean, are you sure?"

"It'll take me forty-five minutes, tops. We could be here all night. We've got to get the rest of the horses home. I mean, unless you want to leave him with Mr. Fleming's mares."

She held her breath at her own audacity and faced Mrs. Hunt square on, half expecting to be fired in the woman's next breath. And then she thought, *No. She's lucky I don't walk out right now.*

And on the heels of that thought, *She knows it, too.*

To her surprise, Mrs. Hunt didn't seem to be annoyed at Lynn's maneuver. Instead, she looked out toward the woods and patted a strand of hair back into place. She looked at Lynn and back at the woods.

"I don't think, that is—I'm not sure . . ." Her voice trailed off. Lynn was boggled. Mrs. Hunt—*flustered*? She didn't think she'd ever seen that.

"Oh come now, Kathy," Howard said. "Just say the word, and I'll have Geoff fix a box for him." He smiled indulgently. "We can drive down to the Continental for dinner. My treat."

Lynn felt a pang of sympathy for Mrs. Hunt. The woman looked trapped.

Ignoring Fleming's invitation, Mrs. Hunt said, "At night? Are you sure it's safe?"

"It's less than an hour, practically door-to-door. I'll bring a flashlight, and I won't jump anything. I promise."

Mrs. Hunt dutifully acknowledged the little joke with a polite smile, but still she hesitated. "Those stories . . ."

Lynn stared at her. The *stories*? The summer camp stories that said Gordath Wood was haunted? Was Mrs. Hunt serious? "Stories, yeah. The summer camp kids get a kick out of them . . ." She hastily improvised. "It's really not that far. I ride these trails twice a week or more with clients. I really think we should be getting the horses home."

"Yes, of course, the stories are nothing but stories. They're nothing."

Lynn waited while Mrs. Hunt tried to convince herself.

Finally Mrs. Hunt took a deep breath. "Very well. Ride him home. We will see you back at the barn. Howard, I believe I left my hat at the owner's pavilion when it collapsed."

As he escorted her off, remonstrating with her, Lynn let out a silent breath. She and Joe exchanged glances. *What have I gotten myself into?* She shook her head.

"Well," she said. "Let's tack him up."

While they got busy taking off Dungiven's shipping blanket and bandages, Lynn got the first aid kit from the van, fished out the aspirin bottle, and shook out two, thought a moment, then shook out one more. She swallowed them dry. They would have to do to stave off the migraine that had been threatening all day.

Lynn went around to the front of the van and slipped out of her hacking jacket, laying it across the passenger seat. The evening was growing chilly; she shrugged into her down vest and checked for her cell phone in the pocket. The reassuring display glowed at her.

Dungiven was ready. He turned to look at her with his ears pricked and gave a low whinny as she took the reins and flipped them over his head. Joe gave her a leg up, and she boosted lightly into the saddle, gathering her reins and settling her feet into the stirrups, trying to hold back the headache. Joe held her ankle for a moment.

"Listen—are you doing this because she didn't let you ride him in the Classic?"

She leaned down to adjust her stirrups and to whisper in his ear. "All I want is to get these horses home. Are you okay with that?"

He stepped back. "Fine by me, you pull a crazy stunt like this."

She immediately felt sorry. "Look—I'll see you in an hour, tops. Okay?"

He accepted it grudgingly. "All right. Go."

She took the helmet he handed her, strapped it on, and gathered the reins. Before she set off, he called out, "Hey."

She stopped and turned in the saddle. "What?"

"You're not going to have one of your damn horse show headaches tonight, are you?"

She felt herself smile, and he smiled in return. She stood in the stirrups and dug her apartment key out of the tiny front pocket in her breeches. She flipped it to him, and he caught it. "See you in an hour, Joe."

Darkness dropped almost as soon as they entered the woods. "Shoot," Lynn said under her breath. She had forgotten the flashlight. After the first quiver of uneasiness, though, the peace of the dark woods fell around her. Insects buzzed and twanged, and a breeze fanned her cheeks. The trail was a pale smudge in front of her, the footing solid and even. Dungiven's walk was strong and quick. He knew he was going home. They'd be at the barn soon, and she'd call the emergency vet out right away to make sure there were no hidden strains or bruises from his fall.

Her headache faded a bit, and she smiled again, thinking of her implicit promise to Joe. They'd been seeing each other for a few months. He had started at the barn last spring doing the general handyman stuff, painting, fixing grain bins, mending kicked doors and downed fences. She found herself drawn to his quiet manner, his polite Texas drawl, his dark eyes and dark hair. All that summer she had tried to treat him with professional courtesy, and all the while she had half her mind on him when she was teaching lessons, supervising the farrier visits, or schooling the young horses.

Now he was a part of her life the way no other boyfriend had ever been. Lynn thought about the last guy, a bartender at the local riders' hangout. That had been a mistake from the beginning and had ended quickly. Rumor had it Mark had gone back to Colorado. *Thank God,* she thought, shifting in the saddle. Joe was about as different from Mark as a person could be.

Dungiven flicked an ear, his head a ghostly vision in front of her. She patted his shoulder, letting the reins go slack, and eased her boots from the stirrups for a moment. She couldn't wait to get home, get out of her tight breeches and boots, and take a shower. She let the peace of the night woods lull her, then picked up contact again.

With a crashing of the underbrush, a deer exploded out of the woods and leaped across the path, disappearing into the trees.

Dungiven bolted. He probably didn't even see the three-rail fence; she knew she didn't. He ran straight through it and brought it down in a splintered, crashing wreck. Lynn was launched off his back and landed hard on the forest floor.

She sat up, groaning. Dungiven stood nearby, his head hanging down to his knees. "Oh *Christ,*" she sobbed. She tried to get to her feet but sank back down; her knee flared with pain, and she was shaking. After a few moments her heart slowed, and she pushed herself to her feet. She hobbled over to the horse. For a moment she just hugged him, his neck damp with patches of sweat, whispering an apology. He was unresponsive. Painfully, she reached down and began to feel his legs. His left foreleg had a warm spot—probably a bruise, she thought. He flinched and yanked his leg away when she ran her fingers down the long bone under his knee. Right where he must have hit the jump, she thought, and looked behind her.

She had to look twice, but it did no good; the jump wasn't there.

It was dark, yes, but it wasn't that dark. She could still make out trees and brush. The path had been visible as a slightly paler trail along the ground. Now there was nothing. No path, no fence, no short ride home.

Lynn's hands shook so hard she could barely hold on to her cell phone as she fumbled it out of her pocket. She punched in the number to the barn phone and pressed Send, imagining what she would say. *Not the truth,* she thought grimly. She would save that for later. The phone beeped and flashed No Service on the display. "Damn," she muttered, and canceled the call, trying the main house. Even if the van weren't quite home yet, Mrs. Hunt surely would be. Once again the phone beeped unhelpfully. Dungiven cocked his ears forward, his nose at her shoulder, his warm, oaty breath misting on her vest. Lynn canceled again and dialed 911.

Nothing. In the middle of a dark forest, she stared with a sinking heart at her useless phone.

The forest is full of gate magic tonight, thought Captain Crae. He looked out over the forest from the walls of Red Gold Bridge, his back to the torches that lined the stronghold's stone stairs and walkway. The forest was a mass of darkness in the night. He could sense the restlessness that it hid at its heart. Red Gold Bridge may have been carved out of the mountain ridge that backed up against Gordath Wood, but it quivered beneath his boots.

Generations of strongholders had chipped away at the caverns that riddled the mountain, smoothing walls and carving out windows in the stone. Beams of oak and other hardwoods harvested from the forest shored up walls and ceilings. Outside the main stronghold stood a stout, high wall of carven stone, its mortar well-tended against time and war. The wall and the iron and wood gate that buckled it would never be neglected, for even if there were peace in Aeritan, there was still the Wood.

The guardhouse housed his men, and it was hot in the dim, small space. All twelve stood around the walls, leaning against the stone, their arms folded across their chests or one hand held near a sword hilt. They wore green coats, the muted red stone insignia naming them Tharp's. Lord Tharp himself sat at one end of the long wooden table that took up most of the guardhouse. He sat back in his chair, his coat thrown over the back of it, his rich brown shirt open at the throat, and his sleeves rolled up. Despite the lateness of the hour and the waning of the year, sweat beaded his forehead and darkened his hair. Crae knew he sweated the same, as did all his men.

Some days the Wood breathed out hot air like a man with a fever.

At the other end of the table sat Bahard. The stranger man was sulky, annoyed.

"Look, I shouldn't of shot him, I know that now," Bahard said, his words heavily accented. "But you wanted the damn thing open, and he was trying to close it. He *would* have closed it, if I hadn't done something." His sulkiness increased. "I was just trying to get his attention."

Tharp looked at him over laced fingers. "Did he say anything to you before you shot him?"

Bahard threw up his hands. "He was pissed as hell, yeah. I don't know—I couldn't begin to tell you what he said. He was mad, though."

Tharp sat back as if he were holding half-monthly grievances, his mouth a thin line. Crae knew he must be seething. There had always been an uneasy truce between the citizens of Red Gold Bridge and the guardian who kept the gordath quiet. The arrival of Bahard already upset that balance; shooting the guardian—Arrim—could only make it worse.

"Are you sure you didn't kill him?" Tharp said brusquely.

Bahard lifted his hands. "I told you. I just winged him. He took off into the woods."

"We followed the blood trail as far as we could," Crae put in. "The guardian crossed at the stream west of the old morrim, and we lost the trail in the water." Even wounded, the guardian had shown cunning woodcraft. Crae hoped that's all it was. He hoped that the Wood hadn't turned full against them by concealing the guardian. Then again, the Wood's capricious nature had been sorely tested these past months. The constant earth shakings had made that clear, and earlier that day, the violent shaking of the earth when Bahard shot Arrim had been enough to put cracks in the stronghold's walls. This night the air fairly hummed with the energy from the gordath.

As if to emphasize its malice, a soft rumbling came out of the heart of the forest, and dust sifted down around Crae's head. *It toys with us.*

Tharp pinched the bridge of his nose. "South and west," he muttered. Crae knew what he was thinking. Arrim's course would take him to the Council's army, the one that amassed outside Red Gold Bridge in a show of strength against Lord Tharp. If Arrim reached the Council, told them how Tharp was getting his weapons—Crae had nothing against Arrim, even thought him a good man, but he could do nothing to save him from his treason.

Then again, a guardian gave his allegiance to the Wood and the portal he guarded, not the lords.

Tharp shook his head. "Halfway measures. If you had to be such a fool, Bahard, would that you were one who went all the way to foolhardy without restraint."

"Yeah, whatever," Bahard retorted, holding his ground. His mottled green jacket and trousers made him look bulkier than he was. "Look, all I want is to be paid for the guns, just like we agreed. You wanted this thing open, and this guy was trying to close it. I took care of that. You want me to kill someone for you, that's separate, and anyway, I'm not sure I'm gonna do it." He scowled. "I have to sleep at night, too."

Tharp ignored him. He turned back to Crae. "What do you think?"

"If he's still in the Wood," Crae said carefully, "we'll find him. I've set up scouts around the gordath itself, in case he means to come back and try again."

Tharp nodded. "All right. Take your men back on the hunt." He threw another disgusted look at Bahard, but he addressed Crae. "We still need him, Captain, so I expect him returned alive. For now, all goes on as it has been. The gordath remains open. My lord Bahard, take your wagon and meet the weapons merchant at the cottage as planned."

"Yeah, don't want to keep Garson waiting. You have the first payment, right?"

Tharp eyed him without comment. The stranger man did not look cowed; Crae had to give him that much credit. Tharp stood. "The wagon has been loaded with goods that should please your merchant. Captain Crae, make haste."

They bowed except for Bahard. Tharp ducked out the small guardhouse door, followed by the stranger man. Crae gestured to his men, and they filed out as well.

A breeze came from the river, refreshing him and for a moment cooling the night. Crae paused to savor it. Summer always lingered near Gordath Wood, but the promise of fall and winter hung on the winds from the river. In his home country of Wessen, autumn had already come. Or so the wind said when it blew in from the water.

In the dim torchlight the stranger man disappeared down the stairs cut inside the wall. Crae watched him go. He hadn't looked like much for a bringer of war, Crae thought, but he had carried trouble with him the day he arrived at Red Gold Bridge under heavy guard. He also brought his weapons and the promise of more. It had not taken Tharp long to see their potential. Crae had served Tharp long enough to know how the man chafed under the reins of the Aeritan Council. Red Gold Bridge, by its position on the long banks of the Aeritan, could control trade along the river, and with it most of the country, if the balance of power tilted enough. With Bahard's strange weapons providing leverage, Lord Tharp stood ready to push.

The wounded guardian had a different view, one that saw not the opportunity for Red Gold Bridge to become a true power in the region, but the danger of arousing the gordath. He might have paid for his dissent with his life, unless Crae could find him, and time was running out.

Crae cast one last look over the wall at the night-dark woods and hurried down the stairs after his men.

Two

It was full dark by the time Joe pulled into the parking lot at Hunter's Chase. He maneuvered the big van next to the indoor ring and cut the engine and the lights. Night fell around them. He could hear the small grunts and whinnies of the horses, eager to get out of the cramped compartments and into their comfortable loose boxes. From inside the barn another horse neighed a greeting.

Beside him in the cab, Gina stretched. She had been riding shotgun, Lynn's usual spot.

"What a day," she said. "I'll be glad when Lynn gets back and this is over." She opened the door and hopped out. He heard her talking to Kate, who had ridden in the back, watching over the expensive horses to make sure they didn't get tangled in their lead ropes or throw a fit out of fear or boredom.

Joe got out a little slower, throwing a look across the fields for a bobbing flashlight coming through the woods. Instead, the trees hulked thick and indistinct, a greater darkness in the night. He had never grown used to the woods. Nothing like them in Texas, and sometimes he felt like they were watching him. He'd be at work in the fields or even behind the main barn, and have to look over his shoulder constantly. *God's earth, my ass,* he thought, dropping the ramp with a muffled scrape. That's what people round here said the name for the woods came from. Maybe, like everything else, God was different in Texas, too.

While the girls unloaded the first horse, he pushed back the big bay doors to the ring and turned on the small lights that illuminated the walkway around the arena as well as the floodlights that beamed down on the parking lot. The thick, warm smell of horses, hay, oats, and manure wafted over him. Joe had seen Lynn breathe it in deep like it was the best smell in the world. All he could smell was shit, but he could allow the peacefulness of it, of drowsy animals, warm and well-fed. One of the barn cats twined around his leg, and he nudged it aside with his boot. It meowed indignantly, and he snorted. Speaking of well-fed—"Go catch a rat, you," he said.

A car rolled up on the gravel drive. He could hear voices, and Kate answering. Alarm tightened in his belly, and he headed back out, squinting against the outdoor floodlights.

"But Mom," Kate said. "I can't go yet. Lynn's not back. It's just Gina and me."

Mrs. Mossland nodded over at Joe coming out of the barn. "What about Joe? It's just that it's nine o'clock, Kate. We need to be going."

Kate's father frowned. "She'll be here soon, Kate. I don't understand why she didn't drive back with the van. Doesn't she usually?"

Kate hesitated. "She rode Dungiven back. He didn't want to load, and she thought it would be quicker to just ride him."

Kate's parents exchanged quick glances. Joe hastened forward. They were nice enough folks, but they were clients, even if Kate worked off part of the bill for her little horse, Mojo.

"If Kate needs to go, that's fine," he said. "Gina and I got it covered." Out of the corner of his eye he saw Gina flounce off, clucking to a tall chestnut thoroughbred named Piper. He remembered her talking about having a date that night.

Mrs. Mossland said, "I suppose—well, we can stay a bit longer. I'm just not sure I understand why she rode the horse home. Was it part of the show?"

"Mo-om," Kate said. Her face reddened with embarrassment.

"All right," Mr. Mossland said. He clapped his hands once. "Let's go. Get these horses put away, so we can get out of here."

"Is there anything we can do to help?" Mrs. Mossland added politely, clearly relieved when Kate and Joe assured her that no, the best she could do was to just wait; they wouldn't be that long.

Joe thought that unloading took longer than it should have, even though they were all anxious to go home. He kept stopping to look out toward the drive.

Why isn't she back yet?

More than an hour later, when all the horses were safely tucked away, the three gathered in the tack room while Kate's parents waited in the car.

"She should be back by now," Gina said. She fiddled with her car keys.

"Maybe she called in when we were in the hill barn?" Kate ventured.

"I thought of that. I checked the messages on the barn phone, but there weren't any," Gina said. "I could go look again."

"Do you think she just got lost?" Kate said. "I mean, it's not likely, but—"

"If she did, she would have called. Unless—" Gina didn't finish. *Unless she couldn't.*

"Maybe she stopped in at one of the other barns, High Hollow or Stone Brook," Kate said, still desperately hopeful.

No one said anything. The words *But she would have called if she had* bounced around the dimly lit barn.

"I'll call around," Gina said finally. She headed back to the tack room, stuffing her keys in her backpack. In a moment they could hear her on the phone. Kate looked as if she were going to cry.

Joe fidgeted. "Look, you need to go home. I'll drive around all the places she would have come out."

"Shouldn't we call the police?" Kate said.

Joe felt his stomach tighten extra hard. Call the police, and Lynn stopped being just a little late and apt to ride in any moment now. Call the police, and it got serious. *She's fine. She knows these woods.*

"Maybe we should check with Mrs. Hunt first," Joe said. "Is she back yet?"

Kate made a face. "She went out with Fleming, remember? They went to the Continental."

They could hear Gina in the tack room say, "Thanks anyway. If you hear anything, let us know, okay?" She hung up and came back, shaking her head.

"Damn," Joe said under his breath. Louder, he added, "I can go look, but someone should stay here, in case she tries to call."

"I can," Kate said promptly.

"What about your parents?" said Gina.

"Absolutely not," said **Mr. Mossland, when** Kate broached the subject, trailed by Gina and Joe. "Kate, it's after ten o'clock. For God's sake, let's get out of here."

"She should be back by now," Kate said. She turned to her mother. "Mom, listen. It shouldn't have taken this long."

Mrs. Mossland looked indecisive. "David, I don't know. Lynn could be in real trouble."

"Then we need to call the police," he said. "Where's Mrs. Hunt?"

"She went out," Kate said. "With Mr. Fleming."

Again her parents exchanged glances. Joe wondered if they knew him. More likely knew of him. The Mosslands were hardly poor, but they still worked for a living.

"What do you think?" David turned to his wife. "Think it's time to call in the cops?"

She nodded. "I think so." She pulled out her phone and stepped aside, and after a moment they heard her say, "Janet Mossland here. Hello, Daniel. We have a problem out at the Hunter's Chase stables. We think you will need a search crew to come look for a missing rider." Her gaze fell on her daughter. Mrs. Mossland lowered her voice. "And possibly an emergency response team."

Joe had just enough time to wonder why Kate's mother was on a first-name basis with the police when another set of headlights turned off the road and into the drive. This time the car swung toward the main house. Mrs. Hunt was home.

When she got out of her fancy convertible, she saw their little huddle and came over, her tall figure still arresting in her horse show clothes, but her face was drawn and pale in the yellow lamplight. She looked around at all of them, unknotting the kerchief she wore over her hair, and her expression changed—to Joe it looked like dawning fear. She addressed him directly.

"She isn't back."

He shook his head.

"We've just called the police," Mrs. Mossland said. Mrs. Hunt swung toward her, her eyes wide with shock. Kate's mom looked taken aback at her reaction. "We thought—she should have been back by now. We were worried."

Mrs. Hunt took a moment to collect herself. "Of course. But Dungiven is in capable hands."

"Yes, well," said Mrs. Mossland after a moment of judicious thought. "We're actually more concerned about Lynn."

"Umm," said Gina. "Do I have to wait for the police?" She added hastily, "I will if you think it's necessary. It's just . . . well, if I get going, I can swing by the trailhead and see if I can see anything there."

"Go," said Mrs. Mossland. She seemed to have made a decision to take charge, now that she had seen Mrs. Hunt's reaction. "If you see anything, please call right away, both the barn and the police. Do you have a cell phone?"

Gina patted her backpack.

"All right. We'll wait here. Katherine, should we wait at the house for the police, or do you think it better to stay here at the barn?"

Her challenge dripped courtesy. Mrs. Hunt's lips tightened at the rebuke.

"Let's all go in, shall we?" Mrs. Hunt said. "Joe, please wait at the barn in case she calls in."

Joe kept his temper down.

"Beg your pardon, ma'am," he said. "I'm heading off to look for her myself. I'll call the house phone when I come across her." He looked around at the others, touching the brim of an imaginary hat. "Miz Mossland. Mr. Mossland. Kate." He gave the kid a real smile, and she went shy and turned away.

Alone outside the barn, Joe turned off the outdoor lights and let his eyes adjust to darkness. One by one the katydids came out, sawing away. The rush of traffic from the highway wafted over to the farm, and the trees of Gordath Wood massed indistinctly across the field. Two or three tall trees poked at the overcast sky, like sentinels.

He couldn't see a thing. No rider coming out of that blackness, no sound of clip-clopping hoofbeats drumming a tattoo over the trail.

"Where are you, Lynn?" he said out loud.

The katydids stopped. The sentinel trees quivered against the sky, independently of the rest of the woods.

Faintly, from far away, the ground rumbled beneath his feet.

It wasn't like the earlier earthquake, more like a big truck passing by, rattling the windows of an old house, but he knew it came from the Wood. *She's out in it,* he thought. *She's hurt, and she's alone, and I don't have nothing to help her with.*

After a bit he got in his old car and started it up. The dusty old Impala bounced over the graveled drive, and he pulled out onto the road. He didn't know how he was going to find her, didn't even know the first place to look. The woods outside his window were a blur of dark; he could make out nothing in them, not even the narrow trailheads that twisted into the deeper dark. They were hard enough to find in broad daylight, some of them, barely a hoof-pocked track that wound through ferns and brush.

Hang in there, Lynn, he thought.

Lynn woke up slowly, aware of wetness and chill air. She stirred and groaned; sunlight struck her eyes. Lynn winced and turned her head, rubbing her cheek into the loamy soil and decaying leaves, breathing in their musty aroma.

Something scurried over her collar. She staggered to her feet, helmet askew, batting at her neck and hair, spluttering in disgust. She tore at her vest, throwing it aside and tugging at her shirt collar. Finally, a large beetle crawled out from underneath the stock pinned at her neck and flew off. Nearby, watching her antics with a calm, interested expression, stood Dungiven, his ears pricked at her.

With slightly shaking hands Lynn unbuckled her hard hat and looked around. She spotted the trail, a wandering, narrow path, nothing like the broad trail they had taken last night. Washed-out sunlight rippled lightly through the underbrush, backlighting the bushes and limning the earliest autumn leaves with pale gold. Birds called endlessly in the forest. The early morning air held a chill.

Lynn let out a breath. "Oh, *crap,*" she said.

She hadn't meant to fall asleep. After trying to call 911 and getting no signal, she had tried the barn and the house again until she gave up. She sat down, telling herself it was just for a few moments, sure that she would see flashlights bobbing through the woods, people calling her name and Dungiven's.

And now it was morning, and there was no rescue to be found.

In the aftermath of her creepy wake-up call, her knee had begun to sting and throb. That reminded her of Dungiven's crash, and with sharp chagrin she turned to check on him. "Wow, what a night, hey, old man?" she told him, sliding a hand down his neck. He bent his head to look as she knelt and felt his knee and cannon bone. She felt his warm breath on her neck as she probed a little harder.

He jerked up his leg, almost banging her in the eye. Lynn struggled to her feet.

"Okay, that smarts," she said. She patted his neck. "Nothing an ice pack and a shot of bute won't fix, though. And that goes for me, too."

The knee of her breeches was smudged and frayed. She could see a bit of blood seeping through the fabric. She must have landed on a rock. She didn't want to pull off her breeches to take a look; the thought of peeling off the tight pants over the injury made her cringe. *I'll do it when I get home,* she thought.

The sooner they got out of the woods, the better. She looked around, considering. By her reckoning of last night's ride, she hadn't come that far from Pennington. Barely an hour at most. She looked back the way they had come. The strange trail wound into the woods and disappeared into green scrub backlit by the sun. So far it looked like it was her only option. She gathered up the reins under Dungiven's chin and led him back along the trail.

Less than an hour later, she pulled up. For the past several minutes she had been forcing a path through nigh impenetrable brush and pricker bushes. Thorns snagged at Dungiven's braided mane, snatching bits of yarn so that the path behind them was littered with blue tufts, and several scratched the leather of his expensive saddle. Lynn looked at it, winced, and tried to rub out a scratch.

Finally she forced her way into a small clearing in the woods, a tiny creek trickling through the rocky terrain away from a small knoll. Sweaty, hungry, and miserable, Lynn got them unstuck from the last of the pricker bushes and only looked up at Dungiven's alert whinny. She gasped and jumped.

A man lay sprawled at the foot of the knoll. At first she thought he was dead; then he turned his head and mumbled something that she could not understand. He moved his hand limply. It was stained with blood and dirt.

Oh my God. She stayed where she was and raised her voice. "Are you okay?"

He said nothing. Heart pounding, she approached cautiously, Dungiven clopping after her. He was not a big man, and his clothes were ragged and worn. No, not just ragged; they looked homemade. His shoes were thick and clunky, as if he had stolen them from some poor old lady. Blood seeped from a ragged hole in the shoulder of his shirt, darkening the dull material to black.

He opened his eyes when she drew near. Stubble masked his face, and his hair was matted with sweat and dirt. She thought it might have blood in it, too.

"Hey," she said. "Hey. What happened? Are you okay?"

He mumbled something she couldn't make out.

"What?" she said.

He said, more clearly, "The gordath is open."

His accent was strange, but she understood that—except that it made no sense. He was rambling. She had to bring him back to reality.

"Hey. Hey. I can help you, but you have to help me," she told him. "You have to stay awake, okay?"

His expression cleared a little, and the fog seemed to lift a bit from his eyes. "Are you lost?" he asked.

Lynn nodded. "Do you know the way out?" she asked.

He closed his eyes, let his head turn aside. "If you are lost, we may already be too late."

His wounded shoulder seeped. His skin was sallow under its tan, and she could feel heat radiating off of him. If he died . . .

She would be more alone than before, even.

"Hey," she said nervously. "Don't fade out on me here."

His mouth moved in a tired smile. "Help me, and I will help you."

Fair enough, she thought. She propped him up against a boulder, tucking her vest behind him as a cushion. She filled up her helmet at the little trickle of water. His fingers were hot against hers as he helped hold on to the helmet and drank clumsily. She took off her stock, tucking her little hunting horn pin into the front pocket of her vest, then gently pulled back his rough shirt from the small, jagged hole below his shoulder. He shivered and cried out, clutching her fingers.

It was a gunshot wound; she was sure of it. She had seen enough TV to tell. The skin around the hole was inflamed and puffy, and though the bleeding seemed to have slowed to a trickle, that probably was not a good thing. This guy needed a hospital and an antibiotic IV, and fast. She leaned close to the wound and took a sniff, wincing at the smell. Definitely infected.

She unfolded her white cloth stock and laid it against the wound, nudging him to rise up a bit so she could wrap it around his shoulder. Poor enough first aid, she thought, but it would have to do. And it would help to stanch the bleeding at least, though it would do little for infection.

"My thanks," he rasped, his eyes still closed. He had not opened them during her ministrations and moved little except when she needed him to.

Lynn squeezed his hand. "You're going to be okay," she said, glad he couldn't see the worry in her face. She didn't think he could walk. His face was pale, and he couldn't keep his eyes open. He would have to ride. She glanced at Dungiven. If they took it slow, it shouldn't hurt the horse too much. And the guy seemed scrawny enough. Taking a big chance here, she told herself, but she could hardly carry the man herself. Dungiven would have to do his part.

"Hey," she said. He opened his eyes. "Think you can get on his back?" She nodded at Dungiven.

The man squinted at the horse. He nodded, his expression changing. He's more alert, she thought. Good. It wouldn't be easy if he were completely out of it.

She helped him up. He leaned on her, supporting as much of his own weight as he could, and they hobbled slowly over to the horse. A nearby boulder served as a mounting block, but Lynn still had to push him into the saddle. He slumped over

Dungiven's neck, sweating and trembling, and touched his forehead to the horse's mane.

Relief came over Lynn. One hurdle down. "Great!" she said. "Well. We're on our way." She would be home soon; she knew it. She snaked the reins over Dungiven's neck and handed them to the man. "Here," she said. "Let me get my vest."

Even as Lynn took half a step, some caution made her stop. *Ooh, that probably wasn't*—she spun around in her tracks. "No!" she shouted.

It was too late. The man gathered up the reins and kicked Dungiven clumsily in the ribs. The horse threw up his head and trotted forward out of the clearing, the man bouncing in the saddle.

"Stop!" She lunged forward, but the man kicked again, and it was clear Dungiven had had enough. The big horse bolted up the treacherous hillside, scrambling through leaves and rocks, sending an avalanche of debris down into the clearing. The horse made it safely to the top, and the man, riding hunched over with his legs out in front of him, bounced in the saddle but stayed put. They disappeared over the top of the ridge until all she could hear was the sound of Dungiven crashing through the forest and her own sobs of rage.

"Stop! Stop!"

Don't leave me here alone!

Three

The day after Lynn's disappearance was one of those glorious days when the September air goes chill and the sunlight sparkles. The pots of geraniums that graced the dark entrances of each of the three barns at Hunter's Chase Stables were bright splashes of red against the white stables with blue trim.

As Kate led Mojo out of the top barn, she shivered, wondering if it had been a mistake to wear a tank top for her ride that morning. She kept an extra jacket in her equipment trunk in the tack room, but she was too impatient to go back and get it.

Last night's search had turned up no sign of Lynn, despite emergency vehicles that trundled along the roads outside the wood and a helicopter with a searchlight chattering overhead. Search parties with dogs had gone into the woods, starting from the Pennington trails. They found nothing, not a trace of her.

Kate and her parents waited at the farm until one in the morning, her mom in close contact with the police. Kate knew her mom, a prosecutor in line for a judicial appointment, was important. The night of Lynn's disappearance was the first time she realized exactly how much. Finally they made Kate go home after being assured that someone would call as soon as Lynn and Dungiven were found. The last Kate saw of Mrs. Hunt, the cool woman was staring out the beautiful front window of her living room, as if she could see into the dark center of the forest.

Mojo bumped her shoulder with his muzzle, reminding Kate to get a move on. She smiled and reached up and stroked his long, elegant nose. Mojo tossed his head and pricked his ears, eager to move. She gathered the reins under his chin and walked him down the drive, nervously expecting someone to stop her at any moment. The farm was quiet though—new search parties had already gone out that morning, so except for one rider warming up her horse in the main training ring, no one was around to take notice of Kate.

All for the best, she thought. If anyone knew she was planning to ride off to conduct her own search for Lynn, she would be stopped in half a second. The thing was, she knew the trails, probably even better than Lynn. Kate rode out there all the time. The search parties probably stuck to the main trails. Kate knew the shortcuts. If Lynn had tried to take one of those last night, the searchers would never find her.

She hastened the rest of the way to the ring, Mojo's head nodding next to her. Kate halted at the bottom of the drive and tightened Mojo's girth, then pulled the stirrups down to the end of the leathers. They slid into place with a satisfying smack, and she mounted with an easy movement. The other rider, a skinny blonde woman named Carolyn, trotted over, pulling up her horse on her side of the fence.

"Did you hear about Lynn?" Carolyn asked avidly, her eyes gleaming under her plush cap. "She stole Dungiven. Did you hear? I heard she took him to Canada."

Kate settled her helmet on her head, tucking in her pale, flyaway hair, and buckled the chin strap as Mojo tossed his head and turned in circles, eager to be off. She pretended he was giving her too much difficulty to answer. She didn't like Carolyn, and she didn't like her horse, a weedy thoroughbred mare named Allegra, either.

"I don't know," she said finally and neutrally. She gathered up the reins and nudged Mojo toward the gate.

Carolyn followed on her side of the fence.

"You were there last night, right?" she chattered on. "What do you think? Do you think she did it?"

A spurt of anger shot out of Kate's mouth in words. "She didn't steal Dungiven!" she retorted. "I have to go, Carolyn."

With that, she pushed Mojo into a trot down the gravel drive, leaving Carolyn speechless. Not for long, Kate thought grimly. She knew that Carolyn would add her outburst to her store of gossip. That would be all over the barn in no time. Kate wondered if Carolyn herself had started the rumor about Lynn stealing Dungiven.

Kate hurried Mojo along the drive behind the main barn and turned down the lane toward the trails, casting a nervous glance behind her. She wanted to clear the stables before she caught anyone's attention. Her heart sank when she saw Joe, driving the tractor up from the lower barn with a load of hay in the trailer. *Busted.* He stopped and cut the engine, and she pulled Mojo up next to him. He looked pale under his tan, his eyes red-rimmed and his face rough with stubble. He had looked for Lynn the night before on his own and then went out with the search parties earlier that day. *No,* she thought. *Of anyone, Joe would understand.* She straightened in the saddle and gathered her courage.

"Where do you think you're goin'?" Joe demanded. Kate was almost always tongue-tied in Joe's presence. This time she answered without her usual shyness.

"I'm going to retrace her steps," she told him.

"Now, you need to leave it to the police."

She shook her head before he even finished. "I know those trails better than anyone. I know what to look for—all the shortcuts, all the dangerous parts."

He sat and looked at her. Kate held his gaze defiantly.

"First damn time I ever wished I could ride," he muttered. "Kate, I don't think you should go alone. Whatever happened to Lynn—"

"They aren't looking for *her*," Kate said. "They don't care about Lynn. They're just concerned about Dungiven."

"Ain't that the way you horse people are?" he asked. "Horses first, right?"

"I'm not worried about Dungiven," she said. "If Lynn stole him, he's in good hands."

He laughed, and she blushed. Joe said, "Listen, I still don't like that idea. You know you ain't supposed to ride alone on those trails."

"I know, but—look. I won't go far. I'll be careful. All I want to do is check a few places. I'll come straight back if I see anything."

Yeah, like a dead body, thrown from the back of a horse. Neither of them said it, but they both thought it. Just a few years before, an experienced rider had been killed in a fall on the trails.

"I promise, okay?" she said. He held her gaze for a moment, his dark eyes serious, then started the tractor again and nodded.

"I'll be waiting for you, girl," he told her and let the tractor roll toward the stable. She gathered her reins and pushed Mojo up the driveway.

Two old stones marked the trail entrance, buried in the dirt so that they only showed as gray, rough mounds, stained with moss and eroded by time. Sparse weeds grew up around them, yellowed by the summer's heat. Kate turned Mojo's head and rode him through. The trees closed in, and she shivered in the twilight, goose bumps prickling the skin of her bare arms. She put Mojo into a trot, and he moved out with his usual bouncy energy.

The little horse, a blood bay with black points and a black mane and tail, was compactly built, his Arabian and quarter horse ancestry combining to form a strong, round, powerful horse, barely fifteen hands tall and full of spirit. Mojo, her dad called it. He was the perfect size for Kate, who wouldn't be getting much taller than five foot three. She longed to have Lynn's willowy figure. *Instead,* she thought, *I turned into a tree stump.* It didn't help that she was late to fill out; she felt like she went from being a stick-thin kid to a woman overnight. Sometimes the back of a horse was the only place she felt comfortable, where the embarrassment that colored her entire life, about her hair, her acne, her breasts, her period, melted away, and for a few hours she could forget the horror that was high school.

Kate pulled up Mojo as they approached a stream, running silver between the brown banks. Sunlight flashed. He stopped and drank, snorting at the water and pawing it a little. Kate leaned forward, giving him rein, and patted his moist shoulder. Mojo tossed his head in the air and snorted again, his bit and curb chain jangling. Light flashed off the silver metal, the glare hurting her eyes, and then he splashed strongly through the water and up the opposite bank, following the well-worn track.

They came this way often. It was stupid to ride alone—everyone knew that—but Kate felt confident that she knew the trails well enough to keep out of trouble. *But so did Lynn.* She pressed Mojo on, hurrying now. He quickened his pace to match her mood, and they came up to the first fence. Firmly Kate held Mojo in. He tossed his head, making his disgust clear, but though Kate might ride alone, she knew better than to jump alone. Besides, the turnoff was coming up, and she could let Mojo run there, where the trail widened and the footing was soft and easy. Sure enough, he leaped forward at a touch of her heel against his flank and galloped steadily and happily up the slight rise through the wide field, his hoofbeats drumming a muffled tattoo. They galloped for about a hundred yards, the air streaming by, when a sense of wrongness impinged on her consciousness.

Kate pulled up and gasped. Startled, Mojo crouched and shied sideways. Kate rode it as if he stood still.

What should have been a short stretch of open land had become an endless field. They were midway up a sloping hill, with nothing but blue sky and a few puffy clouds above them, and behind her a sea of green and golden grasses. *I've taken a wrong turn,* she thought. *Somehow I made it to the other end of the trails, by Aspen Farms.* But she should still have been able to see the woods.

She turned in the saddle, craning to see behind her. Still no trees.

If I find anything, I'll come straight back. Kate remembered her promise to Joe. This warranted a swift retreat. She turned Mojo back the way they came, pushing down her niggling doubt. We *had* to have come that way, she thought. It's behind us. We *had* to have.

Twenty minutes later, she pulled up Mojo again, panic bubbling. They had reached woods—*finally!*—but it was all wrong. There was no trail. The woods were rough scrub, hardly the woods she knew. She had never been here before.

"Come on, Mojo," she said, her voice trembling. "What's going on? Don't you know where we are?"

I need to call home. She reached for her cell phone and remembered. It was still in her jacket pocket, and her jacket was in the tack room. Her stomach clenched with fear. *Stop it,* she told herself. *There's nothing to be afraid of. I'll just ride to the next farm and call from there.*

She dismounted at once and loosened Mojo's girth. He heaved a sigh, and she did, too. She hated walking, but he needed a break. "Sorry about this, Modgie," she said, patting his neck. At least she wore her paddock boots, not her tall show boots, but it wouldn't matter if she had to walk for too long. She could feel the blisters starting already.

As she walked beside her horse, she stripped off her riding gloves, stuffed them inside her small saddlebag that carried her lunch, and took off her helmet, hooking it onto the back of the saddle. Her damp, crushed hair moved listlessly, strands that had pulled free of the french braid straggling around her face. Kate blew up at her bangs in frustration. No matter how she pinned it, she never could get her hair to stay in a braid.

Her hair was another source of embarrassment for Kate; she sometimes wished she could just trade in her whole outside self for a new one. Like Lynn's, she thought. The consensus among the women at the stables was that Lynn Romano could have been a model. Carolyn said she had heard a rumor that Lynn was a recovering crack addict. Carolyn had added ominously that if Lynn took any drugs, *any* at all, she would fall back into a drug frenzy. Some of the other boarders took Carolyn's assessment seriously. If Lynn was aware of the gossip, she ignored it, another ability Kate envied of her hero. She wished she had the inner serenity, the balance that Lynn had that let her not care what other people thought.

Kate sighed. *Fat chance,* she thought. *People like me and people like Lynn—we're whole worlds apart.*

Once the woods closed in overhead, she felt better. It was cooler, for one thing, and Kate felt like she could think again, out of the hot sun and that eerie field. Even better, she came upon a trail. It was an old, comfortable track through the woods, worn by hooves and other traffic. It was unfamiliar to her, but it was so well-traveled that she supposed it would come out to a farm or to a paved road soon enough. She wasn't even going to complain about the tongue-lashing in store for her when her parents found out what she had done.

The air beneath the trees was cool, but where sunlight stabbed down in slender columns, the dust motes danced and the last of summer's heat bathed her shoulders. Despite the cooler temperatures, the dim light started the panic niggling at her again.

One good thing: no one would think she had stolen her own horse. Her parents would make sure there was a full-scale search on the trails for her. That way, they might also find Lynn. And Joe knew where she had gone. The thought comforted her a bit.

"We'll get out of this, Modgie," she said, and this time her voice held firm. She patted his shoulder, and he flicked his ear at the sound of her voice.

Suddenly his head shot straight into the air, pulling the reins taut. At the same time a musky odor reached her on a wayward breeze, so faint that Kate first registered it only as a familiar smell, without identifying it.

Mojo snorted and jumped sideways.

"Hey, settle down," she said, catching the reins under his chin. Kate frowned and breathed in. *Oh!* she thought. *Someone's burning leaves.* She always loved that smell, and more so now, signaling as it did that they were close to civilization. She turned to Mojo happily. "See? We're almost ho—"

She looked twice at her horse. Mojo's shoulder was slick with lather, and he was trembling, his eyes showing white. Kate gasped.

"No," she said out loud, her voice holding the merest tremor. "Just someone burning leaves. It's got to be." But the breeze that washed against her cheek carried the smell more strongly. Mojo whinnied. A series of branches snapped like gunfire. Deep among the trees curled tendrils of smoke carrying the smell of burning wood. The crackling sounds came louder, until she saw the flames licking up through the underbrush.

Fear made her clumsy. With shaking hands she tightened Mojo's girth and pulled down the stirrups. She unhooked her helmet from the D ring on the saddle and put it on, and scrambled into the saddle. She reined Mojo around, trying to figure out which way to go. He half reared, fighting her control, and she closed her eyes, said a prayer, and let him bolt. His instincts would have to save them both.

Colar of Terrick sat his nervous horse easily and watched the fires race up the backbone of the ridge leading into Gordath Wood. The dry grass of the hillside took no time at all to catch, and the low-running flames were almost instantly obscured by thick smoke. It was fascinating; the fire moved as if it were alive, consuming the hillside. A breeze off the Aeritan River at his back harried the flames, sending them off into the woods.

The other scouts shouted as yet another runnel of flame tore away up the hill, and then another, and another. Over the rising crackling of the fire, Colar heard the whistle and turned in the saddle. Captain Artor waved his sword and shouted, signaling them all to come back. Colar nodded, though the captain could not see him, and threw his torch into the grass away from his horse's feet. The torch smoked dully and then sparked, setting up a gout of flame from the oil-soaked end. Colar turned his horse on its haunches, cantering back and joining the rest of General Marthen's outriders.

They gathered around their captain. Artor scanned their handiwork from horseback, resting his forearms on the saddle-bow, the crow's-feet around his eyes deepening as he watched the fire's progress. He was as old as Colar's father, his close-cropped hair and beard salted with gray, his pale eyes red-rimmed. The captain looked around at his men.

"Good work," he said, and his face lightened somewhat. "That should smoke him out."

"Or chase him back into the Wood," Jayce grunted, his narrow jaw jutting out pugnaciously. "Waste of time."

Colar caught the expressions of a few of the other scouts. Some lifted their eyes briefly, a few exchanged glances and acknowledged Jayce's comment with an unspoken *There he goes again.*

True enough, Colar thought. Jayce always had something to say, and as often as Artor cuffed him down, it never seemed to have an effect. This time Jayce said what they had all been thinking—or at least Colar had been, but he knew better than to open his mouth. At fifteen, he was the youngest scout, the least experienced. This was his first campaign. His father had told him, "Mouth shut, boy, and eyes and ears open." He wondered sometimes how Jayce got away with questioning orders outright.

This time Artor didn't cuff the scout. Instead, he just shook his head; but Colar caught the way his lips tightened. *This question angered him more than usual,* he thought. He puzzled over it a moment and then realized: Artor hadn't liked this order either.

"The river bends to the west of us, and this fire will go straight through the Wood and meet it on the shore," the captain explained. "If Tharp's man is truly in those Woods, it'll drive him straight into our arms." He emphasized *if* ever so slightly.

But the captain grinned, looking back at the fire behind them, and a few of the scouts laughed. Colar remained silent, looking back uneasily at the Wood. He had grown up far away from Gordath Wood but had heard the tales nonetheless. He could not imagine traveling through it. Tharp's runner had more to worry about than fire. A shudder ran down the young scout's back, and he was thankful for the leather half coat that concealed his involuntary shiver, and his sparse beard, just coming in, that he hoped hid any expression of fear.

"Look at that," said Jayce gleefully, and Colar's heart jumped into his mouth. But the scout was looking toward the Wood, and the others followed his gaze. The fires had gained speed up the slope and combined at the top of the hill to create a wall of flame. With the help from the river breeze, and with little resistance from the dry, drought-ridden wood, the fire began to climb to the outskirts of Gordath Wood.

Captain Artor let them watch a moment longer, awed at their handiwork, and then said, "Right. Let's go."

He wheeled his horse and started them off along the river road, the fire roaring above them into the Wood and the sparkling waters of the Aeritan rippling on their other flank. They rode at a fast trot along the shell-covered road, leaving the fire behind them. They would meet it around the river bend and from there try to pick up the man's trail.

If, as Captain Artor had intimated, there really was a runner. Colar knew that according to General Marthen's spies, a man from Red Gold Bridge had set out two days ago, but to what purpose no one seemed to know. Setting the fire to smoke him out was like taking a hammer to an ant, except that even Colar knew there was more to this fire than just driving a wayward courier into the right direction.

The weapons. Colar hadn't seen them, but he heard the sto-

ries the soldiers brought back. Loud, thunder-cracking weapons
with shot not even plate mail could keep at bay. The few skir-
mishes between Marthen and Tharp had been small, sporadic,
and inconclusive, but the weapons had everyone uneasy. A fire
might be a hammer to catch a courier, but it could be the right
tactic to stop an enemy from arming himself, distract him, and
keep him from his supply lines.

Colar patted his sword hilt as he sat his horse's long trot.
He wanted to get his hands on one of those weapons. The soldiers' tales all said the weapons had a longer range than even
the longbows the archers used, let alone the short, powerful
crossbow bolts. More accurate, too, said they. *If we had a few
of those weapons,* Colar thought, *it might make all the differ-
ence in this war.* Then again, it was probably more to the point
to find a way to defend against them.

Captain Artor picked up the pace, and the scouts pushed
their horses into an easy, ground-eating lope, alternating with
periods of walking to rest the horses. It was a good way to
make up distance. They had a several hours' ride before they
reached the river's bend. Colar looked back a few times over
his shoulder. The fire had raced into the Wood, and the only
thing to see was the smoke pluming above the forest. The way
the fire had moved, Colar thought that it would beat them by
hours. He felt excitement push him on; he wanted to gallop
full out to the bend where the river approached Red Gold
Bridge, but he knew better than that. The horses could not
travel far at such a punishing pace.

Even with the breeze from the river, the air was hot and
sweat dripped into his eyes. His leather coat grew unpleas-
antly heavy, but Colar knew that if they were riding to war he
would wear a mail shirt and a helm and would have to withstand the heat and the exercise of battle. He straightened his
shoulders stoically and was rewarded when the breeze from
the Aeritan did him a favor and blew his red brown hair back
off his forehead.

The small relief revived him, and Colar's excitement
surged. *This is it,* he thought. *This is war.* He hadn't been in
battle yet for sure, but he was truly here. Just remembering being ordered by the general to report to Captain Artor made his
stomach churn all over again. His father hadn't said anything,

but Colar thought that for a moment the old man had looked on approvingly.

For the dozenth time he mentally checked off his gear: sword, dagger, mail shirt under his shirt and jacket. He thought about capturing the runner. His eyes were sharp; he knew he could catch the sight of some movement deep into the Wood. He could slip off his horse and signal discreetly to Artor with hand signals to tell him: *I see him; he is deep in the Wood. I will bring him to you.* The man tries to hide from Colar but the scout pounces, and after a brief struggle subdues him, places his knife at his throat—

"Hold up!"

Startled, Colar pulled his horse to a sliding stop, and the horse threw his head into the air and squealed. All around him the other scouts halted less precipitously. Jayce gave him a disgusted look. Artor looked him over but said nothing. Colar felt heat slip up his cheeks. They had arrived at the outskirts of a small village, just before the river's bend. The fire and the Wood were now behind them, rather than off their flank.

"Dismount here. Fan out and empty the houses, and then torch them. We'll have no hiding places left for our man."

The small group of stone houses, whitewashed and gleaming in the light of the afternoon, nestled against the foot of the hill that rose into the Wood. A well, water spilling merrily over its lip and running down toward the river in a stone channel, cut a glittering path in the ground. Goats browsed along the edge of the field. A few people watched warily as the soldiers suddenly entered their midst. Colar swung his leg over his saddle-bow and dropped to the ground, snaking the reins over his horse's neck and letting them fall untied. His horse stood obediently along with the others. They would remain ground-tied until the scouts returned.

The butterflies in his stomach returned, but it was less pleasant. Next to him, Jayce had already begun stalking through the village. So had the others, swords drawn, though the smallholders could be no threat. Colar swallowed back the bile in his throat and drew his own sword. With no plan of his own, he followed Jayce.

Colar ducked into a small house behind the other scout, cool in the shadows with only two small windows to let in the light. Outside he could hear the rising cries of panic of the smallholders. It took him a moment for his eyes to adjust to the darkness, and he felt a moment of stark fear. *Think, boy!* he heard his father say. *Don't just react.* Colar gripped his sword and resolved not to enter the next small house like that. Too much of a disadvantage, even though Jayce had gone in as if there were no danger.

He was likely right, Colar thought.

"Everyone out!" Jayce said cheerfully, grabbing an old woman by the collar and apron of her blousy shirt. She began to wail and protest, but he pushed her toward Colar and the door. Feeling stupid, Colar stepped aside as she stumbled over the threshold. He wondered if he should have helped her—or turned and kicked her harder. The thought made him sick. Turning back at him Jayce laughed. "We'll just keep the pretty maids, right, boy? Some of these have to be good for a bit of fun."

Colar didn't respond for a moment while he tried to get his voice to work again. "Any sign of him?"

Jayce had taken a poker and raked the fire out of the small hearth, throwing a small chair with a caned seat onto the scattered flames.

"Him who? Oh, the runner. Not likely. We beat the fire here, so even if he's on his way, he won't be here for a while. This is just for fun."

He stood back to watch the fire catch. "Love to watch the flames. Something about it . . ." He grinned. "On to the next one. Ready, boy?"

I'm not a boy, Colar wanted to say. *And anyway, you aren't much older than me.*

He couldn't make the words come. Instead, he just nodded and ducked out the little cottage, letting Jayce follow. He had a moment of blessed fresh air, then smoke billowed from the windows and a random spark caught on the overhanging thatch. Jayce came out, hurrying and coughing, but his eyes were bright and he grinned. "Come on, boy!" he shouted, and Colar followed, but not before he caught sight of the old woman, standing off to the side, her wrinkled hand covering her mouth. She never even looked at him, as if he were beyond her notice.

Colar stumbled backward, his long legs suddenly as awkward as a newborn colt. He found his balance and hurried off, scurrying to catch up with Jayce.

While they continued their destruction, the Gordath Wood fire caught up with them, and smoke began gushing out of the forest, hanging at the top of the hill. The villagers, caught between the scouts and an even bigger threat, left off protesting and began to pull out their belongings as quickly as they could. Colar watched their exodus with the rest of the scouts, the line of refugees dwindling around the bend.

Only the old woman and a few others lost everything. Artor and the rest of the scouts let the villagers go in, get their few things, and pack out. *I should have done that,* Colar thought, ashamed that he had not showed mercy and restrained Jayce. He thought of what his father would have said and winced.

Afternoon sun glinted on the waters of the Aeritan. The sun lowered behind the trees. The well still bubbled, and except for the scouts, the little village was now deserted. Colar scanned the top of the hill where the trees formed a dark line and shook his head. Even if the runner did come through the woods, there was nothing to say he would come to this exact spot.

Evidently Captain Artor thought the same thing. He waved a hand, pulling everyone in.

"Doubt we need to stay," he said. "It was long odds, anyway, that our man would come this way. Let's finish the fires here and go home."

There were a few mumbled "aye, sirs" and nods, and everyone dispersed. Colar took one look back at the Gordath Wood, then looked again.

"Soldier's god," he half whispered, an oath he had recently learned. "Captain!" Artor, already heading back to the horses where they were grazing by the shore, turned and also looked twice.

A rider came galloping out of the woods, followed by smoke.

"Down!" Artor ordered, and they all dropped at once behind the small stone walls and the houses that were still standing.

The rider dismounted at a gallop in one neat movement, sliding on his heels as he sought to keep his balance and check his momentum down the hill. The horse, a small, neat, well-built little horse, looked to have been ridden to the edge of exhaustion. The rider pulled him up, looked behind them at the fire, and looked again at the village in front of him.

He's suspicious, Colar thought, daring to take the smallest look over the top of the midden heap he crouched behind. *He knows something's wrong. He's*—

A girl. Colar almost stood straight up in his surprise. The rest of the scouts were exchanging astonished glances. Jayce's expression had gone from confusion to glee. Colar remembered what he had said about maids. This girl was no village maid nor even one of the noble class, like the girls he knew. She wore no kerchief over her hair, just a strange white helm. Her thin, short shift was white, too, or had been. Now it was gray with soot and dirt. She wore light trousers and short boots—he had never seen such ridiculous clothes. Had she had to leave her home before she had gotten dressed?

This girl had decided to take a chance on the village. She clicked to her horse and led him over to the well, letting him drink and washing out his nostrils and his eyes of the smoke and soot. She stripped his saddle and threw it off to the side and unstrapped the strange helm, tossing it down, too. Light, flyaway hair hung damply around her round face.

Colar felt pleasantly uncomfortable. He glanced at Artor. The captain seemed as astonished as his men. He looked around and caught everyone's eye, then jerked his head toward the girl. They rose as one and began to advance.

She never even noticed their approach. Her horse tended to, she began to drink, gulping in handfuls of water, splashing it onto her face and letting it run down her front.

Jayce reached her first, grabbing the back of her shirt and dunking her into the water. When he pulled her up, she gasped and choked, trying to cry out. Whatever protest she planned to make died in her throat as she looked at all of them, wiping away the water still streaming into her eyes.

"Where is your saddlebag, courier?" Jayce said in her ear. He tightened his grip on her hair. "Or do you need another swim to help clear your head?"

Captain Artor came forward

"Stay your hand, Jayce," he said curtly.

Colar thought Jayce would disobey. For a moment he held
her, then growled in frustration and released her, shoving her
hard into the lip of the well.

"What are you doing?" she cried out, her accent strange,
barely intelligible. "Let me alone!"

Skayler, Artor's second-in-command, came up with the
contents of the girl's saddlebag.

"No letters," he said crisply. "But look at this." He held out
a soft, thin cloth, completely transparent, and a light bottle.
He shook out the bottle, and a few drops flung out of it, gleaming in the sun until they vanished into the grass. For an instant
Colar smelled something sweet and fragrant, and then the tan-
talizing scent was gone.

Jayce turned toward her.

"Where are they?" he advanced on her. "Where are the dispatches you're carrying for Tharp?"

She shook her head in confusion. "I'm not—"

He slapped her, and she gasped again. Colar jumped a little
and hoped no one noticed.

"Jayce!" Captain Artor snapped. "Hold! She can't tell us
anything like this." He nodded at her. "Now, girl, tell us who
you are and what you are doing out here by yourself. Be quick
about it, and no sniveling."

Colar had heard that tone before; he'd been on the receiv-
ing end of it himself. It evidently had a bracing effect on the
girl, because after only a quick glance at Jayce, she said with
some calm, "My name is Kate Mossland. I—I'm lost. I was
riding on the trails, I was looking for a friend, when I got lost.
We ran from the fire. My horse—" She nodded at the little
horse, his reins now held by Skayler. "He was very tired and
thirsty, and I had to tend to him. I'm sorry if we did anything
wrong. I thought it would be okay to get a drink. But, if I
could borrow a phone, I could call my parents and have them
come get me. Please?" she added hopefully.

No one said anything. She looked around at all of them,
and as if she could see herself through their eyes, the color
rose to her cheeks, and she crossed her arms uncomfortably.
Jayce hooted softly. The other scouts remained emotionless.
Colar did his best to act like the older men.

"A young girl, out here alone—" Artor said. He shook his

head. "For your own protection, we're going to have to take you with us."

"No," she said quickly. "No, please. If you could just tell me how to get home. I don't want to be a bother . . ."

Artor looked her over, his own arms crossed. He looked as if he were trying to stare into her thoughts. Colar shifted uncomfortably.

"Your parents," he repeated. He scanned the village and the Wood. "Are they here?"

"No . . . no. I told you, I'm not sure where—I mean, if you had a phone, I could call them and they could come get me."

"So call them," Jayce smirked. "How loud can you scream?"

She looked at her tormenter, and Colar felt a shiver. She was lost and frightened, certainly, but the look she gave Jayce was neither. It was anger, the kind of anger that was born of desperation, perhaps, but there was nothing subordinate about it. *She is no village maid.*

She turned back to Captain Artor and waited, as if Jayce were of no importance. Artor caught Skayler's eye, and Skayler shrugged the least bit. Artor turned back.

"I don't understand half of what you say, girl. I'll leave it for the general to decide what to do with you." He turned toward Jayce and Colar. "You two. Take her and her horse back to camp and report to General Marthen. The rest of you, split up and finish torching the houses."

The girl's eyes went large at that, but she made no sound and no struggle as the scouts saluted and set to their work. Colar took the reins of the little horse from Skayler. The sandy-haired scout handed over the saddlebag with the strange bottle and cloth in it and nodded at Jayce. "Watch him," he said, his voice low. "Could be there's more to her than first glance sees. She needs to go to the general in one piece, now."

Colar nodded back, glad to have the commission. He clicked to the horse, and it fell in beside him.

"Here," he said to the girl. "Saddle him up." He did not trust himself to say anything else, though questions pounded with every heartbeat. *Who are you? Those strange things in your saddlebag, what are they? Why are you here?*

She barely looked at him as she did as she was bid, tossing the small saddle lightly onto the horse's back. He watched her fumble with the buckles with shaking hands, so frightened she made a mess of it again and again. He was about to take over when finally she gave a short, frustrated "Oh!" took a deep breath, and let it out before trying again.

It was something Colar did; it looked so odd to see a stranger girl use the same trick to calm herself.

Jayce bumped him with his shoulder, and Colar started and turned around. The other scout had a length of rope in his hands. He raised a brow and looked at the girl, a grin of antic-ipation on his face. "We should tie her, right? I think we should tie her."

Colar lifted his shoulders. "Where is she going to go?"

Jayce made a dissatisfied expression at his response. "I'm going to tie her," he said. He turned around and looked at the rest of the scouts, busy at their work firing the houses. When he turned back to Colar, he said, "We'll make a stop after we clear the bend. I don't see why this has to go beyond the two of us." He cocked his head, regarding Colar. "You can go first," he offered, grinning.

The blood thundered in his head, and only when it cleared could he trust himself to speak. Colar forced himself to look at the other scout and tried to act like the captain.

"We aren't touching her, and we aren't tying her."

Jayce stared at him, incredulous. "You don't give the or-ders here, boy."

Colar almost couldn't breathe. Instead, he put his hand to the hilt of his sword. He hoped that was enough of a threat. He hoped he wouldn't have to say what was struggling to come out from behind his teeth.

If you touch her, I'll tell my father.

When Jayce sneered and turned away, Colar knew that it was that last unspoken threat that he responded to.

The girl was watching them silently. If she understood what had happened, it did not appear on her face. She stood next to her horse, patting his neck, and he had to bark at her to make his voice work.

"Mount," he said tersely. Jayce made an under-his-breath oath and swung into his saddle. The girl mounted lightly, swing-ing easily up onto the small horse. The rising evening breeze flared up, and the girl shivered in her inadequate clothing. Colar shrugged out of his leather coat and handed it to the girl. "Here," he said, and for the very first time, she really looked at him. Her eyes were pale blue and rimmed with red from the smoke. Her skin was blotchy and smudged but looked like it was fair under the dirt and tears. She had a sprinkling of spots on her chin. She had to swallow before she could get her voice to work.

"Thanks," she said and put it on and hugged it around her. The breeze that came off the river felt good against his fevered skin.

As a precaution against her trying to flee, though he doubted her tired horse could make it ten strides at a gallop before falling over, he shook the reins over its head and led her away. Jayce followed. The back of Colar's neck itched, with the man riding behind them like that. No—Jayce wouldn't dare try anything against the blood of the House of Terrick. Colar sighed. So there went his chivalry.

Jayce'll get over it, he told himself hopefully. *When we get back to camp.* Jayce didn't have a woman in the camp, but he always found one of them to lie with when he wanted, and he rarely had to pay coin—though Colar wondered if the girls had a choice in that.

Colar glanced back at his little train. The girl hunched up on her horse, holding the coat closed at her throat. Jayce sulked behind them. The lowering sun turned the Aeritan to glowing gold, and the pall of smoke rising over the forest was tinged with it as well.

It was going to be a long ride back to camp.

Four

Climbing the ridge after Dungiven and the horse thief brought Lynn out of the shadow of the woods and into sparser cover. After the twilight of Gordath Wood, it was almost bright. The air on the ridge was crisp, and the insects that had been harassing her ceaselessly in the damp woods were blown away.

She swiped her hair back and made a face when she saw how grimy and sweaty her hands were. *A little dirt never hurt anyone,* she thought gamely and limped out into the open.

She had come out onto the backbone of the ridge, skirting a jumble of rocks that tumbled precariously back down into the woods. One massive boulder had been split in two. Vines crawled over it, and a sapling came up in the middle. It balanced on three smaller rocks, settling onto them the way a pot settled on a stove.

A tongue of rock thrust out from the ridge over a wide bowl filled with trees. Far below ran the silver line of a stream. On the other side of the valley, a swath of green field swooped up toward the sky. The wind picked up a bit, and Lynn closed the collar of her vest, staring at the distant field and scanning the rest of her surroundings. She couldn't see any roads or telephone wires. Electrical towers should be marching up that field, carrying wires along outstretched arms.

She looked up at the dulling sky swept with wisps of cirrus clouds. No planes.

Her knee hurt, and she was getting cold, the sweat from her hike chilling her in the cool breeze. Lynn turned away from the ledge and back toward the forest, limping over to a gnarled tree. She slid down, wincing a little.

Sparse grass cushioned her, warmed by the sun. Taking advantage of the warmth, she drew off her boots. The hot leather slid away grudgingly, exposing her sweaty toes in their shredded nylon socks. Blisters were rubbed raw all over her feet. The cool air flowed over them, but Lynn already knew what it was going to feel like when she had to put her boots back on.

She sighed, shrugged out of her vest, and folded it under her feet. Couldn't be helped, she thought. She wasn't going anywhere without a rest, and she closed her eyes.

Without sight, she was lulled by the rest of her senses. The smell of sun-warmed grasses filled her nostrils, and the faint sound of the wind in the trees washed over her.

Lynn was reminded of a late-summer evening in her apartment over the top barn, the curtains lifting in the open window, letting in an evening breeze. She kept her eyes closed, indulging the memory.

She can smell the familiar barn aromas of horses and tanbark, dusty hay and leather, and breathes in deep. Joe stirs next to her. She doesn't want to burst the illusion by reaching out to touch him, so she just concentrates on the familiar aroma of him. Over them the white curtains waft gently, billowing out from the cool air.

He says something she can't hear, and she says, "What?" and he says, "Where are you?" "Right here," she says and wants to put out her hand but holds back. He doesn't answer, and she realizes that he's falling asleep, falling and falling, and she lets herself fall with him.

Lynn jerked awake. The shadows stretched across the little lawn like thin fingers, spilling out from the edge of the woods. The breeze picked up, raking her, and the afternoon sun paled, taking the day's warmth with it. Lynn peered into the woods, sharply uneasy. The broken boulder hulked under the trees, the sapling swaying in its stone prison, the vines fluttering.

She heard whispers from the stone, voices just beyond the reach of her hearing. *Just the wind,* she told herself, looking harder and seeing nothing. She pulled on her boots, her blisters stinging, and got to her feet. The wind, or whatever it was, faded, like a conversation she was listening to on a distant radio. She thought that if she strained, she could almost hear what the voices were saying. It wasn't the wind. She knew that. The whispering emanated from the split boulder, rising and falling, and she felt cold shivers spike along her spine at the sense of malice that tinged the distant words.

Run, she told herself. *Run. Jump if you have to. Just run.* She edged away from the boulder toward the ledge, glancing down at the valley below. The ridge wasn't a sheer cliff. It would be a tough downward climb, but Lynn knew, looking back at the whispering boulder, that there was no way in hell she was going back into the woods.

Back anywhere near *that.*

The whispering stopped. The ground began to tremble, so gently at first she only registered the movement as a vibration in her boots, and then the ledge shivered out from underneath her feet. Lynn dropped to her hands and knees. The sapling lashed violently in the crack, far out of proportion to the almost gentle earthquake.

Lynn wormed her way over the still-shaking ledge and let herself down into the brush feetfirst. For a heart-stopping moment she hung over the air, her toes trying to contact the ground. The ledge gave a last, violent shake. Lynn's fingers slipped, and she crashed into the brush backward.

She fell, windmilling wildly, grabbing for brush or rocks, scraping herself as she slid down the hill. Rocks bounced past her. She managed to twist herself around, got her feet beneath her, and sat determinedly, plowing boots first through the brush. She hit a small tree, stunted by the barren hillside and the wind, and braced herself against it, the impact jarring her into the hill.

Her descent halted, she looked around, gasping for air. She was about halfway down the hill. Above her the ledge still sent down a few pebbles, dislodged by her flight. Lynn ducked as one bounced past her. Below her, she could see the stream and what she had not noticed before: a dirt road that ran alongside it.

She saw the horses first, milling about on the road. Then she saw their riders, all watching her, some pointing.

It's about time, she wanted to say. *What took you so long? Can we go home now?*

Lynn grabbed the tree with a shaking hand and began to

edge her way down the hill, sliding and stumbling in a cloud of dirt and dust.

When she reached the dirt road, one of the riders detached himself from the group, gesturing the others to stand back. He was tall, sandy-haired, with light eyes, clean-shaven. He wore the same kind of clothes that her horse thief had worn, but his coat bore a reddish brown insignia.

He carried a sword at his belt along with a sheathed knife. Lynn's eyes flicked along those weapons, and she took an involuntary step back, but she knew she had no strength to run. He stopped, making sure there was distance between them.

"Are you hurt?" he called out, his accent as strange and lilting to her ears as the horse thief's.

She almost burst into tears or laughter, or both. She was bleeding from several scrapes, she was covered with dust, and there was plenty of dirt down her shirt and breeches. Lynn got herself under control and said, "Nothing broken. I think I'm all right."

He nodded and glanced up at the hill. "Are you alone?"

She was silent for a long moment, not wanting to say, but her silence gave her away. So she pushed back her hair, and said, "Look, where am I? Is this North Salem?"

He shook his head. "This is Aeritan."

Aeritan. She had never heard of it. That must have shown on her face, because he said, "I am Captain Crae of Red Gold Bridge. You should come with us."

Of what? Of where?

She tried one last time. "Look, my name is Lynn Romano. Isn't anyone looking for me? Are you sure you haven't seen my horse? This guy—I thought he was hurt, but he managed to ride off. Only I don't think he'll get very far . . ." She trailed off. How could the man have a gunshot wound when all these guys carried swords?

He stared at her. "A—*gae*?"

Comprehension dawned. The first thing he had asked her when she fell down the mountain was, *Are you alone?*

They were looking for her horse thief.

With two long strides the captain reached her and grabbed her by the shoulders. "This man. Which way did he ride?"

"Hey!" She tried to shake him off, but he kept hold of her. *"What does your horse look like?"*

"He's a big gray, seventeen hands—stop!" She was becoming frantic herself. "And I don't know which way he went! I followed him up the ridge to that *thing!* And I am *not* going back in there! Let me go!"

He released her, stepping back. He help up a hand. "Stay there," he ordered, as if she was in any shape to go anywhere. He turned toward his men. "Brin, take up the track. We follow. Tal, take our guest up and bring her back to Lord Tharp. Have her tell him what she knows."

Lynn shook her head before he finished. If he thought he was taking her prisoner . . . "Wait. No. Stop. I need to find my horse, get to a phone, and get home. I am not going anywhere *without my horse!*"

"I am trying to find your horse!" he bellowed. "When was he stolen? How far are we behind him?"

If I hadn't fallen asleep, if I had just kept after him . . . She was going to cry, and she never cried. "Hours," she managed. "It's been hours."

His face went cold. He made a clipped, quiet remark that she couldn't recognize, then turned to the short, wiry man he called Brin. "We follow." The man nodded and sketched a quick salute. The captain nodded at Tal. "Take her to Lord Tharp." He glanced at Lynn again but forebore to say anything more to her. "Everybody up."

Heartsick, she had no choice but to comply. The young man called Tal brought his chestnut mare over to her. Lynn gripped the gloved hand the soldier reached down to her. He kicked his foot free from the stirrup, and she stepped into it, pulling herself up behind the saddle like a crippled old woman. The horse humped her back against the added weight, then settled. Loath to hold on to the man, Lynn gripped the raised cantle in front of her and looked around.

The road was rutted with cart tracks and hoofprints, horse prints interspersed with the tracks of narrow, cloven hooves from oxen and cattle. The river was shaded with trees and brush, but the road itself was dusty and sunburned. Lynn turned to look back up at the ledge. Behind the ridge rose the trees of Gordath

Wood, their tops just lit with the sun. She remembered the shadows and the whispering rock and shivered. Tal said over his shoulder, "Hold on to my coat if you need to."

"I'm fine," Lynn said.

Tal pivoted the mare neatly, and they rode away from the others, the mare in a smooth running walk that would eat up the miles. After a quick glance back, Lynn concentrated on keeping her seat behind the saddle. Her knee hurt, her feet hurt, her face and hands stung with cuts. Still, she couldn't help but feel that anything, *anything* beat being lost in Gordath Wood.

Crae was grimly impressed that the woman had managed to come down the ridge in one piece, but his horses could no more climb it than they could fly. He left a couple of men with their mounts, and he and the others climbed. The sun was hot on their backs, and they sweated hard by the time they reached the top. The unquiet ridge still trembled and sent rocks and debris at them; he and his men cursed when struck, slid a few feet, and kept at their climb.

The trembling increased when they achieved the lawn. In front of them, shadowed by the outskirts of the wood, the morrim hulked. It whispered and hummed. Crae swallowed. His men, stalwart all, were pale under their beards. He signaled them into the wood, and they faded back, away from the danger. Arrim had told him once that the morrim were not the danger, that the gordath was. They were anchors, he said, that held the gordath between them.

"Between?" Crae had asked. "There's another morrim?"

Arrim gave a grin, slightly mad in the way he had. "Not in this Gordath Wood."

"There's . . . another?" Crae had asked, feeling stupid.

He didn't want to look too closely at the morrim; it vibrated with energy. But he couldn't resist throwing back one glance as they filed away into the forest as softly as they could. The earth was gouged up at its feet, the loam still wet and dark.

The anchor was being torn from its moorings.

Brin cast about at the edge of the ridge and lifted his hand. Crae and the others followed. They could see the hoofprints leading away from the morrim back into the cool forest. Brin knelt and put his hand into one of the hoofprints and held it up to Crae. One of his men whistled softly, and Crae nodded. The woman had not exaggerated about the size of her horse. The hoofprint was half again as big as Briar's, his own sturdy gelding.

The hoofprints led southwest. They followed.

The castle rose out of the distance like an ex-tension of the mountains, a central tower rounding in front. Long walls fell away on both sides like irregular wings. The stone was gray and weathered but with a tinge of pink to it, the tower windows long, narrow slits. The dirt road led up to a curved bridge that soared over the river toward a vast gate. The mare trotted briskly over the stone bridge, and the gate ground open at their approach. The courtyard was crowded with soldiers and horses, wagons and oxen.

Tal brought the mare to a stamping, blowing halt. He swung his leg over the front of the saddle, dropping to the ground. Lynn followed more painfully. He looked around, spotting a small group of boys watching the activity with wide eyes. "Hey!" he shouted at the kids. "Take the mare and walk her for me."

They darted forward and, tired though she was, Lynn had to smile at their eagerness. The young soldier's cool was undeniable. Tal pointed. "This way. The lord will want to see you."

The lord, huh? She followed him across the courtyard, aware of the many eyes on her. The tower loomed overhead, and she craned back to see, hurrying after Tal when he got a few steps ahead. He led her through a somber archway; she caught a glimpse of the carvings, beautifully etched-out leaves and vines, and then they left the courtyard behind.

The corridor led to a wide hall. A fireplace ran the length of the long room, the fire set but unlit. Knots of men stood there, their voices echoing up to the ceiling. All turned to look at Lynn and her escort. Tal scanned the room until he found who he wanted. He pushed Lynn in front of him.

"Sir. Lord Tharp," he said.

Tharp turned from his men. He looked to be in his early forties; his dark hair, cut severely short, was graying at the temples, as was his beard. He wore a dark red padded vest over a brown tunic. Brown blousy trousers tucked into his boots. He smelled of sweat and woodsmoke. He looked at Lynn, and his gaze sharpened.

"Who is this?"

"We found her in the Wood, sir. She said that the guardian stole her horse and fled. Captain Crae and the rest of the guard are tracking him now."

Tharp took that in. His expression went from harried to furious.

"He's *mounted*?"

"Yes, sir."

Lord Tharp cursed. "From dead to hale in the space of a day. Damn Bahard! Damn guardian!" he said; his wrath reminded her of her worst clients. "You, woman. Tell me of the guardian. Be quick, for I do not have all day."

She knew how to deal with assholes. Her voice clipped, she said, "Look, all I know is, yesterday I rode my horse through the woods and got lost, and today some guy stole him and I was left to find my way on foot." She couldn't keep the bitterness out of her voice. "He was badly injured, or so I thought—I stopped to help."

"Who gave you the right to interfere?" he roared.

Lynn's own rage and tiredness boiled over. "Hey! Look—"

"Sir! Lord Tharp!"

They all turned to look. Several men hastened into the hall, carrying another. A swirl of smoky air came in with them. "Water!" one shouted. "Water and a wet cloth!"

Someone brought water, and they poured as much of it into the man as they could, swabbing away the smoke and dirt from his face.

"The gordath closed on its own," he croaked. "We couldn't get near it to keep it open. The fire—" He started coughing again, and this time it looked like he was coughing up blood. "We couldn't stop it. Bahard tried to drive through the gordath, but the fire got there first and pushed him back."

Tharp dropped to his knees beside the man and put his arm under his shoulder. The man gulped more water, and his breathing became more even.

"We tried to keep the fire off the gordath, but it was no use. Without the guardian, it slammed shut on its own against the flames. Then there was a new danger—Bahard made us move the weapons and the reloading supplies into the root cellar to protect against the blaze. He said they would explode if the fire got to them."

Tharp's expression steeled. "What of the house and the weapons cache?"

"Safe for now. When the gordath closed, it cut into the flames. Some flames got through, I could see, but then the worlds were divided once more. But the fire surrounding the house was easier to put to rest after that. I came as soon as the smoldering was under control."

"How much of the weaponry did you save?"

"All of the guns, sir, but we had not finished carrying the ammunition across the gordath."

"Forest god," Tharp said under his breath. He made an effort, collected himself. "Where's Bahard now?"

"He's on his way across the south encampment," one of the men said. Tharp gave his support of the man to another soldier and stood.

"See to him. The rest of you, to your duties. You, guardsman, have the woman put somewhere for safekeeping, then for the sake of all the gods, man, go back and find that guardian! Or any guardian, the useless, lordless rabble that they are, and harry them at end of your sword if necessary, but just *bring one back!*"

His anger swept the hall, galvanizing all of them. "The rest of you, with me. We have a war to fight, with new weapons to get used to. Lord Salt." He looked around, and another man stepped forward. "We may need the smiths after all. Would you do me honor and oversee their progress?"

"With a good heart, Lord Tharp," said Salt.

Tharp took one more look around and then clattered off with his men. The hall emptied, leaving only Lynn and the young man, Tal. *He looks like he's a college kid,* she thought. She gave what she hoped was a winning smile.

"You know, you all look very busy here. Why don't you just let me go back into the forest, get out of your hair?"

He was young, but he wasn't stupid. He gave a rueful grin.

"You know I can't do that. Besides, you heard. The forest is afire."

And Dungiven is out in it. Too bad she didn't cry; it felt like all she had energy for. "Are you going back to look for my horse?"

"The guardian, yes."

They had their priorities, but at the moment their priorities meshed. She followed him back out into the courtyard. The smoky air was stronger outside, and Lynn's eyes watered. The boys were still diligently walking the mare, weaving her in between wagons and barrels. The young man guided Lynn up the spiral tower stairs carved into the outside of the wall, draped in trailing brambles bright with red rose hips.

The stairs were the hardest thing she had ever done. She was so tired she felt as if she could fall asleep standing upright on the second step. Her knee throbbed at the abuse, and her boots pinched her unmercifully. Tal waited for her as she negotiated each step.

If she wanted to go home, if she wanted to ever see Joe again, she had to stop reacting and start thinking. So the Gordath Wood spooky stories, about phantoms and unsolved disappearances, were true. She had come through some kind of gateway. The trouble was, the fire had closed off her only way home. But she wasn't alone. This Bahard was from home, too, evidently. *And running guns from North Salem to here.*

Bahard is my key, she thought, trudging up the stairs. *Find Bahard and find out where the weapons are coming in, and that's how I can get home.*

Lynn heard the snick of the latch behind her as Tal left her alone in the room and pulled the door closed behind him. From the other side of the door came the dull clunk of a lock tumbling into place. She shivered, holding her arms around herself, thankful for her vest. Cold seeped through the soles of her boots. The round tower room jutted out from the wall of the mountain, brick masonry laid in flattened curves. Two narrow windows were set in the bricks, letting in cold air streaming with smoke. Set beneath the windows was an enormous wooden chest. Dust motes danced in the narrow beams of the setting sun lancing across the chest to the stone floor and onto the bed, a low-slung frame covered with heavy woolen blankets. A fireplace was set into the opposite wall, a fire laid but unlit.

She tried the door, but it stayed locked. The doorjamb was carved with a decorative scroll, long blurred now. The lintel and the threshold were decorated with faint rosettes, reminding her of the rosebushes that trailed over the entrance to the stairs. She tucked her hands back in her pockets and slouched toward the window. Peering through it, she looked out, squinting as she got a faceful of the setting sun.

Her window did not overlook the courtyard and the forest but instead looked out over an encampment of tents and fires. Tharp's army. Men and horses swarmed about, dark dots in the hazy sunlight. Beyond the camp flowed the river, its far bank lost in the distance, its near bank a flat and sandy beach.

Lynn sighed and pulled back from the window. She was tired, hungry, and aching. The bed lured her, and she gave in to its seductive call.

She was sitting on the edge of the bed and taking off her boots when she registered a familiar sound, one so familiar that at first she did not recognize it as out of place. A second later she flew to her feet, holding a dirty boot in one hand, and leaned out the window, craning around the wide stone sill.

A Jeep, trailing dust behind it, drove along the edge of the army encampment and disappeared down the curve of the riverbank.

Five

The news of Lynn's disappearance traveled fast. Joe had to get his chores done amid a crowd of search teams and gawkers and clients. The barn phone rang constantly, and after a while Joe stopped trying to answer it. There were plenty of teenage girls who wanted a chance to report the news, so he let them manage the calls with breathless importance.

The insurance adjusters showed up about the time the news stations got wind of Lynn's disappearance. The adjusters went up to the farmhouse to talk to Mrs. Hunt about Dungiven's coverage, and Joe had to tell the news trucks to return to the main road and stay off farm property. After that, his temper started to get short, so he decided to take the tractor out to the far turnout pasture to repair the fence line. He would have preferred to be around when the search parties reported in, but then again, it didn't look like they were having much luck.

It still burned him that when he asked to go out with the search parties, the police turned him down after he admitted that he didn't ride and didn't know the trails better than they did.

"You better wait this one out," one of the cops said. Joe, still trying, said, "Look, I tried to search last night. I think she could have come out along by Aspen Farms and gotten turned around."

The cop looked at him.

"You searched last night?"

Joe, surprised, said, "Yeah. Didn't get far though."

The cop cut him off. "We'll handle it."

Joe took his temper out on the clapboard fence, kicking out

the rotten piece of wood. It snapped off, and he pried the rest of it with his hammer. One of the horses browsed up to him curiously—Piper, the chestnut gelding. He watched Joe with interest. Horses held no real attraction for Joe, but he often thought Piper was like a big ol' dog; he preferred humans, he was calm and happy, and he had a goofy sense of humor.

The horse clopped over to the tractor where Joe had left his tools and pulled out another hammer. He couldn't get his teeth around it and it dropped to the ground. He looked at Joe.

"You better not take them all out," Joe said. He jerked his head toward the gate down the hill. "Beat it. Get out of here."

Piper shivered, his red skin twitching as if a fly had touched down on his back. He swung his head to look at the woods, his ears standing at attention. Then, inexplicably, he snorted and spun, cantering off toward the gate with his tail held high.

Joe shook his head and finished nailing on a new board. The day had turned damp and humid, the sky burned white by the sun. Joe straightened his back and twisted, trying to loosen the kinks, and dumped his tools into the cart on the back of the trailer. A cooling breeze lifted off the slight hill that he was working on. It carried a hint of woodsmoke.

Shit, he thought suddenly. *Is Kate back yet?* He started the tractor and chugged slowly back to the main barn.

Things had quieted down some. The searchers were still out, but the insurance guys had gone, and most of the clients had finished riding and gone back home, leaving their horses to the stable girls. Someone had posted a printed message on the tack room bulletin board in the main barn: "Police request that riders stay off the trails until further notice. Thank you. Mrs. Hunt." Joe's guilt deepened.

He hurried up to the little hill barn where Mojo boarded. His first glance at the tack room made his heart sink. Kate's equipment trunk was open, brushes and equipment flung everywhere. The sleeve of her jacket trailed onto the dusty floor. Mojo's saddle rack, mounted over her trunk, was empty, a plastic saddle cover tossed carelessly on top of it. Joe checked Mojo's box anyway, but he knew it would be empty.

Great. He'd have to tell Mrs. Hunt.

The farmhouse front door was open, the screen door slightly ajar. Joe rapped on the doorframe, and the door rattled as much as knocked. He peered inside at the dim interior. He'd never been inside her house but once, when he helped some deliverymen bring in a new washer and dryer. As his eyes adjusted, her elegant living room appeared out of the gloom.

With a start he realized she was in there, sitting quietly in one of her wing chairs, looking not at him but out the tall windows overlooking the farm and the woods beyond.

Joe didn't think she heard his knock. He rapped again, holding the flimsy door so he could knock hard. She shifted in her chair and turned to look at him.

"Come in," she said.

He let himself in, feeling awkward in his sweaty T-shirt and faded, dusty jeans, and stood just inside the door.

"Ma'am," he said. "I think Kate Mossland is missing."

She looked at him, and even in the dimness he could see the dawning knowledge in her expression.

"She went out on the trails this morning," he went on. "I, uh, didn't think there was any harm. I just now realized she hasn't come back."

Mrs. Hunt put her fingers against her temples as if to push back a headache. "Very well. I will call the police and let them know they are now looking for two riders." She nodded her dismissal. "Thank you."

He turned and let himself out, holding the screen door so it wouldn't bang shut, when one of the clients came pelting up the drive and onto the porch, running awkwardly in her tall boots and tight breeches.

"Where's Mrs. Hunt!" she said. "Does she know the woods are on fire?"

Joe spun around and followed her gaze. Smoke billowed out of the woods where the search parties had been combing all day. Behind him Mrs. Hunt heard the commotion and came out to look. She whispered something that he could not decipher.

The horses in the turnout fields came cantering in, manes and tails flying, to stand by the gate where Piper was waiting. The distant wail of sirens grew louder every second.

Joe's heart sank to the pit of his stomach.

Someone didn't want Lynn or Dungiven found. Someone

set the woods on fire to hide what they had done. Someone was playing for keeps—and he had let a fifteen-year-old girl ride out there by herself.

Kate was grateful for the jacket the boy had loaned her. The breeze off the river had risen and stung with cold. The sun had almost completely set, turning the river briefly alight, but it carried no warmth with it.

Mojo trudged along sluggishly. The two soldiers kept wanting him to move out, and she wanted to scream at them, *Can't you see he's exhausted?* Instead, she kept her leg behind the girth and kept pushing at him, making him stumble into a trot. *I'm sorry,* she told him silently. *I'm sorry, Modgie, but please hurry; you have to.*

She didn't want to make the mean one any madder than he was. She concentrated on keeping Mojo on the move, all the while focusing her anger on Jayce. *Jerk. No. Asshole.* There. That was better.

It was almost dark by the time they reached camp, a sprawling expanse of people, tents, horses, and oxen. Cooking fires dotted the ground. The air was thick with smoke, the smell of horses and manure, people and sweat, the musty smell of heavy tents. The air was filled with shouts, screams, talk, constant movement. Kate was dazed.

Colar and Jayce pulled up, and Mojo stumbled to a halt, his head hanging to his knees. Kate went to dismount when Jayce barked at her.

"Hold!" he snapped. "I haven't told you to move."

Kate was shocked into stillness.

Jayce dismounted, stretching extravagantly, a relief he denied her. Kate got the message. The knowledge that she was dealing with a petty tyrant emboldened her. She dropped her stirrups and stretched out her legs, trying for some relief while staying put.

Colar was already on the ground. He held Mojo's reins under the horse's chin, not that the horse was going anywhere, and nodded at her.

"You can dismount."

"Okay." She slid out of the saddle, biting her lip as she landed. Her ankles were stiff. She hesitated, looking around at the gathering crowd, then steeled herself and shrugged out of Colar's jacket. "Here," she said. "Thanks."

He looked startled but took the jacket.

The crowd included women among the men. The women hooted and laughed at the sight of the girl captive.

"Eh, lad, whaddaya get this time, eh? A little fancy for your bedroll?"

"Just big enough to warm the blanket, eh, boys? Won't do to take up too much room!"

Kate's cheeks heated up.

Jayce took her by the elbow and pulled her along. "Let's go."

Kate pulled back. "Hey, wait! My horse!"

Jayce made to slap her, and she shrank back. He smirked and dragged her on. Kate took one last look at Mojo and the other horses, now being taken up by a few of the men, and struggled to keep up.

They escorted her to a makeshift stockade. "Hold her here," Jayce said to the sentry at the gate. "She'll be wanted by the general for interrogation."

"The runner?" the sentry asked, taking Kate by the neck and the wrists and pushing her into the jail. Inside a few chained prisoners stirred listlessly.

Jayce shook his head. "We don't know. Here, you girl! Tell us now what news you've got. It'll go easier for you if we don't have to beat it out of you!"

She stared back at him for a moment, taking in his cruel eyes and thin face. The slow burn that started when he first hit her gave her strength. Evenly she said, "If anything happens to my horse, I'll kill you."

She could tell it took Jayce by surprise, though an instant later the scout sneered dismissively and turned away. She sat against the edge of the palisade, hugging her knees, shivering in the cold night air. She wished she hadn't given the jacket back. She thought of her promise to Joe. "If I see anything, I'll turn back," she had told him. Neither of them had considered that turning back might not be possible.

She glanced at her fellow prisoners and looked away. Two of the harder-looking men stared deliberately at her, and one of them shuffled as close to her as his chains would allow. Kate scooted herself farther away.

She huddled against the rough planks and waited, tense and frightened, and once again pricked by anger. She couldn't afford the luxury of weakness. Not now, not with men like Jayce or like those two prisoners. She missed her parents, her home, her horse, she even missed herself, the old Kate who loved horses, dreamed about boys, and lived for her solitude. That Kate could not help her now. Tears welled in her eyes even as she scolded herself. *Get a grip.*

She bit her lip against her fear until she tasted blood in her mouth. Kate allowed herself one last thought of home and waited.

Marthen looked up as the scouts reported in. His tent was lit by a few lamps clustered over his table where he pored over maps of the Aeritan Valley. Darkness closed in from the edges of his tent. A brazier flickered over by his camp bed, warming the little space against the evening chill off the river.

"Report," he said. Lord Terrick's son Colar saluted and handed him a saddlebag and helmet.

"No sign of the runner, sir, but we found these. A girl rider came out of the Wood, chased by the fire, she said. Captain Artor didn't think she was a courier or a spy. She said she was lost, sir."

"Lying?"

Colar took a breath. "I don't think so, sir. I don't think anyone could dissemble so well."

"You'd be surprised," Marthen muttered. "Continue."

"Begging your pardon, sir," Jayce broke in. "She would have stood out too much to be a spy, the way she was wearing nothing but a shift and breeches that left nothing to the imagination." He smirked.

Even in the soft light Marthen could see the Terrick boy turn red. The young scout hastily nodded at the saddlebag and helmet. "She was carrying those things. Strange, sir. And this—cloth as clear as glass, but lightweight and strong. I've never seen anything like them. And the helm—it's light as well, but strong. I tried to crush it, and the outside part just dented and sprang back. Here."

Marthen handed him back the helmet, and Colar demonstrated. The lightweight material gave under his hands, then regained its shape. Marthen took it back.

"Have you searched her?"

"No, sir. It was clear—she was not hiding anything," Colar said.

Again Jayce sniggered. Marthen looked at him expressionlessly, and the scout's giggle faltered into silence. Marthen let the silence lengthen until Jayce bit his lip and began to fidget.

"Dismissed," Marthen said shortly, and turned back to Colar. "Continue."

Jayce hesitated, then saluted and ducked out.

"Her horse, sir. A breed I didn't recognize. Very neat and small. Cobby, but with a fine head and small feet. Powerful, too—big square haunches. The only thing is, he's only about fifteen hands, not much more, if any, so he might be of limited use." He smiled, remembering more. "She took good care of him, when they came out of the Wood, made sure he was walked cool and watered before drinking any herself."

Marthen sighed. "The code of Terrick," he murmured and eyed Colar as the young scout looked uncertain. "You are all taught that how a man treats his horses and hounds speaks volumes about his character. One of these days it will get you killed."

Colar opened his mouth but hesitated. "General, I only meant—" He broke off as Marthen held up his hand to stop him.

"Never mind, scout. Anything else?"

The young scout gathered himself, then said, "Yes, sir. I think she's from across the Wood, sir. I think the gordath's been opened."

Marthen regarded him. The scout held himself at attention. *A Terrick through and through,* he thought. He looked over at the corner of his tent, lost in shadow. "Have her brought to me," he told his lieutenant sitting there. Colar started; he clearly hadn't seen the silent man who rose and left the tent. "All right," he told the young scout. "Get some rest. I want you back out with the patrol at dawn."

Colar saluted and ducked out, and Marthen waited, turning over the bottle in his hand. It was of an odd material, molded, not blown. The helmet was of some strong material, neither wood nor metal, for it was very light. It looked ornamental rather than useful. He held the small, transparent cloth bag to the golden light. It was torn and crumpled.

These were not from Aeritan or from any of the countries that traded with it. Whatever they were, however they were made, they were not forged in any smithy that he knew of. Like Tharp's strange weapons, he thought. Like those "guns" his spies brought tales of, these were foreign.

Gordath Wood had always had a reputation for eeriness, for sly stories. "Don't go in the woods alone," the peasants said. "You'll never know where you're going to end up." Now this. And he had a feeling, looking at the strange artifacts, that they were just a precursor. *Something big is coming through the Wood,* Marthen thought. *I was right to torch it.* His aides had protested the order, objecting to the mass destruction it implied. The loose coalition of lords that he answered to were emphatically against it as well, yet he knew that he had to stop whatever was coming through in order to cut off Tharp's advantage.

He looked up as the lieutenant came back with the girl, ducking through the tent flap. She was no longer a child by a few years, but old enough to marry, if she were of Council blood. Her hair was a colorless, tangled mass, her face streaked with layers of grime. Her sleeveless shift had once been white; now the tight-fitting shirt was streaked more black and gray than any other color. Her breeches were covered with soot. She cast quick glances about the tent, afraid to look at him.

Something is coming through the Wood, Marthen thought again, tossing the helmet onto his camp bed. *And just my luck—Tharp gets powerful new weapons that will cut my army to ribbons unless I can find a way to stop him.*

I get a girl.

Kate stood straight, hoping that her new strength would carry her through whatever came next. She looked at the general in quick glances, taking in his pale eyes, dark black hair, tall frame. He was wearing a plain white shirt with wide sleeves, fastened with buttons at the shoulder. His trousers were black; instead of boots, he wore soft slippers.

He raised his brow at her inspection, and she flushed and looked down.

"You may go," he told the lieutenant, who saluted and faded out. Kate braced herself, thinking of the men in the stockade.

"So you are the mysterious spy," he said to her after a moment, watching her. "What is your name?"

"Kate Mossland. I'm not a spy," she whispered to her feet.

"What were you doing in the Gordath Wood?"

"I was lost. I—I was running from the fire."

"Lost? Where are you from?"

She looked up at him then, hesitating. Would he even know where she came from? She doubted it. Wherever *here* was, she knew she was a long way from home. He sat back against the desk, waiting.

"North Salem. New York."

Marthen raised an eyebrow. "I am not familiar with it," he said politely. "Is it a small village?"

"No, you would have burned it then." The words burst out of her, and she raised a hand partway to her mouth, horrified.

His expression did not alter at first, then he cocked his head to the side and said, "Perhaps. I have burned a lot of villages."

She said, "I rode out this morning, and all of a sudden, I wasn't where I was supposed to be. It was like I had taken one step too many, or to the side of the trail. And then when I let Mojo have his head to let him find his way home, I would have sworn that he was lost, too." This time she looked straight at him. "I have never in my life seen a horse who didn't know the way home."

His mouth quirked, and her face flamed. She hadn't mean to sound funny.

"You told my scouts you were looking for a friend," he prompted.

She nodded. "I think the same thing must have happened to her," she said. "See, she rode Dungiven—that's Mrs. Hunt's big jumper—home from the show the night before. Only she never got home. And everyone thinks she stole the horse. But she didn't. She wouldn't have."

Marthen nodded again, and heat rose into her face.

"I'm not a spy," Kate said. "Or a courier. I just want to get my horse and go home."

"Spy or not, girl, you are in the middle of a war. I'm not sure what your part is yet, but I think I will need to keep you around for awhile to find out."

"This isn't my war," Kate said, her throat tight with tears.

"No. It's mine. And I intend to use any weapon at hand to win it." He looked her over once again, and she looked away from his gaze. Marthen went over to a small chest at the foot of his narrow bed and rummaged through it. He tossed a shirt at her, and she clutched it to her chest. "Cover yourself with this. Try to run away, and I'll hang you for desertion. Understood?"

She nodded without saying anything, and feeling his eyes on her, she fumbled with the shirt, pulling it over her head. She had to cuff the sleeves many times. It hung practically to her knees, and she realized that was probably the idea.

"What about my horse?" she asked. She was tired, hungry, and sore, and all she wanted to do was sleep. But if anything happened to Mojo—

"He's been drafted, too," Marthen said without a trace of a smile. He lifted his voice. "Grayne."

The man who had fetched Kate ducked back into the tent. "Sir."

"Have a tent pitched for this girl. Make sure everyone knows she is under my protection and is not to be touched."

"Yes, sir." Grayne took her by her sleeve and led her out. Kate shot one look back at Marthen as she left the tent. He met her eyes, his expression bland, and she hastily turned away.

Her tent was musty and cold. Kate crawled her way into it in the pitch dark, and sat for a moment on the bedroll the orderly had tossed inside. She listened to the sounds of the camp bustling around her, men shouting, tools clanking, horses clip-clopping by. She could hear low voices, harsh laughter, and voices surprisingly carefree. Fire flared up outside the wall of her tent, and she could see shadows of figures huddling close to it.

She had to clamp down hard on a flood of despair that suddenly overwhelmed her. Kate put one hand to her mouth and bit down, and the pain brought tears to her eyes. But it also gave her strength and took the edge off her panic. *I will not lie here in the dark.* She wriggled back out of the tent and stood up. The air was brisk, and no one seemed to pay her any mind after first giving her a curious glance or two. Kate cast around and then began walking to where she thought the horses would be. She could not sit in the dark, cold and frightened and alone, when her horse needed her.

The night was cold and damp, starless. Kate shivered in her borrowed shirt, tucking her hands in the sleeves. She discovered that if she didn't look directly at the fires, her eyes adjusted to the dark somewhat. Still, she stumbled over the uneven footing toward the bulky silhouettes of the dozing horses. Kate smelled their warm scent, mingled with grain, manure, and leather tack. The familiarity eased her nervousness. She knew horses. She knew this.

She bumped into the makeshift corral, a simple structure of rope and slats, that surrounded the horses. Nearby, several men squatted around a firepit, holding their hands close to the small blaze and talking in low, tired voices. No one saw her. Kate ducked under the rope and sidled around the perimeter of the small corral, now and again whispering to one of the horses and giving it a soothing pat.

She found Mojo on the far side, bedded down with the others. He nickered low at her approach but didn't get up from where he lay, legs tucked underneath him. She knelt beside him and stroked his neck, feeling his chest. It was coarse but dry. His back had the caked outline of the saddle left on it, and she wished she could brush his coat soft and clean. He would need to be exercised gently tomorrow, but she doubted she was going to be able to tend to him the way she knew she should. Kate wondered where her tack was; they must have stored the gear somewhere else. In any event, she couldn't flee that night; Mojo was too tired, and she thought that the general was expecting her to try.

She didn't want to go back to her drear and empty tent. Kate wrapped her arms around herself, trying to pretend the loose sleeves were a blanket, and closed her eyes to the growling of her stomach, leaning companionably against the solid warmth of her equally tired horse.

Six

Kate woke up from a shallow doze when Mojo heaved himself to his feet with a rumbling whinny. She scrambled up herself, trying to stay out of the way of his hooves.

Mojo stretched his neck and shook from nose to tail. Kate looked around. It was still dark, but a line of light edged the horizon to the east. A few dark, indistinct sentries stood on the camp's perimeter, hardly visible in the early morning darkness.

The rest of the horses began to stir, getting on their feet and nickering for grain. Mojo whinnied again, deep in his chest.

Kate had to go to the bathroom. She knew that she had better do it while she had the cover of darkness—but where to go? She looked around, taking in the circle of supply wagons and the crowd of bodies wrapped in blankets nearby.

Stiffly, she walked over to the wagons, stepping between prone bodies wrapped in shawls and dresses. As she stepped over one woman, she moved, muttering, and sat up, pushing at her crooked kerchief.

From the smell of things, she wasn't the only one to use the area behind the wagons as a toilet. Kate hurried to pee.

The camp came more and more alive, the raucous chaos from last night beginning again. Here and there campfires began to spring up, crackling and spitting on the damp wood. Kate could smell food being prepared. Her stomach rumbled.

"If it ain't the general's pet," remarked one of the women, sitting up as Kate came back through. "Whotsamatter, luv? He toss you out with the rest of us?"

"Thought she was better than us!" another woman pealed with laughter, rocking back and forth, her blouse untied to show off her sagging breasts. Kate looked quickly away. Mistake.

"Ooh, ain't never seen 'em before, eh, pet? Least not on yourself, you've not!" She laughed again while the other women cackled, and Kate walked back to the horses, head up, miserable. She half hoped Grayne would come to drag her back to her tent.

Mojo whickered at her, nipping at her long sleeve eagerly the way he did when he was hungry. The ostlers were up, their low voices grumbling over their tasks. The horses neighed more insistently.

"Here, you!" someone shouted at her. "Get away from the horses!"

The sky lightened enough for Kate to see an ostler with heavy whiskers glaring at her. The others gathered around.

"He's my horse," she explained. "I'll take care of him."

The ostlers gathered round.

"Oh you will, will you, girl? Get off with you! We don't want your kind of trouble!"

A horn sounded a series of trilling notes, and the ostler threw up his hands.

"Call to saddle for the scouts," he said. "Either clear out, or I'll clear you out, girl. General's orders be damned, this army is going to the dogs."

Still grumbling, the grooms forced themselves into action. A big, husky man with huge hands and enormous boots hauled down three sacks of grain from the supply wagons, dumping them on the ground. He slit one sack with a heavy knife, and men dug into the grain and piled handfuls for the horses. Kate hesitated for half a second, and then sprang in to help. This she knew. This was familiar. The scent of grain soothed her. She dumped two handfuls in front of Mojo but hurried to help feed the others. If the call to saddle, as the lead groom had it, meant that the scouts were riding out soon, the sooner the horses ate and watered, the better.

She got a couple of looks from the grooms, but she ignored them and soon they ignored her. She fell into the routine. When she saw one of the ostlers lead two horses over to a watering trough filled by a giant barrel in the back of a wagon, she grabbed the halters of two others and took them for their turn. The chestnut man, as she took to calling the one with the bushy red whiskers, gave her a baleful glare but said nothing.

The sun was almost completely up when they finished feeding the horses. Kate, sweaty and hungry, smiled tiredly at the sight of the horses eagerly eating, switching their tails against the flies. It had been a good morning's work.

The men trailed back to the cooking fire, and Kate followed, not knowing what else to do. Big-boots turned to look at her and waved her off.

"Not you, brat," he said curtly. "Eat with the rest of the doxies."

"Ah, get over yourself, Mykal," said the chestnut man. He jerked his head at Kate. "Sit, girl. Tell us how a slut like you got stuck with the likes of us."

Kate gasped in outrage. "I am n—" Her protest was drowned out by their laughter. The chestnut man wheezed alarmingly. It was a moment before she realized that he was laughing, not having a heart attack.

Hunger outwrestled her anger, and she sat down. Almost instantly, she regretted it. The pot held an unappetizing stew, smelling of old grease and rancid meat. There was rock-hard bread, and she took a piece, and something was crawling in it—yes, in it—and she set it down quickly.

One of the other ostlers jostled her elbow.

"Here. Like this." He broke off the bread, flicked off the bugs, and dunked it in the stew. "Heat kills the rest of them."

Kate smiled wanly, took a deep breath, and copied him. She swallowed the lumpy, wet mass without chewing and hoped she wouldn't throw up. Her body was not so picky, though. With the first bite of the loathsome stew and bread, her appetite awakened fiercely. Saliva flooded her mouth, and she ignored everything and everyone, taking another dip in the stew before it was the next man's turn.

She was not the only one focused on the business of eating. No one spoke as they passed around the bread and sopped it in the cauldron. Big-boots—Mykal—was the enforcer; he growled or cuffed at the ones who took more than their share or tried to sneak a turn, including Kate, to her chagrin.

"Ow!" she said, rubbing her hand where he had rapped it

for a too-big bite. She looked around for sympathy but got nothing but scowls except from one young man. As she caught his eye, he beamed a ragged smile at her. She smiled back tentatively, sensing something strange about his expression.

"Mooncalf!" Mykal bellowed, picking up a rock and throwing it at the man. He cringed and flung up an arm too late, and the stone struck him solidly in the chest.

"Oww!" the man began to cry and moan pitifully, rocking back and forth like a child. *Ohhhhhh,* Kate thought with a sinking heart. *Mooncalf.*

She had gone to middle school; she knew what was going to happen next. She knew that she could try to protect this poor man and become a fellow victim, or she could join in his persecution and gain herself a spot in the group. She looked down at her soggy bread, wishing for strength. *But I'm only fifteen,* she thought desperately. *No one would expect me to stick up for this guy. And anyway, who wants some idiot around all the time, grateful for attention?*

She glanced over at the idiot boy and knew she was doomed.

"Don't do that," she muttered.

Mykal grinned. "Don't do what?" he mimicked.

"Don't hit him." She looked around at all of them. The ostlers were frozen with anticipation, and the camp followers had gathered around. Even the idiot had uncurled to watch the proceedings. Mykal raised his hands, pretending to ward her off.

"Ooh, the doxy has taken a fancy to the mooncalf, boys! Perhaps you want to teach him how to bed a wench! Go on, Torm, give her a kiss; show her what ye know!"

Torm, having understood at least that he was no longer being pelted with rocks, grinned enthusiastically and moved in on Kate to kiss her.

Kate, furious and frightened, balled her fist and punched him in the nose. Torm stopped, gasped in confusion and pain, held his nose, and burst into tears again. Everyone oohed.

"Ah Tormie, she's a cruel woman," said one of the grooms, wheezing with laughter.

"How's yer nose, man?"

"I'd stay clear of her, there, Torm. She's a bad 'un."

"Bad 'un," Torm repeated thickly, holding his nose and sidling away from her.

"Look what you did to Torm," one woman shouted, a stick-thin wraith with almost all her teeth.

"Yeah, did you see her hit him!" said Mykal self-righteously.

"Wait—I didn't mean—" Kate started, but the others all hissed and booed, their eyes bright.

"All he wanted was to give her a little kiss!" one of the ostlers called out, and they roared with laughter. "Led him on, she did! And see what it got him!"

"Ostlers!"

The noise broke off abruptly as everyone turned. It was Colar and Jayce, ready to ride. Jayce kicked at the nearest man. He flinched and staggered back. In the abashed silence the camp followers scurried off. Torm made to follow, but the chestnut man grabbed him by the arm and made him stay. Jayce drew on his gloves with an irritated gesture. "Stop this *now* and saddle the horses. And give me a halfway decent mount this time, not that plow horse you gave me yesterday—" He broke off as he caught sight of Mojo. Jayce glanced at Kate and nodded at Mojo. "I'll take that one."

"No!" Kate said. "He's too tired."

Jayce smirked. "Shut up. You don't give the orders here."

"You can't take him." She knew he would spur Mojo and yank at his mouth, just to spite her. She might be under the general's protection, but she doubted that it extended to her horse.

"I said, shut up, bitch."

She stared, her mouth open in astonishment. Then all the fear, hunger, and pain she had been experiencing boiled over into rage, and Kate started for him. Whatever he was expecting, he was not ready for her tackle. Jayce went down backward, Kate on top of him, fists flying.

Kate barely heard the shouting and excitement as the ostlers drew a crowd again. Jayce cursed and hit her in the face, and she saw sparks as something warm spurted down her nose. Struggling to get free, Kate landed a lucky blow with her knee, and Jayce bit off a scream. Then someone pulled her by the collar of her oversized shirt, and she was up, stumbling backward. Kate held her nose, and blood trickled through her fingers. She glared at Jayce, now being helped to his feet by the chestnut man, through one eye. The other was already swelling shut.

"Tilt your head back," advised a voice in her ear. She obeyed, and coughed as blood trickled down her throat. She sprayed red down her shirt. "Here. Press down." From out of nowhere a wet cloth was pressed into her hand. Kate applied it to her nose, kept her head back, and forced herself not to cough.

"You crazy bitch," Jayce said hoarsely, as the other scouts dragged him away. "Don't ever let me catch you alone. I'll teach you a lesson you won't forget."

Colar came into her field of vision and took the cloth, rinsing it out in a barrel and handing it to her again.

"Nice mouse," he said. It took her a moment to realize he was referring to her eye. He grinned. "Do all stranger girls fight like that?"

She winced against the stinging pain. "Don't let him ride my horse, okay?"

Colar stopped smiling. "He's just a horse. And Jayce can be a bad enemy."

"I noticed." She winced again, touching her nose. The bleeding seemed to have stopped.

"Well." He shifted uncomfortably. "I'll try." He sounded doubtful about it.

Kate sat down by herself on a wagon's tailgate, holding her head back and the cloth stuck to her nose. She couldn't hear their words, but she saw Colar remonstrating with Jayce, who was still spitting mad. Kate sighed. *Way to go,* she told herself morosely. *If Mom and Dad could see me now* . . . She screwed up her face to stop the sudden flow of tears. When she regained her composure, she felt a warm drop hit the front of her shirt. Her nose had started bleeding again.

The riot of noise and laughter caught the at-tention of officers and lords breakfasting with the general. Marthen gestured at the lieutenant. Grayne stepped forward smartly, always at attention.

"See to the commotion, Grayne," Marthen ordered, and the man saluted and disappeared. Marthen turned back to his guests. A map graced the center of the table, held down at the corners by fruit and a pot of honey.

"My son gave me to understand a courier was brought in, one of Tharp's spies," said Lord Terrick, a tall, lean man in his midfifties, his graying hair sweeping back from his brow and his mouth framed by a neat, pointed beard. His mouth was thin, perpetually grim.

Marthen frowned. He made a note to have Grayne remind young Colar Terrick that he reported to him alone. "Not a spy," he replied with equanimity. "A lost villager." He had no intention of telling them that she came from beyond the Wood.

"A girl, wasn't it?" Terrick persisted. "I would not put it past Tharp."

"She carried no dispatches and was searched and interrogated. I talked to her myself and had her detained."

He could see the raised eyebrows and surprised smiles of the lords and suppressed his rising irritation, striving to keep his face emotionless. *Some men can think of nothing else but bedding,* he thought. "Now, gentlemen—" he raised a hand to forestall more questions. "We have a campaign to plan."

As he had hoped, it distracted Terrick, a man of action himself, and he leaned forward to better see the campaign map. Marthen moved a pear deeper into the corner of the map so he could see the mouth of the Aeritan River. All along the spidery length of the river rose Gordath Wood, an indistinct mass of forestland, empty at the center. No roads, no cities, no settlements. Was that what it was like on the other side? Marthen thought. An endless forest serving up hapless travelers to different worlds.

Marthen was seized with the desire to leave behind this war and lose himself in the vast, untouched emptiness of the map of Gordath Wood. He shifted restlessly to throw off the unsettling urge. An officer, misreading his mood, coughed.

"Tharp is likely to be entrenched behind the walls at Red Gold Bridge," the officer suggested quickly. He pointed with his knife at the elaborately drawn fortress on the map, representing the northern territories held by Tharp's lord. "I suggest a feint along the Temian foothills, harass him along those borders. He rides out to meet that threat—and the rest of our force moves in here." The line drawn by his knife dripped grease. The breakfast map had many such campaigns drawn on it.

Lord Terrick frowned. "Fighting in Temia is easier on paper than fact. Winter is coming, and those hills become icy and treacherous."

"They are the back door to Tharp and the city," the officer objected. "Once the crows join us, we'll have the forces necessary to push Tharp into fighting on two fronts."

Terrick snorted. "The crows solve nothing. The bulk of the army will be forced too far north. No, we should come up the river, meet him straight on."

"I am uneasy with our alliance with the crows," Lord Shay, a fat, graying man, objected. "Lawless rabble fight only for themselves."

"But how they do fight," said a young Lord Favor, slim and bright-eyed. He grinned. "Can't argue with their tactics."

The objecting lord muttered and subsided, but Lord Terrick's lips tightened. Marthen knew that he agreed with Lord Shay. He had argued loudly and at great length against the crows with Marthen and the other lords, and only gave in when it became clear they stood against him. Marthen knew he took a risk in commissioning the crows. Lord Favor was right; they were fearless in battle, ruthless during the aftermath. But problematic at all other times. He had but to lead them astray, and they would turn.

Sometimes the risk was all that made the game worthwhile. He wondered if Lord Terrick understood that.

He is my greatest ally—and my greatest enemy, Marthen thought. Terrick would be staunch, but he would only yield his principles so far.

Soldier's god, save me from a good man.

The rest of the lords still argued. Marthen let them debate without listening. He sat back in his chair, turning the strange light bottle over in his hands.

How was Tharp doing it? Marthen cursed the lost runner. His spies had told him that the man was making his way to him with an accounting of how Tharp was managing to bring over his armament. But the man had not come, and the word was he was dead. Marthen could hold off no longer; he gave orders for the Wood to be torched, hoping that a fire in the dry season would close down whatever operation Tharp had set up. He thought he had lost his chance to learn the truth in the expediency of the thing. But now his thoughts turned to young Kate Mossland, with her strange men's clothes and her frightened eyes. She might have answers to some of these mysteries.

It wasn't advanced weaponry, but it would have to do. And maybe, after he took care of Tharp, he could put those answers to a new use. Marthen had been a soldier since his boyhood, but he did not think he had to remain one. He looked up as Grayne came back, slipping through the tent flap and standing at attention before the combined leadership of the Aeritan army. Lords and officers looked up at him, for the moment silenced.

"Report," Marthen said.

"Hazing, sir. The—new ostler."

What was he talking about? "All right now?" Marthen asked.

"Yes, sir."

Stout Lord Shay grunted through his whiskers. "Hang one. Always sets an example."

"I'd rather not do Tharp's work for him," Marthen responded tartly. He stood. "Have we all broken fast adequately, noble sirs? Then we need to ride out at once."

They stood hastily, pushing back the small chairs in the cramped tent, one or two grabbing an extra bite. Only Lord Terrick looked at Marthen with as much amusement as his dour features could allow.

"And what direction are we are riding, General Marthen?"

Marthen met his eye and knew that Terrick had understood the debate was for show only; Marthen had his plan and wasn't about to let a group of loosely connected lords change it. He almost smiled.

"Straight up the river, my lord, behind the fire. With a good wind behind it, no doubt it will burn Gordath Wood to the ground and take Red Gold Bridge with it."

Terrick nodded his head in curt approval and swept out with the rest. After they had filed out, Marthen turned to Grayne. "What happened down there?"

He could tell his lieutenant was uneasy.

"The stranger girl was being hounded about hitting the fool," Grayne said. "Then on the heels of that, she got into a fight with the scout, Jayce. He had wanted her horse saddled for himself."

"All right," Marthen said. He set the bottle down so he would not crush it. "What was she doing down there, Lieutenant? Why wasn't she in her tent?"

Grayne hesitated, then bobbed his head, acknowledging his error. "I put her in her tent, sir. I heard later that she slept in the corral with her horse and helped the ostlers this morning at their tasks. They said she worked willingly."

"You never checked on her."

Grayne turned pale beneath his beard.

"No, sir. I thought—she seemed exhausted, sir. I didn't think she'd move from her tent."

"Because she seemed like a young girl, like every young girl that you've ever known, perhaps. So of course she'd be exhausted."

Grayne said cautiously, "Yes, sir."

Marthen threw the bottle at him. It was so light that it almost floated, and Grayne caught it before it struck him, his eyes wide as if Marthen had thrown the table knife at him. Marthen drew closer until they were almost nose to nose.

"She comes through the Wood carrying this bottle and this helm—" He turned and grabbed it off his camp bed and threw it at Grayne, too; it hit harder, bouncing off his head. "And you think she is just a common young girl like any other you've ever met."

Grayne stood rigid, eyes forward, a red spot on his forehead where the helmet hit.

"You stupid son of a bitch," Marthen said. "She might be our only hope of winning this war."

He turned around, trying to get himself under control, gathering up the maps on his desk. With his back to Grayne, he added,

"Was she hurt?"

"A black eye."

Black eyes would heal. Marthen knew that by blind luck he had skirted disaster. She wasn't a camp follower, though Grayne and the rest of the army no doubt saw her as one. He should have known only he would see it. There was something about her, something he recognized in himself, and he let it lead him into folly. It never did anyone any good to be treated as half noble and half common, he thought. He would have to study the girl more closely to settle on where he would place her.

He rolled the maps into a tight scroll. Still with his back to Grayne, he said, "She rides with me today. You say her horse has been saddled?"

"Yes, sir."

"Then give her yours, and you catch a ride among the supply wagons today."

Grayne gave a small gasp at his demotion. "Yes, sir."

"Get out."

He heard the faint rustle as Grayne bowed in salute and the louder sound of the tent flap drawn back. Only when he was sure that he was alone did Marthen turn around. His rage no longer contained, he kicked over his camp chair, sending it flying into the wall of the tent.

It took Colar and two of the other scouts sev-eral long minutes before they could calm Jayce down. They kept him walking in circles, much as they would a horse, and every once in a while he would try to break free of their grip and lunge back to get at the girl. Colar managed to send her off to sit on the wagon, out of his sight, but he didn't know how long they could keep Jayce at bay.

One of the ostlers led up a skittish chestnut mare, already saddled. He tugged at his forelock.

"Here, sirs, perhaps the young sir would be ready to mount."

Jayce shrugged off his handlers, and swallowed hard before saying hoarsely, "I'm done. Let me go. I'll kill her if she comes near me, but I'm done for now."

Skayler grabbed him by the front of his jacket. "You will not, not if you want to keep your head. The general's put the word out—she's off-limits."

"If she comes near me—"

Skayler yanked him harder. Jayce glared at him, then subsided. He jerked himself out of Skayler's grip and grabbed the mare's reins. She tossed up her head in alarm as he jammed his boot into the stirrup and mounted, pulling hard on the reins. Jayce spurred the horse, and she crowhopped sideways while he took his anger out on her with his spurs and hands.

They gave him wide berth to punish the mare as the other

scouts were mounted. The girl's horse was brought out. Colar hastened forward.

"I'll take him."

The horse waited patiently under his heavy saddle. The girl held his reins, stroking his mane. Her eye was almost swollen shut, red and sore. Her nose had stopped bleeding, but it still looked tender. *Kett,* she was called. It was a hard, short name, hardly feminine at all.

Skayler had chivvied Jayce and the mare off toward the rest of the scouts. Colar threw a glance back at them. He needed to go. He wished he hadn't offered to keep Jayce from riding the horse. Still, with the mood Jayce was in, he would have half killed the animal.

Kett held out the reins. She glanced over at Jayce, still bullying the mare. "Thanks."

Colar just nodded and mounted. He gathered up the reins and felt the horse come together beneath him, despite its exhaustion.

"I'll take care of him," he promised and almost immediately wished he hadn't. If Captain Artor needed him to ride at speed, he couldn't coddle the horse.

She still had her hand on the bridle, and he felt all eyes on them. He was about to tell her to let go, when he heard, "Colar!"

His heart sinking, Colar turned to see his father, already mounted on his big blue roan gelding Storm. He was glaring at the both of them, his icy eyes flicking over Colar and the girl and back again. Colar sat still and turned the horse on his haunches. Leaving the girl behind, he trotted over to his father.

"Yes, sir," he said quietly, burning with embarrassment. *Why do you have to treat me like I am only eight years old? I am going to war with you. I am not a child.*

Terrick glared over his shoulder, and Colar knew he was staring at the girl. "Hmmph," was all he said. "Get on your way, boy. Captain Artor is waiting."

"Yes, sir." Colar bowed his head and pushed the little horse toward the rest of the scouts. Jayce had already been sent off with another group, and Colar was relieved. Twice he'd faced down the scout over the girl. Neither of them needed it to happen again.

Artor's eyes flicked over him as he rode up on the strange horse, but he said nothing about it. "Right," he said, when the remaining scouts had ridden up. "We ride out to the south, make sure there are no surprises creeping up behind us on the march." Artor glanced back at Colar again. "Let us know if we need to fasten stilts to your pony's legs, Terrick."

Colar's face flamed as the rest of the scouts laughed. Artor gave a whistle, and they were off.

Kate balanced on the side of the nearest sup- ply wagon, watching as column after column began to march off, but the rear guard still was doing no more than milling about. Camp followers scurried about, gathering up belongings and children and hurrying after their men.

The supply wagons were ready to go before all the men were. Drivers whistled up their teams and cracked their long whips in the air. The horses and oxen surged against the traces, and the wagons lurched forward. Kate was almost dislodged from her perch and grabbed wildly to hold on.

A shout rose from the army, and Kate started at the sudden surge in volume. Men banged their swords and lances against their shields, and their voices rose in a strange ululation. The women shrieked. Oxen lowed. Kate craned to see.

Out of the smoky morning crawled another column of men to intercept them. For a wild moment she thought they were at war right then and there, and then she understood. The shouting was in greeting to these new men.

They did not look like soldiers. They were wild, ragged, skinny, their beards and hair unkempt. Their weapons were laughable, too—Kate could have sworn that they carried iron pokers and mauls, not real swords.

The shouting continued, although whenever these new men turned to look at someone, the commotion faltered in that direction.

Kate held on, fascinated. She couldn't take her eyes off the spectacle, peering through the dust and the crowd.

It never occurred to her how exposed she was until she caught the eye of one of the newcomers. He looked at her and smiled.

A sudden sickness hit her in the pit of her stomach. The

sheer malevolence made Jayce seem kind—at least he didn't look on her as prey.

She thought, *They just got here. They don't know . . .*

Marthen's orders were worthless.

She couldn't help it; she looked again. The man still stared at her, laughing, and he pointed her out to his friends. Swaggering, they sauntered over toward her.

She jumped and landed on the ground with a thud. Desperate, Kate looked around for somewhere to hide. Not the wagon—they would find her in a moment. She began to jog, threading her way through the line to get away, pushing desperately through the crowd. One of the women grabbed onto her shirt, and wild with fear, Kate smacked the woman to get away.

She could feel them close in on her. As she ran, beginning to clear the crowd, she became aware of three separate groups of pursuers. Every time she tried to make her way to the front where the officers were, where she knew she would be protected, she had to turn to avoid running into one of her pursuers.

They're herding me.

The crowd suddenly thinned, and Kate bolted. She dodged wagons and people by instinct, her flying feet taking her across the single-minded forward motion of the army as it trundled along the borders of the Wood. Her breath came hard as she sobbed, trying to hold back the panic. Through her blurred vision she could see the dark trunks of the trees on the forest's edge beckoning her with freedom. Kate threw her head back and ran harder, boots thudding against the hoof- and foot-packed dirt, jumping wagon ruts.

Kate was almost under the eaves of the forest when she heard thudding hoofbeats behind her. She risked a look back—a rider, hard on her heels, and gaining fast. Kate stumbled as she tried to push herself more, but she was spent. In three strides the horse had come even with her, so close she could reach out and touch the rider's boot, heading her off, forcing her to turn, to stumble, to slow. Kate made to stop and turn direction, to feint a sharper turn than the horse could manage, but the rider leaned in, and the horse's sweaty shoulder bumped her side and Kate fell flying, hands out, straight into the charred soil.

No no no no.

She scrabbled for anything to use as a weapon, a rock or stick. She pulled herself to her feet, a handful of useless dirt crumbling in her fist, and stopped.

It was Marthen's lieutenant, Grayne. He dismounted. Her breath exploded in a spray of relief.

"Oh God," she sobbed. "Thank you. Thanks—" Her legs gave way, and she sank down. The lieutenant reached down and pulled her to her feet, and for a moment she had to steady herself against him.

"Oh God," she said again. "Who were they? Where did they go?"

"The crows," he said. "Stay away from them."

She half sobbed and had to push down hard on her rising hysteria. She cast a longing look at the forest.

"Oh, I want to go home," she muttered, more to herself than Grayne. He answered nonetheless.

"You can't." He swung the horse around and held out the stirrup for her. "Mount."

She had to stab her boot a couple of times at the stirrup before she was able to pull herself into the saddle. Once aboard, she began to calm down a bit. Grayne held the reins beneath the horse's chin and led them back toward the army, still untangling itself from the campsite. There was no sign of the crows.

The horse suddenly stopped and flung up its head, dancing in a circle. Kate, taken unawares, grabbed with her legs and sat deep in the strange saddle. The horse stood stock-still, ears pricked at attention at the Wood, and then gave out a clear, bell-like neigh.

From the Woods came an answering whinny, and out of the shadows loomed a great gray horse.

Kate's heart leaped.

"Dungiven?" she said. The big horse took a careful step forward. His coat was darkened with soot and sweat, and the blue yarn that had been braided into his mane hung scraggily along his neck. He had lost his bridle, and his beautiful noble head was bare. His saddle hung beneath him, stirrups dangling. Kate struggled to dismount, but Grayne held her tight.

"No! Let me go! You don't understand—that's Dungiven!

Lynn!" She kicked furiously, trying to wriggle free, and to control her, Grayne pulled her out of the saddle. She landed on the ground with a thud, and he fell with her.

When they looked up again, Dungiven was gone. "No!" Kate stumbled toward the forest even as Grayne grabbed onto her shirt and hauled her back. Cursing and crying, Kate grabbed a clot of mud and heaved it at the lieutenant, splattering it across his leather shirt. "That was Dungiven!" she shouted. "Don't you understand? You ugly, *stupid*—I hate you!"

His face set, Grayne cuffed her against the side of the head, much as Mykal did. "Don't run away again!" He bellowed. "You useless brat! Stay put, or I will throw you to the crows myself!"

It didn't matter anyway; Dungiven was gone. Tight-lipped, Kate remounted, looking backward as he led her away, but there was no sign of the big horse in the shrouded woods.

Seven

Almost a week after Lynn's and Kate's disap-pearances, the headlines still screamed, "Hunt Country Fire!" and "Fire Marshals Investigate Arson." A few die-hard reporters stood at the entrance to Hunter's Chase, taped by the news trucks that broadcast "live from this horrified enclave of wealthy equestrians." Fire response crews from New York and Connecticut mopped up the last smoldering hot spots and prayed for rain, and the search crews waited for the all clear before they could resume searching for the missing riders.

Except for the dust, the farm was back to normal. The horses had been returned to their comfortable loose boxes, the owners had been appeased, and plans for Mrs. Hunt's annual gala and horse show were still under way. Joe had a lot of work to do.

As he came out from the main barn, he saw that he wasn't going to get to any of it right away. A small group of police officers awaited him on Mrs. Hunt's lawn. She stood with them, and they all looked at him as he walked over, his stomach knotting.

They found them. Sweet Jesus, they found them. He almost turned tail and ran. He didn't want to know.

Instead, he kept on walking. When he came up to the group, Mrs. Hunt indicated one officer, a plainclothesman in a gray suit with salt-and-pepper hair, and said, "This is Lieutenant Spencer, Joe. He would like to ask you some questions. I've told him you have a great deal of work to do, and he agreed to question you while you get your chores done."

Joe waited a moment for his stomach to settle down. He could feel Spencer's eyes on him, taking in his hesitation.

"Yes, ma'am," he said. "I had my mind on trimming up the hedges on the cross-country course."

Spencer followed him without comment across the drive to the rolling green field dotted with stone walls, hedges, and other obstacles. From the top of the highest rise where the first hedge hulked, they looked down on the barns, bright in their fresh white and blue paint and dark gray roofs, ash notwithstanding. In the ring below, riders practiced as an instructor called out commands. The smells of hay and horses wafted over to them, intermixed with a cold tinge of coming fall. Flying over the burned-out Gordath Wood, a search helicopter quartered the woods. The sound faded as the chopper dipped away, but Spencer's words were lost in the dying roar as he sat down on a tumbling stone wall intermixed with hedge.

"Beg pardon?" Joe asked, intent on evening up the wildly overgrown hedge.

"I asked, where are you from? You aren't from around here, are you."

"Town called New Braunfels, Texas," Joe said, clipping away.

"No kidding," Spencer said with the tone of one who has never heard of it. "That near Dallas or Houston?"

Joe stepped back to look over the hedge. Straight. He kicked the clippings underneath and walked to the next, Spencer trailing him. "Neither," he called over his shoulder. "Outside San Antonio."

At the next hedge, Spencer asked, "What brought you to North Salem?"

"I was traveling for awhile," Joe replied. "Been on the road about five years now, working where I could. This seemed as a good a place as any to stop."

"How long have you been here?"

"Goin' on six, seven months now. I've been working here for about six months."

"Where did you work before?" Spencer asked.

"Toomey Feed and Supply."

Spencer had a little notebook out, but he wasn't writing in it. Joe tried to keep a smile off his face. Just two ol' boys having a chat. He wondered when the bad-cop routine would start.

"Did you know Lynn Romano well?" the investigator asked.

Joe kept clipping, his head down. He wondered how much this officer knew, if the grapevine had told him there was something between Lynn and Joe. He didn't want to talk about it if he didn't have to, but he didn't want to appear to be lying.

In the face of his continued silence, Spencer said, "She was a very pretty girl, wasn't she?" Despite himself, Joe looked straight at him. The lieutenant held out a small snapshot for him, as if Joe needed to be reminded what she looked like. The picture was one Lynn's parents had given the police, Lynn looking pretty and informal. Her hair was down about her shoulders, and her eyes were laughing. He had seen that picture before; it had been reprinted in the paper next to one of Dungiven soaring over a jump at Nationals. Joe handed it back, wondering what his face showed.

"We were seeing each other."

Spencer's eyebrow raised. "Really." It wasn't a question.

"Really," Joe said, his voice dry.

"Any idea where she is?"

Joe shook his head. "Wish I knew." The words echoed inside him. *Wish I knew.*

"But you were seeing her, right? Didn't you talk? Get to know each other first?"

Blood pounded in his head. Joe tried to control his anger. "That's our business," he said, low-voiced.

"Now it's my business," Spencer snapped. "She's missing, Joe. So's a little girl who had nothing to do with whatever you got going on here. I'm investigating arson, insurance fraud, theft, kidnapping—murder? You think I care about your hurt feelings? Your privacy? Where is she, Joe? What happened? Where's Lynn Romano?"

"I don't know!"

The hilltop was silent for a moment, and a breeze swept through the long grasses, turning them gold for a moment.

Spencer said: "Did you kill her?"

Joe shook his head and laughed. It had very little mirth in it.

"Aren't you supposed to read me my rights?"

"You want me to arrest you?"

Fear gripped him. He didn't say anything. Locked up . . .
Joe pushed the thought away.

Spencer watched him expressionlessly. Finally he said,
"You try to leave town, and I'll make sure you spend the rest
of this investigation in jail."

Joe watched him walk down the hill, gray suit flapping in
the breeze. After a minute he picked up the trimmers and
started on over to the next hedge. He wondered what the detective was going to do next, wondered why he hadn't been ar-
rested. Sure, he had an alibi for each disappearance, but he
doubted that counted for anything. He as good as told Spencer
he was a drifter. Joe grew up in a small town; he knew that
made him a convenient suspect. He doubted Spencer was just
playing fair.

Time to move on, Joe, a small voice whispered. He ignored
it and began shaping the next hedge.

He drove the back roads from the farm, wind-
ing his ancient Impala around the narrow country lane, a cold
beer between his knees. He passed Balanced Rock, hulking
off the highway, a massive boulder sitting lightly on three
small rocks. He shivered for a second. His grandmother had a
saying: there's a goose walking over your grave. *Every time I
drive by that damn rock,* he thought. Gordath Wood crowded
in on both sides of the road. Another thing he had never gotten
used to. The roads were so narrow, compared to the wide
country roads of his native Texas. And there was no sky to
speak of. Nothing to let a man look at anything bigger than
himself. Sometimes when Joe was feeling poetic, or just a little drunk, he thought that the narrow view translated itself into
a narrow mind, and that was why Yankees thought the way
they did.

Of course, he had to admit that if that theory held, then his
father, owner of more than a thousand acres of prime farm-
land, would be the broadest-minded individual on God's green
earth, instead of the bigoted horse's ass he was. But Joe still
did miss the sky in Texas. He even thought that he might want
to go back, just to show it off to Lynn.

When he first came to the farm he couldn't help but take
notice of Lynn. He dredged up a word he didn't even think he

knew: exotic. Dark hair, olive skin, dark eyes. Tall and slender in her blue jeans and T-shirt and scuffed boots. So serious that when she smiled it was like the sun came out.

The night Lynn invited him home, he had been sure she was the reason he came north. A sudden thunderstorm had opened up, and the hayloft over the main barn was still open, a shipment of expensive hay still only half-loaded, ready to be ruined. Joe hastily threw a tarp over it and headed down to close the big bay doors against the thunder and lightning. Lynn grabbed the other door and hauled it closed, and they stood in the darkness for a moment, listening to the rain hammering on the metal roof and the faint nervous whinnies of the sensitive horses.

"I didn't know you were still here," she said. They stood so close he could feel the rain on her arms. Water dripped down the walls, and the smell of tanbark and horse manure was thick and unpleasant in the wet air.

"Had to get the hay covered."

He felt rather than saw her nod, heard her draw in a breath.

"You, um, you want to wait this out in my apartment?" They ran out of the dark indoor arena, getting soaked in the short distance to her apartment over the barn. Upstairs, the windows had been left open, curtains flying, letting in the cold, wet air, smelling of thunderstorms. Rain splatted on the sill. He pulled her close and tasted the rain on her mouth, warm and cold at the same time.

The worst thing was, he didn't know if he'd ever find out if the strange restlessness that pushed him his whole life was Lynn. He didn't know if he'd ever be able to show her the Texas sky. He couldn't even say if this was love. All he knew was that if he had to look up at the white curtains flying in the windows of the barn apartment, and it was no longer her home, it would be more terrible than anything else he could imagine.

Joe parked the Impala off the street in front of the tired brick buildings that lined downtown and headed for the feed store, the order for Hunter's Chase crinkling in his back pocket. The little bell tinkled as he walked into the old-fashioned store, the aroma of feed and leather and gear intermingling in the dim light. Jim Toomey, the owner, looked up at his approach, an easy grin on his face.

"Hey Joe," he said. "Got an order?"

"Right here," he said, pulling it out and handing it over. "Big one this time for the gala."

Jim scanned it. "No problem. Helluva thing about those two girls," he added. "Any news yet?"

Yeah, the police think I did it. Joe just shook his head. "Nothing yet. How about you?"

Toomey had gone out with the search parties on his big palomino gelding that he rode western. "Not a thing. The woods are all burned to hell, but that's about it. She's probably up in Canada by now, got that horse stashed away on somebody's stud farm. Shame about that little girl—" His voice faltered, as he remembered that Joe was the one who had let Kate disappear. "Uh—"

"Yeah. A shame," Joe said.

Jim scratched his jaw, uncomfortable.

"Well, look, I'll take care of this and deliver it before the gala," Toomey said hastily. Then, obviously thinking that he had been too abrupt, he added, "Say, you tell that friend of yours . . . What's his name, Mark? Tell him he owes me twenty bucks on the Sox."

Joe was nonplussed. "Mark Ballard?"

"Yeah, yeah. That's him. Bartender at the Continental."

Joe shrugged. "He left town. Went to Colorado, I heard."

Toomey laughed. "Did he? There goes twenty bucks."

Joe tried to smile, and the little bell tinkled again when he left. The grapevine had it that Lynn and Mark Ballard had been going out before he and Lynn got together. Lynn herself never mentioned Mark. Joe didn't want to think about her and Mark together; from the little he knew of the man, he could be an asshole. Not a friend at all, and he wasn't sure why Toomey thought so. He wasn't all that sad when he heard Mark had gone out West.

Would Mark know where she was? He didn't want to think of Mark and her *sleeping* together. Still, if there was a chance that Mark knew something . . . Joe started the engine and pulled away from the curb. The Continental would probably have his forwarding address, maybe even his phone. The only thing it would hurt to ask would be his pride.

The Continental in New Canaan was the local hangout for the horse community. The young people who kept the stables going hung out in the bar, the owners in the upstairs rooms. The restaurant was decorated with wood paneling with brass accents and tasteful hunt scenes. In the dim lighting, deer, elk, bobcats, pheasants, and other wildlife stared down from the walls.

Joe parked the Impala on the bar side of the building and walked into welcoming coolness. It was only about three, and the bar was deserted except for the bartender. The jukebox played "Thunder Road." He had once bet Mark that he could walk into the bar at any given moment, and the jukebox would feature Springsteen. Mark had laughed and refused the bet.

Joe straddled a stool and nodded at the new bartender, a heavyset young man with a round, calm face.

"What can I get you?" the bartender asked, turning away from the TV high in the corner of the bar. He turned the sound down, and the news anchors finished their wide-eyed report in talking-head silence while an old video of the Gordath Wood fire ran in the background.

"Budweiser," Joe said, fishing out some bills.

"Cooling off out there," the bartender said when he slid over the bottle.

"Fall's coming," Joe agreed. He forestalled the questions about his drawl and his origins with a question of his own.

"Is Mike Garson here?"

The bartender nodded at the short stair leading to the front entrance to the restaurant.

"In the hostess area. Getting ready for the rush."

"You think it'll be okay to head on in and find him?"

The bartender frowned. "What's it about? Maybe I can help."

"I need to see if he has Mark Ballard's address," Joe said, which was pretty much the truth.

"Oh. Yeah, you'll need to ask him." He nodded again at the door. The door opened again as a few early birds swirled in, and Joe headed for the restaurant.

Garson was a smallish man, dressed in tan slacks and a golf shirt, his strident New York accent booming as he talked to someone on the phone by the hostess station. He gestured to Joe to wait. Joe pretended to be absorbed in looking at the hunt trophies. Garson made no effort to modulate his voice, and Joe overheard part of the conversation on deliveries. Garson's end seemed mostly expressions of bonhomie. The conversation wound down, and Joe turned toward Garson as he hung up the phone, shaking his head.

"Never should've gone into the restaurant business," he said to Joe. The whole thing had been a performance for his benefit; under the social veneer, Garson's expression was wary. Joe put on a performance of his own, kicker grin, country boy, dumb as dirt.

"Howdy, Mr. Garson. I don't know if we've met. I'm Joe Felz. I work at Hunter's Chase. I'm a friend of Mark Ballard."

"Yeah, yeah, Mark's friend," Garson said expansively. He reached out a hand. "Tell me, why'd that son of a bitch never tell me he was quitting?"

"Well, that's what I wanted to ask you about, sir," Joe said. "I was wondering if you had a phone number or address where I could reach him?"

Garson frowned. "No, no, I don't think so. Wait a minute—" He began to search through the papers at the cash register, as if he would find it there. "No, no, I don't think we have it." His voice was expansive again. "I don't do much letter writing. Ask my wife. She does the thank-yous and Christmas cards."

"What about an address to send his last check to?" Joe suggested, his voice as neutral as possible. Garson looked up from the desk straight at him, all good fellowship gone, and Joe read that look as if it had been spoken. No check had been sent; Garson had no intention of ever sending it. Then the restaurateur's brow cleared as he thought of a plausible explanation.

"No, I believe my accountant sent that to his address in town," he said. He smiled. "Sorry I couldn't help you," he said, tones heartier, dismissive. "Maybe the post office." He waited as Joe nodded and turned to go. Then suddenly he turned back. Garson was still staring at him, a half smile on his face overlaid with irritation.

"Jes' one more question, Mr. Garson," Joe asked. "Did Mark Ballard ride?"

As soon as he asked it, he wished he hadn't. He didn't need to know that riding had brought Mark and Lynn together.

Garson was obviously expecting something else.

"I don't ask my employees how they spend their free time," he said finally. "Good-bye."

Joe pushed open the heavy door and walked out into the afternoon sunlight.

It was stupid anyway, thinking that Mark Ballard would know anything about Lynn's disappearance. The only connection was that he and Lynn had dated awhile. *Forget it,* he told himself. But as he headed back for his car, he saw a rusted green Volkswagen pull up in a big hurry. The car was still sputtering when the driver got out, grabbing a bulging knapsack. Angie was one of the waitresses; as a regular, Joe knew her casually. A glimmer of an idea came to him as she hightailed it for the employee entrance. Joe looked at his watch. He had stuff to do at the farm, but it could wait until tomorrow. It wouldn't hurt to see if Angie knew anything about Mark's whereabouts.

The bar was filling up when he went back in. Joe took up his seat at the corner. The bartender looked up from an order, surprised.

"Did you find Garson?" he asked, sliding over two collins glasses topped with limes to a pair of suits at the bar.

"Yeah." Joe pulled out another couple of bucks. "Might as well have another beer before I head back."

He sat nursing it, waiting for Angie, wondering if she would have time to talk with him. All of a sudden the place was packed. The bartender looked up at the clock just as Angie burst in, tying her apron around her waist.

"Sorry sorry sorry," she panted, pulling a tray from behind the bar. Joe watched her in action, admiring her trim figure in dark jeans and the hunter-green polo shirt that was emblazoned with The Continental in gold across the back. He sipped his beer in quiet, nodding to a few people he knew, waiting for Angie to get a break.

It was a couple of hours before business settled down enough to where she could take a breather. Joe spent the time chatting with some of the other horse people, mostly young women. The jukebox blared, and a few brave and tipsy souls slid out onto the tiny patch of clear floor to dance to Bruce.

When Angie was finally standing at the bar, totaling up the happy hour receipts, he slid across to join her. She looked up, surprised.

"Hi, Joe. What's up?"

"Hey. Mike Garson said you might have Mark's address," he lied. Her mouth made an O of surprise.

"Mike said that?"

Joe watched her narrowly.

"Yeah. I think he just didn't know himself and hoped you might."

"Well, I don't. Sorry."

"Angie," Joe said. "This is gonna sound dumb, but did Mark ride?"

Her face sparkled suddenly. "Mark hated horses," she confided, looking around her as if confessing to a crime. "You should have heard him talking about the horse girls around here." She made a face. "Why not? They're so stuck up, you know?"

Joe nodded, but he wondered how Mark and Lynn had been going out. Horses were her life. Angie gave him the answer in her next breath.

"You should have seen him talk about that girl where you work, the one who took off with that horse." She giggled, shaking her head as she finished paying out. "He said if she'd just shut up about the horses, she'd be fine."

A flush of heat crawled up his skin. As she picked up her tray and got ready to go back to work, he caught her elbow. "Angie, do you know where Mark lived while he was here?"

"He had a place in town," she said promptly. "Those little apartments off Main Street. I know because I asked him once to tell me if there was ever a vacancy."

With that she swooped up her tray and headed back to work. He slipped out of the bar into the soft evening and crunched across the crowded parking lot to his car.

Shit, he thought, *what am I doing?* Mark didn't have anything to do with Lynn and Kate; he didn't ride. He hated horses. Hell, he didn't even like Lynn. It was crazy to think the disappearances were connected. Except . . .

The expression on Garson's face came back to him. Why *didn't* Mark tell his boss that he was leaving?

Joe parked at the grocery store lot and walked over to the big old house that was cut up into apartments. Sure enough, there was a vacancy sign out front.

No one was around as he walked over to the side door of the house. Off to one side was the row of tenant mailboxes. As he turned away, he saw a metal trash can brimming with circulars and other discarded mail. Joe began picking through it. Most was addressed to Occupant.

One entire stratum, three-quarters of the way down, was addressed to Mark Ballard. Joe hauled it all up, scattering junk mail, and began flipping through it. Circulars, bills, a hunting catalog, nothing more. Joe put everything back, then drew out the hunting catalog. Without knowing what he was looking for, he flipped through it. Nothing but ads for hunting and fishing gear. Waders, camouflage, hunting rifles, sights, the usual. Back home, he used to pore over these as a kid; as an adult, he would look through them with restless boredom.

Joe turned the catalog over to look at the address label.

Mark Ballard, it read in fuzzy computer print. The rest of the address was crossed out, and in neat block handwriting was printed the address of Mark's apartment. Joe squinted, then realized it was hopeless. Adding mail theft to his sins, he gathered up the bundle of mail, circulars and all, and headed quickly back to his car.

He turned on the dome light to look at his booty. Under the handwriting he could see the original address printed there: Mark Ballard, 127 Daw Road, North Salem, New York.

For a man who hated horses, what the hell had Mark Ballard been doing, living in the middle of the riding trails?

Eight

Gordath Wood held fast to its secrets, and as the fire encroached on Red Gold Bridge, Crae and his men had to turn back, soot-covered and discouraged, without the guardian. With the fire and the near-constant earth shaking, the mood of the stronghold had shifted more toward fear, even as Tharp's army grew.

All the signatory lords brought their men. Camrin, of course, and Salt, and now Trieve. More than seven thousand men camped outside the stronghold, a sea of them, bound between the river and the mountain. Seven thousand men and a few hundred weapons that were expected to make Tharp's point for him.

At summer's beginning Tharp's emissary delivered his message to the Council sitting in convocation at Kenery. He had ridden out on a chestnut warhorse, in full battle armor, carrying a banner with the colors of Red Gold Bridge. The emissary had been flanked by two riders, more plainly dressed, carrying Bahard's weapons. Crae wished he could have been there when they fired the weapons into the air at the beginning and at the end of the emissary's speech.

No more do I yield to the Council, nor am I bound by Council laws. Accept this or not, submit or not, fight or not, I care not. But be warned. For I will yield no more.

Forest god, damn the man for his pride. He would break up the Council out of nothing more than pique. Had the weapons not come his way, Tharp might have let his wounded pride over his lost wife simply fester, the way most men would. But then Bahard had come, and that was that. Tharp had set his course on war.

Crae and his men came in from their fruitless search, covered in ash, dirt, and sweat, and dismounted in the courtyard, their horses blowing and snorting in the smoky air.

"All right," he told his men, tossing one the reins of his horse. "Get rest and food. We ride out again at Lord Tharp's wish."

"He's running you ragged, then," came a cheerful voice. Crae looked around and brightened.

"Stavin! Have you just arrived?"

Lord Stavin of Trieve came over, still in his riding dress, the gold of his House a muted pattern on his shirt. The two men gripped hands. "Not half a day earlier. I never thought he'd really go ahead and do it."

Crae winced, wishing his friend would lower his voice. "How many of your men have you brought?"

"Trieve is depleted. Jessamy was not pleased, but in the end, she told me to take all the armsmen. All in or nothing, I always say."

Tharp will not thank you for the sacrifice. Crae tried to keep the worry from his face. Leaving Trieve vulnerable in a time of war . . . What had Stavin been thinking?

Instead he said, "Well, he has some tricks up his sleeve."

"I heard," Stavin said. "The weapons. Have you seen them?"

"I have. They are impressive, though few."

"Perhaps a lowly bond lord will get a chance to try one."

That's all any of the men had been talking about. Those who had seen Bahard's demonstration were the most eager—including Crae, even after Bahard had aimed directly at the insignia over Crae's heart. Some days Crae had visions of himself returning the favor.

Stavin turned to walk into the stronghold with him. "So tell me everything," he said. "Tharp, this Bahard, even this woman I've been hearing about."

Crae shook his head. "I was hoping for a meal and an ale, myself."

"You can eat and talk, right?"

A week after they lost the guardian and found the stranger, Crae took Stavin hiking. At the foot of the stronghold, the mountain stream that coursed beneath the

bridge plunged down a short cataract as it crashed on its way
to the Aeritan River. The little waterfall set up a constant
spray. Crae's hair and uniform were damp from scrambling
around the rocks at the foot of the great cliff. He left his boots
and socks back on dry land, and his feet slipped and slid over
the rocky boulders. The water was sharp as ice, but he gritted
his teeth and bore it.

Behind him, he heard a splash as Stavin caught his balance
but not before planting a foot in the stream. "Crae," he growled.

"Come on," Crae shouted over the water. "It's not far." He
scrabbled for purchase over the rocks until finally he made it
to the far side, where the mountain rose straight up in front of
him.

Cursing and splashing, Stavin made it to the narrow strip of
land right behind him. He shook his head like a dog, sending
droplets flying, and wiped spray from his face. Crae squinted
through the water, peering at the wall of rock. He pointed.
"There."

A fine line, like the etching of a pen, traced its jagged way
up the rock until it was lost in the heights above them. Stavin
looked at it for a long moment, then turned to Crae. "Crae, I
love you like a brother, but it's a crack. The mountain is full of
them."

"This wasn't here two days ago. You remember that last
earth shaking?" Stavin's expression made it clear that he had
and it had not been a pleasant memory. "This crack showed up
after that day." Stavin raised a brow, and Crae shrugged self-
deprecatingly. "I come here a lot." It was peaceful for one, but
he had added a regular foot patrol around the outskirts of the
stronghold out of a sense of the mountain's vulnerability.

"You need to stop brooding," Stavin said. "All right. Where
does it pick up?"

"If it's the same one, all the way down at the shore. It
comes out by the docks."

"Have you told Lord Tharp?"

"I'm telling you. Now."

Stavin shook his head before he even finished. "I have no
influence with him, Crae. You know that. I'm just a bond lord
fulfilling the terms of a convenient alliance."

Crae raised an eyebrow. "Did he tell you that?"

Stavin snorted. "His message was, 'Come if you want.' The implication being that he didn't care much one way or the other, thank you very much." He hesitated. "He isolated himself long before this. When Sarita—" He broke off, and Crae hid his impatience. *Just say it. She vanished under my protection.*

He looked out into the Wood. They were almost inside the forest, and the trees pressed ominously around the foot of the mountain. The fire that swept through the Wood had been kept back by the little river, and the trees were unharmed, though the air reeked of smoke. The stream was loud here, a constant rush, and their backs were to solid stone. It was the most private place in the stronghold.

"I think he knows how dangerous the gordath has become," Crae said. "He just refuses to acknowledge it. He wants these weapons so badly, he wants the gordath to stay open, he won't see what it's doing. And it's getting worse. The earth shakings are happening almost every day now, and this." He gestured at the crack.

"It's just a crack, Crae."

"Listen to me. Red Gold Bridge was built to withstand the gordath, and now the walls are cracking. How many more earth shakings will it take to pull these walls down?"

"Impossible. You always look for trouble."

"And you deny what is before your eyes."

"Crae, the gordath is closed." Stavin met his gaze with a forthright one of his own, his face wet with spray. "The fire has prevented Bahard from even going to the weapons depot, and the guardians have gone to earth. How is it opening?"

Crae threw up his hands and blew an exasperated breath. "I don't know. Something must be going through. And each time it opens the gordath . . . Do you feel it? The mountain shaking?"

Stavin nodded. Crae went on.

"You know the woman? The day we found her, she came crashing down the ridge from the old morrim as if the forest had spat her out. She told me later that she heard something from the Wood. The morrim was whispering at her, she said." Crae paused. "Now, she could be mad."

Stavin shrugged.

"But I don't think so. I think the gordath soon will be out of anyone's control, whether we find a guardian to put a hand to

it or not." He reached out and put his own hand on the cool
mountain rock. "I think it's out of control now."

Stavin was silent for a long time. Finally he said, "This is
why I prefer the forests of the east. In Trieve, rocks don't
whisper, and the earth doesn't shake."

Crae tried to sound lighthearted. "Never a dull moment,
that's us."

Stavin just grunted. He looked back at the fast-rushing
stream with distaste. "Let's go back. If I am going to confront
Lord Tharp, let me get back in time to dry my clothes."

They splashed back over to where they left their boots and
socks and sword belts. Putting his on, Stavin said, "So what of
this wandering woman of yours?"

Crae wiped wet sand off his feet and drew on his socks.
"Safe for now."

With Tharp and Bahard preparing for battle, they were too
busy to consider the interfering stranger. He thought that Bahard might not even know she existed, and as far as Tharp was
concerned, she was out of the way in the tower room. Out of
sight, out of mind.

"Good," said Stavin. "But that's not what I meant. I know
you, Crae. You are taken with her; I can tell."

Crae tried to keep any expression off his face. "Oh?" he
said as noncommittally as possible.

"Yes, oh."

She had been lost, dirty, frightened, and hungry, and trying
to keep her mind through all of it. His first impression of her
had been tall, thin, plain. Her tangled braid, scandalously uncovered, looked as if a tree imp had snatched it to shreds with
long, twiggy fingers. And her clothes! Yet, as outlandish as she
was, he found himself intrigued. He had known prettier women,
kinder women, and had fallen in love with more than a few of
them. But he kept on coming back to her, wondering about her.
Curiosity, he told himself firmly. That's all. But he thought he
should keep away from her, just in case. He glanced at Stavin.

"No. I'm not."

Stavin looked as if he were fighting a smile. "Good. Because Jessamy has been making a list of possible women for
you to marry. She would be very angry with me if I let you fall
in love with an unsuitable woman."

Crae nodded, and they began to make their way out of the forest to the shores of the river. "Do I even want to know who's on this list?"

"Three widows—all young, don't worry! One or two spinsters, but still of childbearing years, loosely counting. Tevani, of course, but that one was my addition."

Tevani was Stavin's daughter. Crae snorted. "Stavin, she is only three."

"Four. You've waited this long, what's another twenty years?" He said it lightly, and Crae just rolled his eyes.

"No. Besides, she deserves someone young."

Stavin snorted. "I know what young men are like; I was one once. I am not entrusting her to a young man. It's you or no one."

He was serious. Crae stopped and looked at him. Stavin held his gaze.

"Truly, Crae. I wish she were older, because then I would give you both my blessing. She doesn't get to choose—none of us do. Why not you?"

Because I do get to choose.

Not being one of the governing lords, any marriage he made was through his own desires rather than the laws of the Council. Even so, he had to choose well, for only married men could be eligible for the governing convocation, and only if the marriage was deemed responsible.

Crae said, selecting his words carefully, "Even if she were older, even if the marriage were approved by the Council, it still wouldn't be right."

Stavin sighed and began walking again. "Jessamy was right. She said you'd never agree." He waved off Crae's apology. "No, you're right, you're right. I'm trying to save her from all the wrong things. But if she ends up in a bad marriage, I'm blaming you."

"I think between the two of us we'll be able to keep any son-in-law of yours in line."

"We'll have to stand behind Jessamy."

"True enough."

Stavin fell into a rare silence as they headed back toward the river, leaving Crae to his own thoughts, that somehow, unaccountably, always returned to the woman in the rose tower.

The forest thinned out, and they made their way to the shores of the Aeritan. The wide river lapped against the shallow water by the docks. Out in midstream, several broad-beamed boats sailed south, their sails bellied out in the wind, oars poking out of their hulls like spider legs. They rode high in the water, their cargos offloaded onto the docks that bustled with men. For many merchants, this was the last voyage of the season, and in their haste to sail home before the autumn storms, they chose to sail light. In less than a month, the merchant boats would not be able to make it down the river without running into the first bad weather, and a month after that, the river would be iced over. Red Gold Bridge would stand alone until spring.

The breeze off the river was stiff. The two men put their backs to it and walked back up toward the shallow steps that led up to the stronghold.

"Do you ride out with Lord Tharp in the morning?" Stavin asked.

Crae shook his head. "No, the glory of battle is not to be mine." He gave the words a wry twist. "I am no longer in favor."

Stavin grunted. "Lucky man."

Crae kept his doubts to himself. Ever since his failure to find the guardian, Tharp's disappointment in him had been as thick as the smoke-filled air that still surrounded Red Gold Bridge. *My insignia is of the stronghold, not the man,* he told himself. Still, it burned every time he thought of it. Crae knew what his men were saying under their breath, and it wasn't good for his command or Tharp's: the stranger man had brought down the wrath of the Wood on Red Gold Bridge. Finding the guardian would have gone a long way to dampening that talk.

The steps grew steeper until they were climbing up and around the corner tower of the wall. The breeze grew stronger, carrying the scent of the burned Wood. From the top of the wall they could see over the trees into the blackened patches where the fire had struck first. Crae was used to thinking of the forest as a single mass, but now he could see more of the contours of the terrain, where single trees stood out on barren hillsides.

Boots clattered along the stone walkway before them, and Tal came round the curve of the wall.

"Captain! Sir!" he said, saluting them both. "We've gotten word of the horse."

The stooped and wrinkled farmer glanced from one to the other of them, Crae, Stavin, and Tal, in the little antechamber off the hall.

"My son saw him first, in the field with the cows and our old mare," he said. "I knew at once he was one of the lord's horses, or one of the fine ones from Wessen, gray as a ghost. So we brought the gate closed at the end of the pasture. We thought we'd keep him there until someone could bring him home."

"Did he have a rider? Anyone with him?" With difficulty Crae kept from describing the guardian. All he needed was an eager-to-please farmer telling him what he wanted to hear.

The farmer shook his head.

"What happened?"

"We couldn't get close to him. He was too wary. And then—he flew, sir. Or so it looked like. He trotted over to the fence when he saw us coming, and then he broke into a gallop and he flew into the air and was gone. I've never seen anything like it."

Crae kept his expression calm and interested. "How high is your fence?" he said, regarding the man. The farmer looked up and held his hand about a foot over his head. He squinted up at it and moved it about six inches higher.

Stavin snorted and turned it into a cough. The farmer reddened and brought his hand down quickly. Crae hid his dismay. Stavin was a good man and a good friend, but if he thought it, he said it.

"All right," Crae said. "Tal—" He gestured to the young man to come close and turned them both so their backs were to the old man. Guardians were well-trusted by the farm folk who lived on the outskirts of the woods; they faced its secrets and its dangers so closely, they knew what they owed the protectors of the gordath. Crae would rather not trust this oldster with his orders. Speaking low, he told Tal, "Take Brin and two others and ride out at once. Search where the horse was last sighted; see if you can find where the guardian might have fallen." He took a deep breath. "Even if you just find the horse, be sure to bring him in. He's almost as important. Do you understand?"

Tal nodded, his young face intent upon his responsibilities. "Yes, sir. Who should I choose?"

"Use your judgment, but go."

Tal saluted and spun on his heel, practically bolting for the door. Crae turned back to the farmer and Stavin, both watching him go with some surprise.

Crae half bowed to the old man, which the old man returned with stiff courtesy. "My thanks for bringing this news. I will have someone escort you back to your smallholding. You may go, and if you ever sight the horse again, send word."

The old man nodded, then added forthrightly, "We need to know, sir. Is the guardian well? The earth shakings have been getting worse, and the fire destroyed the harvest of some of the outer smallholders."

Willing Stavin to keep his mouth closed, Crae said, "The guardian is working to calm the forest. The fire was the doing of Lord Tharp's enemy, General Marthen."

"We know that," the crusty old-timer said. He glanced at Stavin, clearly a lord, and lowered his voice. "We need to know that the guardian is caring for the Wood."

Crae chose his words with care. "He is. And we are searching for another, any other, who can help."

The smallholder nodded. "No one with the skill has been born to the forest smallholders for a generation now," he said.

Next to Crae, Stavin started, clearly bursting with something to tell. The old man clamped his jaw, and Crae knew he would get nothing more out of him. He bowed again. "Send word if you sight the horse again, or anything else amiss."

When he had sent the farmer off with one of Lord Tharp's men, with orders to give him a few coins and provisions from the kitchen for his trouble, Crae closed the door behind him. He looked at Stavin. "What?"

"I told you, the woods of Trieve don't shake, quake, mutter, or talk."

"Yes. And?"

"I think, we, uh, have a guardian."

"What?!"

Stavin shrugged sheepishly. "He's another old-timer. He wanders around the woods, talking to himself and scaring the daylights out of anyone on the road to Trieve. We've never called him anything except for the guardian. I never knew it meant anything until just now."

Never knew it meant anything . . . Crae didn't know whether to laugh or punch his friend's easygoing face. "High god, Stavin, write to Jessamy. I'll carry the note myself."

"Crae, he's older than dirt. You come at him like that, he will die of fright before he gets a mile from Trieve."

"We need him, Stavin. Don't you understand?"

A sudden rumbling of the mountain cut off his words. As the stone floor jerked out from beneath them, they grabbed the table and held on. Outside the room they could hear shouts and cries of folk taken by surprise. As the shaking went on, dirt sifted down from the ceiling, caught in the shaft of sunlight from the small window.

"Damn it," Stavin half whispered when the shaking subsided. He was pale under his beard and held on to the table very tight. When it finished completely, they looked at each other, Stavin clearly a little sick. "Nothing like an earth shaking to make you realize you are underneath a mountain."

His words fell flat. Crae laughed hollowly nonetheless.

"Write the note, Stavin," he said. Stavin nodded. He rummaged in a small cabinet by the door, finding paper and pen and ink. He wrote quickly, the words flowing. "Jessamy will think I've gone as mad as you," he said, waving the paper to dry the ink. He folded it and handed it to Crae. "My commission." He raised a brow. "What will Lord Tharp say?"

Good riddance. Crae didn't say it out loud, just took the letter. "Just be very convincing when you talk to him, Stavin."

Stavin nodded. "Sweet as honey, that's me."

He left Crae alone in the little antechamber, and the captain sat at the end of the table, looking out the window, thinking hard. He had to ride to Trieve at once, find the old man that Stavin called guardian, and bring him back to Red Gold Bridge. There was little time to waste; tomorrow Tharp went to war. Stavin had only one chance to convince him to abandon the gordath and any other weapons that came through it.

Crae knew that his friend would have to be honey-tongued indeed to turn Tharp from his course. He pushed himself away from the table. The old guardian of Trieve had damn well better be alive when he got there.

The long rumbling of the mountain faded away, and Lynn got to her feet. Sand sifted down from the ceiling, and she brushed it off her hair and shoulders and got back to work on prying the hinges off her door with the poker from the fireplace. *At least it keeps my mind off the earthquakes,* she thought, half-wry, half-grim. She didn't like to think of them shaking the mountain and the stronghold, and the sand from the mortar in the ceiling didn't help.

A week's imprisonment had been a week too long. She had watched from her window as the army dispersed from its encampment, draining itself of men, wagons, and horses. She never saw the Jeep again or any other vehicle other than ox-carts and wagons. The maids who brought her meals and took away the chamber pot looked blank when she asked about other cars.

Looks like it's just me and Bahard, she thought. The poker slipped, gashing the wood frame of the door. "Crap," she muttered.

She had to find Bahard. He had to know how to get out of there. The poker caught underneath the crude hinge, and she pried with all of her strength, the metal shrieking. But the wood splintered, and the plate began to pull away from the door.

If she couldn't find Bahard, she needed to find the supply depot where he was storing his guns. There had to be a road for the Jeep. All she had to do was stick to the road, follow the tire tracks. She'd be home in no time. She shied away from thinking about what came next. How to explain what had happened to her, to Dungiven. "First things first," she grunted, and pulled at the hinge, working the poker under the metal. After she got home, she could figure out what to say to Mrs. Hunt. To Joe.

The plate pulled away with a final shriek, leaving behind shredded wood and thick nails. Lynn gave her arms a rest and then began work on the second hinge. This one gave way more easily, and the door listed drunkenly. It was still locked on the other end, but she could reach one arm through and feel for the bolt. She strained, her fingers slipping on the bolt over and over again.

God dammit, she wanted to shout. She didn't. With determination she pushed at the door with her shoulder, forcing her arm to reach as fully as it could. Her shoulder ached where it was pressed by the heavy door. She caught the bolt, pulled with all her strength, and grudgingly it came free, sliding along the rusty channel. It caught her fingers for a moment, bringing tears of pain, but she pulled her hand back and pulled the door open, leaning it against the wall.

Lynn pushed back her hair. She was free. She sucked her throbbing fingers and cast a look into the corridor. There was no sign of anyone. Usually the maids came only in the morning and at night, and she was left alone all day. She began to gather up her things.

The second day of her captivity the maids had brought her a basin for washing and a change of clothes. They had provided her with a long split skirt, once blue but faded gray, and thick tights and socks that felt good on her blistered feet. She wore her vest over her white shirt, which the maids had washed for her and mended. Of her expensive breeches there was no salvaging; they had been badly torn at the knee and the seat. Her underwear was still useful, and the maids had washed that as well, but they had been reduced to fits of giggles at the sight of her bra and panties.

Dressed for escape, Lynn bundled up her telltale vest in the thin towel she had been given for her bath. She hoped her boots would escape notice; the skirt came down to her ankles, but the expensive leather paddock boots peeked out brazenly. She tied the blue kerchief on her head, praying she got the little bow just right. Out of habit she felt for her cell phone. For a moment, she let herself think about calling Joe, hearing his voice. *Hi, honey, I'm home.*

Lynn shook her head. *Concentrate,* she told herself sternly. She gathered up some flatbread she had hoarded and after one last look around took a deep breath and ducked out the door.

Confidence, she told herself. *Walk with confidence.* Her heart hammered as she headed toward the tower stairs, following the daylight that fell across the dark corridor from the archway to the outside tower. A sharp wind blew keenly, almost whisking the kerchief off her head. Lynn grabbed at it and nearly dropped her bundle of clothes. "Crap," she muttered, and ducked against the wall, trying to put herself back together. Looking both ways, she stepped through the archway and the crisp air of daylight, the sunlight shining on the red gold stone and the fluttering vines. She had not gone two steps before she heard voices. Lynn froze. Men, coming up the stairs, their voices loud and bold. She couldn't understand what they were saying, and for a moment she hesitated. Then she thought: *No. That's not right. The only place to go up here is to my room.* She felt suddenly sick to her stomach. She backed up into the corridor, then bolted.

She left behind all pretense of acting with confidence. Lynn ran down the stone halls, clattering down the stairs. From behind her she heard shouts, and then running footsteps echoed through the mountain. They found the door, she thought grimly and hid in a small niche, pressing her body into the shadow. There was a pause, then booted feet thudded past her down the corridor.

She peered out and saw a cluster of men milling about at the far end of the corridor. She plastered herself back against the niche again. *Think, Lynn.* They would backtrack, call for reinforcements. If she didn't move, she'd be caught. *I need a distraction.* She reached into the bundle and wormed her hand into her rolled-up vest, pulling out her cell phone.

It always took forever to program the damn thing, but fear gave her focus. She set up the alarm for one minute hence and, hands shaking, leaned out of her little hidey-hole and slid the phone back along the corridor the way she had come. It scraped along the stone until it was lost in the darkness, but the little noise it made caught their attention.

"What was that?" That was clear enough. She waited, sweating, pressed up against the cold mountain rock. Footsteps approached her niche, paused, and then passed her, back up the corridor. She heard more voices, exclamations of discovery, questions. Her fingernails carved dents into her palms.

An unearthly rippling shriek began repeating itself with piercing insistence. Even Lynn, who knew it was the phone, jumped; down the hall the men practically exploded with fright.

In the resulting hubbub, she ran off, the phone shrieking its fool head off behind her.

In the south tower guardhouse, Crae looked up from packing his gear when Lord Camrin came bursting in, followed closely by his men and three of Crae's guards.

"My lord?" Crae said. Lord Camrin was wild-eyed, disheveled, and red-faced.

"You had better do something, Captain! Your prisoner has escaped."

Crae dropped his pack and picked up his sword, buckling on the sword belt as he hastened out the door. Stavin's commission would have to wait. He would need to set up a guard on all the gates and the lesser-known posterns, as well as send searchers through the outbuildings. He shouldered through the door as he fired questions at the old lord. "What happened? Did you see her? When did you discover this?"

The short, stout lord panted hard, struggling to keep up. "Her door was shattered, torn off by the hinges. We chased her down the corridor, but she gave us the slip." He shook his head. "She set off a weapon, a shrieking weapon. I—I don't know what it was. But she got away."

Crae stopped to look at him. "A shrieking weapon?"

Camrin reddened even more than usual. "Yes, Captain. Do you doubt me? It shrieked. You would have run, too."

What in the unspoken name of all the gods was she carrying? "Was anyone killed or hurt?"

Camrin made an impatient face. "Did you not hear me, Captain? It shrieked. It did not shoot."

Oh, a *shrieking* weapon. That explained all, then. Perhaps something of his derision leaked into his expression, because Camrin began to bluster.

"You had best do something, Captain! You brought her here, and now she's on the loose! You said she didn't have any weapons, but she's somewhere in the stronghold, and you need to do something!"

Crae reined in his temper and bowed. He scanned the gathering crowd for his men and with a few terse orders dispersed them on their search.

"My thanks, Lord Camrin. If you could set your men to searching as well, we should soon recover her."

Camrin nodded grudgingly. "All right, Captain, but if she has another one of those . . . things, don't blame me if my men find other places to be."

Yes, such discipline, Crae said to himself, just as another thought struck him. "My lord, it is well you found her missing in her tower room, but why were you there?"

Lord Camrin's eyes flickered, but he stared Crae down. "Does the lord answer to the captain?" he growled.

You are nothing more than an elevated smallholder, only here at the will of Lord Tharp and your own petulant whims, Crae thought. *Yet you sought to meddle with one of Lord Tharp's prisoners, no doubt to impress your men . . .* This time he let his unspoken rebuke reach his eyes on purpose, along with a satisfying anger.

Camrin still blustered, but his voice faltered. "It is none of your concern, Captain. Just find her."

He turned his back, and Crae let him go. Just find her, indeed. Well, she could hardly mix in . . . Then he remembered. He had asked the maids to bring her a bath and a change of clothes, as a courtesy, and he admitted, hoping that she would think of him fondly. It was too much to hope that she had kept her outlandish clothing. If she had played her cards right, she was probably outside the gates already.

Crae set the searchers combing the mountain and the surrounding terrain while he took one of the search parties into the stronghold itself. Inside it was dim and cool, the only light from the rows of windows in the outer balconies. The fresh air mingled with the musty smell of the cavernous hold. Crae and his men moved without speaking, fanning out through the many corridors.

They heard the weapon before they saw it, its rhythmic squalling drawing them near. It got louder and louder until finally Crae saw where the sound came from, a small gray device lying on the ground. He could understand why Camrin had described it as a weapon. The noise set his teeth on edge. Warily, he picked it up.

It fit in the palm of his hand. It was hinged and came open easily. Inside it gleamed with lights and symbols, arrayed in a pattern. The little thing shone with a cold, hard beauty. His thumb pressed one of the buttons, and the symbols changed. Curious, Crae kept pressing at random, watching the symbols change, almost mesmerized. He was barely aware of his men coming up behind him, cautious in their approach.

The dreadful shrieking stopped in mid-voice. Everyone started at the sudden silence.

"That's better," Crae managed. He closed the little thing awkwardly. "Now let's find her."

But before they could move on his words, an unwelcome voice stopped them.

"First the guardian, now the lostling," Tharp snapped. "Captain Crae, what is happening here?" He was flanked by the outlander, Lord Bahard, along with Lord Camrin. No doubt Camrin had given Lord Tharp an earful on the way back from the field.

Crae bowed deeply to Lord Tharp, trying to keep his face wiped of expression. He glanced once at Lord Bahard, dressed as always in his mottled green, standing just beside Lord Tharp as if he were his equal. Not even Lord Camrin stood so.

"We have the stronghold under heavy watch, sir. The postern gates and the outbuildings are all being searched. We will find her."

Bahard snorted. "You better. She can't go back, Tharp. If she gets through, she'll find the guns in the house on the other side. Once she goes to the police, that's it. They shut us down." He lifted his hands. "We just got the damn thing open again. You said yourself, you don't know how long that will last. We don't have a lot of time. If she gets through before we can stop her, it's all over."

Crae stared at him. "The gordath is open?" *So we are too late,* he thought. Stavin had not even been able to talk to Tharp, let alone convince him to turn from his course.

"That is not your concern, Captain," Tharp said even as Bahard said, "If you ask me, I don't know what we need a guardian for. The damn thing opens and closes on its own." He shuddered.

Tharp threw up his hands. "Well, if she goes through, you'll have to go after her."

Bahard shook his head. "And then what? Believe me, it's better if we stop her over here. Anything I do over there—let's just say, it's not so easy to get away with—stuff."

"What do you mean?" Crae asked, although he was beginning to understand.

No one answered, though both Lord Tharp and Bahard exchanged glances.

"Just find her, Captain," Lord Tharp said finally. "Just bring her back, and bring her to me when you have her. She's a prisoner of Red Gold Bridge and will be treated as such."

Crae watched them go, tucking the little device into his jacket pocket. If he brought her back, she would soon be dead. Not by Tharp's hand or even Bahard's, perhaps, but somehow she would meet with her death.

He turned to his men. "You heard my lord," he said evenly. "The man who finds her and brings her to me will be doubly rewarded."

He didn't wait for their salutes but walked off, his strides long and purposeful. As he walked, he pulled at the insignia on the shoulder of his jacket, tearing at it until the stitching came loose and it was free, just as he reached the courtyard. Crae threw it on the muddy stones where it would get trampled into oblivion and took a deep breath of cold forest air, still smoky but sweet with the promise of winter.

After he found her, he would fetch his pack and replace Stavin's commission with his resignation; no need to compromise his friend's standing with Tharp. Getting her through the gordath would be another trial, but for now, he only had to keep her alive.

To do that, he had to find her before Tharp or Bahard did.

The cold wind blew the cobwebs from his head, leaving him with clarity. She had arrived by horseback; she would seek a mount to return home. He would find her in the stable.

Lynn peered out from beneath a long feed trough, lifting her head out of the damp and moldy straw just enough to see. The old mare in whose stall she hid flicked an ear at her but otherwise ignored her.

I'll have to stay here till nightfall, she thought. Several search parties had swept through the stables, looking in the stalls, though not in the shadow under the mangers, and up in the hayloft. She gathered from the sounds she heard that they had grabbed pitchforks and shovels and were jabbing them in the hay.

The barn was silent now. She waited, trying to hear over the thrumming of her heart. Nothing. The calm and peace of the stable rose around her as horses dozed, ate, shifted their weight. The warmth and smells of the stable were comfortingly familiar, and she found herself relaxing.

With a long scrape the main stable door opened up again. Lynn tensed. Footsteps. Someone walked in and stood in the center aisle. She let the hay cover her again, shutting out the dim light until she was in a scratchy cocoon of hay.

"Lostling," a voice said. She held her breath.

"I am not here to capture you," the voice went on, the lilting cadences hard to decipher. She recognized it: the captain's. "You are right to escape. Lord Bahard sees you as a threat and means to have you killed so you cannot return through the gordath."

It took her a moment to understand, then her heart sped up. What was he saying? Bahard wanted to kill her?

"Come with me; I will help you live."

She hesitated in a torment of indecision. Believe him? Stay hidden? She had trusted him before, but look where it had gotten her. No. She was on her own now. She could only trust herself. She willed herself into stillness.

He was silent, then she heard him say something under his breath. He walked back to the door, and she heard it open and close. She breathed out a sigh. Good. He was gone.

She had halfway thrown off her covering of hay before she realized that it was a trick. By then it was too late. The footsteps came back, then there he was, staring at her hiding place in the back of the stall.

"Shit," said Lynn under her breath.

Nine

Grayne had the girl with him when he came back, leading his horse with her in the saddle. Marthen sat his black, keeping a tight rein on the irritable stallion, and took in his lieutenant's muddy, disheveled uniform. The girl looked worse for wear herself. The shirt he had given her was soiled and torn, and her hair was tangled around her face, which seemed to have collected a few more bruises.

"Report," he said crisply as a disgruntled Grayne came up and saluted. The girl had a mutinous expression.

"She tried to run off, sir. I caught her before she got into the Wood," he said. Marthen raised an eyebrow. The black shifted restlessly under him and bared his teeth at Grayne's horse.

"I thought I had given you an order," he said to Kate. She jerked her head to indicate the crawling army behind them.

"You need to give *them* orders," she shot back. So the quiet mouse of the night before was gone; she was frightened and furious.

Marthen looked at Grayne.

"The crows," he said. "She thought they were chasing her."

"They were!"

Marthen's face tightened in distaste at the squabbling.

"Enough. You should thank Grayne; he saved your life. If I had had to send someone to track you down, I would have brought you back to be hanged." She made to protest, and he said sharply, "Thank him."

For one long moment she said nothing, and then, grudgingly, "Thanks."

Grayne bowed his head the least bit. "Also, sir. We saw a

riderless horse in the Wood. She knew him, and called him by name."

Marthen looked at Kate.

She said, "It was my friend's horse, the one I told you about. Something happened to her. Dungiven lost his bridle, and the saddle's half off. She's lost in there now."

Her voice caught on unshed tears.

Marthen looked at Grayne, who nodded, affirming the girl's description.

"We do not have time to look for lost riders," he said. "But I will have the scouts keep a watch for her or the horse. Now," he added, and nudged his horse with his heel and reined him around. "You will ride up next to me." He looked at Grayne. "Work with the quartermaster to coordinate the supply train movements."

Grayne bowed his head and flipped the reins over the horse's head for the girl to gather up. Marthen watched his lieutenant walk away with his shoulders slightly bowed. He glanced over at the girl, now sitting quietly on the horse, her boots a few inches above the stirrups, which had been set for Grayne's long legs. Who was she to cause so much disruption? Yet she sat the horse so competently, the reins perfectly gathered, the horse standing at attention, waiting for her orders.

Without another word Marthen pushed his horse into a trot and rode up to the head of the line again. He heard her follow at a prudent distance.

When they encamped he would ask her what he needed to know about the weapons that Tharp was bringing through. He still didn't know how she could be of use, if any, but it would have been a shame if the crows had gotten hold of her before he could find out.

It was the hardest ride of Kate's life. Once the army got fully under way, Marthen and the officers pushed them at a brisk pace along the river road that wound along the eastern edge of the forest. Like him, she ate and drank in the saddle, taking only a few minutes for short breaks. It was only when she relieved herself in the scant cover of underbrush at the edge of the woods that she realized that she had lost any sense of modesty. *Almost,* she thought, yanking up her breeches, now loose about her waist. She wasn't going to go as far as the women and men who merely turned aside off the road.

As she rubbed her hands on some leaves in a vain attempt to pretend she washed them, she thought to herself, *Give it time.*

When she ducked out of the brush, she gathered up the reins of Grayne's tall chestnut gelding, patting him on the shoulder. He was sweaty but holding up well under the pace. Kate wondered about Mojo, then tried not to worry about him. He was part Arabian; stamina was his birthright.

She swung on board, wincing as her sore butt hit the saddle. She had figured out the stirrups and managed to shorten them to her length, but even so, the long ride was taking its toll. Kate never rode all day.

She collected the horse with her hands and legs, and he gathered himself under her. He was a good, responsive horse, alert and spirited. For a moment she thought about what it would be like to ride him over fences and felt disloyal to Mojo.

Under a dreary gray sky, the crawling army marched up the river road, rising to the top of the high bluffs overlooking the river. Kate craned out to see the water, running flat and fast between its broad shores. Several ships sailed out in the middle, heading downstream, their sails belled out from the wind and spidery oars dipping and rising in the water. She saw tiny figures crawling in the rigging, standing on the spars to watch the advancing army.

It was strange to think of people going about their business, so removed from her life that they could be in a different—

World.

And yet, they were closer to her than her parents.

Kate watched the ships as long as she could, until they sailed around the wide bend in the river back the way the army had come.

When night fell, the army halted with the forest at their back and the valley of the Aeritan spread out around them. Off east of their position was Red Gold Bridge.

Marthen knew that Tharp's scouts were already aware of his presence. He kept a guard on his perimeter and ordered out a new team of scouts once darkness fell and the others had come back in.

Their reports were sparse, telling only of the smallholders fleeing their steadings in the edges of the Wood, gathering at Red Gold Bridge. Marthen gave orders for a small squad to move ahead to burn the fields surrounding Tharp's stronghold. It would increase the panic and disorder in the stronghold and lessen any chance Tharp had of sitting out a siege. A few men with torches in the dark should make short work of the harvest.

None of the scouts had seen a white horse or another lost rider, but then he knew that they dared not venture deep into Gordath Wood but kept to the outskirts where they could watch the roads.

He looked out over the spreading army from his door flap, the sea of tents, wagons, and men dark shapes against the dark night. The word had gone out: no fires, no torches. Only the officers had light, the thick walls of their tents masking the dim lamps. Marthen ducked back into the semidarkness of his tent.

The lords crowded into the small space, the junior officers sitting in shadow in the corners. A small lantern hung over the map table, and their faces were lost in darkness. The air smelled of men and sweat, horses, and musty canvas. Under the lamplight, sitting on a small camp stool, was Kate Mossland, small and uncertain in their company.

He had given Grayne orders that she was to wash up, and as best he could tell in the dim light, she had complied. Her hair was braided, and it looked as if her face and hands were clean.

At the other end of the table, Lord Terrick cleared his throat.

"Child. We mean you no harm." He looked pointedly at Marthen. "Answer our questions honestly and with goodwill, and we will treat you in kind."

Despite himself, Marthen nearly laughed. The girl looked almost more frightened at Lord Terrick's ill-tempered kindness than before. *Enough,* he thought.

"Tell us, Kate Mossland, how do they wage war where you come from?"

Grayne escorted the girl back to her tent, and the rest of the lords filed out, all save Lord Terrick. Marthen poured a bit more oil in the lantern and turned up the wick so they could see the map.

"What do you think?" Terrick said, his gruff voice low.

Marthen sat back, his fingers steepled. He had been mulling over the girl's tales since she had been sent back to her tent, trying to make sense of the strange words she used. Airplanes, machines that rained down fire from the sky. Tanks, armored wagons that rolled inexorably over all obstacles. Aircraft carriers, ships so vast they were like floating cities. He knew that she had been trying to impress them, but he had not gotten the sense that she was lying.

"Fantastic tales, all, but she confirmed the reports of the weapons Tharp's gotten. Common, where she's from."

He had not asked directly about guns; she had brought them up on her own. She was almost offhand in her description of them. If all Tharp had were guns, Marthen was confident in the ability of his army to withstand them.

If he had any of the other weapons she described, they were doomed to hell.

As if he could see Marthen's thoughts, Terrick said, "We're sure he only has these guns?"

"Not anymore." Marthen noted Terrick's surprise. "I won't lie to you, sir. The tales she brings change everything. How would our spies know what to look for, if we never knew there were such things? The guns—they sound as if they are but a kind of bow, much like a crossbow or a longbow. But who would have thought to armor a wagon?"

He had a sudden image of an armored wagon, drawn by armored oxen, rolling invincibly over a battlefield, men shooting arrows from slits in its carapace. He thought about a large wooden flying machine, with wings of cloth to catch the wind, soaring over Red Gold Bridge, spewing fire from above.

No. That's not it. He knew he didn't have it right; she described something he had no words for. He knew there were no oxen in the war that she described, and however the airplanes flew, it was not with wings of cloth. He wanted to shake her, beat her, force her to use words he knew to make him understand.

He wanted to see for himself. His eyes were drawn to the whiteness at the center of the map, where such wonders hid themselves.

"Yes. Well. In light of what she told us, I think we should change our strategy."

Marthen started, brought back to the moment by Lord Terrick's words. The man stared down at the map, absorbed in their tactics, and missed Marthen's inattention. Marthen composed himself and said, "I agree. A smaller force to test those weapons?"

Terrick nodded. "Seven hundred, I think. Plus the crows."

"We draw him out here," Marthen said, pointing to the drawing of the wide wall that encircled the stronghold. His finger traced a line back a few miles east of where their dark encampment lay. "The rest of the men wait here. We fall back, and call for a bigger charge when he is in range."

Terrick nodded. "It could work. It could work. He would have to take the bait, though."

Marthen snorted. "If I had weapons like those, I'd be itching to use them."

Terrick laughed, and for a moment they exchanged a look of understanding. Then the man sobered.

"And if the girl's tall tales are true? If he has more weapons than just those damned fancy crossbows?"

"Well then, how are your knees?" In the face of Terrick's surprise, Marthen went on, "You will be on them, sir. You will be on them."

The lord's face reddened with anger, and he stood.

"You have a way with you, General; I don't deny it. But a word to the wise: if I am to kneel, I will be sure to do it on your back."

In the darkness of a little clearing off the forest road, Lynn dragged the saddle off her borrowed mare and propped it next to Crae's against an outcropping of rock. Her muscles ached, and her mind was heavy with exhaustion. She slid down against the outcropping, her eyes closing.

"There are hobbles attached to my saddle," Crae said, from where he was setting a small fire. An orange spark glowed dully, and she could hear him blowing on it to keep it alive.

"Okay," Lynn said, pushing herself up with effort. She rummaged through the gear hanging off his saddle and came up with the ropes, hobbling the horses' forelegs, making sure they were bound securely but not too tightly. The horses were used to it; as soon as she had them secured and took their bridles off, they dropped their heads and began to nibble at the sparse grass.

The little fire flared and began to crackle. Lynn stumbled across the clearing and sat down opposite Crae. The night air was brisk, and the fire felt good.

He reached out a long arm behind him and rooted through his pack, coming up with a small kettle. He got to his feet.

"Water, about fifty steps in that direction," he said, nodding off into the darkness.

She squinted at the dark. "How do you know where we are?"

"When I patrolled with my men, we would stop here," he said. "A bit of shelter, water nearby. I'll be back soon." He disappeared outside the fire's circle.

Lynn's eyes closed against her will, and she curled up next to the fire, resting her head on her arm. Just for a few moments, she thought, but she woke to his hand on her shoulder and sat up, disoriented. He loomed in shadow over her, waiting patiently, something in his hand.

She mumbled something even she could not decipher. He handed her a cup.

"Drink this," he said. "It will keep you warm and soothe the aches."

She nodded vaguely and sipped. The drink was rich and herbal, with a taste she could not place. It reminded her of something dark, like earth, that smelled better than it tasted. She swallowed politely, then put her hands around the cup. She had grown cold, and the drink helped a bit.

Crae sat back down, looted through his pack again, and handed her a thick flatbread and some pungent cheese.

"Thanks," she said. He got some for himself, and they ate in comfortable silence, the horses tearing peacefully at the grass, occasionally stamping a hoof or switching their tails. Lynn took another sip. The drink was growing on her. The cold receded a little, though the wind tousled the top of her hair with greedy fingers.

"So what do you call this?" she said. "It reminds me of a drink we have back home called coffee." Mostly by omission, but she felt she could stretch the truth a bit.

Crae made a disparaging noise through his full mouth. When he could speak, he said, "Bahard said it tasted like horse piss."

"What a guy," she said, voice dry. She took another sip. "Tell me about this Bahard. What's up with him?" *Why does the bastard want me dead?*

Bahard had come in the spring. Snow still whitened the hollows beside the road, and the ice on the river crashed and creaked as the river threw off its imprisoning sheets. The sun shone warmer though, even if the night left puddles of dangerous ice in the early morning. It rained, a thick, steady rain that turned the tributary streams into crashing torrents. Red Gold Bridge dripped with rain over its balconies and inside its windows.

The stronghold dripped with winter fever, too. Not just illness, though there was plenty of it, but with the aggravation that comes when men are cooped up in tight places with no relief. Several merchants had been trapped by the ice in the dark of winter during one last attempt to sail the river, adding to the mix. Crae and his men spent most of their time breaking up brawls and scuffles.

When the word came that smallholders on the edge of the Wood found a stranger, Tharp ordered Crae to escort him across the border to Terrick rather than add one more man to the havoc that marked the stronghold. Crae and his men walked the distance to the smallholding on the edge of the Wood, trudging through the snow, laughing at what they would find: a lost peddler, perhaps, or a smallholder himself, led astray by the mischievous Wood. They joked about escorting a confused farmer to another lord's lands.

The jokes died when they saw the tall stranger in bulky trousers and jacket, his boots the same drab color. He waited

for them by the snow-capped Xs that made up the smallholding's fence. He had a peeved expression Crae would come to
know well, and he held a stick of wood and metal.

Crae had known without knowing that the metal-and-wood
stick was dangerous. He kept his men from attacking and
talked with the stranger. The man's accent became easier to
understand as they kept talking, though sometimes his words
were still incomprehensible.

I am called Crae, he told the stranger man. Captain at Red
Gold Bridge. How are you called?

Bahard let forth a stream of speech of which Crae deci-
phered only one or two words. Then he raised the weapon and
aimed it straight at Crae.

Later, after Bahard demonstrated the power of the weapon
to Tharp and the other lords, Crae sometimes thought about
how close he had come to death. By then the deal was sealed,
and Bahard was an ally to Red Gold Bridge and a large part of
Lord Tharp's war.

At the end of his story, Lynn nodded and took
a sip. She still looked drawn and tired, but the vesh had revived her. He almost had not wanted to wake her when he
came back with the water, but he knew it was better for her to
eat and drink than go to rest with an empty belly. She was skin
and bones as it was. "So I guess Lord Tharp liked the idea of
the guns," she said.

Crae looked down at the fire, nudging a glowing log with
the toe of his boot.

"Yes," he said. "Lord Tharp saw a chance with the guns, if
he had more of them. He bargained with Bahard to bring more
guns, better guns, in exchange for land and most of the wealth
of Red Gold Bridge—much of his wife's dowry, in fact."

"Tharp is married?" She sounded surprised.

"Is—was. Seven years ago, Lady Sarita went into the
Wood, never to return."

For long moments the only sound was the gentle cracking
of the fire, and the dozing movements of the horses.

"Wait—what? She *wanted* to go?"

He still couldn't believe it, himself, though it had been so
many years.

"She must have," he said. "She left a message with a strongholder, not even one of her own maids. The message said that she had gone home for a visit." He looked over at Lynn. "She had been unhappy; it made sense. So, we rode out, thinking we'd catch her on her way. We never caught her up. I sent an envoy ahead to Wessen and returned to Red Gold Bridge to see if she turned up, but—" He lifted his shoulders. "The guardians say the Wood has a way of calling folk to bring them to it, then it draws them into itself," he said at last. "I think her reasoning was more—prosaic. She and her lord did not get along. She miscarried, and the rift widened. I think it was that, more than the gordath, that drew her into the Wood."

His protection did not extend to her heart, though sometimes he wished it had. Remaining silent while they argued, and later standing outside her door when she wept, sometimes he wished he could go before the council and demand an annulment for them.

If anything, he thought, at least he would get some sleep at night.

He wondered if she knew that when she left, all the spirit went out of Red Gold Bridge. Had she died, they could have mourned, as they mourned her miscarriage. She had probably fled unaware that she had become such a piece of the stronghold's foundation.

He heard Lynn yawn. Crae set down his empty cup and dragged over his saddle, pulling at the ties that held the bedroll. "Here," he said, handing it to her. "We have a long way to ride tomorrow."

She laid out the blanket and wrapped herself in it. Crae took out his sword from his saddle scabbard. He got out his crossbow and two bolts and set them on his other side. He piled sand on the fire, smothering it, and night fell around them, the stars brightening in the cold, dark sky. Only then did he roll out his own thick blanket and wrap himself in it, lying back against his saddle. He heard her soft breathing slow and let his muscles loosen as he tried to get comfortable on the hard ground. He was sure she slept when he heard her voice, hopeful and sleepy in the darkness.

"Hey, Crae," she said. "If she did go to our side, she'll be okay. It can be a little rough, but you know, it's not so bad."

He smiled ruefully at the sky. "My thanks."

She made no answer except for a snore, and he knew she slept at last.

Ten

Kate watched the army preparing for war from the door flap of her tent. The men were mostly silent, the only sounds the clanking of armor as they geared up. Every once in a while she would hear a low voice or a laugh but little else. She wrapped her arms around herself and danced in her boots, trying to keep back the creeping cold.

Grayne loomed out of the dimness, a stranger in armor, holding his helm under his arm.

"The general wants you," he said.

"All right," Kate said, surprised at how calm she sounded. She followed Grayne to the officers' pavilions. Marthen's serving man dressed him out. His shoulder armor made him appear bigger than before. He wore a breastplate that came down over his abdomen and greaves over his legs. Thick gloves covered his hands.

A commotion caught her eye; Marthen's peevish war stallion bucked against his two grooms. Kate caught her breath as the big horse threw his body into one of the grooms, knocking him to his knees. The man bit off a cry of pain. Instinctively, she jumped forward to help.

"Back him up!" the groom said, and she grabbed the horse's bridle and rein and began pushing him backward. The injured man rolled out of the way, cursing behind gritted teeth. The stallion's eye rolled, his nostrils flared red, and he huffed at her, his teeth bared and his ears flat against his head.

"Ho, now," she said. "Ho, baby, settle down." Kate continued speaking baby talk, the other groom giving her a look of surprise. The horse must have been as shocked; his ears pricked, and he came eye to eye with her, his resistance broken for the moment. Kate seized the initiative, taking a deep breath and blowing it back at his muzzle. The war stallion huffed again, then brought his muzzle delicately to her face. She held her ground. She and the horse breathed back and forth at each other, then the stallion knocked her in the face with his head, hitting her on the cheek. Kate stumbled back, and the groom hauled off and yanked on the horse's rein, hurting his mouth. The horse squealed and reared, the moment of understanding lost. Kate groaned, hanging on to the reins. The stallion hadn't meant to hurt her; it was his version of Mojo's affectionate rub. The stallion skittered and squealed, and they dragged him to the mounting block. She still didn't see how Marthen was going to be able to mount, covered in armor as he was, but he merely gestured at two or three other men.

"Hold him steady. Girl, come here."

She waited until she was replaced and then walked over to the general, breathing hard and rubbing her cheek. He regarded her, his helmet under one arm looking like an ornate skull.

"I don't need a tamed horse. I need one that will fight."

"You need one that will fight with you, not against you," she shot back. He set his helmet on his head. The nosepiece flattened his features.

"This is war, Kate Mossland, not a pleasure jaunt. I didn't have you brought here to pet my horse and braid its mane with flowers." He ignored her gasp of outrage. "You will stay back with the camp followers and others. I cannot spare Grayne or others to keep an eye on you, so do yourself a favor and do not see this as an opportunity to run back into the Wood. I've ordered that your horse be ridden out to carry messages behind the lines. He can earn his keep for the both of you for now."

Marthen did not wait for her reply. He turned and stepped onto the mounting block, and with three men holding his horse, he mounted up. Someone handed him his sword, and he sheathed it in the leather scabbard at his side. He took his shield and the reins and spurred the horse forward. The animal ducked his head and tried to buck, but his heavy load defeated him, and Marthen muscled him to the front of his army.

The sky had just lightened on the horizon when the camp began to empty. Even the crows advanced, mauls and staffs over their shoulders, taking up position behind the soldiers.

Kate thought about what it would be like to have a crow at her back and shuddered. No deserters in this army, she thought. She fell back with the rest of the camp followers and tried not to think about losing.

The camp was littered with sagging tents, cold campfires, abandoned gear. The supply wagons waited off to one side, their taut canvas cold and damp in the early morning fog. Only a handful of camp followers remained; most of the men and a few of the women had straggled haphazardly after the army, carrying makeshift weapons.

Kate hugged her elbows in the emptiness and looked around. A few of the ostlers stood near the empty corrals, talking among themselves. Torm made bewildered sounds, and they yelled at him irritably. One made as if to smack him, and Torm cringed. Kate looked away.

A young woman sat down on the hitch of the wagon next to her, one thin arm resting on her big belly.

"Oof," she said. "Curse them for making us walk this far. The brat will be born if I have to go another step."

A burly drover looked at her sourly. "Should have thought of your feet when you were on your back, Tiurlin."

His snide remark raised a laugh from bystanders and a gobbet of spit from the pregnant girl.

Kate blushed.

The girl noticed. "Hey you, stranger girl," she said. "Best stake out a comfy spot. When they come back, they'll be wanting to bed. Randy as bulls after a bit of blood, they are." She winked at the drover.

In the general laughter, Kate knew she turned bright red. She waited for a moment to gather herself and then said as coolly as she could muster, "I'll let you handle them; you seem to be good at it."

The laughter turned into hoots and hollers. Tiurlin cocked her head and pursed her lips. "Isn't she an uppity bitch, boys. Who do you think you are, stranger girl? Too good for us?"

Kate, heart pounding, knew she wouldn't be able to come up with a good comeback before nightfall. She settled for a derisive eyeroll and a feeble, "Yeah, whatever." She turned away as the crowd booed and catcalled, pretending to be interested in the mist-soaked camp squatting in a field of crushed, brown-tipped grass. Spindly trees dotted the perimeter, and the clouds met the earth with fog. A few dark, wet tree trunks, the vanguard of the Wood, marked the edge of the camp. Rain fell harder, stinging. Kate's hair plastered itself to her face in dark, thin snakes. She wiped wetness from her cheeks and thought about climbing into a wagon and going back to sleep. *Wake me when the war's over,* she thought. Then Tiurlin's teasing came back to her, and her stomach went queasy again.

Someone nudged her, and she turned around in alarm. It was the drover. He grinned at her. "Brat or no, she'll snatch you bald-headed if she finds you stepping out with her boy. I'd stay away from her, I were you."

Kate made a face. "Thanks. Tell her I'm not interested in her . . . boy." She looked at him suspiciously. "Which one?" If he said Colar . . . *Not that I care.*

"That scout. The bad-tempered one. Jayce."

Kate's jaw dropped. "She likes *Jayce*?!" Her voice rose loud enough for Tiurlin to hear, and possibly half the camp as well. They all turned toward her. Tiurlin, dawning shock and anger on her thin face, started toward her, and the crowd, lured by blood, surged after.

The pregnant girl stomped up to her, fists clenched. "You stay away from him," she said, pushing at Kate's shoulders and making her stumble back a few steps. She unclenched a fist and poked her finger at Kate's nose. "I will split you longways if you make a move toward him. Is that clear?"

"Yeah. Yeah." Kate raised her hands, palms up. She couldn't fight back even if she knew how; the girl was *pregnant*. She continued. "Not a problem. He's all yours." Tiurlin held her gaze pugnaciously, then backed off after one last shove. Kate let herself fall back.

"Remember it, stranger bitch."

Kate watched her go, her breathing slowing. The crowd dispersed, and she shook her head when she was left alone once more. The drover cocked an eye down at her.

"Not too bright, are you?"

She couldn't help it; she laughed, then put her hands up to her mouth to stuff the sound back in. "She likes Jayce," she said again.

The drover began to look a little alarmed. He sidled away. Kate barely noticed.

Oh my God. I'm in high school.

The crack of an explosion made Kate jump. She gasped.

Was that a gun? It was impossible. It couldn't be. Everyone in the encampment was as startled as she was, turning to peer tensely toward the direction of the sound, distorted by the fog. The echoes of the report rolled away.

Hoofbeats thudded out of the fog, growing louder and louder, until suddenly a riderless horse galloped past them, stirrups flapping and reins trailing, and disappeared in the center of the camp.

Another shot sang out. It whined past Kate and splatted.

She ducked instinctively, feeling wetness, and wiped her bloody hand on her shirt. She was puzzled. *Wait. Was I shot?* Next to her the drover crumpled to the ground, and she stumbled away from the body in alarm.

With a roar, a rolling volley exploded in the fog. The camp followers milled briefly, then started to run, pushing and screaming at one another. Kate was knocked off her feet, and she rolled under a wagon, covering her head. She peered past the drover's body to look out toward the battlefield.

Marthen's men had swords, she thought, bewildered. And those short bows. Not guns. How could someone have guns? On the heels of that thought came outrage: *That's not fair!* Another volley of gunfire roared, and she heard more screams, closer. Kate closed her eyes, curled up tight under the wagon, and listened to the sounds of battle all around her. The volleys were intermittent over the din of clashing swords; she could even pick out the somber thunk of crossbow bolts and arrows. Hoofbeats shook the ground. Men shouted or cried out or screamed and fell. She opened her eyes to see the wagon surrounded by a forest of legs from the knees down, crisscrossing her field of vision. A man gave a guttering scream above her head and fell, landing by the wagon tongue and faced her as if he could still see her, and she closed her eyes tight again at the blood and froth that spewed from his mouth.

She heard an odd grunting sound and rolled away from the

dead man. She could see Torm, trying to worm his clumsy
body beneath the wagon. "Unh unh unh," he grunted, his eyes
wide and his round face filled with panic.

"Mmamamamnnnnm," he said, and she saw the sheer terror
in his eyes. Kate reached out and grabbed his hands. She pulled,
and he squirmed, and she got him under the wagon with her.

They held hands for the rest of the battle.

A horn sounded clear and high above the
noise of battle, three long blasts. Men shouted. Kate could
hear the call for retreat. Pull back! Fall back! Regroup! The
wagon dipped and shook as someone clambered onto the seat
and slapped the reins on the backs of the team. Kate forced
herself to her hands and knees and crawled out the back as the
wagon began to trundle forward, Torm squirming behind her.
They stood up, watching as soldiers ran from the field, their
eyes wild and their faces covered with blood. Some held up
wounded comrades, but most just ran by themselves.

Torm stuck close to Kate, one hand gripping to her sleeve.
He gurgled, his voice stuck on the sounds, and he kept pawing
at her arm, trying to pull her along, and she suddenly had to
get away from him. She rounded on him and cried out, "Let
go!" Terrified, he backed off.

A tattoo of hoofbeats caught her attention, and she turned
at the sound. A covey of mounted troops cantered into camp
and drew up their lathered horses. Kate peered through the
crowd, but none were on her little horse.

Mojo. Where was Mojo?

Kate began to run in the direction of the battlefield, pushing through the line of defeated soldiers returning from war.

She alternated jogging and walking for at least
a half hour, pressing her hand against the stitch in her side.
She looked for Mojo every time she saw a horse, but he was
nowhere to be found. She saw only a scattering of dead men,
then too many to count. The crows picked through the wreck-
age, eyeing her now and again but making no move toward
her. She was not alone; other women drifted through the
camp, calling for their men. Kate felt too foolish to call out.

It had stopped raining, but the fog was still thick. Mojo lay near the front, his neck flung out and his forelegs hanging crookedly under his big body. A crossbow bolt lodged just behind his shoulder, piercing his heart. Bloody froth spilled from his mouth.

Kate knelt in the mud and touched her little horse's neck, wet and cold. "Mojo?" she whispered. He was so still. How could it be him? She began to stroke his mane over and over. "Modgie?"

Someone came up beside her. Kate didn't turn around. She couldn't take her hand away from Mojo's mane. Her fingers twisted in the long black hair, her other hand pressed flat against his rain-soaked neck.

Grayne said, his voice sore and tired, "The general wants you."

She ignored him. After a moment he reached down and pulled her to her feet. He looked down at her, his face soiled and stubbled and his armor streaked with blood and dirt. He made an odd gesture, as if he meant to push back her tangled hair but thought better of it.

"One minute," she croaked through her broken throat.

He hesitated, then nodded, and she knelt once more. But when she touched Mojo again, she felt nothing.

Under a heavy rain the camp bustled with ac-tivity as men kept coming in, wounded, bloodied, many screaming, others silent. Grayne pulled her out of the way of two men carrying a third on a pallet. The man moaned, his voice gurgling.

The general stood surrounded by his officers, still in their bloodied armor, in the middle of the camp, as Kate and Grayne approached. She could hear shouting.

"I blame you for this, Marthen!" a big, burly man shouted, blood soaking into his thinning hair. "You and this girl of yours! You knew this was going to happen, and you threw us right into it!"

"I thought the army you brought me was better trained than to run at the sound of a loud noise and weapons that were no more lethal than a crossbow," Marthen said. His voice was raised. Kate had never heard him raise his voice. "The next time—"

"The next time? You can't think we can face him again on

the field like that! We go around to Temia!" the burly lord almost shrieked.

"Don't you think that's what he wants us to do?" Marthen snapped. "Try to ambush him by coming in from the north? You can say good-bye to your short war."

"I want a war I can win, General! Not a slaughter, with these weapons that can kill a man from thrice the distance a crossbow can fly!"

"If we go around by Temia, it will be a slaughter, only we'll be penned up on the wastelands in winter! How long do you think we'll last with fall approaching and winter snows in less than a half month!"

"We can't win against these weapons!"

"We can't win in Temia!"

"We engaged you to obey our command!" the lord shrieked. His face was purple. At his rage, Marthen's voice turned to ice.

"You engaged me to command your army and to win your war. Not to be countermanded at every turn by your fears and whims. If you don't like it, find another general."

His words fell on sudden silence. Kate watched as the officers moved uncertainly, except for Lord Terrick; she couldn't tell who he was madder at, Marthen or the other lord. He stared daggers at both of them.

Never taking his eyes off the other man, Marthen nodded curtly. "If that is all, my lords, I suggest we rest ourselves and restore our bodies and spirits. We have other battles to prepare for."

Dismissed, the lords drifted away, trying to avoid each other's eyes. Marthen snapped his fingers at Grayne, and the lieutenant pushed her forward. Marthen's face was drawn and stubbled, and his armor streaked with blood and dirt. He waited until she was close, then reached out and grabbed her by the front of her shirt, almost lifting her from her feet. Kate gasped.

"You will tell me everything you know," he said, his voice calm and quiet, belying the rage in his eyes.

Kate, Marthen, and Grayne sat in Marthen's tent, hastily erected in the army's new encampment. The orderly served them, providing meat and flatbread, and a hot drink like coffee, with a flavor Kate couldn't place. Grayne, as always, sat silently in the corner of the tent. Marthen ate and drank, but he stared at her the entire while, a muscle jumping in his cheek.

"They're guns," she said. "It sounded like they are fully automatic." Her mom's last big case, the one that all the reporters called about, was about modifying semiautomatics into automatic rifles and how these weapons were currency in parts of the world.

She knew Marthen didn't want to hear about her mom's last case.

"Look, I don't know much about them. But I know something. They need bullets that have to be specially made. Unless the people who brought the guns brought enough bullets, they'll run out, and I don't think they will be able to make them here."

Marthen exchanged a look with Grayne.

"What are they made of?" he asked, and Kate bit her lip and plunged on.

"Lead, and umm, other metals. And gunpowder. The thing is, you need a whole manufacturing process, and you have to make them just right, or they won't work."

She hoped that was the case. She hoped that Tharp's army didn't have someone squirreled away making bullets by hand. She sipped her drink and waited. Marthen swirled his cup absently. He looked up at Grayne.

"Send out the scouts," he said. "Have them scour the battlefield, and ask the crows if they picked up one of these guns. Bring it to me if you can find one. Head out toward Red Gold Bridge after, and see if you can take a prisoner. Find out if they are making these bullets."

Grayne nodded. "Yes, sir." He had barely touched his sandwich or drink. Now he stood, set down his meal on the ground next to his stool, bowed, and slipped out. Kate looked down at her drink, hoping to be dismissed as well. She remembered what Tiurlin had said and felt her bones turn to water.

"What else did you neglect to tell me that will turn up in our next battle? Airplanes? Tanks?"

"I—" She suddenly regretted being so talkative the night before.

"The next time I am taken by surprise by weapons I should have known about, Kate Mossland, you may consider my protection revoked." She opened her mouth to protest when his curt gesture cut her off. "Go to your tent, and pray you remember more about these weapons tomorrow than you did tonight."

She got up and set down her cup, but her hand was shaking so much that it fell over and spilled the rest of her drink onto the ground. Hastily she bent and set it right, fumbling to make it stay. She felt that she spent long agonizing moments until it propped up against the campstool leg, and she fled beneath his gaze.

Her tent was dark and cold, and she curled beneath a thin blanket, shivering. Kate wept into her hands, trying to make no noise. She had owned Mojo since she was ten years old. He had been her constant companion for the last five years, sprightly, spirited, and sweet. Even when other girls her age were moving on to agile Thoroughbreds, the better to win points in the Juniors competitions and go on to Nationals, she stuck with him.

Now she had to let him go, if she were going to survive.

If she were going to get home.

In the dark tent, Kate whispered, "Go play, Mojo." It was what she used to tell him when she turned him out in the fields at Hunter's Chase. *Go play, Mojo.* And he would light out for the pasture, bucking a little for the fun of it.

The evening shadows stretched long over Daw Road where it cut across the trails, dipping and turning through the woods, its surface broken up into gravel, asphalt, and dirt. Joe drove along between tumbledown stone walls that ran along either side of the road. Wild rosebushes, their flowers dried and brown but still exuding a sweet scent, climbed all over them. Poison ivy crept low to the ground, and elderberry bushes hung lush and green over the road. Huge stone houses, many with barns and paddocks, were set back almost into the woods, lush lawns sweeping down to the narrow road, dark asphalt drives flowing through the grass.

Finally, when the road turned to dirt for good, he pulled up into the overgrown driveway of the sagging little house at the end of the road and turned off the engine. He sat for a moment, listening to the buzzing cicadas and the ticking of the engine. In the distance he could hear the sounds of highway traffic. At length he got out, shut the door, and walked on up the overgrown walk.

The front porch steps were crumbling concrete with a rusted rail. He knocked on the peeling door and waited, looking around. There was no answer. He turned the doorknob. The door moved, but the lock held. He knocked again, then leaned over to peer through the picture window, cupping his hands around his face to block out the reflection.

He could just make out an old armchair and a table, but the place was obviously deserted. Glancing around, he bounded down the porch and went around back.

The grass stood taller in the back, waving in the breeze. Several rusty barrels were shoved against the back of the house where the basement rose from the ground, the cinder blocks flaking with faded paint. Away from the house, a rope hung from a tree, a hook swinging from the end over another barrel.

It was a crude abattoir. His father had something like it back home. Shoot the pig, hoist it over the barrel, let it bleed. Farming was an ugly business. Joe doubted that Mark Ballard was doing much farming out here.

Cautiously he peered into the barrel. The interior smelled of decay, but the blood was long dry. Joe jerked back and looked around. Along a leaning split-rail fence was a good selection of deer skulls.

"Shit," Joe whispered. Poaching he could understand; hell, back home, there were plenty of folks who called it putting meat on the table. But he wondered if the owners of those million-dollar homes knew that Ballard was hunting out-of-season deer right in their own backyards.

Had Lynn come across Ballard poaching the night she disappeared? Would Ballard kill her if she had? What about Kate? Joe's stomach knotted.

A car was coming. The distant sound barely registered over the incessant buzzing of the cicadas. The sound of the engine faded in and out as the car negotiated the narrow, winding road. Joe ran to the Impala, jumped in, and started it. It fired at once, a miracle, and he threw it in gear, backing out in a spray of dust. He continued on past the house as fast as he dared, the Impala's aging shocks bouncing mightily over the terrain. The road quickly petered out into a grassy trail with two deep ruts, and the Impala trundled along wildly. A turnoff in the woods appeared up ahead, and Joe slewed the car around, fishtailed, then straightened it out in a sunny clearing. Ruthlessly Joe mowed down brush, then wedged the car into a grove of trees, their wide trunks giving him just enough room to park among them, and stopped. Shrubs and bushes swayed and closed together behind him. Joe looked in the rearview mirror and saw green. He opened the car door and waited. He could hear the other car, still creeping along, then the engine idling, then stopping. After taking one more look at the Impala to see how well it was hidden, Joe walked back, hiding behind the brush.

He watched as someone got out of the car and went up to the front door, unlocked it, and went in. He recognized the car, a green Jaguar, but he wasn't sure from where. Then, as the driver came back out, carrying two gun cases, it came clear: Garson. Joe ducked down as the restaurateur opened the trunk and wedged the rifles in, looking around nervously as he did.

Even from a distance Joe could tell when Garson's gaze sharpened. The dust from Joe's wild flight had not quite settled, and dust motes floated hazily in the air in a long-ago wake. Garson closed the trunk and walked to the end of the driveway, stopping to look at the tire tracks with a frown. He looked straight at Joe's car. Joe held his breath. *Shit,* he thought. *He's seen my car. He saw it just the other day. He's gotta know it's me.*

Garson took a few tentative steps toward the woods, then stopped. He looked reluctant, dithering. Joe risked turning his head to look back where he had lodged his car, and his eyes went wide.

The Impala was gone.

Joe squeezed his eyes shut, then looked again. Nothing.

"Mark!" Garson called, starting out assertively, but then faltering. "Is that you?" He took another step forward.

The woods remained silent. Garson made a face, danced indecisively one more time, and then turned and walked back to his car. Joe crouched in the underbrush, hardly breathing. Finally he heard the car door snick closed and the engine start up with a confident purr. The Jag backed out, turned, and went back the way it came.

Only when the sound of the engine died away did Joe stand up, glancing back once or twice at where he had left his car. Still there. Optical illusion, he thought. His stomach was sick with relief, and he headed back to the house. Garson had locked the door again, but tucked into the concrete of the basement on the side of the house was a little window. Joe kicked it in. It broke with a tinkling crash, and he punched out the shards before sliding inside into the cool darkness.

The basement held a cool, moldy smell. Pale light streamed in from the window, and as his eyes adjusted, he could see a little better. A furnace and water heater hulked in a dark corner. Lumber, scrap metal, and paper, all broken-up pieces of the house's former life, littered the floor, and several stacks of flat, narrow boxes were piled under the stairs. He recognized them immediately. He opened one to make sure, and the arranged cartridges gleamed dully up at him. Joe set them down.

He had to swallow twice before his throat loosened enough for him to call out, "Lynn? Kate?"

Silence. The basement pressed on him. A flight of stairs led to the first floor and creaked when he started his ascent. He pushed open the door at the top. Gray light came in from the uncurtained windows, and the fear he had experienced in the basement receded in the daylight.

"Lynn?" he called out again, but he could sense the house's emptiness. Still, Joe began to search methodically. The living room held nothing except for the table and armchair he had seen from outside. A kerosene lamp sat on the edge of the table. Joe threw a light switch anyway, just to check. Nothing. No electricity, or water, either. Sitting on the edge of a large wilderness area like the trails, it was a poacher's dream. No wonder it had never come up that Mark liked to hunt.

Something gleamed on the floor, caught in a sullen sunbeam from the window. Joe bent and picked it up: an old, battered penny. He slipped it into his pocket.

He finished the rest of his search quickly. The bathroom and kitchen were both filthy. There was one bedroom; it was stale with beer, cigarette smoke, and ashes, littered with magazines and clothes strewn everywhere. Joe picked up a magazine at random—*Penthouse*—and let it fall, then caught sight of another hunting catalog, Mark's name on the address label. He wondered why Mark moved into town and wondered where he was now. In Colorado? Or hiding out on the trails, waiting for some unsuspecting kid on her pony to run across him?

The place was making him sick. Joe tossed the catalog down and left, this time through the front door, letting it bang with all of his anger. His head cleared a bit when he got out into the fresh air, but by the time he walked back to where he left his car, his nausea increased. He shook his head, trying to clear it. The sun pierced his eyes, and he winced, thinking he might even throw up.

With relief he saw light reflect off the chrome fender of his car where it sat between the three massive tree trunks, mostly concealed by the gently swaying weeds. Joe got in and sat still in the heat, sweating, and resting his head against the seat back. After a bit he leaned forward to start the engine, fumbling with the key, but stopped when movement caught his eye.

A man stumbled toward him from out of the woods. He reached out one hand, the other clasped to his side, and croaked something Joe didn't get. The man put his hand on the window, then slid out of sight.

Joe scrambled out the passenger side, kicking hard against the recalcitrant door, and came around. The man lay crumpled on the ground, his pale face turned up to the sky, his eyes rolled back. Joe knelt and tried to straighten him out. The man's breath was shallow, his skin hot. Mud and streaks of old blood covered his long shirt, and his trousers were shredded from deadheading through the woods. Joe fingered the material; it was coarse and thick, the weave loose and irregular. The laces were frayed and torn at the man's throat, and the stitching had worn away. Joe could see the man's feet where the leather had split on his old, heavy shoes. The man groaned.

"Okay, hold on, just a minute," Joe said. He struggled to lift the man's shoulders, and the man caught at him feebly. Joe stopped, staring down at the man's fingers, clutching threads of gray mane intermixed with blue yarn.

Lifting the man was like lifting a dead weight. Joe managed to get him slumped in the backseat, then had to drive to three trophy houses before finding one where someone would answer the door. Even then, the housekeeper eyed his dusty clothes and old car with alarm before consenting to call 911.

Joe's heart sank when he saw Spencer with the response team. The detective took one look at him and tsked.

"You again," the detective said.

Behind them, the EMTs worked to stabilize the man.

"Yeah, me." Joe looked at him, arms folded across his chest. His nausea was gone, but he had a splitting headache. "You gonna listen to me or arrest me?"

Spencer just looked at him. "Okay. Go."

"Did you see his hands? He's got horsehair and blue yarn between his fingers. That's what they braid horses' manes with around here to make them fancy for horse shows."

"Show me," Spencer said. He convinced the paramedics to let him see, and grouchily they stepped back long enough for a look. The man, with an oxygen mask and IV, was unconscious, his hands limp. The threads of long gray and white hair still wound through his fingers, and a bit of yarn hung onto them.

"I watched Lynn braid that horse's mane and tail the morning of the show," Joe said. "That's Dungiven's."

"All right," Spencer said. Carefully he took the strands of hair and fluff and put them in a plastic bag. He muttered something under his breath. "Too bad he couldn't have held on to the horse," he said. "Ever seen him before?"

Joe shook his head. "No, sir."

"The horse has got to be around somewhere then." He sighed, then gave Joe a look. "That still doesn't answer what you're doing out here."

Joe rubbed the back of his neck. "Yeah, that's another

question. Listen, I think there's something going on out here. It might not have anything to do with the girls, but I think you've got a problem with poaching."

"That's nothing new," Spencer said. He eyed him. "What makes you say that?"

Joe made up his mind; might as well be killed for a sheep as well as a lamb, he thought. "I think I better show you."

Spencer and two other officers drove with him back to the little house, with Joe describing how he saw Garson pick up the two gun cases. At his first sight of the backyard abattoir and the silent skulls lined on top of the fence, Spencer began making phone calls for a crime scene unit. The broken window caught his attention, and he squatted next to it, shining a flashlight inside. Joe kept silent about that, but the nausea came back again, and this time he had the sense that he was snared in a trap of his own making. He wondered how long it would be before they figured out that he broke into the house.

"All right," Spencer said, pocketing his flashlight and standing creakily. "We'll take it from here. But if you come out here again, I will lock you up. Stay away from this house, and stay away from Garson. We will take care of him." Joe nodded, and Spencer added, unexpectedly, "This sure as hell makes more sense than she stole the horse, kidnapped the girl, and headed for Canada."

"I think I like the other way better," Joe said. He met Spencer's eyes. "Better chance of them still being alive."

Spencer surprised him again. "I know," he said.

It was almost dark by the time Joe got back to his place in Danbury, a garage apartment near the university. The small efficiency suited Joe just fine. He stacked his few books near his mattress on the floor, and a lamp was plugged in by his pillow. He had three boxes for clothes. He put his one suit in the closet just inside the entrance. On the other side of the room from his bed the landlord had installed a small three-burner stove and a half-size refrigerator.

Joe sat in the ladder-back chair that came with the place to take off his beat-up old boots and toss them in the corner. He made himself a sandwich at the little stove, rummaged for a beer in the fridge, and padded over to his bed.

He took a bite of sandwich and washed it down with a swallow of beer. The long day began to catch up with him, and he closed his eyes and leaned back against the wall, wondering how someone could get lost in the woods about a quarter mile from the highway.

Eleven

Sunlight and shadows dappled the dirt track through the forest. A sharp wind made the light patterns ripple across the narrow path as it wound along a narrow creek bed, now drying to an end-of-summer trickle. Lynn and Crae turned off the trail down to the water, dismounted, and let their horses drink. Despite the sunshine, the air was cold, and Lynn hunched in her vest, grateful for its synthetic warmth. It wouldn't do much against real fall weather though. She wondered how much longer they would wander the forest. *I want to go home,* she thought, holding her vest closed at her throat with one hand. *I don't want to stay here anymore.*

But the Wood stubbornly failed to deliver up the gordath for her, even as the earthquakes happened almost daily. The forest floor was littered with tree branches, and once the trail was gouged with a series of long, jagged cracks.

As their horses lifted their dripping muzzles, Crae looked around, his forehead creasing. His beard had come in dark and grizzled, flecks of gray in the brown. *Handsome guy,* Lynn thought, and immediately scolded herself. *Stop that. Stop that immediately.*

"What is it?" she asked. He glanced at her, and she felt sudden butterflies. She ducked her head and busied herself with Silk's bridle.

"I thought we would find a way to the gordath to get you home safely before I rode to Trieve. But the more we ride in these woods, the more I think they have become too dangerous for travelers. I think we need to go to Trieve at once and bring the guardian back here."

Panic welled up, and she stuffed it back down. "Well," she said evenly. "That's not good. Are you sure?"

"I'm sorry," he said. "I know you are anxious to go home."

"Yes. Just a bit," she said caustically. She sighed. "How much farther to Trieve?"

"Five days, if we push the horses."

They had already been on the road for three days, and the damn forest showed no signs of ending. *He saved my life, and he wants to help me get home,* she told herself. She believed that, she understood that. But her understanding was wearing thin, and it became harder to believe that she would ever get home.

"Look, Crae," she said, trying to keep her voice from fumbling. "Maybe this is where we split up. You go on to Trieve, and I try to get myself lost again, which is how I ended up here in the first place."

He looked at her for a long moment, as if trying to parse her words. She looked at him back, willing him to see that she was serious, that she needed to go home. When he spoke, he spoke with care.

"I do not doubt that you can handle yourself," he said. "But this forest is more dangerous now than anything you can think of. All those stories you have about the treachery of Gordath Wood are nothing compared to the stories we have of its malevolence. Travelers do not just lose their way; they are forced to lose their way, and they are driven mad by the forest's wiles. Even a half month ago I would have let you travel this wood alone, but not now."

A sudden gust of wind blew up the trail at them, scattering leaves and making the horses jerk up their heads. It suddenly got very cold; the sun had gone behind the clouds while they conversed. Crae grinned a bit apologetically. "You see," he said. "The forest god himself agrees with me."

The forest god . . . She shivered. "All right," she said out loud. "You—and he—convinced me. For now. But I reserve the right to duck through a gordath if one comes our way."

He took a breath as if to protest but instead bowed his head with that same courtliness. Her butterflies started up again, and she tried to ignore them. Crae swung the reins over Briar's head, checked the horse's girth, and tugged at the straps that held his sword on one side and his crossbow and bolts on the other.

She paused in the process of checking her own horse's saddle. "Expecting trouble?"

He paused and glanced at her. "I take care only. The smallholders who live out here are loyal, but they are proud and dislike strangers. Still, I don't expect danger, if that worries you."

"It does, a little." She shook her head. Not that her world was worry-free; keeping expensive horses free from harm and their wealthy owners happy had her tossing and turning at nights. But those weren't life-or-death decisions.

She prepared to mount when a bit of sunlight flashed along the creek. "What's that?" she said, pointing. A tangle of something drifted in a shallow pool where the water lapped the muddy bank. Sunlight reflected off metal. Before Crae could answer, she tossed him Silk's reins. Lynn slithered back down the bank and sloshed toward the little eddy, picking her way over tree roots and boulders.

With a sinking heart, she recognized it. She had to struggle to get around the rocks and over the deadwood, and she stepped in the creek once or twice, splashing her skirt up to her knees. Finally she made it to the pool and fished out the tangle of leather and metal, holding it up to Crae.

It was Dungiven's bridle.

An hour later the trail had veered away from the small stream, and the trees closed over them, casting a welcome gloom. The trail widened, but the terrain turned treacherous, winding over roots and around rocks. They dismounted and led their horses. Lynn's sweat chilled in the cold air. Crae stopped in front of her.

She drew up next to him. "What—" she started. Up ahead the trail crossed a dry ravine running downhill toward the other creek. A small stone bridge arched over it, the first sign of civilization.

Had arched over it would be a better description, she thought. The little bridge had cracked and fallen into the dry creek. She scanned the wood nervously. "Crae," she said, and pointed. A massive tree lay uprooted across the ravine, the drying mud clinging to its root system. Lynn could smell rich loam from the forest floor. One of the branches had broken at the trunk, the exposed wood a pale yellow scar. Now she could see that the ground had broken up into waves, rising in humps and spreading out through the woods. Trees leaned everywhere, supporting each other like drunkards.

"Come," Crae said. They led their horses down and up the little ravine, skirting the ruined bridge and the tree. As they neared the smallholding, the signs of destruction came faster. Broken trees. Downed stone walls and fencing. By the time they saw the tumbled houses, the devastation became clear.

The little village lay in ruins.

The horses snorted and balked, so they left them back at the little bridge, tied for real this time; Lynn didn't trust their training in these circumstances. They were spooked enough as it was.

It must have happened at night, she thought. They didn't have a chance. She heard a noise and turned; Crae on hands and knees, peering under a pile of broken stone and wooden shingle.

"Is there anyone alive?!"

He got up, strain around his eyes. He looked sick. "No. I thought I heard—" He stopped that thought.

It's a forest. Plenty of scavengers. She turned abruptly and supported herself against a tree, swallowing hard, willing herself not to throw up. When she could talk again, she said, "We have to do something. We have to bury them."

"No—we need to let them lie for now. But we need to ask the forest god to protect them. Help me."

She helped him gather stones and together they built a rough cairn. Crae kissed stone after stone before placing it on the pile until his lips were covered with dust. It was a rough, uneven pile of clumsy stone, like a child's tower, but somehow, they had placed it in a patch of sunlight that pierced the forest's canopy. At its feet were a few of the first red leaves of autumn.

Crae bowed his head and whispered a few words she could not understand. Unbidden, the Lord's Prayer came to her, and she recited it under her breath and crossed herself.

Movement caught her eye, as a silent leaf fell and landed on the cairn, resting perfectly on the top. The sunlight beamed stronger, and the little clearing brightened with a clean, pale light.

It was perfectly still. A peacefulness stole through her heart.

The sunlight faded, and the clearing dimmed, but the peace remained.

Lynn started to cry. *No,* she told herself. *I don't cry. I don't.* Crae turned her toward him. She let herself be folded into his arms and wept into her hands, pressed tight against his chest, his chin on top of her head.

At length he drew back.

"Lynn. Lynna. We have to go."

She looked at him. His eyes were wet, too, his mouth pressed thin. She sniffed and wiped her nose with the back of her hand.

"This is because of the gordath, isn't it."

"I think so." His voice was clipped.

"Well, we have to stop this." She took a deep breath. "I'll come with you. I'll come with you to Trieve to find the guardian. We have to stop this for good."

Before he could say anything, the ground began to rumble, even as a steady roar rolled through the sky.

Is that a helicopter? Lynn whipped around, trying to see through the forest canopy. The ground surged, and they grabbed hold of one another.

"Where is it?" she shouted. "Can you see it?"

"Run!" He shouted. "Now!" He pulled at her arm, but she shrugged him off, still searching for the roar. The ground swelled, lifting them up in a wave of dirt, earth and roots breaking apart with a wet and ripping sound. Crae went down, and Lynn fell on top of him. The ground threw them upward, and they clung together on the wave of dirt and brush. Lynn got a mouthful of forest floor and choked and spat.

Overhead a tree began its slow fall to the earth, plowing through its mates. Lynn ducked reflexively, flattening herself against Crae, and he rolled both of them over as the tree trunk slammed near where they had been, its branches thrashing.

The shaking slowed and faded. She could hear nothing but the thudding of her heart and his. She lay against him, breathing hard, her muscles strengthless. They were both covered with dirt and debris. She willed her breathing to slow. *My*

God, she thought. *My God.* After a moment she raised her head, brushing away the dirt with a shaking hand. She pushed herself into a sitting position, and he sat up next to her.

"Are you okay? I mean, all right?"

He nodded. "You?"

She nodded. "That was pretty bad. Did you—did you see the helicopter?" He stared at her blankly. She said, "I didn't either; I heard it. It could be here. It could be in this world. Like the car, only it flies. It could be looking for me."

"From your world? Through the gordath?"

She stared at him, her hope fading, understanding dawning. If the helicopter came through the gordath, it could only make the earthquakes worse.

"It's opening the gordath." She could barely get the words out. "It's the people on my side looking for me. Flying—" She broke off. "We should get out of here. Who knows when the next flyover will be." *Could* a helicopter get through? Or was the earthquake the gordath's fight against this mechanical intrusion?

She knew one thing; she didn't want to be around for the next battle.

When Joe arrived at work the day before the gala, Mrs. Hunt waited for him by the entrance to the indoor ring. She carried a pitchfork and wore dirty jeans, heavy boots, and work gloves. Her hair was pulled back in a ponytail. Joe's jaw dropped.

"Don't look so surprised," she said irritably. "It's my barn. I can muck stalls if I want to."

"Yes, ma'am," he said, shutting his mouth with a snap. But he couldn't help but grin, until she gave him a quelling look. Abashed, he looked away, noting the freshly mown grass and the tractor lawn mower sitting in the shade. He took another look at his employer, and this time he saw the smile she had a hard time keeping in check.

"I have several odd jobs for today," Mrs. Hunt said. "We're using the van as the judge's office, so it needs to be cleaned thoroughly. Park it over by the main ring when you've done. I've ordered a load of tanbark for the indoor ring; that needs to be spread and raked when it arrives. I imagine you would use the tractor."

He nodded. She pulled a list out of her jeans pocket and handed it to him.

"Here are some other small things to get to after those are done. The farm is looking very nice, Joe. I'm sure everything will be splendid for the gala."

"Thanks," he said. She picked up her pitchfork and disappeared into the barn, and he stared after her. The compliment was entirely unexpected and sounded a little as if she had to consciously remind herself that the peons needed praise now and again. *But it's a start,* he reminded himself. For someone like Mrs. Hunt, who acted as if she was born mannerly, it represented a breakdown in the natural wall she carried around herself like armor.

Wonder what she's really like?

The thought startled him as much as seeing her mucking stalls did. Joe shook his head at himself and scanned the list. Sagging gates, broken hinges on the grain bins. Little stuff, like she said. Well, he would get the tools he needed from the tool room and get started on the van.

As he fetched his tool kit from the shed, a commotion caught his eye. He looked out the dusty window. Caroline was trying to mount her mare in the drive, and the horse was backing up and bucking in a fit of temper. Both Allegra and Caroline were squealing in rage. Joe rolled his eyes. *Might as well just stay up here till it's over,* he thought.

Another rider dismounted and held the horse still for Caroline to clamber into the saddle. Joe shook his head, grinning, and turned to go.

He almost bumped into Mrs. Hunt. She took a step back, then looked out the dusty window, taking in the scene below, giving him a chance to recover.

"A waste," she remarked.

"Ma'am?" he asked.

"That horse. That rider. One does not have to be a professional equestrian to know how thoroughly she has ruined that mare."

I thought they deserved each other, Joe thought, though he kept that to himself. But she glanced at him as if he had spoken and added, "It is never the horse's fault, remember. And the breed is a good one."

He nodded, not really sure why they were talking about horses. Everyone knew that Mrs. Hunt was no horsewoman. Rumor had it that she had been set up at the farm by a wealthy patron. For the first time, he wondered if it could even be true.

"I had best be gettin' back to work, ma'am," he said. She reached out a hand to stop him.

"Joe." They were very close, thrown together in the little room so they were barely two feet apart. In the dim light from the window, her pale, elegant features glowed, the plain pony-tail pulling her hair away from her face. "Did—that man, the one you found. Did he say anything?"

He shook his head. "No, ma'am."

"I thought not." She took her hand from his arm, and he had to stop himself from stopping her. "You will tell me if you hear anything."

He nodded, but he wasn't sure what she meant. About Lynn? Or the strange man?

"Good." She turned back to the window, dismissing him, and he watched her for a moment before ducking out to get started on his chores.

As the afternoon drew on, the horse vans be-gan arriving, trundling up onto the lawn in straggling rows. The late afternoon sun threw shadows across the phalanx of trailers and SUVs as Joe threaded through the swelling crowd of horses and horse folk up the drive to the house. Mrs. Hunt stood on the veranda with some of her early guests. She had changed out of her work clothes and wore a slim, elegant dress. She glanced over at Joe as he waited in the shadows on the lawn, and excused herself to meet him. He came out into the sunlight and said, "Everything's all set, ma'am."

Mrs. Hunt nodded and asked, "What about the judge's office?"

"All set up," Joe replied. He had stacked the boxes of ribbons, silver cups, and numbers in the van. "You want that locked?"

She frowned. "Yes, do. We should be as prepared as possible."

"It will go just fine, ma'am," Joe said, but her mouth tightened, and he realized he had overstepped his place. Again. The brief intimacy of the tool room was banished as easily as she had changed her clothes. She nodded, dismissing him, and he went down to the trailer to lock it, thinking about the wall that surrounded her and that she could erect at the slightest breach.

The mistake, he thought, as he slid up the ramp to the giant vehicle and locked the doors, is in thinking there's a vulnerable person inside there. It didn't help that she had a way of making a man think he could get over that wall of hers. *Never mind,* Joe thought. *She's your boss. Whatever she was playing at in the tool room, it's nothing you need to get involved in.*

The day of the show, Hunter's Chase frothed with excitement. The rings were bright with jumps, decorated with plastic flowers and fresh paint. Gleaming horses and elegant riders bustled everywhere, popping over practice jumps, waiting at the ring entrances, or galloping off at three-minute intervals over the cross-country course. Horses neighed, the loudspeaker blared, trainers and coaches put their students through their paces. Joe had arrived at the stables at dawn and not had a quiet moment since. Mrs. Hunt had issued walkie-talkies for all the show staff and handed one to Joe that morning when he reported in.

That wasn't bad, but when he found out that Howard Fleming was acting as show steward, he had to work to keep his reaction off his face. As he suspected, Howie took his stewardship seriously. Fleming kept Joe busy with constant orders, interrupting him at most of his tasks. At first Joe was hopeful that if he could just get Mrs. Hunt alone for a moment, she would make Fleming lay off. But he soon forgot that notion when he saw her with her friends. She was standing amid a small knot of admirers, chic in her breeches and boots, the cut of her midnight-blue jacket emphasizing her slim figure. The woman who mucked stalls and traded observations with her stableman disappeared. Joe took matters into his own hands and lost the walkie-talkie in the tool room so he could get some work done.

He broke for lunch about noon and climbed the knoll overlooking the small ring behind the main barn to eat in relative privacy. A rider entered the ring on an elegant bay horse, a long dressage whip in her hand. Joe watched as she began practicing a dressage test, riding in a pattern of lines and circles, her horse's neck arced in a beautiful line. The afternoon began to settle peacefully around him, and the hustle and bustle of the show receded a little.

He caught a glimmer of movement out of the corner of his eye and turned as a red maple leaf drifted down right beside him. He snagged it and smoothed it out, wondering. Autumn was coming, and with it came the call he was half expecting, half dreading. *Time to go?* it whispered, and for the first time he heard the question in it. Could he leave, not knowing what happened to her? He let his gaze go to the white curtains in the little apartment over the barn. He wasn't stupid; he knew the police suspected him. If he stayed, he might never get to leave. And at some point Lynn and Kate would be found, or their bodies, more like, which was the way these things end, despite all the efforts of barn handymen. Their deaths would become a part of the stories about Gordath Wood. And then what? Joe crushed the leaf in his hand, and it folded in his fist, still full of life.

Eventually he heaved himself up to get back to work. As luck would have it, the first person he saw when he came back into view was Howie. The stout man, looking ludicrous in a pink hunting jacket and black boots, glared at him.

"Where have you been?" he demanded, his voice a little shrill.

"Lunch," Joe said.

"The course designers have been waiting to flag the advanced-level course! Go and bring the rest of the jumps out there right now!"

Joe bit back a response and brushed past the man on his way to the tractor. The trailer was loaded with the added poles and standards the combined training club had asked for; it wouldn't take but a few minutes to bring them out to the field. The tractor coughed into life, and he put it in gear, trundling down the hill. He went right by Mrs. Hunt and Howie, who was pointing at Joe and shouting something at her.

One of the course designers, a pleasant-looking, gray-haired lady, waved him down, and he pulled over, idling the engine. She hopped up next to him.

"I'm Sue Devin," she said. "You must be Joe. I'll show you where we need to add the fences."

Once up on the cross-country field, they began setting up the remaining jumps where the land had been marked with lime Xs. They worked according to a wrinkled piece of paper with a crude diagram drawn on it, and soon got the remaining fences up, settling the poles into their supports at heights Joe thought were suicidal, directional flags snapping briskly in the breeze. Overhead, a lone helicopter—a news chopper, it looked like—clattered through the clear blue sky, making a wide turn high over the Wood. Joe's temper began to clear.

"You gonna compete?" Joe asked when the helicopter faded away. Sue shook her gray head.

"Not this time. My horse has been lame off and on all summer. He's fine now, but I don't want to ruin anything. In fact, I was thinking about turning him out from now till the spring, to see if all he needs is good solid time off. What about you?" she asked in turn, looking at him with keen eyes.

"I guess I would have to ride in the little kid's classes," he told her. "I've never been on a horse."

"Not even western?" She was surprised, but for some reason, he wasn't made uncomfortable by it as so often that question made him.

"No, ma'am. I'm just the handyman around here."

"Well, Joe, if you ever want to learn, I will be glad to teach you," she said. Sue laughed at his expression. "Is it such a strange idea? Everyone can learn to ride. You don't have to compete; you can just enjoy riding as a way to enjoy the out of doors."

He said sharply, "Do you still ride on the trails?"

At the sudden curtness in his voice, she faltered. "Why no, I haven't. Not since—no one has been, really. Though I don't know why not—"

"Don't. Just don't."

She looked surprised at his intensity. "All right, I won't." They finished flagging the jumps mostly in silence. The news copter swung around again, the noise cluttering up the bright air. When they finished and were walking back to the tractor, she said, "You know, we're all just sick over it. I knew Lynn

Romano, and she's no thief, but it's easier to believe than the alternative. Do you think they met with foul play?"

Such an old-fashioned phrase.

"Yes," he told her, low-voiced. "Yes, ma'am, I sure do."

They stopped at the gate, and she put her hand on his arm, a sad smile lighting her face. "I'm sorry, you know. We all thought you two made a handsome couple."

He didn't know what to say to that. She went to get on the tractor and stopped in midstep. Joe followed her gaze. Two police cruisers, flashers on, rolled up the drive, parting nervous horses in their way. Howard Fleming waited to meet them in front of the main barn. Joe watched him lean over and talk to one of the cops, then turn around and point straight at Joe up on the cross-country course. Sue gasped.

Joe tried to still the sudden queasiness in his stomach. He patted Sue's hand. "It'll be all right," he said.

He left the tractor at the top of the field and walked down to the police cars, riders turning their horses aside to watch him go. He heard the officer say he was under arrest for the kidnapping and murder of Kate and Lynn, but Joe wasn't listening. He looked at Mrs. Hunt as she stood next to Howard Fleming. She had the grace to blush, but she held his gaze. Joe kept his eyes on her as the officers cuffed him and searched him, then pushed him into the backseat of the car. He caught a last glimpse of Fleming's face, flushed and triumphant, and then the man turned and walked off with Mrs. Hunt, one hand at the small of her back.

Joe settled back into the car, breaking out into a sweat. The officer said a few words in his radio and put the car into reverse. The sound of the chopper came closer, and Joe thought, *They knew.* Why else would the media be back at the farm for a stale story? His fear and shame were replaced by rage.

The cruiser jerked hard to a halt, and Joe slammed forward, then back. It felt like the cruiser dropped out from underneath them. "What the hell?" the cop said, and craned out the window.

The earthquake took hold of everything and slammed it hard. Joe could see horses scatter and run, people fall, and in the air over the cross-country course, the helicopter swung wildly in the sky. The air around it rippled, as if the chopper were leaking fuel. In the next instant the helicopter tipped backward, then plummeted to the ground.

Before he ducked reflexively from the explosion, Joe thought he saw the air shatter.

Twelve

Deep among the tall trees of Gordath Wood,
Marthen's scouts concealed themselves in the thick underbrush,
crossbows and swords at the ready. Colar lay belly down in the
tangled underbrush, his rough clothes blending in with the
leaves and branches, and kept his eyes trained on the soaring
wall that could be picked out between the trees about a quarter
mile away. It was like a wall that kept out the world; he could not
see the top of it. Colar knew that the wall was really the curve of
the mountain from which the stronghold had been carved, that
over time the hands of men had worked it until it held the shape
of rough-hewn bricks.

Nearby, a waterfall crashed down over the rocks, the water
dark and rain-swollen on its way to the river. The rain pattered, and Colar shifted his prone position to wipe his wet
bangs from his eyes. He kept his movements small; Tharp's
men still patrolled here, though most of the lord's forces were
concentrated at the front of the stronghold, facing Marthen's
vaster army. It made sense; an attack from the rear meant going through the mountain, a strategy not likely to hold much
success.

Not that the other day's strategy had been successful either, he admitted. He had not fought but ridden messages to
the different cohorts. His father had come back bloody and
livid. Colar caught sight of him during the battle; the memory
still made him uneasy. His father had been screaming, his face
distorted with something Colar had never seen before. Not
fear. Not anger.

Bloodlust.

Crackling in the brush caught his attention, and his hand

tensed on the hilt of his sword. Then he relaxed. It was Skayler and Jayce, ducking low but hurrying. Captain Artor whistled softly, barely a whisper, and they stopped, finding cover in the brush. Colar tensed, waiting for the signal. Artor had drilled them many times over: the most dangerous time for the band happened when scouts returned to the hiding place. No one knew who they brought with them.

The wait was excruciating. Colar was soaked from the muddy ground and the steady rain falling on top of him. Finally, Artor whistled again, and scout after scout rose from his hiding place. They gathered around Jayce and Skayler, several scouts keeping watch. Colar placed himself where he could listen.

"Well?" Artor said.

Skayler's eyes gleamed, and he smiled a rare smile through his beard. "Wall's cracking."

They stared at him, eyes wide, mouths open.

"Tell me," Artor said.

"Big cracks on the east and south facing the Wood, where the wall extends out from the mountainside. Tharp's got about fifty men with mortar patching them, but the siege engines should take care of that." He turned and waved a gloved hand at the massive wall still visible between the darkening trees. "Smaller cracks on this side."

Artor grunted. "If we can just get close enough. The weapons. Any sign of them?"

Skayler shook his head. "Swords and crossbows only. Lord Tharp's keeping them under wraps." He threw a disgusted look at Jayce. "We almost ran into a few guards and had to pull out before we could get a more thorough look."

Jayce's expression turned sulky. "If we moved at your pace, we'd still be approaching the stronghold."

Everyone exchanged glances and half-rolled eyes. Trust Jayce to argue. Still, Colar thought, he had a point. Skayler's caution was an oft-told tale among the scouts.

Captain Artor's face tightened, but he said only, "All right. Good work. The general will want to know about the walls. Back to the horses and make for camp."

Colar's heart sank, and he fell in behind Jayce as they moved out. He had hoped Artor would send out another mission. *At least I came this far,* he thought glumly. Two scouts had been left behind with the horses on the borders of the Wood.

They made it back to the horses without incident, the sodden animals huddled together at the top of a long rise that fell back into the depths of the forest. Their reins dripped from their bits, tying them to the ground as if they were nailed there. Artor gave his breathy whistle again, and after a wait, the sentries melted out of the underbrush. Colar grinned with relief and some jealousy. It was a good trick; he had not mastered it yet.

He gathered up the wet reins and swung into the saddle, just as a twig snapped in the woods.

Colar spun his horse around as all the scouts around him exploded into movement, drawing swords, the crossbowmen unshipping their weapons and loading up.

"Go!" Artor shouted, as a sudden crack echoed across the little hill. Artor's horse reared on the unsteady footing and then plunged backward down the slope, the captain disappearing under the animal's bulk. Colar spurred after him, his horse sliding down the muddy slope on its haunches. Everyone was shouting.

"Get the weapon!" Artor roared, pushing at his horse's lifeless bulk, its neck a bloody mess.

With a wordless howl, a handful of Tharp's men leaped out from the brush downslope, brandishing swords. Crossbow bolts snapped through the air, and Colar ducked low next to his horse's neck.

Skayler drew his sword and bellowed, spurring his horse at the enemy. Colar jammed his spurs into his horse's flanks and galloped after him. *Stupid,* he thought. *They should have come around us, attacked from the back of the knoll.* One of Tharp's men grabbed at his rein and tried to take his horse from him, attacking with his sword from the side. Colar shifted his weight to sidestep his horse and held his sword arm straight in front of him, spurring his horse with brutal force.

The horse's momentum carried the sword point straight through the man. An instant later Colar lost his weapon, his arm aching with the impact. He picked up the reins again, pivoted his horse, and reached down to grab his sword out of the man's chest. He had to tug it hard; it didn't come easily. He was not surprised to see the point was ruined, but the edge was good. He shifted it for slashing and looked around.

Two scouts were down, one screaming for help. Colar pushed his horse into a short gallop toward him, but another crack sounded, and the scout was silenced in midcry.

Jayce, his narrow face dark with anger, reined his horse around and charged into the underbrush, low in the saddle. A moment later came a scream that ended abruptly.

"Form up, form up!" Skayler screamed. Remembering his training, Colar wheeled his horse. The rest of the scouts regrouped and formed a wedge. They had the advantage of the hill and pushed down at their attackers, swords pointed straight out. With Skayler shouting orders, the scouts held a tight formation and swept down on the foot soldiers. Colar was jammed between two horses, his knee and boot smashed against a comrade's saddle, their spurs hooked. The other horse's shoulder pressed against him, and he shouted wordlessly, letting his horse slide on its haunches down the hill and crash into the men.

A horn sounded, and Tharp's men broke and ran.

"No!" Artor screamed, still pinned. "After them. Get the *weapon*!"

A few scouts took off after the soldiers, but their horses were soon tangled in the brush and had to come back. It began to rain with a vengeance, and the sky got dark. Colar sheathed his bloody sword, but not before the water running off the shining blade dripped pinkly onto the ground. His knee throbbed. He pulled his horse around and trotted over to Artor. He reached down and snagged the reins of the dead horse. With two quick turns he looped the reins around his saddle horn and then spurred his horse hard in the flanks.

The animal neighed and reared, putting all of its strength into its hindquarters. For a moment nothing happened, and then the muddy hillside lent its advantage, and the dead horse half rolled, half slid, off the captain.

Artor screamed.

"Soldier's god be damned," Skayler said, shouting through the sound of the downpour. He grimaced through the blood

and dirt on his face and scanned the clearing, squinting
through the rain. "We need to get out of here. Leave the dead.
Terrick, round everyone up and *go*. We'll follow." He dismounted and pulled Artor to a sitting position. Colar hesitated, but before he could make a move, Jayce came trotting
out of the woods, covered in blood, his dagger streaked with
it. He grinned, his eyes fever-bright.

"Thought that he wouldn't be able to get a third shot off in
close quarters. I must of took him by surprise."

They all three stared at him, Artor included. Jayce was shaking, bouncing in the saddle, still chattering. "I almost had my
hands on it. But he threw it to another man, and then I killed
him, and the rest—they ran off. I almost had it, Captain." His
voice became anxious.

Artor let his head fall back. "I know, boy. I know."

They hoisted the captain, his left leg broken, into the saddle behind Skayler. Unable to sit the horse properly, the captain clutched onto Skayler, and they broke for the road back to
camp, sending up muddy splashes with each hoofbeat.

Pent up, Marthen thought, surveying the
camp, tents and wagons sagging under the rain. Tharp had
him as trapped as if he were in a sheep pen. This prison was as
foul. The ground had turned to a bloody midden, the footing
churned up in some places knee deep in muck. A few fires dotted the area, more smoke than flame. The usual uproar had
been replaced with quiet cries and soft keening. Wounded
men lay everywhere. The few women who had remained after
the rout tended their men.

He said, "Grayne."

His officer stepped up behind him. "Sir."

"Have you set up a burial detail?"

"Yes, sir. We've designated the eastern perimeter for
graves. They're digging now."

The eastern perimeter ran along the edge of the Wood. As
good a place as any, Marthen thought; if they had to retreat,
they wouldn't be running through their newly buried dead. He
nodded.

"And latrines?"

Grayne hesitated, and Marthen turned to look at him.

Grayne raised his chin. "Burial first, sir, I thought. Better to get the dead underground and new trenches next."

Marthen waited for his fury to settle. He forgot sometimes that Grayne's northern beliefs were deeply ingrained; like his countrymen, he believed that battlefield flux was caused by the ghosts of dead soldiers.

"Well. Since I don't intend to shit out my bowels from the bloody flux," he said, "I suggest you put a detail on it, or you will be digging latrines by yourself."

Grayne nodded, bowed, and took himself off.

Terrick limped up to him, his stocky form clothed in thick, warm clothing. He had been favoring his leg since the battle. "Have the scouts returned?" he said in his brusque way.

Marthen turned to him, a bit surprised. Usually Terrick hid his worry over his son better than that. He shook his head. "Nothing yet."

Terrick grunted, scanning the camp, the wrinkles at his eyes deepening as he squinted through the rain.

"Damn Tharp," he muttered. "All this over a dead wife and hurt pride."

If he expected Marthen to comment on *that*, he was entirely mistaken. The general said instead, "Will Kenery join us?"

Terrick threw him a quick glance. "He's made it clear; he's neutral in this."

Marthen snorted.

"Then he has effectively thrown in his lot with Tharp."

"Neutrality is still respected, General. We are a land governed by law."

"And how much respect did Tharp show Kenery, I wonder? Perhaps a demonstration of those weapons, with a promise of a few if he stayed out of it?"

Marthen knew he stepped over the line, but damned if the man couldn't be a stubborn, honest fool. Sure enough, Terrick grimaced.

"I will not win at the expense of losing all that we stand for."

"Then you will not win." Marthen said it flatly. It must have hit home, judging by the way Terrick stared at him. "He has us at an impasse, my lord. We have the advantage in men, but Tharp's is the advantage of weaponry. We need Kenery's thousands if we are to break his defenses."

Terrick remained silent, thinking. Marthen pressed his advantage. "This isn't the end, you know. If Tharp wins, what happens to your convocation? What of your rule of law then, my lord? Back to the days of a high king and lands owned in tenancy, like a commoner?" *Like me?*

Perhaps Terrick picked up on his unspoken comment, because the older man rounded on him, his expression savage. "And what is that to you, General?"

"I want to win."

He surprised himself with the vehemence of his answer. Terrick laughed humorlessly.

"Well. We engaged you for that, after all. I will call a Council, General, and we will give you our answer."

Marthen bowed, then watched Terrick walk away with one hand pressing down on his leg.

Kate spent the morning among the ostlers, feeding and tending the horses and helping mount up the scouts. Even as the horses reminded her of Mojo, the work soothed her sorrow. The ostlers worked quietly around her, accepting her presence without complaint. Poor Torm took one look at her and shouted something, then cringed as if he remembered her socking him in the jaw. Kate patted his shoulder in passing and went on hauling hay. "It's okay, Torm," she told him, and he beamed. He stuck close to her after that, his agitation settling down. The ostlers looked at each other, and then Mykal nodded and said brusquely, "You've a kind heart."

Kate lifted her shoulders. *Whatever,* she wanted to say. Instead, she started in on feeding, the rich smell and warmth of the wet horses easing some of her sadness, though the lump in her throat thickened. It rained in fits and starts, and her hands were stiff and raw with cold. Her belly cramped at intervals, leaving her faintly queasy. Finally all the animals were fed and her work was done. On the pretense of storing the wheelbarrow, Kate gave Torm the slip and went around to the wagon where the saddles were kept. Mojo's little saddle sat by itself off in the corner, dwarfed by the big, boxy saddles used by the army. Kate put her hands on the cool leather, letting tears spill without noise.

It took a moment before she heard the soldier's calm plea. Kate wiped her face and looked around. The voice came from outside the wagon. Kate ducked out.

"Help me," the soldier said again. He lay back under the rain, leaning against the wagon wheel. His whole body shook, but his voice was calm. Kate didn't even think he was aware of her; he spoke as if he addressed someone invisible. He cupped his hand against his side, blood seeping through his fingers, and looked up at the sky, the rain dripping off his black hair and beard.

"Okay," she said faintly. "But I don't know what to do." The soldier didn't say anything, and after a moment she looked at him again and saw that he was dead.

Kate didn't fully understand the impulse that brought her to the surgeon's tent, but she was done second-guessing herself. She put her sleeve over her nose to ward off the smell and ducked inside. The smell of infection and blood, combined with the musty canvas, was thicker inside than out. She could barely make out the figure of the tall surgeon in the gloom; the small lamp hanging from the center pole was barely bright enough to light the wooden table beneath it, the man lying on the table, or the rest of the men surrounding him. The surgeon took no notice of her until one of the men nudged him and jerked his head at Kate. "Talios."

The surgeon looked up. "What is it?" he snapped.

"I want to help," Kate said.

Even in the dimness she felt him assessing her. "All right," he said at last. He jerked his head, beckoning her. "Come here."

In the dim cone of light the man on the table moaned and thrashed. Two of his comrades held him down, one gripping his rough hand in his own. The surgeon eyed her with interest.

"So, *Kett*, the stranger girl," he murmured. "I've heard about you. Show me your hands."

Confused, she held out her hands, wincing as she took a good look herself. They were red and raw, her fingernails rimmed with black. She had resorted to washing them in cold water; if there was soap in the camp, she didn't know where to find it. The doctor grabbed them roughly and looked at them top and bottom. "You'll do," he said. "I need someone with quick, clever hands." He looked at her with keen eyes. "Can you stand blood?"

"I don't know," she said honestly. "I'll try."

"Good." He took Kate's hand and pushed it on top of the bandage. The man cried out. "Here. Feel that lump? That's the metal bit. It has to come out."

She bit back the nausea and pulled her hand away. "You want me to put my fingers in there?" she said, her voice rising.

He nodded. "Oh yes. Small, quick hands." He began to unwrap the bandage.

"Wait!" Kate said. She held up a hand and took a breath. "How—I mean, I need to wash my hands."

She knew it sounded lame, but the surgeon eyed her. "Interesting," he murmured. "You've had the eastern training. Who did you apprentice with?"

Kate laughed nervously. What could she say? "No one. But look; I'm not sure about fingers. Do you have, well, forceps, or anything?"

He raised his hand and put his finger and thumb together in a snapping motion. "Small fingers."

She had wanted to help. Kate took another breath. "All right. But I need to wash first."

Talios turned to one of the men. "You heard her. Go." With a reluctant look he went off.

The surgeon went back to unwrapping the soaked bandage. The man stirred, gasping in pain, and his friend muttered something to him. When the other soldier came back with a bucket of water and some grainy soap, Kate rolled up her sleeves. She plunged her hands in the water and rubbed well with the soap. It hardly lathered but she worked it grimly under her fingernails. Immediately she had to scratch her nose but held back the impulse. The man's thigh was bare now, the wound a ragged hole. *Oh God. I can't.*

Talios picked up one of the knives on the table and doused it in a small basin on the table. Kate could smell alcoholic fumes. He held the narrow knife over the candle, and the knife flared. When it cooled, he took a breath, muttered something, and nodded to the soldiers. Immediately they pinned their friend with all their strength. Talios began to cut, and the soldier screamed. Someone put a glove between his teeth. The knife cut lengthened the bullet hole, and fresh blood oozed out of the wound. Kate whimpered. Talios nodded to her. "Can you see it?"

She looked in. The crumpled lump was embedded in the leg, surrounded by shards where it had smashed the bone. *I can't. I can't.* Trembling, she reached into the leg and began to pull. The man screamed hard, and she lost her grip. Then, steeling herself, she held on to the leg with her other hand for leverage and pulled.

The man's screams sounded eternal. Her fingers slipped over and over again, slick with blood and tissue. She finally had to pry it out with her fingernail until it loosened small millimeters at a time.

The man was still screaming when the little lump lay next to him on the table. Kate crumpled and had to catch the edge of the table to keep from falling. Her fingers smeared bloodily on the table. She wasn't the only one crying; one of the soldiers was, too. Only Talios was unmoved. He grinned, and in the lamplight it looked like he bared his teeth.

"Now let's see how fine your needlework is, my lady."

She wanted to protest. Instead, she watched him sterilize the needle, then thread it. Under his instruction, she poked the needle through the soldier's skin, feeling it resist until she had to push harder. She knotted and snipped the thread as methodically as she could, Talios holding the ragged edges of the wound together. The man cried almost soundlessly, as if he had given up.

Finally she finished, ragged thread poking out of the battered leg. Talios bandaged it, and one of the soldiers patted the wounded man on the shoulder.

"They're done, Sev. It's done. You'll heal fine."

The soldier listlessly pulled the glove from his mouth and groped for her hand. His fingers had no strength to them. "Girl. Pray . . . for . . . me," he whispered.

Kate looked at Talios. He nodded at her to go ahead. The other soldiers waited expectantly.

What should she say? Her family was irreligious; what she knew of God was vague and unfocused. Plus, they had gods here, plural. Should she ask the soldier's god?

For a moment she thought of a wild, grand prayer; *O great god of soldiers, you who are the mightiest of all* . . .

Don't be an ass, Kate.

Feeling inadequate, she said: "Help him, please. He's a good soldier, a strong fighter. A good man."

The wounded man breathed a sigh of relief, and his hand slipped from hers. With confused relief she saw that he slept, his chest rising and falling steadily. *What did I do? What did I do?*

His comrades hoisted him up, and Kate's legs gave way for good.

Talios let her recuperate in the fresh air, and the cold, wet rain felt good on her fevered face. Kate let the water that splashed from the corner of the tent pour over her trembling hands until it ran pink and then clear. Galloping hoofbeats caught her attention, and she looked up. Scouts, carrying one of their own. The riders were shouting, drawing attention from the soldiers and the officers. Even the crows looked up from their tight, insular groups, eyeing the scouts with cold expressions.

They rode straight up to the surgeon's tent. The captain rode double behind Skayler, his leg hanging at a funny angle. He was very pale, his fist clenched tight on the back of Skayler's shirt. "Where's the surgeon? Where's Talios?" Skayler shouted.

The doctor ducked out of the tent. He took in the situation at a glance.

"Get me the blanket from the table. Hurry!" He barked at her. She darted back into the tent and grabbed the bloody blanket off the operating table. When she got back, Artor was out of the saddle and supported by his men. For a moment she and Colar exchanged glances. The young scout looked stunned.

It took Jayce to bring her back to reality.

"Soldier's god, what are you doing here?" the hostile scout said, waving her off. He was covered with blood and rain and gripped a bloody sword. Talios ignored him.

"Lay it on the ground. Don't mind the mud; we don't have a choice."

She put down the blanket as smoothly as possible, and they laid Artor on it. Then, with everyone's help, they hoisted it up and carried the injured man into the tent, Kate alongside the others.

"Another one of those metal lumps?" Talios asked, as they placed Artor on the table. Mindful of the soldiers earlier, Kate held Artor's hand. She didn't know if the captain was aware of who she was, but he curved his big fingers around hers.

Skayler shook his head. "No. His horse fell on him."

"Too bad." Everyone looked at him, and the surgeon jerked his chin at Kate. "She and I, we know how to handle these metal lumps now. But a broken leg, well, that might be tough." He grinned in their astonished faces.

This time everyone looked at Kate, but Talios had already moved on, probing at Artor's wounded leg. He looked up once, his gaze flicking over Jayce. "Any of that your blood?" he asked.

Jayce looked startled but shook his head.

"Then get out. And don't talk to my apprentice like that again."

Colar sat on the edge of his low camp bed, trying to put back the edge to his sword, the stone scraping in long, even strokes. The point was hopeless; the armorer would have to restore it, if it could be restored. He hoped it could. When he showed it to his father, with a sinking feeling in his stomach, his father had only grumped in that way he had.

He would need it on the morrow. Marthen had heard out their reports of the cracks in Red Gold Bridge, and he gave a rare smile. He turned to his silent lieutenant. "Grayne. Bring the siege engines to the front and move them out."

The lieutenant had saluted and ducked out, and the scouts could hear him giving the order. The rest of the army, able to move much faster than the unwieldy catapults, would ride out in the morning and catch up.

Colar knew he wouldn't be dispatching messages in this battle, and his stomach clenched again. Tharp had to know that the secret of his crumbling walls was out and would do everything he could to stop their advance. He would be needed to fight.

He had told his father he killed a man that day, but Lord Terrick had only nodded. Colar wasn't sure if he even wanted his father to say anything. What could he say? He glanced over at his father, writing his quick birdlike script to Colar's mother. When the messenger rode to Lord Kenery, he would carry this letter as well.

"Would you add something for me?" Colar said, breaking the silence. His father's hand paused. Colar took that as a yes. "Please let her know I am well and in good spirits."

A long silence. Then, "That is well thought of."

So. Colar's stomach eased, and he went back to his sword. His father surprised him by speaking next.

"What did Talios want with the girl?"

"She helped him in the surgery. She helped him take bullets out of men." He'd heard the stories from soldiers who had watched their comrade undergo her clever fingers. She had helped Talios straighten the captain's leg, splinting it and bandaging it. Colar overheard her telling him that she thought she knew a way to keep the broken leg from healing shorter or crooked, as bad breaks did. Talios, clearly delighted, asked a lot of questions. Colar added, "Talios wants her for his apprentice, but I think he's hoping to learn more from her."

His father snorted. "Trust General Marthen to overlook the maid's real value. He had hoped that she would help him win this war, never giving a thought that she could help us survive it."

Colar caught his breath and stared at his father. He had never thought—never once given it a thought—that they might not win. *That's why he is sending for Lord Kenery,* he thought. If Tharp won, their lands and all they produced would be forfeit to him. Since the majority of the Council pitched their tents in Marthen's camp, they would not endorse his demands, but as the lords said among themselves, there was nothing stopping Tharp from thumbing his nose at the Council and making an example of one of them. No one wanted to see the effects of those weapons on their people. Colar remembered Heckon's cry and the crack of the weapon that silenced it.

His father looked at him quizzically, and Colar's cheeks heated. He went back to honing his sword.

"Leave off, Colar," his father said. "You'll scrape the blade to nothing. Bring it to the armorer tomorrow, and use my second sword until it's repaired."

Colar nodded and wiped down the sword, then carefully sheathed it. Emboldened by his father's near chattiness, he said, "Sir. If Lord Kenery says no, will Lord Tharp win this war?"

"Hmm." His father put down his pen and folded the letter. "Do you remember the convocation two summers ago?"

Colar had gone with his father and mother to Trieve, which had hosted the great meeting, at which Lord Tharp had requested to have his Lady Sarita declared dead and his marriage over. Colar had been overwhelmed by so many lords and their ladies. Lady Jessamy in particular had unnerved him. She had taken one look at him, then demanded of his father whether he were betrothed. In front of all of Aeritan, it seemed like. He nodded.

"Do you remember who stood with Lord Tharp?"

"The lords of Trieve, Salt, and Camrin," Colar said. His father gave a rare, sour smile.

"Fools, all. For Lady Wessen had the right of the law and the Council, and that is why we stand with her."

Colar remembered the lady of Wessen, Lady Sarita's mother, refusing to declare her daughter dead, forcing all the other lords to bow to her considerable will. She had been ice; Lord Tharp had raged against her to no avail. In the end the colors of Favor, Saraval, and Terrick had massed with her.

"All but Kenery," his father said. "He doesn't border Red Gold Bridge, and his country is more concerned with Brythern and other nations to the west. It was his right to remain neutral, but after this year's convocation and Lord Tharp's demonstration, I think that choice is no longer sitting well."

Again the bleak smile. "Kenery is no fool. If Lord Tharp wins this war, he knows he's next." His father sighed. "Enough," he added. "Bring your head over here, boy."

Inwardly groaning, knowing what came next, Colar complied. He knelt by his father, and the man plucked a hair from the crown of his head. Lord Terrick set it on the folded letter, dripped some candle wax on it, and adhered it to the paper. The hair gleamed in the candlelight. "For your mother. Now go to bed and remember to give thanks to a proper god, not that soldier's god you've picked up."

"Yes, sir. Good night, sir."

The towering siege engines, trundling slowly away from the encampment, blocked the overcast night sky with their angular silhouettes. They were drawn by the heavy horses that reminded Kate of huge Belgian workhorses, eight to a team, their bulging muscles and hairy hooves lifting and straining to move the huge machines. They had made impossibly little progress since the order had been given to move them out.

Kate watched them go and then picked her way around the small campfires that dotted the camp. She threaded between tents, equipment, and men, many rolled up in their bedrolls and sleeping anywhere in the damp, to the surgeon's tent.

"Hey, it's the girl," someone called out from a group by a small, flickering fire. "Hey, stranger girl."

Kate turned warily. "What?" *God, Kate, don't stop and talk to him!*

The man got up, limping. "We heard what you did," he said. "Helping the doctor. That was well done."

"Oh. Thanks."

He turned and gestured back at the group. "Come and have a drink by the fire."

Kate hesitated. "Oh," she said again. She shook her head. "No. I mean, thanks and all, but I can't."

"Leave her be, Fallon," someone said, his voice gruff. "Girl's busy."

"Thanks again," Kate said, not wanting to hurt his feelings. "I was glad to help."

She hurried off, turning over his words. *That was well done.* The words cut through her constant despair, warming her a little.

Complete darkness fell when she ducked into the surgeon's tent. Kate put out her hands and felt her way to the stack of bandages on the shelves in the corner.

As if to rebuke her for her pending theft, her belly cramped again. She knew she had already ruined her only underpants, let alone her breeches. She had nothing to change into while she washed them, either.

Kate counted out three long bandages, calculating that she could tear them into fifths, hoping that would be enough. She stuffed them into the waistband of her breeches under her long shirt and turned, bumping straight into Talios. She let out a little shriek.

The doctor raised a darkened lantern and let a small amount of light flood down on them. He cocked his head down at her.

"Yes?" he said with interest.

Kate's heart slowed. Sadly she pulled out her loot. "I have my period," she said. She was beyond embarrassment. "I didn't know what else to do."

He looked at her for a long moment and then said, "I see."

Several minutes later she headed back to her tent with her bandages cut to the right length, plus an extra pair of breeches donated by a man who wouldn't be needing them anymore.

"Next time, lady, *ask*," Talios ordered her. "Protection or no, this camp is dangerous at night, and there are plenty who would defy Marthen if they thought they could get away with it."

Kate promised, but she remembered the soldier who had given her his praise. *Maybe,* she thought of Talios's warning. *Maybe not.*

She had almost made it back to her tent when she saw that a genial crowd had grown around the same fire, people laughing and talking in low voices. She recognized some of the camp followers and one or two of the scouts.

One was Jayce. He sat on an upended log and had a woman on his lap, holding her tight. She nuzzled her head against the scout's neck, and Kate winced in disgust. She had no desire to be sighted by Jayce and his woman while she carried a stack of rags and a dead man's trousers. She faded back into the darkness, planning to go around the entire party, when someone standing on the outskirts caught her eye.

It was Tiurlin; she couldn't mistake the huge, pregnant

belly. The girl stood in shadow, her eyes on Jayce and the woman. Kate watched for a moment, then tiptoed back to her tent.

Cold mists stole through the outskirts of Gordath Wood, drifting through the trees, chilling Marthen beneath his armor despite the thick padding he wore close to his skin. Wet dripped inside his helmet and trickled down his neck.

He sat his irritable war stallion at the front of his forces. The siege engines still trundled into position, the draft horses blowing huge gouts of steam from their nostrils, like mythical dragons. Ahead the walls of Red Gold Bridge loomed out of the woods. The mountain range that fronted the forest rose still higher than the stronghold, its jagged peak lost in the fog.

They would not be in range of the walls for at least another half hour, and the fog would lift by then. Still, Marthen kept to the slow pace, his spurs pressed against his horse's flanks but his hands pulling at the bit so the horse all but trotted in place, all of his thousands of men arrayed behind him.

Cavalry rode in the middle, some of his horse soldiers in front and some behind the siege engines. Foot soldiers took the outside, where they could continue their forward movement through the outskirts of the woods. Pikemen were arrayed behind the cavalry, archers behind them, and the crows—the crows scattered about at will, hard-to-see, scrawny creatures, wingless yet more like their namesakes than ever in the morning fog. Marthen knew that if he suffered another defeat, the crows would melt away like the fog itself. Wind lifted the trees and tattered the mists. For an instant the walls of the stronghold were clearly visible.

When the first shots cracked, the front row of horse soldiers crumpled to a halt. Still, this time his men were disciplined; the remaining riders plunged toward the wall, drawing their swords in one contained motion. The deep war horns sounded, and Marthen's foot soldiers surged forward, a wave of men in armor, all shouting, a sea of men flowing around the siege engines still inching into range, a river of men trickling through the woods, thousands of men running forward to throw themselves on the walls of Red Gold Bridge.

The *tshurrrrr* of arrows sounded overhead as his archers let loose a volley. They were answered by a rolling series of shots from the walls and more of Marthen's men fell in their tracks. But the attack had momentum now as men and horses outran the dreaded weapons. Another flight of arrows darkened the sky, and this time a few of them cleared the walls. At once a shout went up from his men, and three short blasts blew on the signal horns.

The catapults jerked to a halt. The slow winding began. Another rolling volley sounded from the walls as the stronghold focused on the engines. Two of the heavy horses toppled in their traces, then another, blood spattering their chestnut coats. Shot after shot scored the sides of the machines but did no damage. The winding stopped, and then with a lazy swing, the arm rose into the air and sent a heavy weight soaring at the walls. The catapult bounced on its wheels.

Boom! The crash was louder than Tharp's weapons. The top of the wall buckled against the embedded shot, but held, and Marthen's men roared in response.

An answering roar came from the guns, and a shot sang by Marthen's head. He ducked and pulled his horse back behind the siege tower, still rolling along. Already the first catapult was rewinding as the second sent its heavy burden flying into the walls. Again the deafening crash, and this time the wall shattered along the original crack.

Come out, come out, all the lords and ladies, Marthen thought, the old rhyming song making a noise in his head. Tharp couldn't stay in there forever, not with Marthen battering at his walls all day long. He looked around, found one of his fast riders waiting to carry dispatches, and beckoned to him. The man spurred his horse and galloped over the short distance, the horse sliding to a stop on its haunches. Marthen's war stallion pinned its ears and rolled its eye at the impertinent beast.

"Tell Lord Favor to pull his men around to the river side of the stronghold and wait for Tharp to send men at us from that side. Tell him archers up front and fire first. Go." The dispatcher turned his horse in a tight circle and galloped off with the message.

Tell him to act like an officer and think for himself. A lord did not a leader make, Marthen knew all too well. Terrick and Saraval were no fools, but Favor could be counted on to act one. Perhaps this time it would get him killed—well, a man could only hope. If Favor botched the job of containing Tharp by the river, at least they would have fair warning of the attack.

Another boom as the catapults found their rhythm, punishing the same section of wall. Two more bullets sang by Marthen's head, making him duck, and he grinned. Well, he'd been targeted before. He beckoned to Grayne, and his second pushed his horse over.

"I'm moving to the tower. Give the order to unhitch the heavy horses from the traces and send a detail of men in their place." Men who fell could be replaced; if the horses were shot, the tower would be stuck behind them.

Marthen angled his horse over to the inching tower and dismounted, swinging out of the saddle onto the ladder that ran up the side. He clambered to the second level and held on, the sea of men and horses swarming fifteen feet below him. His chill had dissipated, and he was warm and loose. *Much better,* he thought. He didn't need to be on horseback to command his men. The tower swayed as it was halted, and he tightened his grip, peering around the side to gauge their progress. Another shot whined past, and he ducked.

Several men unbuckled the heavy horses and drew them out of the way, unhooking the tongue from the wagon so the tower could be pushed from behind. A surge of noise caught everyone's attention as a new battle swirled near the river. Marthen grinned again. As expected, Tharp sent out a contingent of foot soldiers.

The tower jerked forward again, and Marthen took off his helmet, the better to fill his lungs and be heard.

"Army of Aeritan's Council," he bellowed. In the midst of the battle he could see men turn to look up at him. He raised his sword high. "Join me to breach the walls!"

Men answered his shout with their own. Several threw themselves behind the tower to push it toward the walls, and others swarmed up its ladders. The tower groaned and swayed under the new weight, but the wagon trundled forward again.

Then the forward swaying of the siege engine took on a

sudden, violent turn that almost flung Marthen from his perch. He grabbed hard as war cries turned to cries of fear. The siege engine shuddered on its wheeled platform, and the whole world began to shake up and down. The earth split in long cracks, and men screamed and ran.

Marthen had one last glimpse of the walls of Red Gold Bridge when the pull of the earth caught hold of the tower. It groaned as it leaned, first slowly, then with a rush, and slammed into the ground.

Thirteen

Crae and Lynn struck out south, pushing the horses into a rolling gallop, stopping to let them blow only as long as necessary. When night fell, they stopped, but they were up before dawn and moved on. A few more earth shakings hit, but nothing like the one that devastated the smallholding, the one Lynn said was caused by a sky mechanism.

Crae glanced over at her. She rode well, that was for certain. She had a lightness to her body that kept the little mare going, and she barely moved in the saddle, even when they were at a full gallop. He grimaced. He wondered if she knew that he picked the gentlest horse in Tharp's stables he could find, then realized, *Of course she knows.* She hadn't said anything then, but he remembered her expression in the stables, irritation chased by amusement. Then she had asked the horse's name, and that was that. *She rode here on a seventeen-hand mountain of a horse,* he thought, *and I give her a lady's mount.* They were paying for it now. Briar struggled under Crae's weight, but Silk was too light-boned for him, and so they could not spell the horses by switching.

As if she heard his thoughts, she pulled up Silk into a trot, then a walk. Briar almost immediately stumbled to a halt, head down to his knees. Lynn glanced back. "Crae, keep him moving."

"I know what to do," he said, nettled, and spurred Briar a little harder than necessary. Still at a walk, Lynn swung her leg over the saddle and slid to the ground. She picked up Silk's reins and flipped them over the horse's head. Crae dismounted less showily. They led the horses along, letting their breathing slow. The horses were both lathered with sweat.

"How much farther to Trieve?" she said, squinting into the horizon. A line of darkening clouds gathered, and the wind picked up, with an edge to it. To Crae, it smelled wet and wild, bringing snow from the mountains.

"A day, and perhaps a half day more. If they can hold this pace."

"That's a big if." She glanced at him. "We're losing Briar. I'm amazed he hasn't pulled up lame." She hesitated. "Maybe we should take it easy on them. I mean, the earthquakes have stopped . . ." Her voice trailed off.

He had been thinking the same thing, but he didn't trust the earth shakings to have come fully to an end. Not if Tharp were still intent upon opening the gordath again for his weapons, or if the machines were still looking for her. No. They could not coddle the horses. "If we rest the horses, Briar will likely still fail, and we would be even farther behind."

"You're saying use them up," she muttered.

"We have no choice, Lynna. What did you think, to ride hard? We have to push them."

She took a deep breath. "It goes against everything I've ever . . ." She trailed off. "You're right. We need to move."

"I don't like it either," he said. He shrugged a shoulder. "Briar deserves better."

She nodded. "I know." Wind picked up around them, bending the grasses so they gleamed momentarily in the light. A few raindrops pattered down, and lightning flashed along the edge of the clouds. Lynn grimaced. "Great. An electrical storm."

Crae scanned the plain. He pointed to the east. "Over there. The land dips into a swale. We'll be out of the way of the lightning, at least."

She clucked to Silk, and the mare picked up the pace. The wind rushed harder at them, and with it came a squall of rain. They hurried.

The swale turned out to be better than he had hoped for. It was more of a ravine, and they were able to back the horses up against the bank while the sky opened with a roll of thunder and the rain came down in a rush. It was so loud they had to shout to be heard. Water streamed down her face, drenching her hair and her clothes. It rolled off her vest in a peculiar pattern, leaving the material almost dry, except at the neck. She hunched against the rain, and he found himself doing the same.

"At least it will be over soon," he shouted.

She grinned, swiping flat ropes of hair away from her face. "The glass is half-full, eh?"

He understood immediately, and grinned back.

At length the rain relented, the thunder rolling off into the distance and the teeming shower turning into a drizzle. The clouds broke, and the setting sun gleamed down on a rain-wet land, pale rays stabbing through the clouds. Somewhere a plains bird began to pipe.

Lynn shrugged off her vest and wrung it out. Crae did the same with his jacket. He looked at Lynn. She hung her vest from the saddle and scraped her wet hair back behind her ears. It gave her face a thin, intense look. She put the flat of her hand on her wet saddle and made a face.

It would get cold tonight and small chance of a fire. They would spend an ill night on the plains, to be sure. He glanced at the sky. Less than a quarter sun of daylight left. One more night, and then a half day's ride to Trieve. *And who knows how long to find the guardian?*

He patted Briar on the shoulder and tightened the girth. He glanced at her. "Let's go."

Without a word, she nodded and swung aboard. They pushed back up the little hollow, onto the plains, and moved the horses out at a fast, ground-eating trot.

Stars. Lynn hadn't noticed them before. Lit-tle of the night sky had filtered through the trees. Now on the plains, she gazed upward at the rain-cleared sky as they pushed the horses on well after nightfall. Only a glowing line remained near the horizon. The rest of the sky was dark.

She recognized none of the constellations. A great swoosh of white brushed across the sky, but it wasn't the Milky Way as she had ever seen it. As she watched, she saw a trail of light out of the corner of her eye. She turned, but the meteor burned out before she could fully see it. A small sound escaped her.

Crae was a shadow hulking next to her. Starlight caught

only bits of him, reflecting off his eye, Briar's bit, a buckle. He turned to her, the saddle creaking. "What is it?"

"Our sky isn't like this," she tried. "It's not—this isn't our sky." Well, that was hardly coherent, but she was numb with weariness. Underneath her, Silk stumbled, and Lynn lurched in the saddle, trying to keep the mare's head up. The mare had been tripping more and more. "Look, they're done," she said. *I'm done.* "Let's stop."

"All right." He sounded grudging. She couldn't blame him, but the horses were dead on their feet. They halted and dismounted, their boots squishing in the wet grass. Lynn loosened the saddles but left them on the horses. The air had chilled, and it would help keep them warm. She winced at the thought of saddle sores from damp saddle blankets. *I'll have to check into it in the morning,* she thought. She hobbled the animals as usual and fed them their handfuls of grain. Crae got out his bedroll and spread it on the ground, and she could hear him arraying his weapons next to him. "No fire," he said, his voice coming out of the dark. "We sleep to last star only."

She didn't say anything, only got out her own blanket and lay down gingerly in the damp grass. Almost immediately the cold and wet spread through her. *Fantastic.* She sighed and tried to get comfortable.

Lynn woke with a start. Her eyes snapped open, and she stared straight up at the sky. The night had wheeled, and the stars had changed. She turned her head. Against the sky, the horses were a darker presence. Briar had his head straight up, his ears pricked forward, the reins making a line from his mouth to the ground.

What's. Out. There?

She heard rustling, something soft and furtive. *Crae!* Slowly she turned her head the other way. As hard as she strained, she could not see the shape of him in his bedroll. Blood pounded in her ears. *Breathe,* she told herself. *Breathe.* One of the horses snorted. Lynn held her breath again. She slid off the heavy blanket, trying to get free. Had he taken both his crossbow and sword? She damned her modesty that made her spread her bedroll a distance away from him and the weapons. The rustling sounded again, and she whispered his name, barely letting it between her lips.

The rustling erupted into charging footsteps. The horses screamed and reared, their forelegs hobbled together, and bumped into each other trying to escape. Lynn rolled over and kicked at her blanket. A silhouetted attacker stumbled over the heavy, wet material and fell, and she used the time to get to her feet.

"Crae!" she shouted.

He rose up on the other side of the campsite, sword in hand. "Run!"

Someone swung at her. Lynn instinctively raised her arm to ward off the blow. Pain exploded across her forearm, and she cried out and fell. *Keep moving, dammit.* She rolled again, sinking into the wet ground, sick with pain. Her attacker rose, a thin, dark figure briefly silhouetted against the sky. Then another shadow merged with him, and he screamed. She could see little more than that. Lynn squirmed back a bit more and bumped something wet. Crae's blanket. She fumbled around one-handed, scrabbling desperately, until her fingers snagged on the crossbow.

She had to brace the crossbow awkwardly, but she was able to cock the bolt. Only one shot, she thought, straining to see. With a keening cry someone rose up in front of her, arm over head, a weapon in hand. Lynn's hand jerked reflexively. The bolt thunked into flesh. The man's war cry turned into a grunt, and he fell. Lynn stared, her breathing suddenly raspy, then unfroze. *Move, move,* she told herself. *They'll know where that one came from.* She grabbed as many of the bolts as she could pick up and scrambled. She set up again, this time quicker, and scanned the men fighting Crae. Dawn had come; overhead, the indifferent sky had lightened, and she could see more clearly. Crae fought two men, and they were so closely entwined she knew she couldn't get a clear shot. Nor was there time to wait for one. Crae stumbled, almost dropping to his knee.

Lynn stood up. "Hey!" she shouted. In their surprise, she got their attention, and in the cold, clear dawn, she could see them fully: skinny, scrawny men carrying mauls. "Leave him alone," she said, and released the trigger.

The shot sang wide, but it didn't matter. Crae recovered first and spitted his nearest man. The other didn't wait; he took two steps back, then ran off. Cursing, Lynn hurried to reload, but Crae, panting, held up his hand. "I'll take him," he said. He laid down his sword, took the crossbow, loaded it efficiently, and aimed. He expertly led the distant running man and released the trigger. A second later, the man stumbled and fell.

Somewhere a bird began to sing. The air was cold, and the wind rustled across the wet grass. Lynn's arm sang with pain, and she swayed, dizzy with it. The devastation of the camp came into focus. Here was the first man Crae had killed, blood pooling around his back. There was the man Lynn had shot. Their bedrolls were trampled with mud and blood. The horses had not managed to run far, but Lynn's heart hammered when she saw them twisted in their hobbles and reins. Crae turned to look at them and said a short, quiet word.

Both horses were unhurt. Lynn kept them quiet, holding their heads with her good hand while Crae unbound their hobbles and set their saddles to rights. He poured out some grain for them, and they dropped their heads and began to eat.

Good. Things are getting back to normal. No, not normal. I killed a man. Immediately, she began to shake and had to sink down, weak with pain. "What? Why?" She couldn't control her voice.

Crae picked up his sword, made a disgruntled face at it. Lynn made the mistake of looking at it. Blood, sure, but there was also cloth and skin. She made a noise, trying to keep from throwing up.

"Crows," he said. "They're crows."

She stared at him blankly. He went on, his forehead wrinkled with concern. "Lordless men . . . mercenaries. I had heard the Council has engaged them for this battle, but I don't understand what they are doing here." He took a breath. "Where are you hurt?"

She shook her head. "My arm. I think it's broken. You?"

He shook his head. "Bruises only, thanks to you. Let me see."

He laid his sword on one of the blankets and helped her ease off her vest. She cried out when he touched her arm. Before she could protest, he took his knife from his belt and slit the sleeve up the seam, and she bit back a scream. Her forearm was blue and purple around a long scrape.

"No bone coming through the skin," he said.

"That's good," she said.

He gave her a quick grin. His face was spattered with blood. "Yes. But though I can bind it, it needs proper care. It will not be easy to ride with this."

Lynn had once broken her collarbone on a cross-country course and had gone back to riding the next day, with a sling and a load of prescription painkillers. *Stupidest thing I've ever done,* she thought. *Except for this.*

She had to lie down for the bandaging process. This time the damp grass felt soothing against her back. Lynn put her good arm across her eyes and tried to will herself away. *Close your eyes and think of Joe,* she told herself, but she couldn't find him; the pain was a wall between herself and his memory. She had to breathe hard through her nose to keep from crying. When it was done, Crae helped her to her feet. Her arm was bulky and still throbbed with every movement, but it felt a little better than before.

"When we get to Trieve, a physician will bind it better," he promised. Lynn nodded, not sure if she could talk. He gathered up the horses and their gear, cleaned his sword and resheathed it, foraged for the remaining bolts, and when they were ready, helped her into the saddle. Lynn swayed and held on. "We'll be there by nightfall," he said. She nodded.

"I'll be all right," she said. "Sorry about this." She meant about slowing him down.

He looked startled. "You saved my life."

She looked around at the remains of the awful attack. The bodies lay where they had crumpled. The grasses were torn and flattened, mud-soaked as their own clothing. She held on to the saddle horn and the reins with her good hand and faced forward again. They had saved each other.

If the police could have charged Joe with the crash of the helicopter along with kidnapping and murder, they would have. As it was, at his arraignment the judge set bail at two hundred and fifty thousand dollars, an amount so far-fetched that Joe's court-appointed counsel sputtered as he tried to object to it on principle. The court did not budge, and Joe stayed in jail.

The lawyer was much more sanguine when he met with Joe to discuss the case.

"The problem is, the kid was Janet Mossland's only daughter," the attorney said, spreading his papers and briefcase over the chipped Formica table between them. "And it was hard to say that you weren't a flight risk, with your history." He was an older man, his thin, graying hair combed over his pink scalp. He glanced at Joe in his orange jumpsuit. "She's got it in for you. You know that?"

"Yeah," Joe said bitterly. "Yeah, seems like everyone does." *I never should have stayed,* he thought. *Never should have slept with Lynn, should have listened to that inner voice, telling me to move on.*

He caught his attorney's eye. The man was waiting for him. Joe threw up his hands. "I was the last person to see her daughter. I wasn't thinking. I let her ride off on the trails by herself."

The attorney nodded sympathetically. "Well, she has the sympathy of the court. We have to take that into account. There is some good news, though." He looked through his notes. "You have an alibi for most of the night when Miss Romano didn't come home, and you were at the barn when the girl disappeared. Ditto for the fire, which the police believe was set to destroy any evidence."

Joe clutched the edge of the table, leaning forward. "And that's all good, right? That's good?"

The attorney took a breath. "And then there's the bad news. It all gets a little more complex. There was the mentally impaired homeless man you found near the site of the disappearance—and, I have to emphasize, *you* found, because the police and the prosecutors will be happy to enumerate for the jury the statistical evidence that the perp often joins in the search for missing persons. There was the evidence of a poaching operation, again, which *you* found out and brought to the police."

"I was just trying to help," Joe said. He was sweating. "That's all."

"I know." The attorney looked genuinely sorry. "I think we have a case here. Without the bodies of the women, or even any evidence they've been kidnapped or killed, it's just going to be harder for the prosecution. But with all the other things I mentioned, well, I just want you to know that it isn't going to be an easy run."

Joe's lips were dry and cracked, but he licked them, wincing at the pain. "Listen. What about Garson? I saw him at the house, I saw him take guns away, and no one knows where the bartender went. That's why I went out to Daw Road! It's connected. It has to be. The bartender is another disappearance!"

He was shouting, and he never shouted. He saw the guard move restlessly outside the visitor's cage. The attorney looked down at his papers again and shuffled them straight.

"That's not the case—"

"Has anybody even investigated? You've got to tell them to look into this!"

"The police have talked to Mark Ballard, Joe."

Joe stopped shouting. "What?" he said.

"Garson gave them his phone number, and they called and spoke with him. He's been in Colorado since midsummer."

"Garson didn't have his phone number," Joe said. He was numbed. The attorney went on.

"Ballard told us that Garson let him live at the Daw Road house; it was cheaper than paying rent on his apartment in town. Garson confirmed it."

Joe closed his eyes. "What about the poaching? The guns?!"

"I don't know about any of that. The guns, well, turns out Garson has a federal firearms license allowing him to buy and sell guns." He made a vague, apologetic gesture.

So there was no disappearance, no connection to Lynn and Kate. Just a guy with a gun taking potshots at deer out of season. The attorney gathered his papers and began tucking them away. He stood and held out his hand. Joe kept staring down at the speckled tabletop, and after a moment the attorney withdrew his hand.

"Look, I know it's hard for you in here. Just try to be patient.

Right now that's the best thing you can do for yourself. Be patient, Joe."

Back in his cell, he felt like Allegra, pacing in her loose box. *Cell's about the same size,* he thought. His cell mate watched from his bunk without comment as Joe flung himself onto his narrow bed, arm over his eyes, willing himself to calm down, to be as patient as his attorney recommended.

Mark Ballard was alive and living in Colorado, just like all the rumors had it. *All that detective shit for nothing,* he thought. There he was, sticking his nose into things, and all he was doing was bringing down suspicion on himself. He thought of the man he had found in the woods off Daw Road, gunshot and weak, with blue yarn stuck between his fingers. Even that had been for nothing. He was recovering in a mental hospital, and word was he was raving, delirious. His attorney had received the transcript of the interview with the man after he woke up from surgery; he had both spoken about stealing Dungiven from Lynn and about warning someone about an impending war. He gave only one name, and so far the police had turned up nothing in their investigation about him.

Joe kept his arm flung up to block out the white fluorescent lights that lined the corridor ceiling. The jail was loud—full of people, smells, anger, and shouting. Harsh alarms signaled doors opening and closing. He kept his eyes closed, blocking out his surroundings. He had to close it all out, or he would go crazy. He'd been in jail once before, years before, in Texas. Never slept then, but he was only in for forty-eight hours until his father came to bail him out. Daddy wasn't pleased, no, sir. Joe was practically hallucinating from lack of sleep, and his father thought he was on drugs. Almost turned around and turned him back in.

He thought about the curtains in Lynn's room, thought about her sweet, strong body held close to his, the taste and feel of her. "Where are you, Lynn?" he whispered into his arm. *I need you.*

Fourteen

A cold winter wind blew across the Temian foothills, bearing snow that dusted the tents and supply wagons of Marthen's encampment and driving the scouts before it. They galloped back toward the encampment, cloaks flying, their horses steaming in the cold air, and pulled up at the corrals, handing off their blowing, snorting beasts.

Skayler led them to Marthen's tent, and they trooped in after him, filling the tent with their cold and sweat, stamping their feet and blowing on their hands. Marthen looked up at them from his bed, propped up with his small writing desk at his back. He nodded at Skayler.

The senior scout said, "They've pulled back, sir. Best we can tell, all the way to Red Gold Bridge. I've left five scouts to follow and report back."

Gone. After three days of harrying them hard, Tharp had pulled back. His weapons, Marthen thought. He had to have run out of the bolts that smashed men's bones through chain and leather, even plate. What had the girl said? The bullets needed to be specially made. Tharp couldn't stray too far from his supply lines, or he would be reduced to using his weapons as clubs.

Cut those lines, and Tharp would fall.

He nodded curtly. "All right. New orders. Find Tharp's supply depot. Fan out; talk to the smallholders and townspeople."

Skayler and the others saluted and filed out, leaving Marthen with his pain and rising anger.

Three days. Three *days* they had retreated in a stumbling, panicked rout from Red Gold Bridge to the empty plains. Furious, Marthen had driven his men hard, wounded soldiers dropping away from the ranks to be picked off by Tharp's weapons or his own crows. He had wondered why Tharp hadn't just attacked but remained content to harry at his heels. If he had been given permission to attack, he could have caught Tharp far from home and out of reach of his resupplies.

The lords had other plans; or, he thought, no plan except to be ruled by fear and indecision.

It had been the same since the day of the battle outside Red Gold Bridge. He had not wanted to run. He had stood before the lords, held up by Grayne, his armor dented and his head and body stabbing from his rushing fall to earth and told them to attack at once, to press on. They could not look at him, except for Terrick. So he had looked straight at the man, letting him see both his contempt and the plea beneath it, but Terrick only shook his head.

Soldier's god, but he wanted to attack something. It burned that the lords had stood against him and forced him to retreat. *We had them,* he thought. *We had them.* Had the earth shaking not taken down the siege tower . . . But it had. And the lords would not yield, or rather, they would not yield to *him.*

Instead, he was left to cope with his injuries and his weakness and his rage. He slept badly propped up in his bed, hardly able to take a full breath with cracked ribs. He found himself irritably aware of his own desires. Once he even woke from a painful doze with the thought of the girl present in his mind and cursed his body's own reasons. She was a distraction, as much for her person as for her value to his campaign and the mystery she presented him with.

And he had little experience with courtship, if such an idea were not laughable on its face.

Still. He made a note to keep more of an eye on her. She was valuable to Talios—nothing to fear on that score, at least, as the doctor preferred men—and with that had come acceptance in the camp. It would not do to have her ally with some common free lance under the guise of love. Perhaps she needed to be reminded that her place in his army was still at his sufferance.

He steeled himself against the pain and called, "Grayne!"

No response. Cursing, Marthen reached out and threw the

first thing to hand: the girl's helmet. It pattered harmlessly against the wall of the tent. *"Grayne!"* he roared, and the force of the cry against his ribs almost made him faint. His head pounded, and his vision grew blurry again.

I will kill him myself. I will run him through. He panted shallowly, the best he could manage.

Grayne ducked in, his face white. "Sir," he said, his eyes wide with panic. "I was—I just—"

"You useless pig. Help me up."

Grayne supported him to his feet and helped him make his way outside his tent. The icy wind made his eyes water and blew his hair across his face, but he confronted it with perverse glee. It took his mind off his battered body. Talios had said that he had at least two broken ribs, and his head pounded with every beat of his heart. It hurt to ride, to walk, to breathe.

He turned stiffly, scanning the camp. "Where is the girl?" he asked.

"She's helping Talios, sir."

Good. He felt a measure of relief.

"From now on she takes her evening meal with me."

"Yes, sir."

That should cement her position in camp. Everyone would make the correct inference, and it would effectively separate her from the rest of the army.

The wind buffeted the surgery tent, and Kate shivered. The tent kept out most of the cold, but the brazier could barely warm their hands as they wound thread for sewing wounds.

She thought longingly of her ski gear back home, last season's lift tags still on the zipper, and sighed. Talios threw her a look.

"Too bad we don't have buffalo chips."

He gave her another look, the one she got when she said something he didn't understand. She said, "When the settlers went West, they crossed plains like this one, and they used dried buffalo dung for fuel for their fires."

"Hmmm. Your people tell the most fanciful stories."

She knew he was kidding, but it stung. "It's true. And it's not a story."

Except it kind of was. She remembered her history teacher, Mr. Winick, talking about the legends of the West and how they had changed America. "We are like no other nation," he said, "because our myths are still half true. Wild Bill Hickock and Geronimo. OK Corral and Billy the Kid. Give it a thousand years," he would say. "Then we can start talking about myths."

"Really." Talios's voice was so dry it almost crackled. "In your country there's a creature whose dung produces fire?"

She couldn't help it; she giggled, the laugh turning into a cough. "Come on. You know what I mean. Don't you have buffalo here? Big shaggy cows?"

He shook his head. "No. What of these settlers? Where were they going? What did they settle?"

He wanted the whole story? *They traveled West and set up towns and farms all across North America, sometimes living in peace with the native people, usually stealing their land and calling on the army to back them up. They brought disease, death, and disaster to native tribes and called it progress. Killed their way of life, trampled on their beliefs. Said it was in the name of God.*

Built the most powerful nation in the world. Perhaps many worlds.

Kate sat poised between the two stories, the one she had been taught from grade school on, and the one Talios would understand, the tale of conquest, of a triumphant nation.

I am part of that nation.

As clearly as if the tent flap opened into the wintry evening, she saw two roads before her. She could accept the role that was being laid out for her, consigning her, if she were lucky, to a small, short life as a soldier's wife, or to a more brutish existence. Or she could take all her potential and put it to use as her parents intended. She *could* still go into public service, accomplish great things to great acclaim. Just not exactly the way they had all expected it to go.

She could barely articulate the possibilities, but for a moment, just a moment, she saw herself as she might become in Aeritan, rejecting the easy myth for the harder truths and bringing something of value to this strange world. She could become great here.

Talios was looking at her with mild interest. She coughed again, swallowing against a dull ache in her throat. "Talios," she said, "can you teach me how to read and write?"

By the time Grayne came to get her, darkness had fallen. He found them at a table littered with scraps of ink-stained paper, heads together under the lamplight. Kate looked up, trying to rub the ink from her fingers. Talios sat back.

"Lieutenant. What errand have you been sent on this time?"

"The general wants her."

Kate looked between the two men. Even in the shadows she could tell something was wrong.

"I see. You've been promoted, then. From errand boy to procurer," Talios said, his voice savage.

"You should know all about that, Talios," the lieutenant spat.

Talios laughed sourly. "Hit a nerve, Lieutenant? Go ahead, take her. Go ahead, my lady—" He jerked his head toward the door flap. "Humor him. The General's in enough of a bad way that you're in little danger. Just stay out of reach, and you'll be fine." At her faint gasp, he snapped, "God's sake, girl, show some backbone!" Almost immediately, though, he relented. "You will be fine. Come back tomorrow, and we'll continue our lessons."

Kate fumbled to her feet and followed Grayne out into the night. A cold blast of arctic—no, she told herself, northern— wind caught her under her shirt, and she shivered and hastened after Grayne toward the soft glow of warmth that was Marthen's tent. She still could not believe Talios's cavalier attitude, but gathered up her determination anyway. If Marthen tried anything, then she would just kick him in the ribs.

Marthen sat stiffly on his bed, propped up, wearing slippers instead of his tall boots. His middle was thicker, the bandages making him look big around the belly. She nodded nervously.

"Sit," he said with his usual curtness. She sank onto the

low camp stool, edging it as close to the door as possible. Meat steamed in the shallow dish on the table. His dinner was on a tray on his lap.

They ate in silence, and Kate relaxed some. Talios was right; Marthen was still incapacitated. She couldn't imagine him trying anything. She wondered how he would manage to ride, if they had to move out. *Maybe that's why we're stuck out here,* she thought.

She felt him watching her and looked up. His eyes were dark spots in the dim lamplight. She suppressed a shiver of revulsion. He seemed so monstrous, even as helpless as he was, with his bulky torso. He had always struck her as a little . . . off-center. *Now I think he's getting crazier.* The silence was driving her crazy now, and she swallowed against the soreness in her throat.

"Thanks for inviting me to dinner," she said. The words sounded too loud in the silent tent. Kate listened to what she said, and winced. *Lame, much?*

He didn't say anything, and she took a breath and went back to the mushy meat on her small plate. Marthen's orderly had made small biscuits to go with the meal, and she picked one up and wiped up the sauce with it. It was surprisingly good, and for the two bites it took to eat it, she gave it her full attention.

"Go," he said. Mouth full, Kate jerked her attention back to Marthen. He said nothing more, and she got to her feet, chewing hurriedly.

"Thank you," she said again. "Good night."

For a moment she hesitated, and his expression changed: fury and something else. She fled, practically tearing through the tent flap. Once outside, she breathed deeply in the cold air, then turned toward her little tent.

She almost bumped into Colar. He stood there in the darkness, just having come from the tent he shared with his father, wrapped in his warm jacket. Kate took a step back, too startled to say a word. He said nothing, too, and they parted, but not before Kate could see by the turn of his body that he looked to see where she had come from.

Not the latrines—that was where he was going.

Kate burned with shame. He had just seen her come out of the general's tent.

The temperature sank steadily throughout the day, so that as Lynn and Crae approached the hills that led to Trieve, she had to zip up her red vest to her chin. The cold wind tore at her hair and went through her fine, thin shirt, the slit sleeve flapping around Crae's crude bandage. It hurt. She had all she could do to concentrate on staying in the saddle. The pain was a constant that took all of her attention. If she moved her arm unduly, she wanted to scream. Crae fashioned a sling, and that helped, but she still rode almost in a stupor.

They could not go faster than a brisk walk. Crae had tried to move them out, pushing the horses into a smooth lope, but Lynn had almost fallen after a few moments, and so without a word between them they kept the horses at a walking pace. At least, Lynn thought, leaning forward in the saddle to help Silk up a steep grade, we haven't had to stop and rest them as often.

The sky had clouded over as the day eased toward evening. *It feels like snow,* she thought. She could almost smell it in the air. The foothills rose toward a jagged line of mountains on the horizon, and the whole effect was chill and dour.

He turned and glanced at her, one hand on his horse's hindquarters. "How are you?"

"Morphine's sounding good." At his look she added, "I'm okay. Let's not talk."

He regarded her a moment longer, then nodded and turned, giving Briar his heel. A few moments later, he pulled up again, and she drew Silk up next to him. They stood at the top of a rise along the road, following as it rose in a series of hills up to a terraced mountain, about six or seven miles away, as best Lynn could estimate. A large house topped the hill, a few lights already twinkling. The road dipped and curved but mostly rose like a pale dirt ribbon through scrub forest and pastureland divided by tumbled rock walls.

The road itself was broken and jagged, the ancient paving stones crumpled upward and cracked. It was hard to tell because of the terrain, but once Lynn knew what to look for, she could detect the rolling waves of dirt caused by the earthquake in Gordath Wood. The series of upthrust earth traversed the fields and cut athwart the road, disappearing in the distance.

Lynn broke the silence first. "Are we too late?"

Crae glanced back at her. "I think if we can still ask that question, we're not." He shrugged the least amount. "I don't know how much time we have, for sure."

She nodded. "Stupid question anyway." She pointed her chin at the distant house. "Trieve, right?"

"Trieve. Where you will be well cared for. I promise."

"Okay." She thought that if she could just get out of the damn saddle, she would be happy enough with that.

Are we too late? Crae thought his reply bespoke too much wishful thinking, but he had no other. He squinted through the darkening afternoon at the lights shining from the House of Trieve. A welcome sight indeed, but if the earthquakes had made it this far, he wasn't sure what they would find when they topped the terraces and knocked on Lady Jessamy's front door. And he had promised Lynn she would be well cared for.

He glanced over at her. She huddled in her red vest like a bird in winter, hunkering down against the cold. Her dove-gray skirt was bedraggled and muddy where it draped over her fine boots, and her uncovered hair was damp with mist. Tendrils curled wildly around her face. Her hands were rough, and the cold had raised the color in her cheeks and also touched her nose with a bright shade of red.

She did not look like the type of guest Jessamy was used to. Maybe she should cover her hair, he thought a bit guiltily. But no—that would raise other questions, such as her family, her holdings, whether she was noble or smallholder.

Whether she was pledged to Crae. He felt warmth creep up his cheeks. He didn't know what would be worse—that Jessamy would assume that he had made a match or that she would know that Lynn was unworthy of one.

At least, his pragmatic side pointed out, Lynn would be unaware of *that* particular insult. And not even Jessamy could fail to give welcome and protection to her, if Crae asked for it.

When they reached the bottom of the terraces, Crae halted.

He always marveled at the engineering that went into the steps, a staircase for giants. He dismounted, throwing his reins over Briar's head. "Stay in the saddle," he told Lynn. "This is not any easy climb."

She nodded. "You'd think the stairs would make it easier."

Crae shook his head. "It's one of Trieve's defenses," he said, and they began walking up. "Deceptive, how hard it is to ride up this hill."

Lynn made a disparaging noise. "First Red Gold Bridge, now this. You people don't seem to like your neighbors."

If you only knew, he thought. "We have our reasons," he said, his words coming short as the climb steepened. "And Red Gold Bridge is walled for another reason."

"The gordath."

He nodded without speaking, concentrating on the steps. Lynn leaned forward, taking her weight off Silk's back, and he noted it, even as his breath came short and he began to curse the imaginative Trieve builders.

In front of the wide gates Crae stopped, breathing hard and leaning against Briar. Lynn kicked her feet from the stirrups and slipped from the saddle, crying out as she accidently jostled her arm. Both horses stood like lumps, their sides bellowing. As they recuperated, a small woman came running out to meet them, her cheerful blue kerchief slipping back from her forehead. She wore a dark blue dress, its split skirt floating around her. "Crae!" she shouted. "Crae!" Behind her a group of men and women spilled out of the house, hurrying after her.

Crae started to bow, but Jessamy would have none of it. She reached up and gave him a vigorous hug. Then she stepped back and said, "What do you think you are doing, leaving your commission and Stavin behind to go to war without you?"

Ah, yes. He should have known she'd have something to say. "Jessamy—" he started, but she shook her head.

"There's nothing you can say that will convince me." She was as tart as ever.

"Jessamy, we beg guesting from you. This is Lynna, a foreigner in Aeritan. She is hurt and needs attention."

He watched with growing dismay as she turned toward Lynn, taking in Lynn's bare head and wild, unkempt hair, then the rest of her. Lynn straightened under her regard, and gave her back stare for stare. "Lady Jessamy," she said, and he was reminded anew of her uncouth accent. "I am pleased to meet you."

Jessamy made no response. She turned to Crae. "I see you have a story to tell. Well, come in, Crae, for we have much to talk about." She gestured to one of the men waiting by the gate. "Take the horses, please."

She turned to go when he caught her by the elbow. "We both ask for guesting, Jessamy."

Her displeasure turned to shock and anger. He shook his head slightly, and her protest died. Finally, though, she did what he expected, though he knew he would hear no end of it. She took both of their hands in her small rough ones and took a deep breath.

"You are welcome here, guests of Trieve. Let no harm come to you within these walls."

He bowed, and Lynn copied him clumsily.

A man came to take the horses, and they followed Lady Trieve's rigid back into her home.

The front doors opened onto the great room as he remembered it, a barren entry hall with a gray stone floor and stone walls that rose about five feet from the floor. The wall facing the terraces had a few glazed windows, the small panes of wavy glass set in carved moldings rising almost to the tall ceiling. At the other end of the room stood a dais with a long, plain wooden table and chairs. It was covered with papers and ledgers.

"Crae," Jessamy said over her shoulder as she headed toward the dais. "You have your old room. We haven't moved anything, though Stavin said that we should just dump it all out, you visit so rarely. Calyne, see to our visitor."

A woman with sternly covered hair came forward and smiled at Lynn. "You look terribly hurt. Come. We'll find a warm bed and have the doctor look. He's got a knack with breaks and has worked wonders with the livestock."

"Oh," Lynn said faintly. "Well. I suppose so long as he doesn't think I need to be put down." She threw Crae a backward glance as the woman put an arm around her and led her off in a gathering crowd of women.

He nodded reassuringly. "I'll come look for you later. You're in good hands," he said.

She had time to smile before she was swept away.

The great room emptied, and it was just Crae and Jessamy. His best friend's wife looked up at him, the kerchief sliding off her head. Impatiently, she reknotted it.

"Tell me what is going on, Crae."

If only I knew where to begin, he thought. "We need your guardian, Jessamy."

The women tucked Lynn into a short bed that barely contained her length, clucking at the state of her. With a chorus of "You poor dear," and "There, there," they helped her off with her boots and her clothing, making small cries at the ruined shirt. "I can mend this," one of the ladies said, taking a professional interest in the seams and the buttons. Lynn cried out when they removed her sling, but they soon had her in a warm, billowy nightdress and turned down the covers. Someone put a bed warmer down at the foot of the bed, and she slid in gratefully, almost bursting into tears. The bed was hard, but the blankets were warm and the pillows more than adequate.

Everyone looked up when the livestock doctor came in, filling the room with his heavy boots and big jacket. He sat down on the edge of the bed and unwrapped her arm.

"Hmmm," he said, holding it with rough hands that matched his craggy face. Lynn took a deep breath, trying to let her tension go. Before she could react, he pulled the break straight. It hurt beyond anything she could imagine, and she almost screamed at the top of her lungs. "Right. Needs a splint, bandages, a healing draft, and you'll be right as rain in a month."

She had been mostly joking earlier, about the morphine. Now, not so much.

When they finished and let her be, all she wanted to do was sleep. The medicine they made her drink tasted of herbs and honey. The room was dim, only a little fire crackling on the hearth. The shutters clattered against the wind, but the room was warm, as was the bed. Lynn lay propped up against the pillows, her splinted arm resting on another pillow, and let herself sink into sleep. Calyne rested at the foot of the bed in a little chair, her feet propped up before the fire, a quiet, comforting presence.

Lynn was barely aware when the door opened, a little lantern light slipping in the doorway. Someone spoke to Calyne in a low voice.

"She is resting," she heard. "The doctor said it will heal well."

Again the voice, and Calyne opened the door a little wider. Lynn heard someone come in, felt them approach and bend over her. "Heal well, Lynna," he whispered, and she smiled.

"Joe," she whispered drowsily, and fell into sleep.

Fifteen

A lone horseman galloped toward the encamp-
ment, tucked low over his horse's neck. Jayce, perched just below the top of the knoll the scouts used as their vantage point,
called back, "Coming into distance. Just one." Colar knelt and
cocked his crossbow, leading the rider. Skayler had his hand
on Colar's shoulder. "Wait, Terrick."

"Can we see who he is yet?" another scout said. Skayler's
grip tightened a slight bit.

Colar shifted his finger on the release but held steady, his
breathing measured.

Something fluttered from the rider's hand and then the
wind snapped it out: a gold and cream flag.

"Kenery's man," Jayce called.

Skayler released his hold on Colar's shoulder. "Let's bring
him in."

Kenery's outrider pulled up when the scouts approached,
fanning around him on blowing horses. He grinned through
his beard.

"Well, well, looks like we've found the wee lost lambs," he
said. He cocked his head behind him. "Fight's that way, you
know."

Skayler said, "Where's Kenery?"

The man gave him a look. "No offense, scout, but my orders are to talk to Marthen and the Council, not some fleabitten
half-pint and his skinny crows. Bad enough I have to ride out
to the back of beyond to find you cowards. I'm not going to
tell my tale to every soldier's whelp I find."

Colar reacted without thought and drew his blade. He was

not alone: six swords scraped out of their scabbards and met at the man's throat. The rider went still. Then he raised one hand and pushed two of the blades away from his neck.

"Enough fight in you now—good. But for the soldier's god's sake, bring me in. The sooner we can get you boys turned in the right direction, the sooner we can all go home."

Skayler looked at him without expression. "Do you have a name, loudmouth?"

"Soldier's god, why should I tell you?"

Colar didn't need orders; he leaned in on his sword the least bit. From the sound the man made, so did the others.

"Samarren," the man said, slightly strangled. "Satisfied?"

Skayler grunted. "Think you can keep your mouth closed till we get to camp?"

Still strained, the man said frankly, "Never have before."

Skayler leaned in close and in a voice just above a whisper said, "Try."

The scouts returned their swords to home, Colar fumbling a bit with his. He still was not comfortable with his father's second blade. The outrider caught sight of his difficulty and rolled his eyes, but mindful of Skayler he said nothing. Colar could only be grateful for his restraint.

They turned Samarren over to Marthen, and Grayne was sent to bring in the Council. Colar and the other scouts were dismissed. Colar and his father crossed paths at the door flap, but Lord Terrick only gave him a once-over and nodded stiffly in greeting. Colar bowed back.

Clear of the door, Jayce slapped him on the back. "You should have shot the bastard when you had the chance. From the hill." He aimed an imaginary crossbow and let his finger release.

It would have been my second kill. Colar laughed to hide his discomfort, hoping Jayce didn't hear the catch in his voice. "I had him, too. Right there."

He didn't want to sit alone in his tent. Why should he wait for his father to come back and deign to fill him in? Colar followed Jayce to the scouts' tents. A long-running game of stars and swords was going on, and he knew the other scouts looked forward to looting his meager purse. His father would have his head if he knew Colar sat in on some hands, but he was getting better and starting to win.

He found a surprise when he got there: in the door to the tent stood Captain Artor, balancing himself unsteadily on crutches. Holding him up were Talios and Kate, the girl looking thin and drawn. She caught his eye and blushed and looked away. He felt a rush of emotions too complicated to understand. All the scouts were talking about it with a mix of ribaldry and admiration: the general had taken the stranger girl to bed.

She's just a camp follower. It doesn't matter.

Except that she wasn't a common camp follower, and somehow it did.

"Captain, you are a fool," Talios said. "This is far too soon."

"Sit me down," the captain bit off. He cursed all the way down to the bed. "When will I be healed? When, damn you?"

"At this rate, you fool, when you are dead. And I will kill you myself if I see you try a stunt like this again. Don't make me waste my good medicine on you."

"What happened?" Skayler said. He reached up and steadied the swaying lantern, knocked about in the excitement.

"Your captain tried to walk on a broken leg."

"On crutches," Artor gritted out.

"Luckily one of the women saw him and got us." Talios gestured, and he and Kate lifted the splinted leg as Artor roared, and shoved a rolled-up blanket under it. "*Stay* there. You can't hasten these things."

Colar watched Kate pick up the crutches and look at them with a pained expression.

"Put those down, girl," Artor growled. He reached out and yanked one out of her grip.

"Don't you dare," Talios shot back. "You can't be trusted with them, Captain."

"Damn you . . ."

Kate spoke up quietly, her voice hoarse. "Mr. Artor, you're falling because these are way too short." Everyone looked at her. She flushed and took a breath, for courage, Colar thought. "I think you should have new ones made. And at home, they're padded here." She patted the crossbar that went under the arms. "We can do that. Then you can practice for longer."

Artor stared at her and then snorted. "And you think I'm going to fall for that."

She tossed a glance at Talios and turned back to Artor and handed him the other crutch. "Okay. But can I have your horse? Because if you keep on this way, you'll never ride again."

Colar had to bite his lip to keep from laughing, and the rest of the scouts ducked their heads to keep from setting each other off. Artor was speechless for a second and then threw the crutch back at her with a huff.

"Get out," he growled.

"Well decided, Captain," Talios said. "I'll be back to check on you later."

She and Talios were leaving with the crutches when Samarren ducked in, filling the tight space. He looked around, grinning. "I heard there was a game of stars and swords. Deal me in, boys. I might even take it easy on you, considering you have a mad general and are led by a Council of small men." He caught Kate's eye and winked, and she turned bright red. "Then again, I wouldn't count on it."

Skayler slid a footstool out and sat at the bed next to Artor. He pulled out the cards and dice. "My pleasure, loudmouth. Who's in?"

Colar was one of the first to find a seat.

The cold air felt good on Kate's heated face. *Who was* that? she wanted to ask Talios, but thought it better to leave the question be. All the scouts looked disgruntled at the stranger's entrance, even Colar. She still twinged in shame every time she saw him. *Why did he have to see me that night?*

"Good work in there," Talios said. "I thought we were going to have to tie him down."

"Thanks." She thought of a way to ask about the newcomer. "That guy, he said Marthen was mad."

"Eh, he doesn't know the man like we do," Talios said absently.

"I think he's right."

Talios didn't respond at first, but he stopped walking. They stood in the middle of the camp, people all around them huddled around meager fires, wrapped in cloaks and blankets. "Well," he said, "it's as easy to follow a madman into battle as a sane one."

"What, is that some kind of adage?" she said dubiously.

"No, chick. It's the truth." He glanced at her and gave a half laugh. "He is less mad than driven, I think. He thinks he must know all the angles of a thing, especially the sides he can't see. He can't see the other side of you, for instance, and it compels him to keep trying."

"Ewwww," she said.

Talios laughed outright. "Well spoken, my lady. Now, as you are my apprentice, carry these back to the surgeon's tent, will you?" He handed her the crutches. "I'll ask one of the carpenters to make longer ones, which I understand can take a month or more to put together."

She grinned and watched him go off on some errand of his own, and with a spirit of playfulness, she took a few steps on the crutches before running out of breath. It hurt to breathe sometimes. She swallowed. Her throat didn't hurt as much, but at night her chest rattled, and she had a deep cough. Nor did it help that she had caught the diarrhea everyone else had gotten in camp. Fully half the soldiers were laid low, and the camp was putrid with it. She drank the drafts Talios made for her, but sometimes all she wanted to do was stay in her bed, as dank and cold as it was. Speaking of which—she grimaced as her stomach cramped again, and she hurried to the trenches.

"This could work," Terrick said, leaning over the map in Marthen's tent. The rest of the council crowded around, giving room to Marthen to sit at the table rather than stand. "We draw Tharp out here, and Kenery brings his army up on his flanks here and here."

"He won't leave the stronghold," Lord Saraval objected. "He has no reason to."

"We give him a reason," Marthen said. He sat very straight, his voice constrained by the bandages strapping his ribs. He scanned the letter from Kenery again. The news was both good and troubling: Kenery was coming from the south, ready for the Council's orders, all to the good. The troubling news was that of Kenery's spies' reports that Tharp had begun recruiting smiths.

Kenery couldn't know what it signified; only the man's thoroughness made him put it in his letter. But Marthen knew. If someone had figured out a way to make metal that worked in the strange weapons, Tharp was no longer tied to his supply lines but could strike at a distance again.

"He knows Kenery's on his way. Can't fail to know," Saraval said. The old lord looked around at them keenly. "How do we get around that?"

Terrick said, "Does it matter who Tharp goes for first? He attacks Kenery, we attack from the rear. He attacks us, Kenery cuts him off."

"Does Kenery know about the weapons?"

Terrick hesitated. "I told him what we knew."

Saraval frowned. "I don't like the idea of Kenery facing down those weapons. I'd rather Tharp turned them on us."

"Noble Lord Saraval," Lord Favor muttered, but his usual desperation to please fell flat.

They all ignored that, Marthen thrusting down his distaste for Favor's presence. Every time the man opened his mouth, he thought. At least Terrick understood, judging by his expression. If Kenery was routed by those earthshaking weapons, that would be two armies penned up.

"Better to draw him to us," Terrick said. "How?"

"We kill the smiths."

They all turned to stare at Marthen. He regarded them with bitterness in his mouth. "He's using the smiths to cast bullets to make up for depleted supplies. He's vulnerable, but only until he builds his supplies back up. We burn all the smithies within Red Gold Bridge and on its western borders and kill all the smiths. He'll come to us."

An uneasy silence gathered in the tent. All the Council looked at him and each other with shock and ill ease. Marthen watched them take it in. These were Camrin's and Salt's smiths, to be sure, but he could see the implications strike home.

Finally Favor broke the silence. "They threw in their lot with Tharp. They knew what to expect."

Lord Saraval didn't deign to look at him, but he answered him nonetheless. "Sorting it out in Council afterwards will be hell."

"We can wage war or we can wage the aftermath," Marthen
said. "I thought to send in the crows, anyway, or what remains
of them. It will keep it clean of your touch."

"No," Terrick said immediately. "They are too hard to control; they will go too far. Bad enough we do this. We live with
the consequences of this decision."

"Very well. Then what do you suggest?"

"We send in trained soldiers and outriders. They can be
trusted to kill only the smiths."

Marthen wondered how the man could be so blind. If he
thought his son's presence ennobled the scouts, he was a great
old fool. The younger Terrick had left boyhood behind with
his first battle, and his father's grip had grown tenuous. Give
him leave to raid a village, and he was likely to go mad with
bloodlust. Then he looked again at the lord. Terrick's visage
had grown haggard, his expression fiercely sad, and Marthen
knew he had not been blind after all.

Lord Saraval shook his head. "Terrick, you don't have to
do this," the big old bear rumbled.

Confused, Lord Favor looked around at all of them but had
the grace to hold his tongue.

Under their regard, Lord Terrick glared back.

Marthen did him the courtesy to ignore his pain. He raised
his voice. "Grayne. Rouse the mounted soldiers and the
scouts. Tell them to prepare for my orders."

"Yes, sir," Grayne said, and he left the tent. Marthen
looked around at the Council.

"We need to move, so that when we flush Tharp out, we are
ready for him."

They all leaned over the map again.

Waves of mounted troops thundered out of
the camp, their armor shining dully where it was not covered
by jackets or cloaks. In the general rush, Kate liked sending
the riders off; everything was louder and faster than usual. She
soothed one bouncy mare as Mykal the ostler threw a saddle
on its back and cinched it tight. Torm stayed glued to Kate,
whimpering a little.

"Hush, Torm," Kate said, trying to keep from brushing him
off. "It's all right."

"He knows what it all means," Mykal said, jerking up the girth. He patted the mare on the rump. "Knows there will be fighting here soon."

"What's going on?" Kate said, handing the mare over to Adyr, one of Skayler's scouts.

"Found out that the smiths are making those metal balls for the earth shakers." Mykal grinned, his teeth a crooked fence line in his beard. "Marthen reckoned we ought to stop them."

Kate frowned. "I don't know, Mykal, it doesn't seem likely. Bullets have to be made in a factory. I don't think a smith here has the technology."

"Doesn't matter what you or I think, girl. It matters what *he* thinks." He cocked his head toward the officers' tents.

Yeah, but, she almost said. She bit her lip. Should she try to tell Marthen that it didn't seem possible? She shied away from the thought. She doubted he'd appreciate her interference. She ducked under the rope corral and picked the next horse, a big, blocky bay gelding with a snip of white on his nose. Kate liked him because he reminded her of Mojo. Sure enough, he rubbed his head against her when she put on his bridle.

When they saddled him up, she said, "So how are they going to stop the smiths?"

Mykal shrugged. "Kill them all, leave their bodies hanging as a warning, and burn down their smithies." He scowled in the face of her openmouthed shock. "Go bring this one out."

Still boggled, Kate led the big gelding over to the next scout. It was Colar.

They looked at each other, and Kate felt her face flame. Even Colar had two spots of color high on his cheeks above his sparse beard.

"Umm," she said. She thrust the reins at him. "Here."

He took them, holding the reins under the horse's chin. The horse snorted and bobbed his head, wanting to be off. "Thanks," Colar said.

"He's a good horse," she said in a rush.

"I'll take care of him."

"No, I meant—" *He'll take care of you.*

He looked as if he wanted to say something, but instead he threw the reins over the horse's head and mounted. With a shout, Skayler formed them up, and the scouts were gone at a gallop.

Kill them all . . . leave their bodies hanging . . . burn down their smithies.

She thought, *But he's my age. They can't make him do that.*

Mykal's cuff upside her head startled Kate out of her reverie. "Ow!" she said, pivoting hard around. Mykal grinned, and Torm hooted.

"Wake up," he said. He jerked his head at the corral. "We need to finish here, else Marthen will have my head—and yours, too. The boy will be back soon enough for you to moon over."

Crae and Lynn had been in Trieve but three days when fall roared in for good, sunshine giving way to rain and then morning frost, and finally light snow. Lynn was still in pain, but he could see that the shelter and warmth had done her good. Her face was no longer so thin and pinched, and her eyes had lost their shadows. Crae still winced when he thought of the strange name she had whispered that night under the influence of the healing draft. He should have known that she was promised, or even wed already. Not that they had any agreement, he reminded himself, but he had sometimes thought she looked on him, well, favorably.

He himself was thankful for the guesting they received, but he fretted as well. The longer they stayed, the more powerful the gordath became, and they were no closer to finding a guardian.

Crae sat on the edge of Jessamy's worktable as she leafed through the enormous daybook that held the House of Trieve's records. He craned to see over her rounded shoulders. She frowned as she searched, her kerchief only nominally covering her light brown hair, the little bow half undone. *Can't keep a kerchief on her,* Stavin half complained, half crowed, and Crae shifted and looked away from her glossy hair. Stavin meant it both ways and didn't care who knew it. "Ah!" she said and sat back. "Here it is." She pushed the book around to Crae. In her crisp dark script she had written, "Midsummer Fifth. Arbac carried fleece to Kenery. We gave Merikard a farewell." Next to the notation was a small calculation of the number of fleeces per sack.

At Crae's blank look, she said, "Merikard is the guardian Stavin was talking about. He went with Arbac to go live with his daughter and her husband. It was a good thing that Arbac was traveling that way, for Merikard had aged terribly since Gerrit died and needed someone to look after him . . ." Her voice trailed off.

Crae rubbed the bridge of his nose. He had a sudden image of himself riding from House to House, asking for a guardian. And behind him, the ground shaking apart as the gordath greedily consumed everything in its path. "Did he leave someone behind who had the knowledge?"

She shook her head. "It didn't seem important, Crae. We're so far from Red Gold Bridge—we didn't really know what Merikard was going on about, anyway." She gave him a guilty look. "If it helps, I am beginning to see that was a shortsighted mistake, if these earth shakings are caused by the gordath."

"How bad have they been?"

"They've rattled the panes in the windows," she admitted. "The road is what worries me. I have not traveled far since Stavin left, but I've seen the broken road."

"You are right to be worried," he said in a low voice.

She pulled the kerchief off and refastened it with an impatient tsk. "I am not always a fool, if that's what you mean. And Merikard—he was old, Crae, and I think his mind had begun to wander in the end. Even if he were still here, it would not have been a kindness to take him back to Red Gold Bridge with you." She looked up at him, pushing the kerchief off her forehead again. "I don't know what's worse, earth shakings or the knowledge that there are crows on the road."

"Did Stavin leave you any men who can fight?"

She sighed. "You know Stavin. We have only a small force of fighting men to begin with, and he dithered so much about what Lord Tharp would think that I finally told him to take them all and just go. He was driving me mad."

"Let me look to your defenses," he said, already devising a system of lookouts in his head.

"I suppose." Her tone was sharp. "It's the least you could

do for Stavin. After all, you abandoned him in Red Gold Bridge."

"Stavin did what he had to do, as did I."

"You have taken your side against your lord and your oldest friend. And you did what you had to do?"

He kept his voice even. "Stavin understood."

She crumpled up a piece of paper and threw it at him. It struck him in the chest. "Don't be so sure. He wrote to me and said you convinced him to speak out. All it did was turn Tharp against him. Against Trieve, and then you were gone." She sighed. "Oh Crae. You've always been this way. You never can just do your duty. It always has to be so . . . complicated." She threw up her the hands. He handed her the paper she had thrown at him, and she burst into tears. "I don't know what is going to happen," she said, taking her kerchief off and wiping her face. "Stavin's letter says that all is going Lord Tharp's way, and the weapons are holding off Lord Terrick and the army of the Council, but now Kenery has thrown in with them, and he has five thousand men. I haven't heard anything else, and I never got to tell Stavin I was with child, because I wasn't sure before he left, and now that I am sure, I don't know if I should tell him. He'll just fret."

Crae stared at her, openmouthed. "You're pregnant?" he said.

She laughed through her tears at the look on his face.

"You should write him, Jessamy. He'll want to know."

"I know. I should. I *will*. But Crae, you need to go back to Red Gold Bridge. You need to stand by him."

"Not without a guardian to close the gordath."

"I don't understand this. He is your friend."

"He'll understand, Jessamy."

"Oh I see." Her voice turned to ice. "I can't understand because of this bond between you that no one else can see or feel. Well, I know Stavin as well as you, and he would come to your aid. He wouldn't leave you to fight alone."

He felt himself close off under her attack.

She went on. "You don't know anything about loyalty." She began tying the damp kerchief over her hair. Her nose and eyes were red from crying.

He knew that she was upset and frightened. Stavin said that

when she was carrying Tevani, he learned to tread lightly around her, as anything was apt to set her off. Still, he had no interest in hearing more. Crae pushed himself off the table.

"Thanks for looking through your accounts," he said. "I'll organize Trieve's defense."

Jessamy rolled her eyes. "Crae, stop," she said, as if he were the one being unreasonable.

And because she was upset and frightened, he relented. "Jessamy, you know that I am not taking this lightly. If I can bring back a guardian to close the gordath, it could go a long way to ending this war. Lord Tharp won't be able to bring more weapons through. He'll have to sue for peace."

"Well enough," she said. "Then that is where it will stand, although I still think you are being disloyal."

Couldn't she just let the argument go? As if in answer, she added, "Besides, if this were all about peace, why did you bring the lostling woman?"

He couldn't think of a thing to say.

"Stavin wrote me about her. And you. This isn't like you, Crae. If you aren't careful, you will lose any chance of gaining property. You've turned from your lord, your friend. A bad attachment can change everything. Think, Crae."

He waited for his anger to settle. When he could speak, he bit off the words, "Thanks. I will."

He walked off, wanting nothing more than to ride off from all of them, Stavin, Jessamy, and Lynn included, and never be found again, the whole world be damned.

Crae stepped outside the huge house, hoping to clear his head in the winter wind. The day was clear, but clouds clustered on the horizon, dark and blue, the kind that brought snow. It was too cold to brood outside, so he hurried over to the barn, pulling the heavy doors closed behind him, surrounding himself in the warm, close odors of horses, sheep, and hay.

A small figure came running down the aisle when she saw him. "Captain Crae!" said Tevani, and barreled full tilt into his arms for a hug. He scooped her up, her thick jacket swallowing her. She had only one mitten. Her cheeks were rosy from the cold, and her sandy hair had come unbraided from under her thick hat.

"Greetings, Tev."

"Hi! Okay!"

He stared at her, puzzled. She giggled.

"I got new words from Lynna."

He laughed ruefully. So, she had already left her mark. Tevani wriggled down. "Come see my pony."

She had shown him her pony every day that they had been at Trieve. Crae admired the small pony in a little stall with a goat. Both animals were curled up together, the pony not much bigger than the goat.

"Will he grow big like the white horse?"

Crae shook his head. "He'll stay small for you. Then when you get bigger, you can ride the big horses."

"But I want to ride the big horse now." She stared down at the little scene with a wrinkled brow.

"Well, Tev, that's up to Lord Stavin. When your father comes home, he can decide if you are ready to ride his horse." Crae heard his own words and frowned. When had Stavin gotten a white horse? He had brought his usual string to Red Gold Bridge. "Tevani, what white horse?"

"He lives with the sheep. Sometimes I see him in the morning from my window. But when the dogs go out to bring in the sheep, he flies over the fence and gallops away."

Lynn slipped her vest over her borrowed shirt, trying to avoid moving her broken arm. Underneath the wrappings and the splint, her arm was bruised and swollen but not infected, and the rigid support of the rustic splint kept the pain bearable. She zipped up her vest to her chin. The House of Trieve was cold. A constant draft blew from every corner. On the little chair in the corner lay her white riding shirt, unwearable now that she had a bulky splint. One of the ladies had washed and mended it yet again, the tiny stitching along the seam almost machine perfect. She had replaced a plastic button with a small white one that Lynn, inspecting, identified as a bit of wood, polished and carved. She swept her hand over it. The shirt had lost its crispness, the collar limp and the cuffs frayed. Lynn couldn't wait until she could wear it again.

Still, her borrowed clothes were warmer, she had to admit. Her thick skirt and leggings and heavy overblouse with its placket that fastened on her shoulder were designed for this weather. She brushed her hair back with a brush left on the mantel over the fireplace, working through it awkwardly with one hand. She was the only woman without a kerchief, as she noticed at breakfast. Tevani, Jessamy's little girl, had stared at her the whole time, her eyes wide as she looked from her mother to Lynn and back again. Lynn had tried to talk to her but gave up after it was clear that Jessamy—Lady Trieve, thank you—did not approve.

Lady Trieve had not approved of Lynn at all.

Just the thought of it, that she was accused of being . . . lesser. *Like I didn't get enough of that with Mrs. Hunt and Howie Fleming,* she thought, wincing as the brush caught on a snarl. Maybe that's why it bothered her so much.

Joe used to say, "Just let it slide. You can't stop them, and they don't have the truth of the matter anyway."

"Yeah, but—" she'd say, and he'd shush her, taking her face in his hands so he could kiss her. Lynn could almost feel that kiss. She closed her eyes for a moment and raised her face, pretending with all her heart that Joe kissed her softly on the mouth, so softly she ached for a real kiss. Instead, a cold draft drizzled in through the shuttered windows, making the lamps gutter.

"I miss you," she said into the little room. "I'm trying to get back. I'm just so lost."

Lost and at Crae's mercy. She liked to think she wasn't, liked to fool herself that she was a valued member of his team, riding with him on his mission to find the guardians. But she knew that she was a charge, not a partner. Her success with the crossbow was pure luck, nothing else. He had brought her here so he could dump her safely and go off on his own. Lynn had a sudden, panicked thought of being in this cold place for years, not quite guest, not quite servant, never going home, the crazy auntie in the spare bedroom.

The gordath closed against her forever.

Her hair was as smooth as she could make it. She let it drape over her shoulder, wishing she could braid it or pin it with her barrette.

A knock came on the door. Calyne, she thought hopefully. Maybe the woman could help. She twisted the ornate doorknob and pulled it open. Crae stood there.

For an instant they stared at each other. He had cleaned up, too, and shaved. He wore a pale brown shirt, a thick vest of dark green, and dark trousers that bloused over his boots. *Ohhhh,* she thought.

"I think we found your horse."

Over Crae's protests, Lynn rode out alone to bring in Dungiven. She wondered if the horse would remember her. He probably would, but whether that would bring him in after so many weeks of running alone, she couldn't say. They had had what she would call a professional relationship; she made his life routine and comfortable, and he sprang over fences and won ribbons. She couldn't say that they had ever bonded.

Well, we'll see, she thought, hunkered down in the saddle, her broken arm tucked under her heavy borrowed jacket, half cloak, half coat, that hung down over her knees. Calyne had found thick leggings for her, and a wool hat and gloves. She was so bundled up she could barely get into the saddle, but she was thankful for the gear when she got out into the wind. Silk walked with her head down against the weather, her mane blowing back. Tiny snowflakes pricked at her cheeks.

The broad, rocky field sloped first down into a valley and then up the other side, scattered with rocks and covered with brown and gray grass. She turned with difficulty to look back at the house. It rose above her, a dark structure blocking out the sky.

God, it felt good to ride out alone. She had been so constrained by her position of dependence, and she had to face it, Crae himself was a distraction. He had wanted to come with her, but she had argued that he would only scare Dungiven away.

Lynn urged Silk into the small valley, and they wound around to the fence Tevani had talked about. The fence followed the hillside down into the ravine and then made its crooked way up the other side, disappearing over the knob. A simple gate, about four feet high, buckled the two sides. The terrain was flat and the approach clear. Lynn knew that was where Dungiven was jumping. Sure enough, his big hoofprints marked the ground. Lynn clucked to Silk and pushed the mare toward the gate. She bent and unlatched it one-handed, and urged Silk through, then turned the mare and closed it behind her, slipping the cord over the top of the post.

"Where to now?" she said into the wind. It was snowing harder and her feet, as wrapped as they were, had begun to freeze. Of her own accord Silk began plodding around the base of the knob. The wind faltered a bit as they got out of the ravine and behind the small hill, and the trail they had been following led downward. Silk got her haunches under her and slid; Lynn rode it easily. The terrain spread out again into another field. Lynn halted Silk and scanned the area. The day was getting dark; the snow and late afternoon made it hard to see.

Silk suddenly lifted her nose and neighed, her sides quivering with effort. From out of the gathering twilight came another clear, bell-like neigh and the sound of hoofbeats.

Dungiven came trotting out of the darkening day, his ghostly gray color looming in the twilight and the snow. He floated in the high carrying trot that horses in the wild have, his head and tail held high. He stopped when he saw them, and snorted. He breathed in, scenting them, and his ears and eyes fixed on Lynn.

He was huge. His winter coat had come in. Usually he'd be clipped and rugged up at Hunter's Chase. Here he looked enormous, his coat a dirty, yellowish gray. He had lost weight, but he was still enormous—seventeen hands and bulky despite his sunken flanks. His eyes and nostrils were dark, and his tail brushed the ground.

She dismounted and left Silk standing with one rein trailing on the ground. She didn't want to spook him by bringing a strange horse over to him, but she also wanted to leave Silk as bait. He watched her come, and his nostrils flared over and over as if he were remembering her by scent.

He let her approach, and she reached out and touched his neck. He quivered, but he bent his head until they were eye to eye. Lynn rested her head against his strong, thick neck, and they stayed like that for a long time, her forehead touching his rough mane. Finally he nudged her with his massive head. "Come on," she said. "Let's get out of this wind." One-handed, she slipped the halter over his big head and clucked to him. He walked beside her as if they had never been apart.

It was full dark by the time they made it back to the barn, Lynn riding Silk and leading Dungiven, following the beacon of a lantern hanging over the barn doorway. At their approach someone pushed the door open and shut it behind them once they were inside. The dim light and warmth made Lynn sigh with comfort and weariness. The small crowd of grooms murmured at the sight of the big horse. Crae came forward from the aisle between stalls. He looked astonished, his mouth open in a little O of surprise. He touched Dungiven on the neck, as if he couldn't believe what he saw. Lynn watched with a tired smile. She knew the effect the horse had.

"Welcome to Trieve," Crae said. He looked at Lynn. "I heard the stories. I know what you told me. But seeing him—"

"I know." She nodded. "He took me that way when I first saw him. And he's not even at his best right now." *You should see him at a show.*

Crae just nodded.

The head stableman said, "We have a box for him with good forage. He'll be warm."

"Thanks." Lynn handed him the lead rope. Another groom took Silk, and she watched the horses go off to warm stalls and hay. She glanced up at Crae and half laughed, suddenly full of joy. "That idiot. Staying out there in that weather. Why on earth didn't he invite himself in?"

"He was waiting for you."

His simple statement took her by surprise, and she felt heat creep up her cheeks. Crae cocked his head at the door.

"Let's go in. The evening meal will be soon."

"No, I think I'm going to stay here for a bit. I'll be in soon though."

She shivered in the blast of cold air that Crae let in when he slipped out of the barn, but was soon absorbed in the peaceful sight of Dungiven eating hay, his jaw moving steadily under his thick white fur, one black hoof pushed forward by his nose.

The warmth of the barn and the peacefulness of the horses, their steady noises, their calm presence, gave Lynn a sense of warmth and peace herself. She leaned on the low wall of the stall and watched him eat.

She had told Crae that Dungiven wasn't at his best, but she thought she might have been wrong about that. Seeing him out there in the snow and the wind, his tail sweeping the ground . . .

Something wild had been captured that night and put away safe.

Lynn sighed and pushed herself away from the wall. He was only a horse, after all, a creature of simple requirements and no regrets. She could do well to adopt his attitude and forget the sense of freedom she had felt by riding alone.

Sixteen

The night of the first raid on the smithies, Tiurlin had her baby. Kate heard about it afterwards—all the women talked about it, their voices full of "Poor thing" and "Who's the father, can you tell?"

"That's women's work," Talios told her when she asked him why he hadn't attended the birth. "They wouldn't want me there." Kate, who had heard her mother's story about her experience—high-risk pregnancy, toxemia, and emergency C-section—shuddered. She resolutely stayed away from the women's tents, but in the end, they found her anyway.

The door flap to the surgeon's tent swung open, and Kate looked up from one of Talios's books that she had been struggling to decode. Oriani, the armorer's wife, ducked inside. The older woman looked tired and stressed. She pushed back graying strands of hair under her tattered kerchief. "Oh, Kett. There you are. If Talios can spare you, can you sit with Tiurlin and the baby for awhile? We're all at our wits' end. She can't be left alone, poor thing, and I've got a cooking pot to tend."

Kate hesitated. "Umm, I don't know." She looked at Talios over the surgery table, where he was cooking up drafts.

Talios nodded.

"Go," he said. "We don't have much to do here for the moment."

"Okay," Kate said. She followed Oriani out, blinking against the cloud-filled sky. Flurries stung her face, and she hunched into her half cloak. Marthen had given it to her at their last dinner. That had been awkward, to say the least. Now she just felt relieved to have it. She was desperate for a bit of warmth. Each night she could hear the rattling in her chest, and exertion made her lightheaded. The entire camp was feverish, and most soldiers were laid low by the flux.

Kate stopped to let a cramp pass, then caught up with Oriani. "You're a dear for helping," Oriani said. They hurried toward the little tent that had been set up for Tiurlin at the back of the encampment. "She has us worried. It takes some this way, especially the ones it's their first. We've all taken our turn, but someone said you could help, since you're the doctor's apprentice and all."

"I don't know anything about this, though," Kate said, panic rising.

"Oh, child, just sit with her for awhile. She might even want a girl like herself to talk to."

Kate kept her misgivings to herself.

The camp followers had a camp within a camp. They settled among the supply wagons, the temporary forge the armorer had set up, and the carpenter's shed. Their tents were small, and if they were with a man, his gear was stowed inside. Some even had simple doorsteps they swept every morning. Food smells rose from the cooking pots that perched haphazardly over small fires.

Kate remembered her first day in the camp when she had bedded down with Mojo. Then all she saw was a crowd of strangers, frightening and overwhelming. Now she saw the community.

From one of the tents came an intense, unending squalling. It sounded as if it had been going on for a while. A woman popped out of the tent at their approach. "Oh, there you are," she said with relief. She lowered her voice, though Kate doubted Tiurlin could hear her over the sound of the baby's raspy crying. "She's done nothing but stare since I've been inside."

Oriani pursed her lips. "Hmmm. Worse than crying. Has she suckled the babe?"

The woman shook her head. They looked at each other, and then Oriani said, "Well, I fear this one is in the hands of the grass god's daughter." She looked at Kate. "Just sit with her, and call if you need one of us. The god knows, we need just a bit of a rest."

Tiurlin was an unmoving form in the dark, squalid tent.

The baby continued crying, a hoarse, desperate sound, broken only when it gasped for breath. Irritation pierced straight to Kate's core. *God, can't it just stop?*

"Tiurlin?" she said timidly. "It's me, Kate. I thought you might want some company."

Tiurlin raised herself and peered at Kate. "Stranger girl. You did always think you were better than the rest of us. Well, do some good and make it stop."

It was hard to think with the baby crying so desperately, as if it knew it had to live its hardest in the little bit of time that it had. Kate looked around, straining in the dimness. A lantern hung from the cross pole, but it was burned out. The brazier was likewise cold. The tent was hardly warmer than the outside air and smelled of blood and urine.

Kate felt a sharp anger. How could they leave Tiurlin like this? "I'll be right back," she said, and ducked out.

When she came back in, she had a flat stone with a hot coal from Oriani's cooking fire and a bit of oil in a small cruet. First she lit the brazier, blowing on the meager bit of wood until it caught. She lit the lantern, adjusting the wick until it cast a warming glow on the tent.

In the light the tent remained slovenly and cold, but it seemed to warm a bit under the firelight. Tiurlin looked terrible. She had blankets at least, but her face and clothes were dirty, her hair snarled, and the baby had soiled her and itself.

The baby was pinched and dirty, its face wrinkled. It gasped more in between cries, and its little head looked dented.

The light seemed to have galvanized Tiurlin. She sat up a little straighter and whispered to the baby, attempting to rock it. "Hush now sweet child, hush now." Tears ran down her cheeks. "I have no milk and he will die, and I don't want him to. I don't want him to. What do I do, stranger girl?"

I don't know. I don't know anything about this! Kate found her voice. "What—what did Oriani and the other ladies say?"

"They told me how he needed to grab my tit, but they were all talking and clucking and he cried so. Then they said I had no milk, and even when I scolded him and shook him, he would not try, he'd just cry and cry. He just wants to die."

"Maybe—well, just try again. I'll be quiet, I promise."

"Oh, just leave me alone! He won't do it! I've tried and tried, and he won't suck!" To prove her point, she raised the baby roughly to her breast and fumbled open her covering blanket. The nipple of her white breast grazed the baby's cheek. Still crying, it automatically turned toward it and latched on.

Tiurlin gave a gasp and sat up straighter. *Don't move!* Kate wanted to shout. Maybe Tiurlin thought the same thing; she quieted her own tears, and even though Kate had made no sound, shushed her.

Kate nodded furiously, her mouth an O of wonder. The baby snuffled and snorted, but clearly it suckled.

The silence attracted attention: Oriani ducked her head in and looked around. She had clearly expected the worst, and the change in her expression spoke volumes. Both girls shushed her and Kate made furious shooing motions. Oriani's head disappeared. There was a flurry of excited conversation outside, and then someone made everyone go away.

As a way to contain her pent-up emotion, Kate began cleaning. The baby's suckling got stronger, and Tiurlin began a droning sort of lullaby, punctuated by sobs. As Kate worked, the tent became a cozy place instead of a dank hole. The blankets that Tiurlin had were filthy; Kate popped out, told Oriani what she needed, and in due time she had clean blankets, a clean dress for Tiurlin, and fresh diapers and swaddling clothes for the baby. Once the tent flap opened by itself, and someone shoved in more wood for the brazier. Kate shoved out soiled clothing and diapers.

The tent warmed up. Clean and full, the baby slept in Tiurlin's arms. Tiurlin wore Kate's half cloak over her shoulders, and she gazed down on her baby.

"Isn't he the most beautiful baby ever?"

Kate nodded. She sat next to Tiurlin and touched the baby's silky hair, tufting out of his snug swaddling clothes. He felt soft and small. "He's great. What's his name?"

Tiurlin's smile faded. "I didn't think he'd live."

Kate could have kicked herself. "Well, you can think about it now," she said.

Tiurlin looked doubtful, but she looked down at her baby as if the little boy would blurt out his own name. Kate straightened up a few more of Tiurlin's belongings and found a wooden comb with most of its teeth. She held it up, and Tiurlin looked startled, but she nodded. Kate began to work it through Tiurlin's long hair. She started from the bottom, patiently picking out dirt and snarls.

To her dismay, Tiurlin began crying again, but it was quieter. She wiped her eyes with one hand, and sniffled as she said, "I think it might have been better if he did die. He'll have a sorry life with me in this place. Only now, I love him so, and it will only make it worse. If he had died before, I never would have known."

"Don't say that!" Kate said. "Tiurlin, it will work out." She thought hard. "Can you go home? Won't your parents want to see the baby?"

Tiurlin craned around so she could look at her in shock. "Go home? What kind of foolery is that? They'd drown him, if I didn't."

Kate bit her lip and kept combing. She wondered who the father was. From Tiurlin's position in camp, it could have been almost anyone. Jayce? Tiurlin had a crush on him, but Kate thought that might have been worship from afar.

Combed out and neat, Tiurlin's hair was a dark gold, almost red. It caught the firelight and softened her features. Despite her swollen eyes and red nose, she looked young and pretty.

"You have pretty hair," Kate said hopefully. Tiurlin shook her head and put up her hand, as if to ward off compliments.

"Yes, that and my bosom are what bring men buzzing about." She gave a deep, tired sigh. "Take the baby and help me up. I need to pee."

Kate took the small bundle. The baby had wet its diaper again and was damp. Tiurlin got shakily to her feet and scrambled slowly and achily outside, clutching the half cloak around her. Kate grimaced and laid the baby down on the pallet and reached for a clean cloth. She untied the damp diaper, puzzling out how it was fastened without pins, when the tiny baby peed on her, catching her full in the front of her shirt.

"Yuck!" She darted back. The baby began to cry again. "Oh, shhh, baby, please," she said. She hurried to wipe him clean and wrap him up again, the warm pee turning cold against her skin. Great, she thought. Just great. It wasn't like she could just go change. She didn't have that many clothes. She picked him up and rocked him awkwardly, waiting for Tiurlin to come back. Whether it was the dry diaper or the soothing motion, the baby quieted. Kate's heart settled down.

Tiurlin came back in, walking stiffly and a bit wide-legged.

"Oriani said she would bring stew," she said. "And water, too. I'm parched."

"Good!" Kate said. She was ready to get out of there. She helped Tiurlin sit down and cover herself with the blankets. The baby began to cry again, and Tiurlin, businesslike now, exposed her breast. The baby took it like a pro. Kate looked away, a little embarrassed. "If you're okay now, I should go. I'll come back, if you want me to."

"All right. You can help tomorrow," Tiurlin said imperiously. Oriani came in with a bowl, and Kate ducked out, taking a deep breath of fresh air until she was doubled over with a barking cough.

Who knew it took an army of camp followers to raise a child? she thought, wiping her lips. She thought about what Tiurlin had said, that it might have been better if the baby died. Would she take matters into her own hands like that? Kate felt sick to her stomach just thinking about it. They could help all they wanted, but if Tiurlin wasn't well and content, it might not be enough. She breathed out in the cold air, watching her breath steam in front of her. Maybe there was another way to keep Tiurlin happy.

If she had Jayce . . . the problem was, Jayce hardly knew Tiurlin existed, and he wasn't likely to be much of a father. But then, who was around here?

She took another deep breath. Like it or not, unsuitable or not, Jayce was Tiurlin's heart's desire. Surely the girl deserved a bit of the happiness she craved.

Snow had drifted over the dark bodies of several of Jessamy's smallholders. Crae dismounted with the rest of the hunting party, letting the reins trail in the snow, and looked around. Smoke rose fitfully from windows of the little house, and the thatch was burned away. He heard the sound of retching—one of the Trieve stablemen. Crae knelt by one of the bodies, bludgeoned to death, and covered the dead man with his ragged cloak. He breathed out, stood.

"Who did this, Captain?" asked one of the Trieve men.

"Crows. Come. Mount up, and look to your weapons."

Stavin would have led the winter hunt. In his absence, Crae had wanted to help provision his friend's House before he journeyed on. A change of plans, he thought, stepping into the stirrup. The deaths of the smallholders meant that the crows were getting bolder. He would have to ride out with ill-trained men and hunt them down before they decided to take on the House itself.

He wished for his men at Red Gold Bridge and then put that thought aside. If wishes were horses, he told himself. He whistled, and the grooms gathered themselves around.

"We leave the hunting gear here behind—" He scanned the terrain, pointed. A small outcropping of rock jutted out by a nearby stream. "We can leave it there, come back for it later. Thank the winter god for an early snow. We can track them. Listen." He looked at them all straight in the eye. Too young, too old, too peaceful. "They must not reach the House. You all have crossbows. Use them."

He thought of Lynn's lucky shot with his temperamental weapon and thought, but didn't add, *If she could do it, so can you.*

They would have to.

The afternoon drew to a close before Crae and his riders came upon the first clear sign of the crows, a trampled spot where they had rested in a hollow down from the road. He scanned the debris where they had stopped, eaten, relieved themselves, but he didn't fool himself. Brin would have told them how far, how many, and how armed. He called his men around. "I'm going ahead to scout on foot. Keep your weapons ready."

He wriggled into the brush, following the trail the crows had left behind. They had struck out overland, heading roughly toward Trieve, but he couldn't tell if that was by design or accident. Not that it mattered. They could not be allowed to reach the House.

The sign became clearer and clearer, broken branches and torn clothing. Bloodstained snow. Then a body. A dead crow, impaled on a crossbow, and another stretched out on the ground. Crae stopped, stepped back into the woods. He peered through the woods, a thin line of trees that edged a sloping field of snow, thin yellow weeds poking through the light cover. The field was gouged up and torn; horses had come this way. There was another dead crow, out in the field. Crae glanced around, then looked up. The next tree had an inviting branch. He secured his crossbow, reached up, and pulled himself into the tree. The branch held, and he put himself into a fork, hiding as much of his body as he could behind the trunk and looked out to see what he could see.

On the other side of the field, marching away along the road, was an army, flying flags of cream and gold.

Lord Kenery's army, and it was heading straight for Trieve.

Lynn listened with the rest of the household as Jessamy and Crae argued in the kitchen. He was soaked, his hair plastered down under his wool hat. Water dripped from his jacket and puddled on the stone floor. Their voices rode over each other.

"Jessamy, he has thousands of men. You have no defenses, no men—"

"All the more reason you must go," Jessamy said. Her voice was calm, but her lips and face were so white her eyes stood out darkly, black pupils rimmed with blue.

"I can't leave you here alone to face down Kenery. Stavin would have my head."

"No. You have to warn Stavin. You have to warn Red Gold Bridge."

"Name of god, Jessamy, don't you think they already know! They have spies, they have couriers—"

"And if you are found here, what do you think Kenery will do to us! Lord Tharp's captain, Lord Stavin's friend. All you would do is to give Lord Kenery an excuse to put you to the torturer for information on Red Gold Bridge and put the rest of us at risk. Our only hope now is for you to carry the word to Red Gold Bridge and give them time to prepare."

"I will not leave you unprotected."

"You are a fool, and your presence will do great harm. Leave, Crae. Go back to Red Gold Bridge, where you belong."

He looked as if she had slapped him.

A boy came running in through the great hall, panting. "They're at the foot of the great stairs."

With great deliberation, Jessamy retied her kerchief, centering the bow just so.

"I will meet Lord Kenery in the hall."

Lynn and Crae stood amid the tense, fright-ened knot of householders while Lady Jessamy faced down Lord Kenery and his men.

He was a massive fellow in a dark, tiered cloak. A huge broadsword rested across his back. He towered over Jessamy, who looked up at him with equanimity, her hands folded at the waist of her simple skirt.

"Do you reject my request for men and provisions, Lady Jessamy?" he rumbled.

"By the Council's laws, it is my right to choose to grant aid, Lord Kenery. In better times, you would have been welcomed here and given all that you asked. By allying yourself against Lord Stavin, you forfeit that welcome."

"But you are not Lord Stavin, nor are you Trieve. You are, hmmm, Favor, are you not? You cannot deny aid when you are but a steward here."

"By contract and law, I am also Trieve, Lord Kenery. You were at our wedding, my thanks to you, sir. You witnessed my contract with Lord Stavin."

Could she really make him go away by citing laws? Lynn glanced at Crae, but he did not catch her eye. He was tense, his hand flexing by his side for a sword that was not there.

Lord Kenery bent toward her, and Jesssamy took a step back, blanching for a moment.

"You speak of the Council's laws, but your husband fights to break the Council. You cannot have it both ways, Jessamy."

"I follow the Council in all things, Lord Kenery."

"Then you would break with your husband."

"A wife can disagree with her husband; only the Council can sunder them."

He snorted. "And when we win, I will see to it that we will. Do you hear me, Jessamy? We will win despite the clever weapons Tharp has. The Council will dismantle all the holdings that stood against it, and you will go home to your foolish brother, and your daughter will never marry."

Color stood out on her cheeks, and her eyes were bright with tears. "Lord Kenery. We were never friends, I know, but—"

"This stopped being about friendship a long time ago, Lady Jessamy. It's about war. Your side started it. The Council is breaking up because of it. What will become of Aeritan, I wonder, because of this foolish war?"

"I will not give you men, or horses, or food, or anything else you ask," Jessamy said.

Lynn felt Crae stir against her. He whispered in her ear, barely above a breath, "Now."

When he lifted his head he moved to stand in front of her. Lynn took a step toward the kitchen, and then another.

Kenery was saying, "You are a stubborn fool, Lady Jessamy, and I will no longer ask but take. Horses. Food. Now."

His voice was cut off by the time Lynn made it back to the kitchen. She bolted for the barn through the sleet. Several more of Kenery's men and horses stood in the courtyard at the top terrace, waiting outside, but they were shivering and huddled by their horses, and paid no attention to her as she slipped around behind the barn to the small door that led to the back of the old byre. She had to duck under the ancient stone lintel and scurry into the main barn.

She shook from cold and fear as she dragged down Crae's saddle and began tacking up his horse, mostly one-handed, her broken arm twinging. She left the animal ready to go, and began on Dungiven.

She pulled down the biggest saddle and blanket she could find and pushed open the door to his stall with her hip. He snorted at her entry, his ears swiveling around with interest. If Kenery saw him, she hadn't a moment's doubt that he would commandeer the big horse for himself. She cinched up the saddle and found his bridle, stiff and cold. She shook it out to try to untangle it, and only made it worse. Desperate with fear, she sorted it out, threw the reins over his head, and shoved the bit rudely into his mouth. Dungiven's head shot into the air at her roughness.

She heard noise at the back of the barn and turned around. It was Crae, with two sacks of provisions and a couple of half cloaks. He glanced over her handiwork and got his horse, leading him out of the stall. Lynn followed with Dungiven.

He tossed a sack and coat at Lynn. She tied the sack of provisions to Dun's saddle and shrugged into the half cloak, tying the strings and pulling on her gloves. In the meantime, he shook out his cloak, revealing his sheathed sword. He buckled it onto his saddle.

"Ready?"

She nodded, and they mounted in the tight space, knee to knee. Dungiven danced beneath her, and she collected him, feeling the power in his muscles ready to release on her command. "You better know what you're doing," she told him. He grinned.

"Just follow me."

At length they heard indistinct voices outside the barn and the sound of the long bolts being pulled back.

As the two big doors were pulled open, they kicked their horses simultaneously, a shout bursting from her throat. Dungiven leaped forward, and Lynn had a blurred view of people jumping out of the way. Then they were through the door into the bright, cold winter air.

Riding down the terraces was almost harder than riding up. The horses had to half leap, half gallop. Dungiven got the hang of it almost at once, launching off each level as if he were jumping a combined training course. Lynn stayed still and balanced, tucked into the big saddle. Crae's horse had more trouble, going down to his knees once and throwing him wildly forward.

They made the last leap off the final terrace and turned toward the woods. Lynn let Dungiven have his head, and he surged forward. He was built for power and grace, not speed. Still, his stride was long and measured, and he gave her his all.

She bent over his neck despite the awkward saddle, and his mane lashed her face.

The horses had dropped to a trot, blowing steam and dripping with sweat, when Crae finally pulled into a walk. The wind picked up, and the snow fell thick.

"We can't stop. We have to keep them walking," Lynn said. Her teeth were chattering.

"I know. This way." He led her down a small hill off the path, through the trees. Looking back, Lynn could clearly see the trail they left through the snow, but falling snow was already filling in the hollows. The horses slid on their haunches, and then they were at a stream, the water dark brown against the white, puffy snow on the banks. Ice swirled around rocks that poked out of the water. Crae clucked to his horse and steered it into the water. Lynn took a deep breath and pushed Dungiven after.

They walked downstream, the horses stumbling in the icy water. Dungiven balked, and she kicked him hard and lashed him with the ends of the reins.

"Crae," Lynn said. "We have got to get them out of this."

"Not yet." His face was tight and grim. "Kenery can't find our trail."

He walked them along some more, until finally, he allowed them to splash out of the water and turn onto land. Immediately, though, he made them trot. Lynn shook her head, closed her legs around Dun, and the horse stumbled after.

An hour later, Crae finally let them stop. Both horses steamed. Crae nodded with his chin. "There."

Up ahead was an outcropping of stone with another slab leaning against it. "We cached the hunting gear here," Crae said. "Weapons, food, blankets." He glanced at her. "We can't make a fire."

"I know." She kicked her feet out of the stirrups and swung her leg over the saddle. When she dropped to her feet, she thought her ankles would shatter from the impact. Crae dismounted just as stiffly.

The cache was just as he promised. Lynn unsaddled the horses and grabbed a blanket, rubbing the horses dry with the rough material. Crae checked the weapons and supplies,

gathering up crossbow bolts and knives, and checking saddlebags. He tossed her one, and it landed heavily at her feet.
"Provisions. Put this one on your saddle"

She slid to the bare, cold ground under the leaning rock.
Her arm throbbed, and she held it across her chest. She looked
at him. "Sorry."

He hesitated and then grabbed a blanket and sank down
next to her, wrapping the blanket around both of them. "We
can rest."

"Good, because if we don't rest them, we aren't going anywhere." Outside the little cave the horses hunched under their
draping blankets. She glanced over at Crae. He sat with his
eyes closed, his head resting against the rock. "Will Jessamy
be okay?"

The blanket began to warm up, and Lynn's muscles relaxed. Crae's shoulder was hard against hers.

He replied without opening his eyes. "I don't know. Yes,
Kenery can bluster, but he can't do much to Jessamy. If the
Council wins, her brother will see to it she is treated fairly.
No, worry about us. Kenery will know we've set out to warn
Tharp. I think he'll concentrate on stopping us."

"That's reassuring," she said drily, and she felt rather than
heard his laugh. She had stopped shivering at least. She slid
down until she rested against his shoulder, her eyes closed. Just
for a few minutes, she thought. He put his arm around her and
held her close. He smelled of sweat, horses, and cold snow, his
body warming hers. It felt good to be held. He reached for her
hand and entwined it in his. Lynn listened to his muffled heartbeat. He stirred and kissed the top of her head.

Lynn kept very still, barely breathing. *Don't do this,* she
wanted to say. *Don't.* Instead, she lifted her face to his, and
they kissed. His mouth was sweet and insistent, and she responded.

They kissed for a long time. The blanket fell off of them.
Crae slid them both down until she was half on the blanket
and he on top of her.

Oh, I've missed this. She started to unbuckle his belt, trying to ignore the voice of reason reminding her that she hadn't
been on the pill for weeks, that she could not allow herself to
become pregnant.

"Lynna," he half whispered, half groaned against her neck.
It won't just be sex to him.

Oh, how she wanted to ignore that voice.

He wants what he cannot have: marriage, a holding. A place to belong.

Instead, he would be outcast forever, and she—she would never ever go home.

Still, she didn't pull back. Crae did.

When he released her, she scooted back against the rock wall, her mouth throbbing and her face raw from his beard. When he spoke, his voice was rough.

"I am sorry. I should not have done that."

"No. Me, too. Shouldn't have, I mean. No harm done, right?" She gave a shaky laugh.

"No," he said. He pushed himself to his feet. "We need to be on our way."

When the guard came to fetch him, Joe thought he was meeting with his lawyer again. Instead, his visitor was Mrs. Hunt. Droplets spotted her raincoat, and her blue kerchief was wet. The smell of cold, wet air came in with her, for an instant overwhelming the sour odor of the jail. Joe was confused. What the hell was she doing *here*?

The guard ushered him in and took up his position by the door. The other inmates and their guests kept eyeing Mrs. Hunt. She was wildly out of place in her fine coat and long, elegant pantsuit, with her bag and matching shoes. Generally not even the lawyers looked so good. She looked uneasy though. She untied her damp kerchief and smoothed down her gleaming brown hair, then thoughtfully and diligently folded the kerchief several times before crushing it between her fingers.

He gestured at the plastic chair on her side of the table, and she sat, still twisting the scrap of blue.

"I'm sure you're wondering why I'm here," she said, her voice giving no hint of her distress. Only her hands gave her away.

"The thought did cross my mind," he said, sliding into the orange and metal chair on his side. He leaned forward, chin on steepled fingers, elbows on the table. "This doesn't seem like your kind of place."

She raised a brow. "No, not generally. Nor yours." He was startled by her firm conviction. He had become used to everyone's suspicions. Now she was saying she believed in him.

"No," he said. "This isn't my kind of place."

"Then we need to get you out of here."

His heart leaped, then he remembered his bail. At his change of expression, Mrs. Hunt allowed a small smile.

"I had the bail process explained to me. Interesting. I will see to it you are released. But in return you have to do something for me."

He became still. He didn't want to hear. She rolled out the kerchief, a pretty, embroidered piece of material, and smoothed it out on the table as if ironing it with her fingers. Joe could see the pattern sewn on it, blue on blue, a running horse rampant on a blue field.

The silence lengthened between them until Joe ventured, "Ma'am?"

"The homeless man, the one you rescued from the Wood. Can you find him again, do you think?"

Joe stared at her. "What? Why?"

"Because it's necessary to return him where you found him."

"Mrs. Hunt, if I go anywhere near that guy, if I go near Daw Road, I'm back in here for sure. I can't go looking for him. Plus, he's locked away in a mental hospital somewhere."

"You have to try, Joe."

"I don't see what good it will do," he said. She looked at him straight, tears in the corners of her eyes. She didn't try to hide them or even draw attention to them by dabbing with her kerchief. They gave her brown eyes a dazzling intensity.

"Please," she said.

It was a Get Out of Jail Free card. Forget the crazy homeless man. He was by God going back to Texas; hell, he planned on driving straight through for Mexico. He'd had enough of this place, enough of jail. Enough of whispers, rumors, accusations, and fear. *Enough,* the voice whispered. *Time to move on.* Joe took a deep breath and looked her straight in the eye.

"Yeah," he lied. "I'll find your guy."

She nodded, and stood up and left without saying good-bye. *God,* he thought. *It will be good to get out of here.*

"Mr. Rosetti?" Joe called, standing on his landlord's front stoop. He rapped on the rickety storm door. Under the rainy November sky, the place looked seedy, run-down. The windows of his apartment stared blankly over the cement block garage. Long cracks zigzagged across the drive-way and up the walls of the structure.

He heard noises, and the door opened. Mr. Rosetti, hunched and dour, looked back at him. The aroma of a heavy tomato sauce rushed out at him in a flow of heat.

"Mr. Rosetti, it's me, Joe Felz. I wondered if you rented out that little ol' space over the garage, or if, well, I could come back for a bit."

The old man said in a crusty voice, "You were in jail."

"Yeah, they let me out. I just need a place to stay for a day or so. I can't pay, but I could do something around the place."

"I stored your things." Mr. Rossetti jerked his head at the garage. "I should charge you for that."

Joe waited hopefully.

"Eh," Mr. Rosetti said and flapped his hand with disgust. He turned back inside and then came back with a key. He handed it to Joe. "You can stay tonight, move your stuff. Where's your car?"

His car sat in its parking spot next to the barn at Hunter's Chase, unless Mrs. Hunt had it towed. "I took the bus from downtown. Thank you, sir."

He hurried up the stairs around the side of the garage and unlocked the flimsy door. The garage room was clammy and cold. He dug through his boxes for his blanket and came up with his tattered jacket.

As he pulled it free, a coin came flying out of the pocket and rolled onto the floor, circling madly until it rattled flat beneath his chair. Joe stared at it. In the gray afternoon light it gleamed dully, and he remembered: the beat-up penny he had picked up from the house on Daw Road. It hadn't brought him much luck. He left it there and continued to search for his blanket, finally pulling it out and wrapping it around himself.

Joe lay back on the stained mattress, rolled up in the blanket, and listened to the pounding of his heart.

The voice was quiet now that he had made up his mind, but the usual urgency was missing. He thought about what he needed to do. Pack his stuff. Take the bus out of town.

See how far you get before the police bring you in for jumping bail.

See how long it took to forget about Lynn.

When he woke, it was full dark, and he was disoriented, heart pounding. He lay there for a moment, then sluggishly struggled out of his blanket, sat up, and fumbled for the light, wincing as it flared against his eyes. When he could see again, he got up, stumbling for the bathroom.

The penny caught the light again, winking at him. Joe made a face and finally bent creakily and picked it up. Frowning, he turned it toward the light, catching the inscription. It wasn't even a penny after all, but a foreign coin. The lettering was worn, and he couldn't make it out. Russian or something, he thought. He flipped it over.

On the other side of the little coin was a raised image of a running horse rampant across a coppery field.

Seventeen

The wind caught Colar full in the face as he
bent over his horse's neck, galloping at top speed toward the
village with the rest of the raiding party. Mud and snow from
their full-tilt charge spattered over his armor and coat. He
rode with his sword held high over his head, guiding his horse
one-handed as they drove down toward the little town. He
could hear nothing over the sound of the thudding hoofbeats
and the war cries of the raiding party. Up ahead people came
out of their houses, milled around a bit, and then began to run.

Colar swept down on a cluster of running smallholders,
gaining on them with every stride of his horse. They turned
and screamed, scattering as he burst through them.

He drew up his horse in a spray of mud and water, froth
breaking off the horse's bit. The village was in chaos. Scouts
threw torches into the little houses, and smoke began to pour
forth. Colar spurred his horse forward and blocked a villager.

"The smithy!" he shouted. "Where is it?"

Wild with fear, the man pointed. Colar scanned the area
and saw a cluster of outbuildings set away from the rest of the
village. Habits were ingrained; he bowed his thanks to the
man, realized a split second later how foolish that courtesy
was, and kicked his horse toward the smithy.

Smoke rose from the forge, but the smithy was untouched.
The smith stood in front of it, a huge man in a leather apron.
He almost came up to Colar's head even on horseback. His
muscles bulged, and he held a hammer in one hand and a
crowbar in the other. Colar swallowed, wishing for the others
to get there. He held out his sword.

"Well, they send a boy," the smith rumbled. "I'm insulted."

"You are a prisoner of Aeritan's army, sir," Colar said. "You must come with me."

"I think not," said the smith and threw his hammer. Without thinking, Colar raised his sword to ward it off, and the blade pinwheeled out of his grip, almost taking his wrist with it. He cried out in pain and fury. *Another broken sword . . .*

The smith smacked the end of the crowbar in his empty hand. "Come and get it, boy."

From behind Colar a bolt smacked into the man's shoulder. The smith grunted and stepped back.

It was Jayce, with a handful of others close behind. The scout slung his crossbow over his saddle horn. He scowled at Colar. "What are you doing?"

The smith charged them with the crowbar, battering at their horses. Colar's horse bucked and squealed and dumped him to the ground in one ignominious fall.

The melee was vicious; the smith fought hard. Colar took a whack on his helmet that made his ears ring and his eyes water. The scouts swarmed and finally held the big man to the ground, stabbing him brutally until the smith lay still, covered in blood. Colar watched from the back, breathing hard, his head pounding, his wrist aching, trying to keep from vomiting.

When it was done, Skayler rode up, looking down at all of them, disgust in his narrowed eyes and downturned mouth.

"Have you finished the butchery, boys? Then let's get on to the next village." He turned to look at Colar, taking in the tears and the blood. "Next time you hesitate, Terrick, remember this: it could have been avoided, had you *done your job.*"

No one looked at him as they mounted up and rode to the next village.

The raiders came back bloodied over the next several days, many of their own men wounded or slung lifelessly over their horses. Kate heard the stories: the smiths did not die quietly. Word had gotten out, and at one village, smallholders ambushed the raiders. Retribution was long and painful, and after that, despite orders, the raiders showed no mercy.

The raids took their toll on the survivors. Skayler seemed to have aged overnight, strain etching deep grooves in his

forehead and around his eyes. Jayce and the other scouts lost
their swagger. Colar looked tired, strained, and thin. Angry,
like his father. Kate heard them fighting one night in their tent
until Lord Terrick smacked him. The next time she saw the
boy he had a bruise on his cheek and a split lip to go with the
knot on his head.

Please make it stop, she thought. *This has to stop.* She didn't
know if God could hear her in this place, or if the soldier's god
was the one she was praying to. In the end, she supposed it was
the latter, because the raids worked. She was eating dinner in
Marthen's tent when Grayne burst in, followed by Skayler, covered with dirt and blood.

"Sir. Tharp's on his way."

The day of the battle dawned clear, and the
sun rose red over the plain. A cold wind snapped out the
banners—blue for Terrick, green for Favor, midnight black for
Saraval—that waved over the wide half circle of earthworks
the army had raised on the frozen field.

The rest of the camp drew away from the front as the soldiers and the mounted troops took up their positions. Kate
went from helping Talios set up the surgical tent to helping the
ostlers mount up the final wave of horse soldiers. Torm, the idiot boy, clung to her, pawing and crying.

"Torm. Stop. Stop," she said, to no avail. Mykal snorted,
grabbed Torm by the arm, and slapped him hard. The boy just
screamed and then cried harder. Rolling her eyes, Kate took
him by the other arm and said, "Torm, let's go to the supply
wagon. Let's go, come on." Gradually she coaxed him away
and got him to crawl under the wagon. "See, just like we did
the first time," she said, squatting down to look at him. He
peered back at her through the wheel spokes. "Now listen. You
stay here. Don't move. I'll come back later, okay? I promise."

He whimpered, but he stayed. By the time she got back to
the ostlers, though, they were done.

"What's this?" Mykal bent down and picked up a dispatch
pouch, covered with mud. They all crowded around.

"That has to go up to the front," Kate said, excitement rising in her voice.

"Oh no no no," Mykal scowled. "They dropped it, they can

come back for it." Kate unbuckled the little pouch and pulled out several papers. Shocked, Mykal said, "Don't look in there! That's for the lords!" She ignored him and scanned the spidery writing that still didn't come easily to her. "These are orders." A wave of pure excitement swept over her. "I'll take it."

It was a measure of how much they did not want to be caught with the pouch that they agreed at once. One of the few horses left behind, a rawboned bay mare, was brought around. Kate ran and got her saddle.

It lay in the corner of the tack wagon, cold and small. She lifted it up, cradling it and feeling the familiar lightness of it. A strand of Mojo's wiry mane was caught in one of the D-rings. Kate closed her eyes for a moment, a flood of memories coming back with the smell of leather and with it shame that she had not thought of him in weeks.

The saddle fit the mare. She was taller than Mojo, but he had been a wide little horse. Kate tightened the girth and took the reins, and Mykal threw her aboard, the way they'd been tossing riders all morning. She adjusted the pouch strap over her shoulder. "Shouldn't be hard to find them," he said, squinting up at her. "Big army and all that. You look fine up there."

She grinned, gathered the reins, and gave the mare her heel. The mare snorted and leaped forward.

Sure, it was cool to watch the riders thunder off, but *damn*, doing it was even better.

Kate cantered over a low rise and gasped. The army spread before her, cohort upon cohort ranged in formation, pikemen, and archers, and foot soldiers and cavalry, waiting behind the earthworks. Beyond them, marching steadily forward out of the distance, was Tharp's army. A drumbeat rolled out, shaking the ground. Her muscles turned to water, and all of her excitement drained away. She steadied the mare into a trot and posted toward the battlefield, scanning for any sign of Marthen or any of the other lords. She thought she could make out his banner standing above the others.

She had expected chaos, but the soldiers held almost completely still as she trotted through the ranks. They turned to look at her but soon returned their attention back to their captains, awaiting orders, clasping and unclasping their swords or bows or long, spiky lances that poked into the sky.

She pulled up near one captain and lifted the pouch to catch his attention.

"Soldier's god, what are you doing here?" he snapped.

She found herself whispering in the waiting quietness. "Someone dropped it back at the camp. It's orders. I don't know where it should go."

"God's sake girl, not here. I've got mine."

"Well, where should it go?"

A horn sounded, and the speed of the drumroll picked up. Someone gave a shout, and the men shouted in return and clashed their weapons against their shields or thudded them on the ground. A massive wall of sound burst from thousands of throats. The mare lifted onto her hind legs and squealed. Kate rode it easily. "Where do I take it?" she shouted.

"Hide your head, girl!" he shouted back, and the men streamed past her, roaring a battle cry.

She decided to take his advice and found a place behind one of the embankments, pulling the mare behind the supporting timbers. The roar of battle was deafening. Rolling volleys shattered the air. Automatic rifles, she thought, and bent over the horse's neck. Men cried out and fell back to earth as they leaped over the earthworks, bullet holes tearing into their leather armor.

A soldier shouted at her. "Hey!" he said. "Take this to Lord Terrick! Quick now, not a moment to lose!" He thrust a pile of paper at her. She reached down and took it in shock. *He thinks I'm a courier.* With shaking hands she picked up the orders and shoved them into the courier bag. She flattened herself against the horse's neck, and the horse pinned her ears back as she burst into a long-legged gallop. There! Kate spotted a blue and red flag on the other side of a broad ditch. Kate gathered the reins, put herself into a half seat and leaped the mare over the gash in the earth. She had a blurred image of nasty stakes underneath, then they landed amid a splash of mud and ice.

Colar's father's only reaction was to widen his eyes under his helm. Panting, she pulled out the papers. "These are for you," she said. "And, sir, someone left this back at the camp." She held out the pouch.

He read his orders first and shouted a brisk command. Then he scanned the others. He made a face. "Lord Favor's." He pointed. "I can't spare another in your place. See the green, girl? Head that way. Keep your head down, and stay behind the ramparts."

She nodded and wheeled the mare toward Lord Favor.

The rest of the battle was a blur. At times the action hit a lull, and she could water the mare and let her rest behind one of the ramparts. They were both covered with mud. Then someone would cry out, "Courier!" and she would mount up again.

They were losing; she knew it. The guns had a longer range. Every time Marthen tried to advance, his men got beat back by the relentless automatic fire. They had to retreat behind the embankments, and they were not sufficient to protect all of the men. Kate sank down behind an earthwork and held her hands over her ears. The mare rested next to her, head low, reins drooping.

The horns rang out a different note, and Kate looked up. All around her men were pulling back, milling around her like a wave.

"What's going on?" she asked. *Please say we're leaving.* No one answered, and she dared to poke her head over the wall. The army was re-forming, and out behind the ramparts came an odd thing. Kate stared until it registered, and a soldier pulled her back down.

"What is it?" he said. "What did you see?"

Kate dredged up the words from Mr. Winick's fifth-period class, Intro to Western Civ, when they covered the Romans.

"Shield wall."

I have my tanks after all.

Marthen sat his horse and watched as his seven shield walls advanced slowly but steadily across the battlefield. All around them fleet-footed horse archers zipped to and fro, harrying Tharp's army.

It had taken them days to modify the shields and train the handpicked men to carry them. The natural inclination of each man was to place the shield in front of himself. Instead, each shield had to overlap the man next to him. In the middle, soldiers held their shields overhead, encasing them all in the protection of the armor.

The men trained for days, practicing throwing the shields aside once they had closed in, when Tharp's weapons no longer had the advantage.

Tharp brought his guns to bear on each wall, and the weapons took on a different note: the zinging noise of bolts ricocheting off the reinforced shields. As the walls drew closer, Marthen knew, the bolts would start to make their mark. He nodded to Grayne, and the lieutenant gave the command.

The horns sounded again, and Lord Saraval sent his men out to Tharp's left flank, a long, streaming flow of foot soldiers and horses.

The gunfire broke up into single shots but rallied. The enemy formation wavered, and the two lines flowed into one another.

A sustained volley brought down one of the shield walls, turning it into a crumpled pile of men and armor. Then another. Tharp was taking one after the other, hoping to kill them all before they reached his defenses. Still, the others moved forward inexorably. Marthen grinned. Tharp was running out of time; his line was breaking up, pulling toward Saraval's attack.

Now. He held up his hand and closed his fist. This time all the horns sounded, a mournful, overwhelming signal that rolled on and on until even Tharp's army paused to see what that awful call would bring.

The men threw off their shields. The rest of the army surged forward out behind the earthworks, swordsmen and pikesmen and crows, all howling like bears. Marthen closed his legs around his horse and spurred it hard in the flanks. The black horse reared and leaped forward. Up ahead, Tharp's line wavered and dissolved as the colors of Aeritan bled into it, black, blue, gold, and green. A few more shots rang out, but not many. Now the song of battle was the familiar one of sword on shield, the cry of wounded men, the singing cry of arrows overhead, the thunder of hoofbeats that matched a racing heart.

Marthen grinned behind his helmet, letting the madness of

battle flow through him and the world narrow to a single point. The only way out was straight ahead. He aimed his horse straight for the center of Tharp's army, carried along by the raging flow of five thousand men.

The moon rose over the snowy wilderness east of Trieve. The creek Lynn and Crae followed ran like a black ribbon through the land, moonlight sparkling over the top of the water. There was little forest here; the land was rough and wild, littered with brush and rock, with no cover. They followed the creek because Crae estimated that it would cut off their travel time by a few days at least and keep them off the road. By day they kept their eyes on the distant mountains that rode the horizon: the range that backed up to Red Gold Bridge. At night he kept track of their direction by the stars.

That troubled Crae. They were too exposed, he said. He pushed them hard, moving them night and day with only short breaks to sleep. Most of their provisions were grain for the horses, and Lynn got used to going on a meal of flatbread in the morning and one at night and all the creek water she could drink.

At night they rolled up together. That might have been part of the reason breaks were so short, Lynn thought with wry tiredness, but the truth was, she didn't feel like doing anything other than sleeping, and she thought that probably went for Crae as well. They said nothing, wrapped the blanket around themselves, and dozed until it was time to get going.

On the fifth day of their flight, they came upon a vast, shimmering lake at the bottom of a low, long bowl. The wind had swept it clear of snow so that the gray ice showed through. The same wind threw snow in their faces. Lynn gathered her hood around her face.

"I don't trust it, plus the wind is against us," she said. "We should go around."

He nodded. His face was bearded again. "Too early in the winter for it to have frozen long."

Both horses stood stoically in the wind. Dungiven was a massive puffball of dirty, off-white fur. Briar had turned from a shiny chestnut to a dull, plain brown. Lynn dismounted and began digging snow out from Dungiven's hooves. He had lost his shoes during his freedom, and his hooves had grown long and uneven, with cracks in the outside walls. She shook her head and remounted. They had more important things to worry about now.

They heard the arrow before they saw the men who shot it. It thunked into Crae's saddle, and Briar snorted and shied sideways. The next arrow caught the horse in the neck, and it reared and crashed down. Crae kicked his stirrups free and rolled clear. Lynn wheeled Dungiven around and kicked her foot out of the stirrup. Crae reached up and grabbed the saddle horn and the cantle, and pulled himself up behind her, grabbing her around the waist. She gave Dungiven her heel, and he bolted forward.

Another arrow flew overhead but missed.

"How did they find us?" Lynn screamed, bending low over Dungiven's neck. Crae held on to her waist, pressing against her.

"It's not Kenery," Crae shouted. He turned to look, and Dungiven stumbled at the change in balance, then regained his stride.

"Sit still!" she hollered.

"They're gaining on us," he said in her ear. She risked a look. Their attackers galloped toward the fugitives at an angle and would cut them off soon. Crae had his sword, and Lynn carried the crossbow and bolts on her saddle, but she knew she would be unable to get a shot off.

"Stop and let me down. I'll hold them off," Crae said.

"No," she said.

Dungiven began to slow, stumbling as he galloped out of the bowl up the hill. The riders had closed in until she could count all of them: eight, their horses big and well-fed. *Oh God.* The men were well-armed.

Lynn kept Dungiven trotting until they were completely surrounded, and then, when it was clear they had lost, pulled up. "Crae," she whispered.

"Stay calm," he said in her ear.

Dungiven snorted and breathed hard, steam pulsing from his nostrils.

"Hand off your sword, Aeritan," their leader said. His voice came from deep inside a hooded cloak, its accent strange. His men were all similarly dressed, their faces wrapped, only their eyes showing. The leader waved a hand, and one of his men reached forward and took the crossbow and bolts from Lynn's saddle. He gestured toward Crae's sword, and after a moment's hesitation, Crae unbuckled it and handed it to him. He inspected it and handed it to one of his men. "Dismount," he ordered.

They did as they were told, Crae first and then Lynn. Crae looked up at the leader.

"Men of Brythern," Crae said. "What brings you across the border?"

The leader eyed him up and down. "Whose man are you?" he demanded.

Crae hesitated, and a strange expression quirked his mouth. "No lord's, it seems, but I have recently served Trieve."

"The only men who are lordless in Aeritan are dead or bandits, or so I've heard."

Crae swept an arm out, encompassing Dungiven and Lynn.

"I must be dead then, because I could not claim to be such a poor bandit."

A chuckle rose from the Brythern men. Even the leader made a noise behind his mask that could have been a laugh.

"Why were you shooting at us?" Crae pressed.

"We're tracking bandits," the leader said. He stood in his stirrups and reached into the pocket in his jacket. "They've crossed the border into Brythern from Kenery and Red Gold Bridge, and they bear weapons of considerable power." He held out his hand, and Lynn craned to see.

Bullets.

The Greyhound station was nearly empty at that time of morning. A tired family huddled around one row of chairs by themselves; over in the corner sat a woman with a kerchief and two big shopping bags. Joe knew he looked just as worn-out. He kept to himself, his backpack between his boots, watching the rain slide down the high windows. He shivered in his light jacket. He had never spent a winter this far north. The cold morning air held a wintry chill. He hoped that by the time the first snows hit, he would already be in Mexico.

From the way the weather was going, that could be in less than a week. Fair enough. If his luck held (and he laughed sourly at the thought), he could be across the border by then.

Lynn and Kate were gone, and no amount of wishing or investigating would change that. Mrs. Hunt was an intelligent person; she'd figure it out that he had run off. If she really thought about it, she couldn't blame him, and even if she did, he didn't care. As he sat there, waiting for his bus to be called, he put his hand in his pocket and pulled out the coin, turning it in his fingers in the morning light. It was a dark brown, worn unevenly around the rim, and was roughly the size of a penny but thicker. The lettering was like no alphabet he'd ever seen. The horse running across one side of the coin copied the horse embroidered in Mrs. Hunt's kerchief. On the other side was the head of a man: short hair, straight nose, rigid mouth.

Over the intercom blared the announcement for his bus. Joe stuffed the coin back in his pocket, picked up his backpack, and headed to the lone pay phone next to the ticket counter. Just because he was going to bring the coin to Mrs. Hunt and see if she knew why it matched her blue kerchief didn't mean that he was going to stick around.

A cheerful fire crackled in the living room of the old farmhouse, cutting the chill. Rain rattled the windows, sliding down the old glass, blurring the view of the barns and fields. Mrs. Hunt brought out two mugs of coffee and handed one to Joe. His said Toomey Feed and Supply on it and had a chipped lip. He sipped around it. Mrs. Hunt sat cupping hers, her eyes distant. Her face, though still beautiful, was drawn, worried. Her lips were dry, and her hair even seemed to have lost its luster.

After a moment he set down his mug and placed the coin next to it on the coffee table. It took a moment, but she finally came back from wherever she was brooding and looked at it. Her expression changed from distant and worried to one of recognition and something Joe thought was relief.

"So," she said finally. She put down her cup but didn't move to pick up the coin.

"So I reckon you know what that is," he said.

"Where did you find it?" she asked. "Here, on the farm?"

"Daw Road. Garson's house. Mark Ballard was living out there. Bartender at Garson's place."

She nodded.

Joe went on. "What is it?"

"Money, of course."

"I never saw money like this before."

"Of course not. You wouldn't. The country is very far away."

"Are you from there?"

She looked away, out the window and through the slashing rain. "Joe, do you believe the stories about Gordath Wood?"

"Ma'am, after this summer, I'll believe just about anything."

"I knew someone once who didn't believe, but she hoped they were true. She wanted to be very far away from where she was. Her marriage had become a sham, but she had no recourse—nothing like here. No divorce, no settlement, certainly no alimony." She laughed. "And she couldn't go home, because her House was closed to her. So she went forward, the only way she knew how, into Gordath Wood. Over and over again she tried, hoping that the stories were true. Until one day she realized how to do it. It wasn't enough to just walk out into the woods. She had to *disappear*. And so she took some of her jewels and clothes and had her maids pack them into her trunks, and she set out through the Wood toward her family home. All she had to do was disappear between her husband and her first family. Out of sight between one and the other."

She looked at Joe. "As soon as Lynn rode off into the twilight, I knew we had lost her. The young girl, Kate, took me by surprise. Did you watch her go, by chance?"

Joe stared at her. Mrs. Hunt smiled. "Never mind. I'm sorry I confused you. The stories they tell about Gordath Wood are true. I should know. Seven years ago I disappeared, never to be seen again."

Joe found his voice. "Ma'am, are you saying that you know where Kate and Lynn are? You've known all this time?"

She picked up the coin and looked at it, her expression somber. "It's funny, isn't it? We all believe only in the fairy tales we want to believe. I didn't want to believe that the rest of the tales of Gordath Wood would also come true. That once opened, the gordath would become stronger and stronger until it burst a hole between the worlds. Lately I've been thinking how strange it was that for some reason, on this side of the portal, you people only know about the disappearances, not the dangers." She sounded irritated. "That's why we have to find the guardian, Joe. We have to close the portal once and for all, and he might be the only one to do it."

She was sounding dangerously like the homeless man. Joe licked his lips and tried again. "Mrs. Hunt," he whispered. "Where are Lynn and Kate?"

"They're on the other side of Gordath Wood. Seven years ago I opened a portal that swallowed them up, and it is trying to take the rest of the worlds with them."

A rumble of thunder rolled muted and distant across the fields, and for long seconds the windowpanes rattled. Joe looked down at the coffee table and the cooling liquid in his mug rippled. Mrs. Hunt looked out the window. "And, I'm sorry to say," she continued in her even voice, "that it appears that we are running out of time."

Joe followed her gaze. Across the fields toward Gordath Wood he could make out through the driving rain something dark flickering between the trees, creating a gap where none had been before.

A whispering took hold of him, thrumming along with his heartbeat, and he swallowed against sudden nausea. A wave of malice flowed from the gap, malice and something else.

Recognition.

Eighteen

The map table had to be pulled out of Mar-
then's tent and set in the snow to accommodate all of the officers who gave their reports. The camp buzzed with activity as
men reported in, received their orders, and set out again. The entire army was on the move this time, and men, horses, and wagons streamed past the table, splashing up muddy snow against
the table legs.

Tharp was on the run, and it was time to snap at his heels
all the way back to Red Gold Bridge.

*With the luck of the soldier's god we will drive him into Ken-
ery's arms,* Marthen thought, sitting stiffly at the table, poring
over maps and written reports, listening to his men. Not that he
believed in luck, except for what a soldier made for himself. He
preferred to put his faith in fast riders and dispatches.

And speaking of fast riders . . . He felt a flush of rage that
the girl had gone near the battle and that he had not even
known it until his captains had complained. They spoke with
fury about it. She had distracted the men, they said. She was a
child and could have fouled up their orders.

"It's happened before, General," said one veteran, his grizzled beard cut through with a nasty scar. "A novice does one
wrong thing, and men are lost. You should have seen her, scampering about as if it were a game. She should be disciplined."

Marthen tapped the table with one hand, struggling for
calm. *Do not school me, Captain.* He didn't say it. Instead, he
raised his voice. "Next."

Skayler, the scouts' second-in-command, saluted. "Sir,
we've found something." He glanced around at the crowd and
lowered his voice. "Important, sir."

Marthen waved a hand, and all but Lord Terrick backed away. "Go."

Skayler said, "We've found a strange wagon in an outpost not far from here. We've heard tales of this thing. The small-holders call it Lord Tharp's carriage. We watched it as it drove up to the camp without horse or oxen to pull it. It's carrying boxes, sir. Bullets. They take them out and load them into the weapons right there."

Marthen's breath stopped. He exchanged a glance with Lord Terrick.

"He's resupplying," Terrick said, something in his voice sick with understanding.

Marthen's chest tightened with rage and pressure. The spies had lied or been misled.

Terrick slammed his fist down on the table. It shuddered and settled deeper into the slush, as men all turned to look.

"It wasn't the smiths after all, General." His weathered face was drawn and strained. "Now what do you want to do? Kill the weavers? The shepherds? Perhaps all the milkmaids? What now, General? What butchery do you have in mind now?!"

It was Marthen's habit to let other men lose control, but he could feel the fury welling up in him until the blood pounded in his temples. He turned to the scout. "What direction does the wagon come from?"

"Southwest, from the Wood. They've cleared a road. We followed it but couldn't get too close. We were leaving tracks in the snow. We should take the girl, sir. She can tell us more about this."

Marthen considered, decided. "Take the girl. Make sure she comes back with a list of all of its strengths and its vul-nerabilities. Go."

The scout saluted and left. Terrick stared at him, an awful expression on his face. Marthen looked at him a moment longer and then said, "If I have to kill milkmaids, Lord Terrick, then milkmaids are the next to die."

They tacked up in early morning darkness, feeling their way around the horses' warm bodies as the animals huffed and stamped and finished the last of their grain.

Kate tucked her hands under her jacket, wishing she had thick gloves. Instead, cloth wrapped around her hands had to do. Snow hissed against her clothes, stinging where it struck her face.

"Scouts up," Skayler said, and they swung into their saddles. She wanted to ask Skayler dozens of questions about the strange wagon, as he called it, but he only glanced at her and said curtly, "No talking."

They rode in silence for several hours until they reached the outskirts of Gordath Wood, alternating walking and trotting. Their horses' hoofbeats were muffled by the snow, and she knew enough to be thankful that it would cover their tracks. She curled her toes inside her boots, wishing she had thicker socks. It would be warmer to walk, she thought. She took one hand from the reins and tried to tuck her jacket tighter around herself. Skayler called for a walk, and they pulled back from the steady trot, their horses blowing and steaming under the trees.

"The snow will stop soon," Colar said, drawing up beside her. He gave his chestnut mare a long rein, and she stretched out her dark red neck, wet and steaming. Kate looked around nervously to see if Skayler would yell at them for talking.

"G-good," she said, her teeth not quite chattering. She took a chance and asked, "Did you see it? This machine?"

He nodded. "At first I thought it was a wagon. But there was no hitch, and nothing to pull it. It made a huge noise, and the horses spooked and almost betrayed us."

Someone had a car, Kate thought. Could it be Lynn? Had she gone back through the Wood and come back with a car?

To look for me? Kate tried to keep her face composed, pretending to concentrate on her reins. She had to see this car and see who was driving it. If someone knew how to get a car through the Woods . . .

She could go home.

It felt remote, unreal. Didn't she want to go back? Of course she did. Of course.

So why did it feel so strange?

"You're deep in thought," Colar remarked.

Startled, Kate jumped. "No, I—I'm not. Not really," she stammered. She turned straight ahead, her face burning.

He looked away, too, and when Skayler called for a quicker pace, gave the mare his heel and trotted off. Kate watched him go, thankful for the snow on her red face, and collected her horse before nudging him into a trot.

An unwelcome voice beside her made the knot in her stomach twist harder.

"Don't even think about him," Jayce advised with his usual smirk. "He's too good for you."

She made a face at him. "Jayce, you're a jerk." She spurred her horse, leaving the scout to laugh at her behind her back.

They stopped twice more in the shelter of the woods, eating in the saddle and letting the horses rest. The leaden sky lightened, and the snow stopped, except for a few stray flakes. Kate couldn't tell how far they had come. She was miserable. Her nose dripped, and her hands were thick and clumsy with cold. One or two of the other riders had gloves; Colar's looked to be leather lined with fur. *He's too good for you.* She knew what Jayce meant. *Even I know that he will be Lord Terrick himself someday.* She stuck the other hand under her jacket again, hoping for some warmth to seep into it.

Skayler raised his hand, and at his signal they halted and gathered their horses in a tight circle. The captain caught her eye.

"The outpost is over that ridge," he said, gesturing at the fields that stretched unbroken and white away from the Gordath Wood. They sloped upward until they were broken by a distant hill, sharp-crested and rocky. "Colar, take the girl from here on foot." Jayce sniggered, and Skayler sighed. "Shut up, Jayce. Now. Keep below the ridge to avoid being seen, and when you get there, have the girl identify the machine and the supplies while you get a count of their strength. And then get out."

Colar and Kate both nodded, Colar with a quiet, "Yes, sir." They dismounted, and Kate winced as she landed on her frozen feet. Colar waved her ahead of him, and they trudged off, snow-encrusted grasses crunching under their boots.

Walking got her blood flowing. Her feet warmed up, and she could keep both hands tucked inside her jacket. She looked back once, and the scouts were gone. They were utterly exposed. The field was like a shallow bowl under the gray sky, the ridge cutting a jagged line into the horizon.

"What if they're watching from up there?" she asked. Co-lar squinted at the ridge.

"Then we are in trouble. They might try to run us down on horseback, or more likely wait till we are on the hill and attack us from there."

"You sound awfully calm about it."

He flashed a grin. "I'm not. But I don't think there's much chance of it. They are expecting an army to come along the road, not scouts from behind them."

Kate frowned. "Behind?"

Colar nodded. "We skirted them in the Wood and are coming up on their rear."

She hadn't known that. Kate nodded. "That's pretty slick," she said, thinking about it. "Still, if I were them, I'd post a guard in all directions."

"And you would be wise to do so. A warrior and a leader never underestimates the enemy." It sounded like something his father would say.

Kate flushed at his compliment, but something nagged at her. "Um, Colar, isn't that what we're doing right now?"

He halted, his face red with exertion and his breath steaming. They were about midway up the slope.

"That is why, when we reach the ridge, we are going to be careful."

She considered that and sighed. "Okay. You win. Let's go."

He looked at her and reached out and took her hand, tugging her along, her hand swallowed by his glove. She felt her stomach do nervous flip-flops.

At the top of the ridge, he led them from boulder to crevice, keeping low and sometimes waiting for long minutes before moving to the next hiding place. This was more tiring than their hard slog across the field and even, Kate thought, harder than their cold ride that morning. She was forever getting tangled in her jacket, and its bottom half was soaked and stiff from the snow, dragging at her. They hid in a tangle of scrub and peered down at the camp below them.

She counted a dozen men and the same number of horses, staked in a makeshift corral in some spindly trees, next to supply wagons. Tents, a firepit, and a pile of wooden crates took up the center of the camp. The crates had stenciled characters on them. Kate's head swam as she tried to read the marking. *But that's from home. Why can't I read it?* She saw the driver at once. His hunting camo made him stand out among the others. From the sound of his voice and the way he was waving his arms around, he was angry about something. She couldn't make out the words.

A small breeze tugged at the bushes, bringing with it a warm, metallic aroma and the gaseous smell of fuel. Kate craned a bit farther over the edge.

It was a Jeep, tucked beneath their vantage point. The ragtop was down, and she could see inside.

Glinting in the ignition were the keys.

Colar tapped her on the shoulder, and they slid back behind the brush.

"Well?" he whispered.

She couldn't stop grinning.

"Well," she said. "How would you like to bring General Marthen that Jeep?"

His eyes grew wide. "You—you can—"

She nodded. She had her learner's permit, and her dad had taken her driving a few times already in her mom's Volvo (he refused to allow her to drive his little BMW sports car). It hadn't gone well—he tended to yell—but she had the theory down, anyway.

This is a bad idea, her sane self scolded her. *Kate, don't do this.* She ignored the little voice, giving in to only one need. She wanted that Jeep. She wanted to show them all that she wasn't just a frightened shadow.

"We'll need a diversion," she said. She peered back out at the camp where the driver was standing at the fire, still haranguing the other men. Her gaze lit on the horses. "I bet if we frightened the horses."

Colar considered that and shook his head. "We couldn't scare them and get back to the machine in time."

"No, but you could, and then start running. I'll get the Jeep and swing around for you."

It was a crazy idea. He was going to say no. He had to. It was a crazy idea.

Colar looked at her, looked at the camp, and then slithered

backward through the brush. "Be ready to act. Meet me along the road heading west." He gestured toward the direction and disappeared.

Kate watched him go and took a deep breath. Her heart was hammering, her mouth dry. *Soldier's god, this had better work*. She worked herself down until she was almost on top of the Jeep and waited for Colar to stampede the herd.

At first the horses snorted and milled in the corral. The men at the fire ignored them. Kate, her heart in her mouth, saw something even worse: the driver waved his hand in disgust at the others and headed back toward his car.

No no no no no, she thought at him, panic welling up. *Go back to the fire.*

He kept walking, and Kate took a deep breath and gathered herself, half sliding, half running down the steep hillside. She reached the Jeep before the man did, even as he saw her.

"Hey!" He started running. Kate flung herself over the door and scrabbled for the keys.

The horses exploded outward in a tangle, frantic. The men jerked up from the fireside, and the driver halted, looked back. The horses bucked and kicked, and then burst through the makeshift corral, dragging ropes and stakes with them. Behind them burned a bright blaze, a tree limb crackling on fire. The men shouted and began to wave their arms and run, trying to contain the stampede, and the driver had to fight through them to get to the Jeep.

She turned the key, but the car didn't start. *You idiot! The clutch! The clutch!* This time she stamped down on the clutch and tried the key again. The engine roared, but she was so surprised she let her foot up too quickly and the Jeep bucked and died. *Oh no, oh no, oh no.* Kate stamped on the clutch, turned the key, and the engine roared to life. She released the brake and put the car into gear. Despite the trembling in her legs, she managed to step on the gas, and the engine revved. Praying, shaking, she let up the clutch and the Jeep spurted forward.

"No!" the man shouted as she wrestled the wheel around and the Jeep slewed in the snow. He jumped in front of her and Kate tromped on the brake and the clutch, barely keeping the engine alive, wheels spinning and throwing out snow and dirt. She shifted again, but her hand slipped, and the Jeep shot into reverse, barreling into the ridge. Kate was thrown forward and back. The engine coughed as the Jeep bucked, and she pressed down on the clutch pedal again and shifted into first.

The Jeep's wheels threw out a curtain of snow but could not get any traction. The man loomed suddenly in front of her, and with desperate determination she held off on the gas, letting the wheels catch up, and the Jeep shot forward.

"Shit!" The man screamed, and leaped out of the way. Kate caught a blurred look at him, and she bumped from the camp toward the road.

Come on, Colar, she prayed, scanning for him. She didn't dare shift; she didn't think she would be able to manage the clutch and the gas without stalling again, and the roar of the engine, the shouts and cries of the men, was overwhelming.

There. She caught sight of the young scout from out of the corner of the rearview mirror. He was running after her, jacket flying, head back, hair whipping in the wind. She slowed, heart in her mouth, as the driver came right after him, shouting and stumbling, roaring his frustration. Colar was almost there, but so was the man.

"Hurry!" she screamed, still trundling along. She couldn't stop, she would stall the engine; she knew she would. The man grabbed for Colar's jacket and missed, cursing himself as he stumbled and caught his balance. Colar jumped, grabbing onto the Jeep and pulling himself over the tailgate. With a breath of relief, Kate stepped on the gas, and as they shot off, she risked a glance in the rearview mirror to see the man standing in the snowy road, dwindling from view. Behind him, the camp was in shambles, loose horses everywhere and smoke rising from the fire.

Colar scrambled over the back of the seat and pulled himself up beside her, holding on to the door for dear life. She took a breath and shifted until they cruised along in third. The instrument panel blurred before her eyes, but she could make out that they were doing about twenty. They had less than a half a tank of gas.

Colar grabbed the roll bar and pulled himself up to stand on the seat, his boots braced and his head thrown back. "Look at us! Look at us!" he shouted. "Soldier's god and all his brothers! Look at us!"

His hair streamed back in the wind, and Kate began to laugh. *Yes, look at him,* she thought. *No seat belt, standing, for God's sake.* And then she thought, *Why not? It's the only way to fly.*

"Woo-hoo!" she shouted and took one hand from the wheel, punching her fist in the air. "We did it! We did it!"

Spewing snow in their wake, they sped toward the camp down the road that linked the two armies.

The ride that took them all day under the cover of the Wood took about an hour in the Jeep on the rutted, broken road. The short winter day had darkened when they approached the camp perimeter. Kate slowed and downshifted.

"Will they try to attack us?" she called out to Colar, sitting now, his excitement quieted. She had convinced him to put on his seat belt. The chill wind still whipped over them, but she turned on the heat full blast. She had tried the radio on a whim, but there was nothing but static on any of the presets.

"I'll show Terrick's colors," he said. He got out of his seat belt and took off the dark blue scarf that matched the one worn by his father, swirling it around him so the interior faced out, a muted heraldic pattern woven into the lining. Once again he clambered to his feet, holding on to the roll bar with one hand, waving the cloth with his other.

They got plenty of attention, that was for sure. The sound of the engine had alerted everyone, and guards and soldiers came running, followed by women, crows, and the rest of the army. Kate turned off the rough road to the rougher fields, bumping over the deep potholes and wagon ruts. Colar almost lost his balance and caught himself, gripping tight. He finally had to abandon his efforts to hold on and slid back into his seat, the cloak in his lap.

"That caught their eye," he said with satisfaction. He grinned at her, and she grinned back.

"I wonder what Marthen's going to say," she said.

He laughed. "Or my father."

It was the first time she had ever heard that impish tone in his voice referring to his dad.

The crowd parted as they headed for the center of the camp and fell in behind them as Kate drove slowly toward Marthen's pavilion. Up ahead she could see the war stallion rearing in a frenzy, two grooms at its head trying to pull it away. She began to cast about for a place to stop and ended up parking the Jeep in front of the officers' tents.

When she cut the engine, near silence dropped. She could hear the frightened neighs and snorts of the black horse, and the men's struggles to subdue him. She could hear the flapping of the tents in the wind and the creaking of the wagons, but none of the people made any sounds except for soft movements and wordless, quiet notes of awe.

The nobles parted, and Marthen and Lord Terrick came through, their expressions thunderous, Terrick's, especially, as he looked from his son to Kate. His eyes narrowed.

Kate bit her lip, and some of her triumph drained out. She avoided looking at Colar and opened the door and got out. She held out the keys to Marthen, and he took them, but he only stared at her.

"It's a car," she said, her voice tentative. "We don't get around on horses; we use these. Well, they aren't all like this one, there are lots of different kinds . . ."

Her voice trailed off at their expressions.

"It was amazing, Father," Colar said. "It was like flying."

As if that broke the dam, their words tumbled out in a rush.

"It's not a weapon, but we could use it as one—"

"It can frighten their horses—"

"You can lead the battle in it—"

"It goes faster than anything—"

"Well, it needs a road; it can't go through the Woods, although I think that's how it got here—"

Marthen raised his hand.

"Whose idea was this?"

"Mine," they both said, and she turned to Colar and scowled. "Stop that," she said. "He's just saying it to keep me from getting into trouble."

"Sir, I'm as much to blame," Colar said at once. Marthen raised his hand again.

"I am not handing anyone blame," he said. He looked at Kate. "Tell me what it can do."

"It has its limits," she said, feeling the excitement surge again."It has just under a half tank of gas. That's its fuel. Once that's gone, it won't go anywhere. It's faster than a horse, and it can carry stuff, as well as people, in the back."

She went around to the back and lifted up the tarp that lay over the small cargo area, and stopped, surprised. One long case lay there, along with several smaller plastic lockboxes. She was so taken aback she forgot to be polite. She held out her hand for the keys. "Let me have those for a moment." Marthen handed them to her, and she sifted through the bunch for right one.

The case lifted, and she caught her breath at the sight of the gleaming rifle nestled in the gray cushioning foam. Next to her, Marthen reached out a hand and caressed the stock.

"Is this one of Tharp's weapons?" he said, his voice calm.

Still staring down at it, Kate nodded. In its own protected space was the sight. She was looking at a sniper rifle.

"This—this is very dangerous," she said, stammering a little. "I don't know if it's loaded. That means has bullets in it. And I don't know how to use one, to load it, I mean. But I think it would be easy to figure it out." From what her mother had said, much too easy, if the defendants she tried were any indication.

"Are there bullets?" Colar asked, hanging over her shoulder.

"Colar, hold your tongue," his father snapped.

Kate twinged in sympathy. She tried keys from the ring until she found the one that opened the lockbox. Small boxes of cartridges were arrayed inside.

"These," she said, pulling out two boxes and handing one to Lord Terrick and one to Marthen. The general poured the gleaming cartridges into his hands and rolled one between his fingers.

"Like an arrow tip," he said to Terrick, handing him the bullet. "Hand me the weapon."

Kate lifted it out. It felt substantial in her hands, not too heavy but not light, either. Though she had no training, she kept her finger off the trigger and pointed it at the ground as she handed it to Marthen. He raised the weapon and pointed it at some distant target beyond the camp. His finger curled around the trigger. Kate picked up the scope.

"Here," she said, and he held it steady as she slid it into place. She stepped back. "Look through that."

Marthen nestled the rifle against his shoulder and put one eye to the scope. It took a moment, then he started and cursed under his breath. Colar and his father pressed in, but he ignored them. He looked at Kate with something like admiration.

"So, Kate Mossland, this is more like it," he said for her ears alone.

She kept a shudder from appearing on her face. Instead, she said, "I think there's more."

Marthen handed the gun to Terrick, who looked through the scope as Colar crowded close. Kate dug through and found a pair of binoculars. Her face brightened. "Oh, cool," she said. "We have ones like these at home." She took them out of the case and looked through them, adjusting the focus. The distant trees of the Wood leaped into clarity. Kate passed them on the Colar. "Here. Just turn this until you see what you want to see."

As Colar fumbled with them, she turned back to the Jeep, smiling a little as she heard his exclamation of astonishment. Then she found the real treasure in the bottom of the Jeep.

"Ohh." They didn't notice and would not have understood when she pulled out the radios. Colar passed the binoculars to his dad, who looked through them from the wrong end and frowned in puzzlement. Kate reversed them for him, then said to Marthen, "This is what you want."

He turned to look at her. The other nobles, exclaiming over the rifle and the bullets, caught on that something was happening and looked over. Kate turned on the radios, checked the channels, and handed one to Marthen.

She walked away by herself about twenty-five paces, out of the line of fire of the nobles who were still aiming in the direction of the Woods, and thumbed down the button.

"Can you hear me?" she said into the radio and watched as Marthen dropped his walkie-talkie into the snow.

She didn't have to explain to him the possibilities, only the limitations—batteries, interference—and watched him confer with Terrick and some of the others, the braver ones who dared to touch the strange new devices, as they talked about the implications for their campaign. Once Marthen looked over at her, his expression uncharacteristically soft, and she felt a nervous twist in the pit of her stomach.

Someone pulled at her hand, and she turned around. Colar nodded his chin away from the hubbub. "Come," he said. "They'll be busy for a while." They backed up, trying to keep from laughing, until they were near the war stallion's stockade. They were both giggling under their breath.

Colar tugged off his gloves and put them on her hands. They were still warm from his hands. "Your hands are cold," he said. His voice sounded strained. He took a deep breath and bent his head and kissed her.

It was an awkward kiss. His mouth felt stiff and strange, and their noses bumped. Kate was so startled, she wasn't sure what she was supposed to do. *Maybe . . . this,* she thought, and opened her mouth the least bit. It seemed to be the right thing. It felt right. She began to feel a whole lot warmer. He pulled her close, and that felt very good, too.

"Colar!"

With a startled leap they sprang apart. Colar whirled around to face his father. Even in the twilight Kate could see the fury in Lord Terrick's rigid form and clenched fists.

"Go to your tent," Lord Terrick growled. Colar hesitated, then with a curt bow he stalked off without looking at Kate. Lord Terrick's gaze swept over her, and without another word, he turned to follow his son.

She stood next to the stockade, utterly alone, butterflies roiling in the pit of her stomach.

Nineteen

Two of the Brythern men pressed in, their swords at Crae's throat, and he held himself still. Sweat chilled down his back, and the winter wind stung his face. The leader tucked the bullets back into his pocket, as if his captives were of no importance, then looked back at them, his gloved hands resting on the pommel of his saddle. Crae's neck prickled with caution.

"Had you ever seen those before, Aeritan?" the leader said.

Crae thought desperately. "I have. They are from the weapons that Lord Tharp has brought from a far nation to wage his war against the Council."

And it seems some have gotten loose. He wondered about that. Who was using the weapons for their own aims?

"Yes, Aeritan's at war within itself. Again. But that Lord Tharp is carrying it to Brythern is a matter of concern to us."

Crae said, "Sir, we may be on similar missions. My companion and I are traveling at haste to Red Gold Bridge to seek to stop these weapons from spreading across this nation and now yours."

"Just the two of you?" The Brythern leader raised a skeptical brow, barely visible under his face mask. "Should I fear for my life?"

"We're no threat to you," Lynn put in. She nodded at Crae. "Is that necessary?"

The leader regarded her for a moment and then nodded. The swords came down. Crae rubbed his neck with relief.

"To be honest, you look as if you are little threat to anyone," the man said. "But go ahead and tell me how our missions are alike."

Crae recapped, tersely. When he was done, the leader frowned.

"Do you know, I've heard a remarkably similar story?"

Crae couldn't conceal his surprise. The leader's eyes crinkled, and he turned around. "Bring the other prisoner," he ordered.

A small man was tugged down from his horse. He was as warmly wrapped as the others, but his hands were tied, and his face was covered completely with a cloth. One of the Brytherners yanked down his hood and pulled away the mask. Crae's jaw dropped.

"I knew I would find you, Captain," said Brin, and he grinned through a swollen mouth.

The wind lessened on the other side of the ridge, and they found shelter under a line of pine trees that bent north as if to point the way to Red Gold Bridge. The Brytherners scraped away the snow and laid a small fire with damp wood, dry tinder, and considerable expertise.

It had not been pure loyalty that had driven Brin to follow after his captain. Crae listened as his tracker filled him in. Watching them over the fire but saying little was the Brythern leader. He called himself Hare; not his real name, Crae knew. *There's something more here than mere bandit hunter.* Hare had called for vesh for all of them and a warm cloak for Lynn. Hare himself draped the heavy cloak over Lynn's shoulders, and Crae pushed down his annoyance. *He's too damned friendly,* he thought.

"Things are bad, Captain," Brin said, sipping his drink. His wizened face was red with cold, and his short gray hair looked more frosted than ever. He glanced at Hare and lowered his voice. "*You* know. And the earth shakings come almost every day now, and are getting stronger."

Crae frowned. "No guardians?" he said in a low voice, though Hare could hear every word.

Brin shook his head. "No sign, and half the forest is in darkness all day and night—and the other half is *shivery*."

"What I want to know," Hare interjected cheerfully, "is the state of the walls of Red Gold Bridge."

They stared at him, shocked silent. He shrugged. "Don't be foolish. We have spies. It's a major port. Something is taking down the walls of Red Gold Bridge, even without the help of the army of the Council."

Crae looked quickly at Brin. The little man nodded. "They brought along their siege weapons, took out the tower over the gate. Another earth shaking brought down the rest, but it frightened the Council so much they lifted the siege and fled back to Temia." He glanced quickly at Hare. The Brytherner waved a dismissive hand.

"I know—it's as if I am at a banquet at which I can't eat. No matter, here's a secret for you in turn. The walls of Cai-sone were rattled by an earth shaking a half month ago. Whatever is tearing down the walls of Red Gold Bridge is threatening Brythern and the lands beyond."

Lynn gasped. "Shit," she said. They all turned to her. "I just realized—it could be getting worse back home, too. Do you know how many people are in New York City alone? Crae, can we even stop this?" Her voice rose.

"If anyone can, Captain Crae can," Brin said staunchly. He jerked his head at Crae. "He knows more about the gordath than anyone who's not a guardian."

Crae's heart sank as they all looked at him, Hare still with that same watchful good nature. "I know little enough, and only what tales I was told by Arrim when I first came to Red Gold Bridge. He showed me the morrim and told me it was the anchor that bound the gordath to this world. He told me to tell my men to walk softly about it, for it was sorely wounded. It was cracked and fallen, weakened, he said, when the gordath opened in a mighty burst generations ago." He paused, remembering. "He said, 'It is the nature of the gordath to be open, for it seeks to live, just as men do.'"

They were all silent. Crae listened to the hissing of the fire on the wet wood and the raspy creaking of the pines. Arrim had pointed out the rise and fall of the forest floor, the strange markings on exposed rock that were signs of the explosive force of that long-ago rupture.

"Is this morrim all that is stopping the gordath from bursting open again?" Hare asked.

"No," said Crae. "He said that the gordath is anchored between the morrim. He said there was another, in another Gordath Wood."

"Another Gordath Wood," breathed Lynn, her eyes wide. "Yes. There is. My God, Crae. We call it Balanced Rock; it's just off the highway. Anyway, it sits on three small rocks, just like the other one, the one in your forest. I've never heard it whisper, but it's got a pretty weird reputation of its own. It's got to be it."

Crae looked at her. "On the other side of the gordath. Holding it down."

"Buying us time," she said. He could hear the excitement in her voice. "If it holds long enough, we could still find a guardian." She turned to Hare. "Will you help us?"

Crae opened his mouth to try to stop her, but Hare shook his head anyway.

"I have my own mission—"

"The weapons are coming through the gordath," she interrupted. "Close the gordath, and you've ended it. There's your mission."

He looked at her for a long time. Crae watched them both. Hare's eyes showed nothing over his mask, and Lynn gave him back stare for stare. Her face was all angles, thinned down like a fox's, her hair tangled around her forehead.

"Perhaps," Hare said at last. "Perhaps."

Crae looked down at his cup, keeping his misgivings off his face.

Marthen looked up from examining the radios on his camp table at Grayne's announcement that Lord Terrick wished to speak with him. He nodded to Grayne, who ducked out, and Terrick swept through the door flap, letting in the cold night air with him. Marthen did not rise, though he bowed his head deeply. Terrick looked at the odd instruments.

"So you have what you want," he said. "Tharp's weapons in your hands."

Marthen nodded. "Did you expect me to turn them down?"

Terrick paced in the small space. "I'm not sure we should use them. They could turn on us. The girl said their range is limited, and they will eventually become useless. I don't like relying on things that I know will quit on me."

Marthen sat back and looked up at him. "Are you concerned about the weapons or the girl?"

Terrick's face blazed. "I grow tired of your disrespect, General. I warn you, it is not too late to bring you before the Council, where you will answer for your conduct and your disgrace."

Marthen kept surprise out of his expression. Lately Terrick had been cranked as tightly as a crossbow, true, but that was out of proportion, even for him. *I will ask Grayne if he knows anything.*

"I mean no disrespect, sir," he said. "Come. Inspect these weapons with me. We can put them to good use the more we understand them."

Terrick gave him the look of a disdainful eagle, but he sat and picked up the rifle and the scope.

"Here," Marthen said. "Let me show you. Loading it was of little concern after all. Captain Tal has chosen five archers to practice with it, and the best one will carry it into battle." The archers wouldn't need their massive brawn to shoot the rifle; what he wanted was their trained sight. If the girl was to be believed about the rifle's range, all one would need was a clear shot to kill a man, without having to leave camp to do it.

If that man were Lord Tharp, this war would be over. And with that done, Marthen could turn his attention toward what he truly desired. On pretext of mapping their route to Red Gold Bridge, he pored over the blank center of the map and all the opportunities that lay beyond it—if a common man had the will and the courage to exchange one fortune for another. After all, however Lord Tharp was bringing weapons through the Wood, the fact remained that a door swung open both ways. With the right alliance, he could set himself up in a new world as lord, not commoner.

He thought of Kate Mossland, and for a moment his heart beat hard. That alliance was in the next tent over.

"Ah, there you are, my lady," said Talios, looking up as Kate ducked into the surgeon's tent. "How would you like to make a man very happy?"

Kate stopped short, her mouth dropping open, her face going bright red. Talios grinned at her expression and nodded over at the corner. Two crutches stood there with padded cross supports.

"The crutches!" she said, forgetting her embarrassment. Captain Artor would indeed be happy. "But isn't it too soon?"

"Eh, he's learned his lesson. I'll scold him severely to not overdo it and then leave him be. Let's go."

As they ducked out, however, Saraval's lieutenant hurried up to Talios. "He needs you—says his wound is not healing."

Talios snorted. "If the old bull would stay off his feet, it would heal just fine. Kett, take the crutches. I'll take care of the old man."

A little abashed, she watched him go and then headed over to the scouts' tent, butterflies quivering. She didn't want to see Colar at all.

The door flap to the scouts' tent was pulled back, and she could see why when she approached. Despite the winter cold, the tent was full of men sitting around the table, the lamp swinging overhead. A funk rose from a row of damp, ragged socks hung from a line strung from the tent's center pole, drying over the small brazier. The scouts were playing a complicated game with dice and cards. The new scout, the one who came from Kenery, had the largest pile of coins in front of him. He appraised her frankly.

Colar was not there, and she sent up a small prayer of thanks. Jayce was, though, his thin face as smug and mocking as always. She was reminded of her plan for Tiurlin, and her stomach went quivery again. She raised the crutches.

"Mr. Artor, here they are."

She knew better than to expect gratitude. The scout captain grunted, "It's about time. Put them over there."

She lay the crutches next to the wall of the tent, feeling everyone's eyes on her. She caught Jayce's eye, grabbed all of her nerve, and said, "I was wondering if I could talk to you."

The tent was shocked silent. Jayce looked at her, laughed shortly, and said, "No."

She felt her face flame up and without another word ducked out, followed by a roar of laughter. But she heard the strange scout call out, "No, no, go talk to her, man. What are you, a fool?"

The rest of the scouts chivvied him out with their laughter and mocking, and she turned as he came out, hopping on one foot as he put his boots on. She could feel the rest of the scouts watching from inside the tent. As was everyone else in the camp, it seemed like, turning to watch them in the cleared space of thick mud between tents. She faced down the scout, arms folded across her chest, and scowled.

"What is it?" he snapped. He had reddened, too. For once she really saw him. Skinny, sick like the rest of them, not much older than herself or Colar. If Tiurlin was the doomed girl at the back of the class, Jayce was the boy right there with her.

"This isn't for me," she said crossly. "Don't think it is. But someone likes you, and I thought you should know, if you weren't too stupid to figure it out yourself." She glared at him.

He looked dumbfounded. "Likes . . ."

"Likes. A crush. She. Likes. You."

He growled. "I swear, girl, you are a stupid cow." He swore, looked away from her, rolling his eyes. "Who?" he bit off, and she could tell it was against his very will.

Kate grinned. "Tiurlin. She's in the women's camp, and she has long blonde hair like you've never seen before." She ran off before he could say anything else, full of impossible happiness.

She still felt the glow when Grayne told her that the general wanted to see her that evening. Kate sat in front of her tent in the pale red light of sunset, scrubbing her boots. The sun threw a rosy tint over the snow, but Kate paid little attention to the view. The snow might be soft and white outside of the perimeter of the camp, but within it was slushy mud, waste, and manure that caked her once-gleaming boots. They were cracked and stained, and she grimaced at their condition. She stopped and clenched and unclenched her fist, looking out over the camp and the snow vista, the rose-red tinge fading with the setting sun. She used her half cloak to cushion her seat, a short stump that had not been chopped into firewood, and tucked her bootless foot underneath her to keep

warm. Her illness had mostly passed, leaving her thin and
weak but no longer at the mercy of her bowels. Her lungs still
rattled with fluid, and she often woke wet with sweat or chills
at night.

It was almost time for dinner. Kate sighed and put her boot
back on, then took off her second boot for its turn.

"Girl."

Lord Terrick stood before her. Kate started and dropped
the boot, jumping up and standing on one foot. She bit her lip
at the picture she must make. "Oh! I—"

He gestured irritably at her to sit, and at her hesitation—
she had learned that much protocol—he snapped, "Sit, girl.
You look like a fool."

Kate sat. Now Terrick looked as awkward as she felt. He
paced a short distance in front of her. She heard him snap off
a curse, then he turned back to her.

"I don't know what my son was thinking," he said at last,
tugging at his gloves and slapping one against the other. "He
had no right to make his advances to you. He is the heir to Terrick. His pledge is not his own to make." Unaccountably, the
dour lord hesitated, and his tone if anything became harsher,
but his expression softened with something like regret.
"Where he cannot give his hand, it is not right that he give his
heart. My son wanted to tell you this himself, but I thought it
best it come from me. There. It is done."

He glared at her as if daring her to contradict him. She
looked down at her boot, turning the worn object over and
over, willing her tears to dry up. When she could control her
voice, she looked up.

"It's okay, Mr. Terrick," she said at last. "My parents
wouldn't want us to get married either."

His expression grew thunderous, and she felt a flash of
self-satisfaction. She hadn't meant it, but she had just turned
the tables on him. Terrick rejected Mossland, and now Mossland rejected Terrick.

"Who are your people, child?" he demanded.

How could she put it? Would he even understand? "My father, well, he's a vice president at IBM and he runs the top-
grossing division there. He always says, try your damnedest

and never give up." She bit her lip, wondering if she had lived up to his credo. "And my mother is a lawyer." She straightened with pride. "She's in line for a state Supreme Court appointment." She missed them fiercely and had to blink back tears, staring straight past Terrick toward the distant horizon. "We aren't noble or anything. I guess that's what you really wanted to know."

"You told me what I needed to know." She turned to look at him at the strange quietness in his voice. For a moment his face was gentle with regret, then the old Terrick was back. "They sound good and well-bred people. Mind you honor them with your obedience, girl." He turned on his heel and was gone, back to his tent.

The campfires started flickering across the camp. The sun had almost set, and her foot was getting cold. Kate tucked her foot beneath her to keep it warm and reached for her other boot.

When Grayne called for her, she took a deep breath and headed for Marthen's tent.

Marthen already sat at the table, his expression stone. Nothing different there, she thought. But the table was barren of dinner. Instead, he was flanked by two men. She recognized them as captains, though she did not know them by name. Kate hesitated by the door flap.

"Sit," the general said. She sank onto the low camp stool. "Captain Sayard, Captain Elevin. Tell me what you saw."

"We saw the girl scampering about on horseback with no regard for her safety or drawing the fire of the enemy, sir," one captain said. "She rode at will, to and fro, distracting us all with her antics."

Kate gasped. "No I didn't! I was trying to help—I didn't—"

Marthen's eyes were dark spaces in the dim light. "Do you understand the havoc you caused? Do you understand that with that one foolish act, you could have destroyed everything we worked for?"

"The courier bag—someone dropped it while we were saddling up. I just thought—"

"There is a penalty for disobeying my orders."

Kate knew that. She had seen the floggings. Some had

been of camp followers. Talios had been barred from helping the victims to recover, though he gave out salve and instructions readily enough. Her outrage turned to fear. *But I was trying to help.*

The captains stirred uneasily, glancing at one another. "General, perhaps a warning—" one said. His voice died at the look Marthen gave him.

"Dismissed," the general said. They filed out, after giving Kate pitying looks.

When he spoke, it took her by surprise. "Grayne told me that the Terrick boy pledged himself to you."

She looked up, startled. Her heart beat harder, and her stomach knotted. "N-no," she stumbled. "He didn't."

"Oh? Are you just a camp follower now? You accept anyone's advances without a promise?"

"No!"

He was relentless. "Lord Terrick will never let you marry his son. Know that. You will never be Lady Terrick. I made sure that you would be spared the usual lot of unattached women in this encampment. That was not so you could make your own alliances. I told you to stay away from the battlefield. You defied me. It is time you learned the meaning of obedience."

"*No.* You have no right." It was hard to get the words out.

He came over to her in one stride and lifted her by the front of her shirt, his face twisted in rage.

"Don't school me on my rights! You are nothing here; do you hear me? Nothing! You walk this camp with impunity because of my protection! And you will obey me!"

He was roaring by the end of his tirade. Kate tried to get herself free but to no avail. Marthen threw her down, and she stumbled against the camp stool and went down.

"*Grayne!*"

The lieutenant came in so fast he almost fell over Kate. The general's face was distorted with rage. "Bring her to the center of camp. She is to be flogged for disobedience."

The steel door had a sign on it: "This door is to remain locked at all times." A keypad with a small display was set in the lime-green wall next to it. The administrator who escorted Joe and Mrs. Hunt punched in a code briskly, waiting for a muted buzzer to chime, and swung the door open, letting them pass through in front of her.

"We were so happy that friends of Mr. Arrim were able to visit at last. So many of our patients get so lonely here," she said, her heels tapping along the linoleum as they followed the corridor toward another set of doors. "He's a very nice man, and we think that once he's stabilized, we can find him a halfway home and get him on his way toward independence. Sometimes they can stay too long, you see." She cast a side-long glance at them under long lashes coated with mascara. "People think it's all about the insurance, but really, a lot of times doctors have to gauge the length of stay that can do the most good."

Joe just nodded, looking around. The institutional feel of the place had him uncomfortable. It was too claustrophobic. Too much like jail.

"Are you a physician?" Mrs. Hunt asked politely. The ad-ministrator laughed.

"No, I help by doing the best I can to smooth things over. There's so much paperwork. That's my calling, paperwork." She made a wrinkle-nosed, self-deprecating smile and pushed open the next set of doors. "Here we are," she announced.

It was a barren common room with several tables, a games cupboard, and an enormous TV. Five or six inmates were watching a news program with the sound off. Joe and Mrs. Hunt exchanged glances. He'd only gotten a brief glance at the man, and that was weeks ago. How were they supposed to recognize him? It would be pretty awkward to try to get that past the ad-ministrator, who was now looking at them, brightly expectant.

"It's all right. You can wait here, and I'll have someone fetch him and let him know he has visitors," she said. "You don't have to worry about being bothered. I know people are so uncomfortable around the mentally ill, but really, they're just like the rest of us. Just need a little extra help." She trilled her laugh and tapped off to the nurse's station, where a nurse and two bored guards waited. Joe and Mrs. Hunt drew to-gether, taking surreptitious glances around the room. It was an eternity before the door buzzed and Arrim came through, let in by another staffer.

He looked better than when Joe first saw him. He had filled out some and cleaned up. He wore street clothes, and his dark beard and hair were trimmed. He favored his right side a bit as he walked, but that was all the effect Joe could see of his wound.

"There you go!" said the administrator. She clapped her hands in delight. "You've got visitors, Mr. Arrim!"

He saw Mrs. Hunt, and his eyes widened. For a moment he fumbled. Joe thought he was going to drop to one knee. Was the man about to kneel to Mrs. Hunt?

"Mr. Arrim," Mrs. Hunt said, advancing on him with her hand outstretched for a congenial handshake. "It is very good to see you again. Please, come sit down."

The man hesitated but then followed her lead, taking her hand, and the three of them sat at the farthest table from the nurse's station. Joe could see the administrator watch with delight and then turn to the others to explain that Mr. Arrim had friends at last. One guard kept his eye on them though.

"My lady," Arrim whispered. "My lady."

Mrs. Hunt looked him over. "You look familiar," she said. "I remember you."

"I am called Arrim, lady. I was Red Gold Bridge's guardian. When you came to be his wife, and before you disappeared." He clutched hard at her hand. "Have you come to take me out of here? I know you must hate me for what I did, but I had to. He was holding the gordath open, and it was becoming dangerous. I had to stop him." He started to cry. "Please don't punish me by leaving me in here."

His agitation had alerted the staffers. Joe could see them break off their conversation and look over at the small group, with Arrim weeping and clutching Mrs. Hunt's hand. Her calm expression was replaced with one of shock and urgency.

"Hey man," Joe said. "Settle down." He glanced back.

"You guys all right over there?" the guard called. He put his hand to his belt, where Joe was relieved to see he did not carry a gun. He had a nightstick though, and what looked like a canister of mace, as well as a radio.

"Yeah, we're fine," Joe called back. "Just a little emotional, you know. It's been a while." He turned back. Arrim tried to control himself, his shoulders heaving. "Take it easy," Joe said in a lower voice. "We're not going to leave you in here."

Although he didn't know how they were going to get him out. As if Arrim could read his mind, the man nodded at the nurse's station, his eyes eloquent with fear and despair.

"Leave it to me," Mrs. Hunt said, as if opening locked doors with influence and wealth had become second nature to her. Still, there was a wrinkle to this she might not understand, Joe thought.

"Mrs. Hunt, you should tell them the money is running out. That's the way places like this work."

She threw him a glance as she stood and gathered up her purse, and her expression was knowing. Her mouth quirked into an almost smile as she nodded.

"Thank you, Joe. I will make sure they know that."

It took a few days for Arrim to be deemed cured enough for a day trip in Mrs. Hunt's care. She and Joe went to fetch him in Joe's old car, the windshield wipers beating against an icy rain. They drove out to the hospital on roads that were almost barren. Most people had fled their homes, and they passed house after house that was shuttered and empty. On one big mansion the roof had slid down like a cracked layer cake. Joe drove along the torn-up roads, once passing an official-looking RV bristling with antennae and instrumentation. He glanced at Mrs. Hunt.

"Must be looking for the source of the earthquakes," he said.

A strange smile crossed her face. "I wonder how they will explain what they will find."

She made him uncomfortable when she talked like that, and he decided not to say anything else.

It was a silent drive. When they picked up Arrim, he slid into to the backseat, his eyes dull. Joe figured that he was still pretty drugged up. Joe looked sidelong at Mrs. Hunt, staring resolutely ahead, her kerchief knotted over her smooth hair. She had taken to wearing it all the time.

"So what now?" he asked. "We've got your guardian. Where do we go from here?"

"Take us back to Hunter's Chase," she said. "The guardian and I will go through the gordath, back to our world, and he will close the portal. With good fortune, it will stay closed.

That is part of a guardian's job, to see to it the gordath stays shut tight."

"But what about Kate and Lynn?" Why wouldn't she be more up-front about where they were?

She was silent for a few minutes, then said, "If the portal does not close soon, it will cause a rift that will grow until it swallows the worlds. You saw what happened to the helicopter. Can you imagine what would happen when the edges of the gordath reach the center of the town? How about New York?"

He remembered the helicopter and the invisible wall that knocked it out of the air in an enormous fireball. But still. The thought of Lynn and Kate, abandoned to their fate, rankled him.

"You get to go home, but they don't?"

"It is not a reward, if that is what you are thinking. Consider it . . . a punishment." She looked as if she meant that.

"I don't buy it. I'll help you close this portal if need be, but not before we find Lynn and Kate and bring them home. I don't know what you deserve, but they deserve that."

"She's right." Arrim's voice was soggy from the backseat. "If we can't find them right away, we're out of time." His voice was quiet with regret. "I'm sorry."

Joe looked up in the rearview mirror. "We're going to take the time. Both of you—you caused this. You fix it."

"Joe!" Mrs. Hunt shrieked.

He turned his attention to the windshield and slammed on the brakes, slewing the old car around. It slid sideways along the icy road, slamming the driver's side into the massive boulder that blocked the roadway.

Balanced Rock had come off its supports and rested in the middle of the road.

Twenty

Night fell early in the barrens, twilight settling over them like lead. Lynn was grateful when Hare decided they would camp under the stunted pines for the night; Crae, she thought, not so much. She wanted to talk to him, get his take on things, but they were never allowed a chance to talk in private. Somehow a Brytherner was always at her elbow or the captain's. *All right,* she thought. *They can hardly keep us from talking when we're riding the same horse.*

Even under the scant cover of the pines the frigid wind found them, bitterly cold and penetrating. A Brytherner passed her bread and dried meat and another cup of vesh. Lynn huddled in her borrowed cloak, sitting on her saddle to keep off the ground, and stared at the fire. She let the warmth of the drink ease her bones. No one talked much. Beyond the fire the horses ate their grain, the munching soothing. She was reminded of walking through the main barn at Hunter's Chase in the evening, when all the clients had gone home and the horses finished their hay and grain in the cozy twilight at the end of the day.

"You finish tucking them in?" Joe teased when she came back to the apartment. He caught her around the waist, pulled her close. *"You smell like horses."*

"Ahem," she said, pretending to be offended. *"At least I don't smell like grease, and oil, and dirt, and—"*

The shower was small, but it fit the two of them, the warm water sluicing away the day's work.

She could almost smell his own aroma right then, the distinct, masculine smell of him. For an instant the here and now was driven away, and she imagined he was right there, right next to her.

A rustling came out of the semidarkness, startling her out of her half doze. Hare sat down next to her at the fire. Lynn felt a pang of loneliness. She had been so sure it had been Joe sitting next to her. "May I?" he said, and took her injured arm. "Can you use it?"

"More and more each day. The horse doctor at Trieve set it pretty well. It's healing nicely." She could hold the reins with her fingertips and move her arm somewhat.

"How did it happen?"

"We were attacked by crows."

"You and the captain?" he said.

"Yes." She became wary. She had thought he was making small talk, but it was starting to sound more like an interrogation.

"Have you traveled together long?"

She cocked her head and looked at him. Hare read her attitude and laughed. "I pried. I apologize. But I admit, I'm curious about you and the Aeritan captain. After all, you are strange companions. How did you come to be traveling together?"

She said, "The gordath brought us together. We saw its effects early on." She remembered the crushed smallholding and the little cairn Crae raised to the dead.

"I see. Shared dangers bring strangers together. And he's no stranger now, I judge. What does he mean to you?"

Oh. She looked around for Crae; he was no longer in sight.

"Where is he?" Hare shrugged; she took that to mean that Crae was relieving himself. "So why do you want to know?"

"I like to know what binds people together."

"Friendship." She said it too firmly and knew he wasn't convinced. *Probably because I'm not convinced either.*

He waited for more, but she held his gaze.

"Friendship," he repeated. "I think he would say otherwise, were I to ask him."

"Then ask him." She turned back to the fire. She could feel Hare watching her. Finally, he leaned over and whispered in her ear, "Who is the man whose face you seek in the fire?"

She stared at him, aghast. *How did he—*

He tilted his head. She couldn't tell if he was smiling. "Ah," he said. "Even the most ill-aimed bolt can strike a target."

"It's none of your business. I don't see why you need to know any of this."

"I need to know about the lives in my command. Your captain is in love with you, and you offer him the warmth of friendship only. Will disappointment turn him? These are all things I need to understand."

We're not in your command. "Like I said, you need to talk to him." She scanned the camp nervously for Crae. Many of the men had already wrapped themselves in their cloaks and slept. A few silhouettes stood guard. Outside the camp the world was in utter darkness. She strained to see, but her eyes were useless; she had ruined any hope of night vision by looking into the fire. *And seeing Joe.*

She scraped snow into her cup and wiped it clean. "Good night," she said with finality.

"A pleasant night to you, my lady," he said with elaborate courtesy. She untied her bedroll and wrapped herself up a short distance from the fire, trying to ignore the seeping cold. She closed her eyes, shutting out the firelight, but she couldn't close out her own confusion. She couldn't love Crae. She couldn't. She willed herself to sleep, trying to wall away her feelings.

Lynn woke with a jerk, someone's hand at her shoulder.

"It's me," Crae whispered against her ear. A shiver ran down her back.

As far as she could tell, the camp was nearly dead silent. Some men snored, but otherwise all was still, not even the sentries making a sound. She raised her head a bit, but she could still see nothing. She turned and rolled over into Crae's embrace. Instantly she was betrayed by her body's reaction.

"What is it?" she whispered, trying to take her mind off things.

"Hare. I don't trust him."

Me either. Not much we can do about it though.

"Why not?"

"Those bullets. I've been thinking about them." He shifted closer and lowered his voice even more. Lynn bit her lip to keep from pressing her mouth against his. "Someone is offering weapons and bullets to Brythern. I think Hare has come to seal the deal, not to stop it."

"What can we do?" she whispered.

"He'll try to stop us from closing the gordath. We can't let that happen."

She thought about her conversation with Hare at the fire. "I think he's going to try to pit us against each other."

He was silent. Lynn's muscles eased despite her efforts. Crae brought his hand behind her neck and twined it in her loose braid, pulling her the infinitesimal distance between them. Their kiss was as quiet as their conversation, and again he ended it.

"Be ready for anything." He slid away, letting cold air under her bedroll where his warm body had been. Lynn lay in the cold, shivering again until she fell into a restless doze.

When the sentries woke them all with low whistles, she sat up, twisting to get the soreness out of her body. It was before sunrise, but the sky had lightened, and she could see. She pulled on her boots and hurried off into the leafless, dry brush for scant privacy. *I will never get used to this,* she thought, finding a spot far enough where she could no longer see the camp.

On her way back, crunching through the snow, she jerked up. The hair on the back of her neck prickled. She could see the camp now, but there was no usual morning bustle. Men stood, but there was no fire, no pot of snow melting over the flames. One of the horses neighed, high and shrill. *Trust your instincts.* She found a tree, pressed herself behind it. They wouldn't have any trouble finding her—her footprints punched into the crusty snow—but she couldn't go back until she figured out what was happening.

She peered around the tree, trying to make out what she could see through the branches and the indistinct light of dawn. Finally the view came clear. Crae, his arms behind his back, a sword at his throat.

Someone stepped to the edge of camp, and her heart leaped into her mouth. "Come now, lady," Hare called out. "We must make haste this morning."

She thought he must be able to hear her heartbeat; she could scarcely hear anything else over it.

"Lynn." His voice sharpened.

What can I do? She thought furiously. She didn't even

carry a knife, let alone a weapon. She would have to elude
capture until she could steal one of the horses. Even then,
what about Brin?

She could run, but it would get her nowhere.

"If I have to send someone out there, lady, he dies. No second chances."

That was that. She called out, "Why are you doing this?"

"He's running out of time. Make haste."

She stepped away from the tree and came back to the
camp, cloak dragging in the snow. When she came up, her
hands were roughly bound in front of her, despite her broken
arm. Crae looked at her. His mouth was bleeding, and his
cheek looked swollen, but she had never seen him look so angry.

"Are you all right? What happened?" What had changed?
One minute they were all comrades, albeit distrustful ones.
The next . . . *He must have heard us talking.*

"We're hostages. He's taking us to Tharp. Probably for
weapons." His voice was bitter. "Gods *damned* Brythern bas-
tards."

Hare walked up to them, finishing a bite of bread. "Believe
me, you left me no choice. Those weapons cannot come into
Brythern in the wrong hands."

"Oh God," Lynn said. "Hare, you don't know what you are
doing. You have to help us stop this, not take your cut."

He didn't answer, just turned and waved a hand. One of his
men led three horses over to them, Dungiven and two others.
Hare swung into Dun's saddle. Lynn let herself be helped on
board the other horse. Brin was mounted up behind her, grabbing the back of her cloak for leverage and almost pulling her
off. Crae had to be wrestled on the back of another horse, still
cursing furiously.

Hare pushed Dungiven next to them, the cloth over his face
masking most of his expression, but she knew he was smirk-
ing by the wrinkles around his eyes.

"Interesting, your idea of friendship."

Fury rose in her. If she could have kicked him, she would
have.

He spurred Dungiven, and the horse half reared into a gallop. The Brytherner leading her horse clucked, and they jerked

forward into a bouncy trot. She thought, *Poor Brin,* and she concentrated on balancing herself on the rough little mount.

"I know where they're going," Brin said, his voice bouncing with every stride. "This is the old part of the Ring Road." The overgrown track ran straight toward the ridge that Crae had said backed up to Red Gold Bridge. It mostly disappeared under the snow but for two sunken tracks where wagons had rumbled. For one long stretch, squat, fat oaks bordered it, their bare branches arching across and snagging at the riders' heads. It would be pretty in summer, Lynn thought and imagined the road shaded by the trees. Someone must have planted them hundreds of years ago for that reason. Now it only looked sad and abandoned, the way winter gardens looked. The Brythern troop trotted beneath the bare branches, the horses clattering along in a stream of bay and chestnut, Dungiven and Hare leading the way.

The road began to climb, leaving the tree-lined avenue behind. The mountains loomed ahead of them, the snow-capped ridge rising out of the dark trees and disappearing in the clouds.

"We should reach the Aeritan River by midday, Red Gold Bridge by evening," Crae said, mounted up next to her. He looked more grizzled than she remembered seeing him, his face hiding behind his furred hood. He rode awkwardly, his arms behind his back. His split lip was swollen and purple, and she winced for him.

Hare shouted, "Aeritani! Come up here."

Their keepers led them to the front of the column, and she could see what Hare saw: a landslide had broken off the rising land and spread across the road, leaving behind a gash of dark brown earth among the snow. The snow on the road had been disturbed as well, the surface of it cracked in waves, like the ripples on a lake.

The ripples moved. Lynn stared with the others, watching the snow slither across the landscape, making a constant shivering pattern as if the surface of the ground were turning liquid. She turned in the saddle to look behind her. In the direction they had come the road was normal, the track of their hoofbeats punched into the solid snow.

Her horse shied and snorted. Lynn rode it as if they were joined and looked down. The snow shimmied around his hooves.

Then she heard it, a deep whispering, words just beyond hearing.

All the horses began to back up, rearing and stumbling in their efforts to run.

"Ride forward!" Hare shouted, controlling his plunging horse with his spurs and heavy hands. "We can't go back; it will only overtake us."

Lynn clucked to her horse. "Come on, let's go." She closed her legs, dropped her hands, urged him forward. He balked, but she insisted, and he took step after hesitant step, moving one hoof at a time. She could feel the ground shivering through his legs. It matched the whispering.

The horse reared, and Brin slid right off the back, landing with a thud on the ground. He screamed when the horse stepped on him and tripped, falling over backward.

With a rumble, the ground jerked sideways, and the horses fell like pieces on a rudely shaken chessboard. Lynn hit the ground hard, the wind knocked out of her. As she struggled to breathe, she could feel the whisper thrumming through her body until she felt it taking over the sound of her heartbeat.

When she opened her eyes, Crae loomed over her. His hood was thrown back; his hair was matted and wet. Cold seeped in at her back.

"She's awake," he called to someone.

Consciousness and memory came back, along with a splitting headache. "Ow," she said. "Is it over?"

"For now," he said.

More memories. "How's Brin?"

"As well as can be expected." He lifted her up, and her headache intensified, then receded. She looked at his hands, free of bonds, and exchanged looks with him. "Back in his good graces?"

"More that he needed all hands."

"Pragmatic, isn't he," she said, her voice dry.

He kept his arm around her though she didn't need it. Lynn

looked around. Brythern men collected the horses, soothing them. She checked automatically for Dungiven, and the big horse stood with the rest, head high, huge and white against the snow. He whickered at her, his nostrils flaring.

"Good," said Hare when he saw her. "We need to move. You can let her go now, Aeritani."

Crae's expression hardened. Deliberately, he said to her, "Are you well enough?"

She nodded. "I'm fine. Thanks." Her bones felt as if they were still humming with the frequency of the earthquake, but the dizziness had mostly receded.

They mounted up, Brin shoved into the saddle behind her again. His breath sounded funny, and he clutched his side. A broken rib most likely, she thought and felt a pang for him. Hare looked them all over and gestured to one of his men. "Untie them. They are too battered to do much mischief."

As the ropes were loosened, Lynn rubbed her arms with relief, and Brin followed suit. Hare, watching, said, "But be warned. If any one of you makes an escape attempt, all of you will be punished."

He didn't have to bother, Lynn thought. Her arm was killing her, and Brin looked as if he were about to faint. She clucked to her horse and pushed him after the others. He pawed and snorted, obviously distrustful, but the snow stayed still, the only remnant of its previous treachery the rippling waves drawn across the road.

Crae second-guessed himself all the way to Red Gold Bridge. By the time the walls of the stronghold rose through the trees, the carved rock streaked with snow, he had despaired of every one of his actions from the moment they left Trieve.

His face hurt, and his heart ached. He had failed— everything. Everything he had tried to fix remained broken beyond repair.

He turned around in the saddle as best he could. Lynn looked miserable, Brin even more so, his face drawn and his mouth compressed with pain. The little man slumped against Lynn and every now and then Crae heard her speaking to him, offering encouragement.

He thought about what would happen when they reached Red Gold Bridge. He had resigned his commission and no longer answered to Lord Tharp, but as Lord Tharp no longer answered to the Council, that might not serve his defense. And then there was the matter of Lynn. Crae felt confident that Stavin would speak for them both, but he had less confidence in Stavin's success. Much depended on Lord Tharp's war; if it were going well, he could afford to be magnanimous.

From what Brin had told them, it was not going well at all.

"Hold up!" Hare called, and they stopped, the horses blowing and stamping in the cold. The sun was a pale disk in the overcast sky. More snow was on the way.

Up ahead, through the trees, they could see movement along the road, a troop of riders cantering toward them.

With shock Crae recognized them. They were his men, led by Tal.

Tal halted his horse and called out, "Identify yourselves."

Hare took his time. "Marai, vice governor of Cai-sone," he answered at length. "I bear gifts for your lord." He swung a hand back at the three captives.

Tal and Crae's eyes locked. Crae sat straight, letting the young soldier—no, captain, now—see his position. A captive. Hostage. The young man hesitated, then nodded.

"On behalf of Lord Tharp, we accept your hostages. Follow me to Red Gold Bridge. Lord Tharp awaits you."

He looked at Crae once more, his eyes widening a bit when he saw Brin holding onto Lynn for dear life, but then just nodded and wheeled his horse.

Lynn stared hard as she approached Red Gold Bridge for the second time. This time the solid fortress looked much the worse for wear. The outer wall had crackled and tumbled. The guardhouses were rubble. The soaring bridge over which she had ridden months ago had collapsed into a pile of stone, and the stream had spilled out around it, flooding the terrain toward the river. They had to enter the stronghold from one of the smaller courtyards facing the river, and even there the walls were shored up with timber and hastily patched.

The ground rumbled, and pebbles bounced down the newly mortared walls. The rumbling subsided but then welled up again. The constant shaking took hold of her bones. *How can people live like this?* she thought.

Four Brytherners stationed themselves around the hostages, but the young man, Tal, called out, "Hey!" The young captain flushed but said firmly enough, "Swords up. My men will guard the hostages. Jevin. Harabal." He jerked his head at two men, and they stationed themselves around the trio. Still aboard Dungiven, Hare eyed them all but grudgingly called his men over.

"Jevin. Harabal. Good to see you," Crae said under his breath.

"Sir," they muttered.

Brin said through the pain, "It's good to be home, eh, Captain?"

Crae shook his head. He looked around at the toppled stronghold. "It all fell apart without us."

"So who the hell is Hare? Vice what of where?" Lynn murmured. She put her arms around herself. Her hair whipped around her face, and her back stiffened with cold.

Crae dropped his voice. "Vice governor of Brythern's largest city."

Hare dismounted Dungiven and handed his reins to one of his men. He walked over to them. "I ask neither forgiveness nor understanding," he said. "I have to do what is best for Brythern."

Lynn and Crae both spoke at the same time.

"Well, that's sweet of you," she said.

"You did the worst for Brythern," Crae said. He shook his head. "Look around you, Hare. Cai-sone is next. All the weapons that Tharp promised you, they won't stop this happening to your city."

Hare's voice dropped. "You ask me to believe a tale of a doorway between worlds?"

"You rode through the earth shaking," Crae said. "You even told us there was an earth shaking in Cai-sone. What more do you want?"

"I want those weapons."

He turned on his heel, his long cloak swirling around him, and stalked off. Crae watched him go, his face twisted in anger. "Just give me my sword," he said through gritted teeth.

Lynn bumped him with her shoulder. "Hey. We still have a chance," she said. "We can still talk to Tharp . . ."

Her voice trailed off at the look on his face.

Someone gave a shout, and they turned to look. Tharp hurried out of the stronghold, followed by his men. "Speak of the devil," she muttered and then looked again. "Holy shit," Lynn said.

Along with the rest of Lord Tharp's courtiers walked Mark Ballard.

They stared at each other in the wet court- yard. Mark's handsome face was sullen, as always. He was dressed in camouflage, a pair of sunglasses tucked into the pocket of his jacket like he was in Special Forces. "Lynn!" he exclaimed. "I knew it. I knew it had to be you! God dammit—"

"Bahard—*Ballard*," she said. "*You're* Bahard? *You tried to have me killed?*"

He made a face, turned to Tharp. "See, this is exactly what I was afraid of. She's not going to understand, and if she goes home, she's going to go straight to the cops."

Lynn boiled over. "Don't you understand what you've done? The gordath is ripping up everything in its path. Over here, probably back home, too. Mark, you have to shut it down."

He threw up his hands. "Oh Christ, not you, too."

"Quiet!" Tharp snapped. He looked older than Lynn remembered, his beard coming in gray and lines drawn like a map on his face. Lynn kept back a disparaging snort. *Yeah, war is hell, buddy.* "I will decide when the gordath is closed or not." He looked at Hare. "Who are you?"

Hare bowed deeply, gracefully. "I am Marai, lord vice governor of Cai-sone," he said. "Bringing gifts and greetings to Lord Tharp."

Tharp snorted. "The gifts are nothing more than my own belongings, misplaced. What do you want?"

"That, my lord, is for us to discuss out of the wind, I hope."

Tharp looked around at all of them. Lynn could see him taking it in, his missing captain and tracker, a lost prisoner, and his pet gunrunner, facing off against each other. She threw a look at Bahard. His sulkiness had increased. He caught her looking at him and scowled. She almost laughed, so happy that they were no longer involved. *What was I thinking?*

"In," Tharp said. "Everyone, even you, tracker," he said, meaning Brin. They all trooped indoors.

They wedged themselves around the table in Tharp's antechamber, Hare included. The Brytherner remained wrapped, though the room was warmer than the courtyard. Everything vibrated, and dust fell on the table.

Mark glared at Lynn. "Trust you to screw everything up. You steal the Jeep, too?"

"What are you talking about? What are you getting out of the deal, anyway?"

"None of your business," he snapped.

"Land," Crae said. "His merchant had him bring back rock and soil and told Lord Tharp where he wanted land."

"Shut up, Captain," Tharp said. "You are treading on dangerous ground."

Lynn barely heard Tharp's warning. Her jaw dropped. "*Really*. That's interesting." She looked at Mark. "Gold? Diamonds? What?"

If he was the Mark she knew, he wouldn't be able to keep a secret.

Mark snorted. "Better than that, if Garson knows what he's doing."

She knew almost before he finished speaking. "Oil."

He grinned. "Garson sent the samples out for testing. According to the geologist, we should start doing core samples someplace called Temia."

God help her, she saw his point. Then she came back to herself. "The gordath, though. It can't stay open."

"Yeah, well, it looks like Garson's gonna get some help with that, too. Once the oil companies saw the samples, they brought in scientists."

"Do you honestly believe that they will one, believe in the gordath, and two, be able to keep it open?"

"It doesn't matter what I believe, babe. It only matters that I get my cash and Garson gets his leases. Speaking of which . . ." He turned to Tharp. "You haven't come through with the rest of the payment—the land grants and the money for the rest of the guns."

"Neither have you, Bahard," Tharp said. "Where is the next shipment of rifles and ammunition?"

"I told you, I can't go back for the reloading supplies just yet. There's crime scene tape all over the place. The police emptied the house, and it looks like Garson is laying low until the smoke clears." He jerked his head at Lynn. "I told you, it's her fault. She tipped off the police."

If I had known, I would have. Lynn kept that to herself. No sense in making Tharp more worked up than he was. She settled on a different tack. "I hope the guns are worth it," she told Tharp. "Because he's getting the better deal, if what he's saying about the samples is true." She added, "And the gordath doesn't blow everything to bits."

As if to emphasize her words, the ground rumbled louder, and everyone held on to the table until it subsided.

Hare spoke for the first time. "What is this treasure that can be detected in rock?"

"Oil," Lynn said. "Fuel. It's worth a lot more than a bunch of guns."

"Shut up," Mark said. "Shut. The fuck. Up."

"Oh, you didn't want Lord Tharp to know that, did you?" Her anger had made her tightly focused, exhilarated.

"God, you fucking bitch. You know why I dumped you? You never could *shut up*."

Crae jumped him from across the table.

They went down with a crash, everyone scrambling backward out of the way, Crae grimly silent but Mark yelling his head off. Tal's men pulled Crae off; Lynn noticed that they hesitated for a few seconds before really trying and stepped in front of him when they succeeded. Tharp pulled Mark to his feet, his throat already turning red where Crae had throttled him. "You son of a bitch!" Mark said. "What are you, crazy or something?"

"That's it, Wessen scum!" Tharp shouted. "You're through here! Just like your lady, treacherous dogs all of you!" Crae shrugged off Tal and the others, still glaring at Mark.

Mark rubbed his neck and scowled back. He tugged his

jacket into place. "I'm telling you, Tharp, you want the rest of the guns, you have got to come up with the next payment. Look, Garson might be willing to renegotiate on the land. But you have to show him you're ready to deal in good faith."

Hare spoke up from his corner. He had not moved during the tussle. "Lord—Bahard, is it? Perhaps Red Gold Bridge and Brythern and your merchant can come to an agreement on our rocks for your weapons."

Lynn laughed. "Better watch out, Lord Tharp. I think Hare is moving in on your deal."

Tharp looked as if he were going to explode.

Hare didn't even hesitate. "I think negotiations will go better without an audience, my lord."

Tharp looked at Tal. "Get them out of here."

Tal saluted, and the guards pushed them out the door.

Kate lay on her stomach on her camp bed, eyes closed, willing the pain and nausea to go away. Her back was wet with blood; she could smell it, feel it matting her hair at her neck. The cold air only stung it more, but she couldn't have clothes against her, so she shivered in her dank tent, her teeth chattering. All around her Tiurlin, Oriani, the other women clucked over her, their voices rising and falling as they asked her if she wanted something to eat, to drink, to wash herself. Somewhere the baby cried, and Tiurlin broke off from clucking with the others to alternately hush and soothe him. *Go away,* Kate thought. *Just go away.*

The tent flap opened, and someone else ducked in. Kate didn't open her eyes.

She felt someone kneel by her, his presence big, masculine. "Well, Kett, what trouble have you gotten yourself into now?"

Oh God. Talios.

He turned to the others. "Bring me those bandages over there. That's right. Have you boiled snow for washing? Good. Give me that now. This is going to hurt, chick, but it has to be done."

The cleaning was dreadful, and she cried all through it. Oriani whispered something, and the rest of the women left, the baby's wail trailing away, but the armorer's wife stayed with them. On Talios's orders she built up the fire in the brazier so the tent warmed up and put blankets against Kate's sides so only her back was exposed to Talios's ministrations.

When he was done, he sat back and sighed. "Someone will have to help her relieve herself, eat, and dress. Her bandages will have to be changed often."

"The women will take turns," Oriani promised. She stroked Kate's hair, and tears leaked from under Kate's closed eyelids.

"Good," Talios said. He shifted again and stood. "You must heal, Kett. I need my apprentice. Do you hear me?" His voice sharpened. "In the meantime, I will have a word with the general."

From the moment the first lash fell, Marthen knew it had been a tactical error. The camp had gathered around silently, with none of the air of excitement that usually surrounded a flogging. A few men had to be held back, and the ostler's boy had howled long and loud until he was hauled off by his fellows. As soon as the last stroke fell, Marthen snapped out a quick, "Cut her down!" and returned to his tent. He sat in silence and alone through the night. Usually his orderly lit his lamps and filled his brazier; that night no one came.

In the morning, when the council filed in for their war-making session, he saw how they averted their gaze. Saraval had a look of astonishment, Favor a gleam to his eye. Only Terrick carried his usual sour expression. It was soothing, somehow, to know that whatever the situation, Terrick would face it as if he had eaten something disagreeable.

"My lords," Marthen said. He had planned all night how he would broach the topic. "The discipline of this army is my charge and mine alone. I know you would agree to this. The girl is a difficult case. She has no House but is not entirely common. I made my decision, basing it on our objective. We cannot afford to play at war."

He watched them exchange glances.

"Your explanation is accepted, General," Saraval boomed. "To war, then, sirs."

"To war," they said.

Too soon, Marthen thought. His heartbeat sped up. "I ask one thing first, Lord Saraval. As I said, the girl is Houseless.

Yet I do not think she is common. We should find a place to settle her, the right place for her."

They all looked around again. Puzzlement entered Lord Saraval's voice. "I think we have broader concerns to contend with, General. You told us your reasoning, and we accepted it. Disposing of the girl must wait."

Marthen looked at him, keeping his expression and his voice neutral. "I petition the Council to grant me the right to marry and representation on the Council and the government of Aeritan in exchange for my duties here."

The lords' faces were mostly blank. Only Terrick's expression was one of dawning understanding. When he spoke, his voice rasped. "You mean the girl."

"Wait," Saraval said, still well puzzled. "The stranger girl? Marthen, you just had her flogged."

Favor rushed in. "And as for any other women, all the women in my family are spoken for, General. I can't think off-hand of any one woman from any family of the Council who is free to make a match with you. I think, sir, that you should not shoot so high. There are many ways for a soldier to get ahead without Councilship—"

"Can you find any reason to deny my claim?" Marthen said, his voice soft again. Controlled. Now that he knew what he faced, he found he could face it with a calm heart. He turned to Terrick. "It solves your problem, at least."

Favor said, "What?" Saraval quieted him, but he stared at Terrick, his forehead creased with confusion.

"I do not need your help to solve anything, General," Terrick snapped. "You have far overstepped your bounds here."

"General, the girl cannot help you become a member of the Council," Saraval said. "High god knows I hate to say it, but Favor is right. This is not your path."

"The girl is not a commoner. She's of good blood." Marthen nodded at Terrick. "Ask him."

"What is he talking about, Terrick?" Saraval said.

Terrick answered as if the very question grated.

"I spoke with her. From what I can tell, her parents hold high positions in her country. She may be the equal of any of us, or more."

"Then he has no claim on her!" Favor cried. "She should

wed one of us! I wish to marry, and I think I would be a better match for the girl!"

Saraval pinched the bridge of his nose. "Favor, be still. Marthen, I don't know about this. It seems a bit fishy."

A commotion at the tent's door caught Marthen's attention. Talios threw back the tent flap, followed by Grayne.

"Get out, you foul abomination!" Grayne roared, his sword at Talios's back. The doctor turned on his heel and faced down the lieutenant, looking down at the shorter man.

"Get off me, you superstitious bootlicker," he said. He took a step forward, pushing the man out the door. Grayne backed up as if he were afraid to let Talios touch him, and Marthen was reminded of Grayne's rustic views.

"Grayne, leave him be," Marthen said. "Talios—"

The doctor swung back toward him, fury in his eyes. Who would have thought the doctor, with his tendencies, would have been so protective of the girl?

"You pig," Talios said. "You coward. You animal."

"Now what?" said Saraval, throwing up his hands.

"To the death, General. Outside. Now."

"Talios, don't be a fool," Terrick snapped. "You can't fight the general."

"Did you see what he had done to her? Go in there and look at her back."

Marthen forced back bile.

"This is not the issue, my lords," he said. "The issue is my petition. Again, I wish the Council to honor it as a marriage with all of the rights that entails."

"And you want to marry the girl," Saraval said with the air of one trying to get things right.

Marthen nodded.

"Who, Kett? You just beat her senseless. Now you want to marry her?" Talios's voice was full of disgust. He looked around at the lords. "Does she not deserve the Council's protection?"

The lords looked at one another. Marthen wanted to speak, but no words came. He thought his heart would burst from his chest.

"It's a puzzle," Saraval said. "If she is noble, it is a crime that he must answer for. If she is common, it's a crime between equals and must be dealt with in a common court. Regardless, we cannot make the decision by ourselves. She will have to go before the full Council to determine her position."

Marthen turned to Lord Terrick. "What of your son?" he said at last, speaking the words as if he had forgotten how. "Do you take his claim before the full Council as well?"

"Leave my son out of this." Terrick was rigid with fury.

Saraval turned to him. "Terrick?"

"My son—in the way of boys—thought he was in love. I ended it. There is no claim."

Saraval shook his head. "In the high god's name, what a mess. All right. This is a distraction from our true purpose. General, we will consider your petition and the girl's status. In the meantime, don't touch her again until we decide. Does that serve your purpose for now, Talios?"

"It's enough for now," Talios growled. He looked at Marthen and shook his head, the disgust still clear in his eyes. With another curse he threw back the flap so violently the whole tent shook and ducked out into the cold morning.

Terrick sat down heavily. "Where were we?" he said.

"Our next campaign," Saraval said, clearing his throat. "General, if you please."

Marthen restrained himself from grabbing at his head to stop the pounding. He leaned over the map, pointing out their next move, willing his voice to obey him. "Attend, my lords. The scouts have word of Tharp's depot. I expect them to return as soon as tomorrow with its location. If we can stop Tharp from resupplying, we can cut off this war."

He had almost lost, but he had not lost yet.

Joe, Arrim, and Mrs. Hunt got out of the car, walking up to the boulder. The crossroads was deserted. There were the lonely half-buried rocks that had supported Balanced Rock, for millennia, Joe supposed. The rock had gouged a hole in the asphalt when it had come to rest. Joe laid a hand on it and jerked it back. The rock buzzed and whispered. It felt warm to the touch, despite the cold rain. He could almost make out the words it whispered at the edge of his hearing. The world faded, and he sank deep into the whispering, letting it take hold of him. It felt good to succumb, and his knees weakened.

He was yanked back, hard, stumbling, and the world came back into clear bright focus.

"What the hell?!"

"A live morrim," Arrim said, letting him go. "Very dangerous to a guardian." He gave Joe a meaningful look. "Be careful."

"Are we too late?" Mrs. Hunt said.

"I don't think so. The pinpricks they gave me in the house of healing are leaving me. I thought I never would feel the gordath again, but it's starting to come back. I think we are in time."

"Regardless, you must try," Mrs. Hunt said. "You are our only hope."

The day turned cold and frozen when they made their way over the cross-country course toward the woods. Joe shivered in his jacket. Mrs. Hunt was bundled in a shearling parka. Arrim wore an old duster someone had left in the tack room. They made an odd group as they went through the gate, closing it behind them, and walked up the long, sloping hill toward the trails. Behind them, the barns remained quiet and closed. Gina and the other girls who came to do the early morning feeding and mucking had been coming later than usual as the strange events occurred, and then left as soon as they could. No one wanted to be around Gordath Wood. Plenty of owners had taken their horses to other farms.

They walked in silence, their boots crunching over the frozen grass. As they followed the contour of the fields, they dipped down into a small decline surrounded by the outskirts of Gordath Wood. Joe was relieved to see there was no flickering darkness up ahead. He wasn't sure what was going on, but both Arrim and Mrs. Hunt seemed to know, and he decided just to follow along and see what was what.

He started to feel a twinge of nausea though, and his forehead sprang out with sweat despite the cold. Almost before he was aware of it, Arrim said, "We're getting close." His voice had become sharp, the sodden druggedness gone. He was no longer weepy and emotional; his eyes were clear and his expression intelligent. Mrs. Hunt nodded. Her face was pale, and the corners of her mouth were pulled down in pain.

"Are you all right?" Joe asked her. She nodded, as if she didn't trust herself to speak.

"It's the portal." Arrim threw a glance at him. He looked fine. "How are you holding up?"

"I think I'll make it. Is this what happened to me the day I found you?"

Arrim nodded. "When the gate pulls on a guardian, that is often the way it feels, for we are more attuned to its spell. But you withstand it well." He smiled. "Perhaps you are the son of a guardian who fell into your world long ago. It is said that it's a talent that is passed from father to son."

Joe grunted. "Not likely," he said. "Daddy was no guardian."

Arrim grinned. "And maybe some sweet-talking guardian visited your mother on a long afternoon. We've been known to do that."

Joe shrugged deep inside his jacket. Nice to think he wasn't his father's son, and maybe it went a long way to explain his mother's wistful sadness. "Yeah, well," he said. "Maybe."

Arrim laughed appreciatively.

Mrs. Hunt looked from one to the other but kept her own counsel.

Arrim went on, "You should come through with me and stay. We could use you."

Joe stopped dead for a step, surprised at the powerful attraction of the idea.

"I thought you were on the outs with that fellow, Lord Tharp," he said. "Not sure that's someone I want to work for." *Lords and ladies,* he thought. *Worse than working for Mrs. Hunt . . .* The thought trailed off as he realized that she was a lady. If he wasn't just being dragged into someone else's craziness. "Guess I'd have to think about it," he finished.

"Guardians have protections. If Arrim took action against my husband to close the gordath, the Council can determine his fate." Mrs. Hunt smiled. "I would step in to lend my support, but I may have little influence once I cross the gordath."

Arrim looked at her sidelong. "He loves you and misses you still."

"Perhaps." Her tone was final; she made it clear the conversation was done.

It took about an hour to get well into the Wood, taking a narrow, twisting trail Joe was not familiar with. Their path cut across several roads, but traffic was light; they saw only one or two cars. It was a weekday, yet it seemed no one was commuting that day. They skirted a little pond, still unfrozen and surrounded by willows, their bare branches trailing the ground, and entered a copse on the other side. Immediately the temperature dropped several degrees, and snow had spilled out along the ground, dusting the tops of the leaves and piling deeper among the rocks and broken-up ground beneath the trees.

"What the hell—" Joe said. "It only snowed under the trees?"

"Snow from the other side," said Mrs. Hunt. She pointed.

Snow was falling up ahead, between the trees, but only in a narrow swath framed by three giant tree trunks. Joe's mouth dropped. The rest of the woods were clear; the sky above was clear. But in between the three giant trees it was snowing hard, with flakes blowing out from a cold, sharp wind. And between the trees—he peered hard. It was as if he looked through a window of air. Forest yes, but a different forest, different trees, a different scene. *My God,* he thought. *My God.*

His nausea reached a sharp pitch, and he swallowed hard against the urge to throw up. Arrim had a strange grin on his face. Joe suspected that he was loving it, and he wanted to hit the guy.

"Let's go," Mrs. Hunt said, and they all three glanced at each other and went forward. Just before they stepped between the three giant trees, they grabbed hands like little kids, took one deep breath, and walked forward into the portal.

Twenty-one

Down a short flight of stairs beneath the grand chamber of Red Gold Bridge were three dark cells. Crae knew them rather well; he had thrown many an unruly merchant or smallholder in them to calm them down before they went to commoner court. Now his boots sank into the mangy straw as he paced in the little space. The windows were just above ground level, and he watched as a few boots went by his range of vision; some horses, rough wagons. There was not much traffic. Too cold, for one, and he suspected that many people had fled the stronghold as war and the gordath pressed in. As if to confirm his suspicions, the mountain shook overhead, then subsided.

Come *on*, he thought. He got up and paced, fretting. His hand kept going to his side, but of course his sword was no longer there, or his crossbows and bolts; he felt the loss of those even more keenly. *Damn Hare. Meddling Brytherner.*

And then, finding out that Lynn had known Bahard. *Balll-lard.* He tried to say it the way she did, but it sounded foreign and strange. It had been only slightly comforting to know that they didn't like one another, once it was clear that they used to be together, perhaps in marriage.

He breathed out a short oath and turned away from the window. Almost immediately he turned back. What was taking so long?

Outside his window, the scarce traffic speeded up. He heard shouting, other cries. At his cell door, the long bolt scraped back, and it opened.

"What took you?" Crae said.

"What? No thanks?" Stavin jerked his head back at the opening. "All right then. Let's go."

Crae hastened out after him. "Thanks," he said.

"It's nothing," Stavin said, handing over his crossbow, bolts, and sword. "Your man Tal said something about a letter."

He had written it when he had resigned his commission. *As your last order, Tal, if I am ever taken prisoner in Red Gold Bridge, bring my plight to Lord Stavin's attention.*

Tal had always been faithful.

Overhead the sounds of panic rose.

"What did you do?" Crae asked.

"Just a rumor. If this damned mountain cooperates, it will take that much longer before things settle down. I'll get the horses. She's in the old rose room."

Her old prison.

"Meet you at the stables," Crae said.

"Meet you at the stables."

Climbing up the stairs to the rose room, Lynn was reminded of her first days at Red Gold Bridge. Then, hobbling up the worn, ivy-covered stairs to the little room, she had been almost too tired to be afraid. Now her stomach twisted in a knot of apprehension. She followed the soldier up the icy staircase that wrapped around the outside of the tower. Snow piled up in the corner of each step where the wind had swept it. The ivy was brown and withered, draping skeletally over the stone.

Lynn shivered, wrapping her arms around her. This high up, the cold pierced right through her. She looked back out over the walls facing the wintry forest, mostly barren under the pale winter sun. The trees quivered constantly, and the knot in her stomach tightened. She paid for her inattention; her boots slipped out from underneath her, and she stumbled to one knee. She scrambled up again as the soldier turned around impatiently.

Lynn didn't know what was worse: to be at the bottom of Red Gold Bridge with the entire mountain poised to come down on top of them or to be locked in the rose room at the top. She looked back again.

"Come on," the soldier said. He held out his hand. She didn't think she recognized him as one of Crae's men—now Tal's—but it had been so long ago since Crae had found her on the outskirts of the forest.

"I'm coming," she said. She gathered herself up and followed him around the last turn. She took a chance and called out after him, "You know it's bad, don't you?"

He stopped at the top of the stairs, one hand on the rough wooden door, its new hinges gleaming.

"I can't talk to you," he said.

"Do you know how he is doing it? How he's keeping the gordath open?"

The soldier pushed the door open, gesturing her inside. She walked into the dim room, as cold as the outside. The fireplace was dark and bare, no neat pile of wood waiting to be lit. The bed was as she remembered it, a pile of heavy blankets and furs on top of the slatted mattress. Cold gray light from the door and the narrow window barely lit the chamber. A sifting of snow lay on top of the windowsill.

Home sweet home, she thought. She swung around.

"Have you been out there? Do you know what's going on?"

Instead of answering, he backed out. She called out to the closing door, "We came back to stop it. You should help us."

He drew the door behind him, and the locks fell into place. Now the only light came from the window. If she closed the shutters to shut out the cold, she would be in darkness. Lynn sighed and sat down on the bed, wrapping herself in the extra blankets. She would shut the window when it was too dark to see anyway. It was no worse than sleeping outside, as she had been these several days.

She shut her eyes, but it did nothing to quiet her mind. Ballard. *Bahard.* She had always known Mark was a jerk, even when they were briefly together. Always boasting about his business deals, alluding to the shady ones slyly and bragging about the next big score.

Stay with me, and I'll take care of you, babe.

She shuddered. *Babe.* That had been the last straw.

She felt the mountain shake again and threw off the covers.

"I'm not staying here," she said out loud to the twilit chamber, her voice quavering in time to the vibrating mountain.

She stumbled over to the dead fireplace, but they had learned their lesson—no pokers. Lynn scrabbled around for the small grate. She pulled it out and hefted it one-handed, and swung it at the door.

At the same time, the door opened. Lynn almost hurtled the grate into Crae's chest. He caught it and let it drop to the floor.

"You have a way with doors," he said.

"Only this one," she said. She grinned. "I was coming to rescue you, you know."

"I see that. Let's go."

She followed him down the stairs on the outside of the tower. The uneven shaking settled down again, but the wind had become razor-sharp with cold. Lynn inched down the stairs, one hand on the rough tower bricks.

"Is this safe?" she called out.

"No," he said.

She took a deep breath and placed each foot with care, trying to hurry. Her boot slipped, and she sat down hard on a step, jarring herself. "Damn." The mountain shook violently, and she slipped down three more steps. "Crae," she said through gritted teeth. He stopped, back against the tower, and hauled her to her feet. "It's doing it on purpose," she said, meaning the mountain.

"I know. Here." He unslung a crossbow and the quiver of bolts and handed them to her. She put them over her shoulder, her heart sinking.

"What for?"

"In case we have to fight our way out of here. Stavin is setting up a diversion, but I doubt it will hold for long. Do you remember how to shoot?"

She didn't think she would ever forget. "Yeah. Sure. What'll you use?"

"I have my sword."

All of his weapons had been taken from him when they were captured by Hare.

"Thank you, Stavin," she muttered.

Crae gave a muffled laugh. "I'll tell him you said so." When the quaking subsided, they continued down the stairs.

When they reached the bottom of the stairs, he unsheathed his sword. The mountain had settled, sullenly, Lynn thought.

Its presence hulked overhead. She gripped the crossbow and the quiver.

"Listen," she whispered. "I was coming to rescue you, but I can't stay. I've got to go back. I'm sorry, but I have to do what I can from my side."

"I know. We've got to go to the stable first, though." She didn't know what her expression held, but Crae gave a slight smile. "You can't go back without your horse, can you?"

The stables were an oasis of warmth; Lynn blew on her fingers and felt her muscles loosen when they slipped inside through a small side gate.

"Psst." Stavin came out of the gloom leading three saddled horses, including Dungiven. The big horse nickered when he saw Lynn.

"Good," Crae breathed. He clasped Stavin's hand, then gestured at Lynn. "Up. Up."

She slung her weapons out of the way and swung into the saddle. "Here we go again," she said. She glanced at Stavin. "We did the same thing in your barn."

He looked at her dubiously. "I am sure Jessamy will write to me about that, too," he said. He mounted.

"You shouldn't come," Crae said. Stavin waved a hand.

"Better if I do. If we're stopped, I've captured you. Or I'm a hostage. No." He forestalled Crae's protest. "Let's go, my friend."

They didn't burst out but rode single file out through the small gate, ducking under the low lintel, their stirrups scraping the doorframe. After that, Crae led them at a quick trot out of the courtyard toward the stronghold wall, where another door awaited them. Stavin slipped to the ground and unlocked it with a huge key. Again they slipped through, bending over their saddles through the tunnel of stone.

When they were outside the walls of the fortress Lynn took a deep breath of cold air. Crae pushed into a trot into the woods. *Almost home,* she thought.

Deep in the forest, with Red Gold Bridge ris-ing through the winter woods, the scouts surrounded a strange house. It rose tall and narrow, made of the same red stone of

Red Gold Bridge, and carried the shape of the mountain with it, as if it had been carved out of a long-eroded tor. Colar, pressed behind the massive trunk of an old oak, watched as Skayler signaled back to them. The lead scout lay prone in the snow. He had the peekers pressed to his eyes. He scanned the camp, his fingers flicking the wheel in the middle to make the view come clear. Every once in a while he would raise a hand, providing a count.

Seven men. Two on the second story. Each had a sword at his side and one of the strange weapons cradled in his arms. About a dozen laborers carried weapons and boxes of bullets and other gear out of the house and loaded them on waiting wagons. The wagons were almost completely full, their horses steaming in the cold and snow. No Jeeps here then, unless they were hidden. Colar wished fervently that Skayler would share the peekers.

One of the laborers suddenly dropped his large box, spilling bullets in the soft snow. He fell to his knees and began to vomit. The others gathered round, some looking nervously into the woods. The soldiers cursed and yelled at them. One kicked the man, and he began to scrabble for the shells, hastening to throw them back in the box.

Soldier's god, what a shot. Colar pressed his finger on the trigger of his crossbow and threw a glance at Skayler. The captain took down his peekers, shook his head, signaling him in silence. *Wait. Watch.* Colar nodded and eased off, but he bit his lip in frustration.

The forest rumbled, sending down a scattering of leafless branches. Colar gave a muffled *oof* as one hit the small of his back. Now he could see two houses, one very strange. Instead of the tall, stone house that looked like the mountain in miniature, he could see a low house with faded green boards on the sides and a pebbly roof.

Skayler capped the peekers and waved them all back, and they melted into the scant underbrush.

They rode fast and hard, galloping almost the entire way back to camp, letting the horses walk at short intervals before calling for another gallop. They pulled up at the ostlers' and dismounted their blowing, stamping mounts.

Colar handed over his reins and looked around surreptitiously for Kate. She wasn't there. *Probably helping Talios.* He wondered if he could find a way to see her. His father had demanded that he no longer speak to her. *But I'm through taking his orders.* Coming up on them that night and treating him like a child—that had been the last straw.

"Terrick," Skayler said. "Jayce, with me. To the general's tent."

They hurried through the freezing camp, a cold gray wind lengthening their strides. Colar ducked into his jacket, looking around for her. When they reached the officers' tents, they frowned. What were all those women doing outside her tent? He thought she kept herself apart from them. He turned to see as he followed Jayce, bumping into the other scout when they stopped outside the general's tent. Jayce scowled at him.

Grayne announced them, and they were met by the entire Council. Colar thought his father looked more sour than before. Father and son locked eyes; Colar turned away first. The general, too, looked as if he were unwell. Beads of sweat dotted his brow, and his hair was disordered. In fact, all the lords looked out of sorts.

"Sir," said Skayler in the uncomfortable silence. "We've found Tharp's depot."

They listened to the scouts' report in hushed silence, taking in Skayler's description of the house and the weapons loading.

Marthen's mind had settled into a cold lucidity. He thought, *Tharp is emptying his depot for one last assault.* The general stared at the white space at the center of the map until his eyes burned.

"We must intercept those weapons before they reach the stronghold," Terrick said. His voice sounded very faraway. "General?"

Marthen turned toward them. They were dark silhouettes against the brightness burned on his eyes. "I will take two hundred into the Wood to the depot," he said. "We leave at once. Saraval, you will lead the assault on the stronghold. Send Grayne to meet up with Kenery; he will attack from the south."

·

"General," Terrick said brusquely. "Two hundred? What is your purpose? That is too many for a stealthy force that can move at speed and too few to pose any threat to Tharp, if he repels your ambush. How do we stop the weapons?"

"I don't intend to stop those weapons," Marthen said. "I do intend to draw Lord Tharp into the forest to protect his supply line, leaving a smaller force to protect his stronghold. Lord Saraval knows how to fight those weapons, and Kenery is bringing so many men, they can stand on the piles of their own dead and still not falter."

He could not see Terrick's face, so he could not tell if the man believed him. The tent was so silent the only sounds came from Saraval's heavy breathing. Finally Terrick's silhouette made a motion that Marthen interpreted as a nod.

"All right," Terrick growled. "But I and my forces will ride with you, General."

"As you will," Marthen said.

In his corner, Lord Favor made a small sound. "And I, noble sirs? What part does Favor play?"

Marthen turned toward him, his cheeks frozen in an unnatural smile.

"You will tell Lord Tharp that we are on our way."

Favor rode off with five hundred of his men, his family's colors tucked under one arm and a letter of defection safe in his pocket. The Council and Marthen watched him go.

Saraval squinted into the distance. "Can we trust him?"

"Even if his nerve fails, as it likely will, he cannot help but deliver the message," Marthen said.

"But will Tharp take the bait?" Terrick muttered. He looked haggard in the cold winter light.

"He will," Marthen promised. He felt again as if he knew all the ways the moves would play out. "He will protect what is most precious to him."

Saraval just grunted and walked off, gathering his captains around him.

Terrick watched him go.

Marthen waited.

Still looking into the distance, the lord said, "Whatever the outcome of this war, General, I will see to it with all of my influence that you do not marry the girl."

Marthen's head started buzzing again, the hateful confusion that kept him from hearing or understanding, and felt a pang at the loss of the wonderful clarity that let him see Lord Tharp's every move.

Kate's back settled into steady throbbing, breaking out into fresh bleeding whenever she moved too much. But she could sit up for a while, and the wounds were healing with little infection, thanks to Oriani and the other women. Oriani had even painstakingly cleaned the mats and the blood from her hair, bringing tears to Kate's eyes, though the armorer's wife had been as gentle as she could be. Her hair was freshly braided now. Talios had moved her to the surgery tent, and she sat up at intervals to mix drafts in a tiny kettle over the small brazier. The tent was peaceful, warm. She could forget about being around Marthen, though it wasn't easy. She had heard the women whisper that Marthen planned to marry her once the war was over.

He thinks so, she thought. She had other plans. "There are always options," her mom said. Talios had spoken about helping her get into one of the schools of healing in Brythern. *It's not Harvard,* she thought, *but it will do.*

The tent flap opened, and Talios ducked in, his arms full of vials. He stopped for an instant, concern in his expression, and then carried on, setting down the small brown glass jars.

"You should lie down. Look, you're bleeding through again."

She couldn't shrug, so she settled for a look. "I need to do something, or I'll go nuts."

He snorted. "Worse than Captain Artor, you are."

She had to smile.

He put down his small vials and inspected the draft in the kettle. "He can't touch you again. The lords put a stop to it."

"Right in time, weren't they." She meant it to be acerbic; instead the words came out weary. When he didn't reply, she looked up. Talios regarded her steadily, and she felt the tears begin.

"I don't even understand why he did it."

"Try not to think about it," he said with an expression that said he knew how inadequate that was.

She made a noise that startled both of them, a laugh and cry mixed together. Talios reached out and pulled her close, mindful of her back. It was the first time he had touched her, and she began to cry more quietly in the comfort and strength of his arms. He rocked her, whispering words she couldn't hear.

Colar and his father dressed for battle in silence, helping each other with their harness. The tent was barely big enough for the two of them in their armor, making it hard to maneuver.

It hadn't taken long since his return to camp before he heard the news about Kate. He didn't know what he felt. Anger, confusion. Guilt. Had the general seen their kiss?

Did my father tell him? He felt a great welling up of rage and yanked hard at the buckles on his father's breastplate.

"Boy," the old man snapped. He caught Colar's arm.

Colar tried to step back, but his father's grip was like iron. Old or no, Terrick was like a bull.

"Save your anger for battle," Lord Terrick said.

"Let me go," Colar said, his voice as low as he could make it.

"Show me respect, boy, or you will sit out this battle with a cracked head."

"Let me go, you doddering old man," Colar said. "I don't have to listen to you."

The next thing he knew, his father had cracked him across the face with his heavy gauntlet. Colar sat heavily, legs splayed, blood spraying. He put his gloves to his face, trying to hold back the blood and the tears. His father watched over him for a moment and then walked out, leaving him alone.

By the time they crossed the bridge and trotted down the snow-covered road to the forest, the clouds were threatening snow. Trees hulked on either side of them, and the forest river rushed cold and gray. When Lynn had come this way last, she had deadheaded through the woods. She scanned up ahead, trying to see where she had fallen down the ridge into Crae's lap.

"Does the road take us straight to the gordath?"

Crae nodded. "We have to ride past one or two smallholds, and the road gets a bit hard to follow in the woods."

Stavin humphed, gathering up his reins and letting his horse prance underneath him. "From what I hear, getting lost in the woods is the only way to find the gordath."

"Not anymore," Crae said. "Tal said they built a road."

Stavin nodded. "Two: one to run supplies to the front, the other leading back to the stronghold." He shook his head. "I went out there once to help bring up weapons to the plains." He sighed. "It didn't do us a lot of good. Say what you like about the Council's general. He may be mad, but he is not stupid. At first we thought he had his own wagons. Then we saw that they weren't machines but men, marching in close formation, their shields overlapping them like a giant plated animal. By the time we felled them, bringing the weapons to bear, the rest of the Aeritan army attacked." He half laughed. "Soldier's god, if you told me they were machines I would have believed you, the way they rolled over the battlefield, every step taken together." His voice changed again. "I lost three hundred men that day."

What do you say to that? Lynn snuck a glance at the man. He had turned his head away from them.

"There," Crae said at last. "The road turns off here . . ." His voice trailed off.

One man after another stepped out of the trees lining the river, armor and weapons glinting dully in the gray light.

Next to them Stavin's sword scraped out of its scabbard, Crae's an instant later. He held Dungiven's rein, bent toward Lynn.

"Take him into the forest, straight up the ridge here, and make for the road by bearing due west. We'll hold them off."

"I—Crae, I don't feel right—I can't do that. I'll get lost." *I'm not ready. How will I say good-bye?*

"Then you'll be sure to find the gordath, remember?" He cast a glance at the approaching men, more and more coming out of the trees. "Run, Lynna. Now. We don't have time." He grabbed the rein again, pulled her close and said, "As soon as you find the gordath, ride through. *Ride through.*" He kissed her hard. "Go."

She gathered the reins and sat deep in the saddle as Dungiven half reared, waiting for orders. "I—" She started. There was too much to say. He gave her a crooked little grin, and nodded, as if he knew.

"I love you," she said in a rush and wheeled the horse. "Go!" she shouted, and kicked him hard.

They went straight at the hill at a gallop. Dungiven gathered himself and leaped at the slope. His hooves bit into the snow and dirt, flinging out chunks behind them. She sat still as his powerful hindquarters carried them up to the top. A couple of arrows whined past them, then they were at the top and sliding down the other side, bearing west as best she could tell.

She couldn't hear anything except the sound of their crashing progress through the woods, that and the pounding of the blood in her head.

Crae hefted his sword and glanced at Stavin. "Are you ready?"

"No." Stavin took a breath and raised his sword. "Let's go."

They spurred their horses forward as one, raising their voices in a wordless cry of battle.

Kate heard voices outside Talios's tent and looked up from the table where she was setting everything up for surgery. She glanced at Talios. The doctor shrugged. He got up and looked out. When he turned back toward her, his face was neutral.

"You have petitioners," he said. "I told them that you were not well enough yet, but they insisted on letting you decide. You need to know, if you accept, I will support you. But I do not think it's the right decision."

She stood, her legs suddenly weak. If it were Marthen . . .

It was not. Lord Terrick and Lord Saraval stood before her, already in their armor.

"Are you able to drive the machine?" Saraval said. He loomed above her, a large man writ larger by the bulk of his chain and padding, and the huge helm he carried under his arm.

"One archer has been trained on the weapon. He must be carried to the scene of the battle at speed," Terrick said. He took a breath. "And General Marthen. He will direct the battle from the wagon, using the voice weapons."

She looked up at him, anger leveling her voice. "I was beaten because I went to battle."

She said nothing else. The two lords looked at each other. Finally, Saraval nodded.

"Point taken," he rumbled. "What do you wish in return?"

"He doesn't touch me. He doesn't talk to me unless necessary." She took a breath. "He certainly doesn't marry me. And when we are done here, I go my own way."

"Agreed," said Saraval. "Though I hope you will not seek a path unworthy of you."

She blinked, surprised to be taken seriously. She looked at Talios, and he gave a small nod.

"All right. We have a deal," she said. "When do we leave?"

When Kate came out of her own tent, the Jeep waited by the officers' tent where she had parked it. Talios had provided her with extra bandaging, and she bulked out under her half cloak. Even that was enough to make her break out in a sweat from the pain. And armor was flat out; the weight would be torture, even if they could find mail small enough for her.

"Listen," the surgeon said, adjusting her cloak. "Be careful. Don't be foolish. Find a dark corner to hide in until it's over. Promise me, chick."

"I promise. I'll see you tonight, help you with surgery."

He snorted. "You'll go straight to bed, is what you will do."

A soft wailing caught their attention: Torm. He huddled next to Mykal, shifting from foot to foot.

"Hey Tormie," Kate said. She went over to him, taking his hand.

"He wouldn't settle down," Mykal said. "Had to see you. Kept going over to the wagon and crying."

"Listen, Torm," Kate said. "You have to hide under the wagon without me, okay? Just like you did last time. It'll be okay, I promise. And the next time, I promise to hide with you, all right? Just not this time. You hide for me all right, and I'll see you when we get back."

Mykal finally got him away, and she turned back to the Jeep.

Her heart beat hard. The archer, Varig, waited next to it, cradling the sniper rifle. He had the muscular, slightly warped build of a bowman. His eyes were clear and narrow, crow's-feet at the corners. Kate had heard about the competition; Varig was a natural-born sharpshooter. She nodded at him, and he nodded back.

Nearby the scouts were mounting up. *Look at that,* thought, Kate, a smile tugging at her face. In the middle of the bustling movement stood Jayce, reins slung over his arm, being sent off by Tiurlin. The baby was tucked in the crook of her arm, and she was scolding Jayce soundly. Kate could only imagine what she was telling him. *Soldier's god, what have I done?* She bit back her laugh and got stiffly in the Jeep. Grayne handed her the keys, and she started the engine.

The Jeep roared into life, the sound harsh in the camp. The nearby horses reared and shied, including Marthen's stallion. Varig leaped over the side of the Jeep and settled into the back. *All he needs is camo and shades,* she thought. *Instant GI Joe.* She looked at Marthen, and he fumbled at the door. He barely fit in the passenger seat in his mail. Kate turned on the radio and handed it to him, keeping the bile down with effort.

"Press this button down to talk, let it up to listen." She demonstrated. "Who gets the other one?"

"My son," said Terrick, coming up next to them. "He will relay orders to me."

Kate steeled herself as Colar came forward, then her jaw dropped in surprise at the look of his swollen nose. *What happened to him?*

The boy avoided her eyes as he took the radio. Their fingers touched briefly, but there was no spark.

Kate released the parking brake and put the car in gear, letting it roll out of the camp.

For a moment Joe was in two places at once: the house at Daw Road and a different house, made of red stone, tall and narrow, surrounded by forest. The scene shifted until his vision blurred and his head ached—forest, road, house, house—until it settled with only a slight quivering. His head still hurt. He glanced over at Mrs. Hunt, who looked ashen. "Are you all right?"

She nodded.

Arrim had the same look of sickness combined with a kind of sharp excitement.

The Daw Road house was gone. In its place was a tall, narrow house made of red stone in a grove of old-growth forest. Snow capped its roof, melting where a smoking chimney poked at the sky.

Joe saw movement around the door; several men came out, some carrying boxes that Joe recognized from the basement of the house on Daw Road. Caution made him back up, gesturing to the others. They all three retreated until they were in the thick of a small copse of young trees and tangled vines. The winter woods gave them scant cover, but the men were intent on their mission and didn't notice any watchers.

"Who are they?" Joe said in a low voice.

"Lord Tharp's men," Arrim said. "They must be removing the last of the weapons and bullets and bringing them to Red Gold Bridge."

Beneath them the ground began to quiver. A dusting of snow fell from the trees. At the house the men began to scurry, shouting to each other. Someone dropped a box of bullets, and they spilled out into the snow. The ground gave a jerk, and Joe was thrown to the ground along with Mrs. Hunt and Arrim.

If it hadn't been for the earthquake, Joe thought he might have noticed that the house was under attack a split second sooner. As it was, he was in the midst of pushing himself to his feet when a crossbow bolt thunked hard into a tree trunk right over their heads. Joe rolled over to look at it and then back at the house up ahead. He immediately flattened himself against the ground, pulling Mrs. Hunt down with him. Arrim flopped back down, too, and they lay there, covering their heads.

Men began pouring out from among the trees, shooting arrows and brandishing swords. In the house, the defenders rushed to the top floor and began firing weapons out the top windows. Some went down right away, but others made it to cover behind trees.

"What the hell?" Joe said. "What do we do now?"

"Stay low and wait," Arrim said. He turned to look at Mrs.

Hunt, flattened in a small depression in the snow. "Are you all right, milady?"

She made a movement of her head approximating a nod.

As the Jeep neared the gordath, bumping along the makeshift road discovered by the scouts, they could hear the sounds of fighting up ahead, the distant thunder of the guns rolling over the distance. Marthen rode with one hand on the roll bar. He had said nothing to her at all during the entire journey. Varig could be heard cursing and praying under his breath from the backseat.

The radio crackled.

"General . . . arthen . . ." Colar's voice came over the radio. Marthen fumbled with the device. The Jeep rattled over the terrain.

"Acknowledge him," she said, wrestling with the steering wheel as the Jeep slewed over the rough terrain.

"Go ahead," Marthen said into the radio. She rolled her eyes.

"Push the button to talk."

Marthen's lips pursed in annoyance, and she was filled with rage at his mannerism. *You have nothing to be superior about,* she told him in her head. She concentrated on driving. Marthen pushed down the button and said, "Go ahead, Terrick."

"We . . . eed help! We're under . . . tack!"

Marthen almost dropped the radio, and the Jeep slid sideways as Kate overreacted. Marthen clutched the dashboard but otherwise regained his calm. He pushed down the button.

"Tell Lord Terrick to send in all soldiers and surround the house. Tell him to station crossbowmen and archers among the trees to pick off any retreating troops. Varig is on his way."

A few minutes later they came upon the battle. Kate tromped on the brake, and the car skidded to a stop in a spray of snow. Bullets whined overhead, and crossbows and longbows sang. The men shot in quick succession, placing bolts with professional ease. There were small battles everywhere, men with swords slashing at each other in close combat.

Varig leaped from the backseat. "Find your vantage point!" Marthen ordered, and the archer slipped into the forest.

Marthen got his sword from the backseat and got out of the Jeep. He thumbed down the button on the radio. "Terrick. Send four handfuls of men to me, at the front of the house."

Bullets sang out, and Kate threw herself down on the front seat, her back tearing painfully. Marthen put on his helm and waited calmly, and sure enough, men streamed out of the woods toward him. Without another word he began running toward the front door, and they followed him. His plan immediately came clear; as he and his men joined battle with the defenders, the close combat kept the others from shooting. They were equal now, sword to sword.

With a crash, a crossbow bolt shattered the Jeep's windshield and stuck in the car seat by her shoulder. Kate screamed, throwing up her hands. Covered with glass, she looked around for a clear path from the fight and scrambled from the Jeep, running low to the safety of a nearby bush, where she could see the back of the house. The fighting was light here. Next to the house was a cellar door leading into the ground. Looking in all directions, she gathered up her courage and bolted across the clearing. Another arrow twanged overhead. Running low but full tilt, Kate dashed behind the house. With trembling hands she lifted up the door enough to slip inside and make her way down the stairs into darkness.

Twenty-two

Lynn didn't find the gordath so much as it found her. She heard distant gunfire, and the earth trembled. The air wavered in front of her eyes, like heat rising from a campfire. *I must be in the right place,* she thought. When she came upon the battle, she held the horse back between the trees.

Dead and dying men lay everywhere, their blood darkening the snow. Men beat at each other with swords. The trees bristled with spent arrows. The men in the tall stone house were shooting from the top windows, but they were not immune to casualties. Someone else was shooting, too, placing shots with careful consistency. Lynn watched as man after man went down. The snow was pocked with blood. A car was abandoned by the edge of the clearing, its windshield smashed. She looked again. *That's Mark's Jeep!* A roar broke from the woods, and hundreds of men came running toward the battle. Tharp had come to defend his weapons source.

And there he was himself, the leader of Red Gold Bridge, riding a chestnut warhorse. Dungiven snorted and went to neigh a challenge, one stallion to another. Lynn grabbed the rein and backed him a few steps to keep him busy, then turned to look again.

Her vision wavered as she sighted the front of the house, where the air seemed thickest. *The gordath. But how do I get there?*

Maybe I just wait until they all kill themselves.

The earthquake that followed knocked her off her feet.

Joe held on to the ground during the violent shaking. With a groan, two tall trees toppled to the earth next to them, pulling up dirt by the roots. "Arrim, we've got to get out of here."

Arrim surveyed the scene. He nodded. "It must be stopped. We're running out of time."

Joe knew what he meant. The air had gathered in front of the house, and it looked as if it puckered like a seam. The gordath grew dark. A slit grew between the seam, and the darkness flickered there. As they watched, it widened.

A soldier, in a sword fight for his life, stepped backward into it and was swallowed up. His scream was cut short, and he disappeared.

It took him, Joe thought. *It's burning a hole between the worlds.*

Men shouted and backed away.

"All right," Mrs. Hunt said. "You begin to close the gordath." She took a deep breath. "I will try to capture my husband's attention."

"Are you crazy?" Joe said. "You can't go out there. You'll get killed."

"Quite likely," she agreed. Her face was pale and pinched.

Arrim, however, agreed. "Time to make things right, my lady," he said.

Mrs. Hunt nodded. She looked unsure of herself, sad, and more than a little reluctant.

"Yes, past time," she said, but more to herself than them. "I don't know if it can be done, after so many years." She got up, dusted the snow and dirt from her front, and took off her kerchief, letting it billow out into a large square. After she was done remaking herself into the calm, cool, person Joe had known for the past year, she stepped out into the clearing, waving the dark blue cloth.

Somehow she caught their attention. Amid the shouting and the chaos, a long, mournful horn sounded, and the fighting slowed and then stopped. Men lowered their weapons and watched Mrs. Hunt come out of the woods in her long, warm coat, her dark hair freed from the kerchief to fall over her shoulders.

"Eyvig," she said in her clear voice, looking at the big man on the chestnut warhorse. He looked at her across the clearing, and though his face was masked, it was clear he was transfixed. He pushed his horse toward her one step, then another, and she held her head up and waited for him.

This time when Mrs. Hunt spoke, her voice dropped into a silent clearing.

"Eyvig, I am back."

The silence deepened. Lord Tharp took off his helmet.

"Sarita," he said.

"Do you accept me back, Eyvig?" Mrs. Hunt said, standing straight and proud in her shearling coat.

Tharp inclined his head, but it was less an answer than further punishment.

"He loves you and misses you still," Arrim had said. Joe could see it, but he could also see that forgiveness was not going to come easy to Lord Tharp.

"I cannot give you an answer now," he said, and his voice rolled out over the clearing. "I have longed for this day, that is true, but it cannot take the place of what we are fighting here. My property has been stolen: my lands defiled, the good people of all the lands of Aeritan have been raided, killed, their livelihoods burned, their smiths killed and forges broken, all by the orders of this man, not even a member of a council but a tool of theirs."

He pointed at the other general, who merely looked at him, his bloody sword bare in his gloved hand. Next to him the other lords closed up ranks.

"The lands of Aeritan rose up against you, Lord Tharp," one growled. He swept his sword around. "Look around at all the colors against you. You brought these weapons to Aeritan. Look what they have wrought. You keep the gordath open against the guardians' counsel, and it is breaking up the world. You know it, my lord. You've felt the earth tremors and the shaking that threaten to take down your fine stronghold. We did not ask for this war, but we will continue to press it." He threw a deliberate glance back at the house behind him. "You might retake this house with all its weapons and bullets and strange materials in it, but even as we two speak, Lord Kenery's main force is attacking Red Gold Bridge."

Tharp smiled. "Your news is old, Lord Terrick. Lord Kenery

has been convinced to return to his neutral stance by the Lady of Trieve."

A mixed gasp and cry rose up among the men amassed against Tharp.

That shocked them, Joe thought. Still, the fellow, Lord Terrick, retained his composure, though his face tightened in disgust.

"That betrayal is a matter for the Council, as is yours, Lord Tharp. We will continue to fight, and we will continue to batter the walls of Red Gold Bridge, while the gordath does its best to tear down the rest of it. If that is what you wish for your legacy, then so be it. But I will not stand by and let you destroy my country. My lands."

"He's right." Arrim got up and came out of the woods. Joe hurried behind him. "Your man Bahard shot me because I was seeking to close the portal against him. But I saw the signs, Lord Tharp. I saw even then what the gordath was doing, pulling open between the worlds. Why do you continue to press this battle? Your lady wife returned, my lord. She saw what the portal was becoming, and she returned to make it right."

As if to emphasize his words, the earth shook, and the gordath spread wider. Now they could see inside, a darkness beyond the darkest night. Men backed away farther.

"Don't lecture me, guardian!" Tharp said. He scarcely glanced at Mrs. Hunt. "And you live dangerously when you speak for my lady."

"He speaks well for me," said Mrs. Hunt. "He speaks truly. All those years ago, when I fled, I thought the gordath had closed behind me. Little did I know—or want to know—that it had stayed open just a crack, enough so that it could be opened again. And again." She stopped and peered around. "What have you done with the barkeep?"

Tharp scowled. "We'll discuss it later."

Her mouth quirked. "I hope to. I hope you discovered his true nature. He was neither well-liked nor well-trusted on the other side of the Wood. But you were always a poor judge of character, my husband."

"I judged you well, and you came up wanting," he said.

She came right back at him. "You were quick to judge me, indeed, but you never even knew me, husband."

"I knew enough, wife."

It had the sound of an old argument. They stopped, but a muscle jumped in Tharp's cheek, and Mrs. Hunt—Joe could not stop thinking of her that way—had a cold edge to her that almost made her pale face glow with light.

A movement from the far side of the clearing caught his attention. Lynn came out of the woods, brushing aside branches. Everyone turned to look at her and the massive horse she led.

Jesus, thought Joe. She was thin, wrapped in strange clothes, her face narrow and her hair unkempt. Her clothes were torn and dirty, and her cheeks were raw with cold. He pushed past Arrim into the clearing. She didn't see him right away. Instead, she held out Dungiven's reins to Mrs. Hunt.

"Mrs. Hunt," she said. "I have your horse." The big horse cocked his ears forward at Mrs. Hunt and whinnied at her as if he recognized her. For the first time a real smile spread across the woman's face, lighting it with delight.

"*Your* horse?" said Tharp, disbelief making his voice rise.

Mrs. Hunt came over to Lynn and touched Dungiven's muzzle. He snorted and rubbed his head against her.

"I am a daughter of Wessen, husband. When I came across Gordath Wood to the world on the other side, I knew only two things: horses and wealth. I used my knowledge well enough, I think." She slid her hand up Dungiven's head, rubbing it beneath his forelock. "I had thought to bring this one with me when I was ready to come back. A gift. I ask only one thing: that you return everyone to their proper place before this war resumes."

She turned to Lynn. "Lynn Romano. When you return, you will find in my house my lawyer's phone number. Call him. He has papers for you to sign that transfer Hunter's Chase to you."

Lynn stared at her, openmouthed. "I—Mrs. Hunt, I mean, Lady Sarita—"

Mrs. Hunt inclined her head and turned to her husband, taking Dungiven's reins from Lynn and holding them out to Tharp.

Tharp hesitated, clearly torn between punishing his wife and accepting her apology. At length he dismounted and took the reins in one hand and her other hand in his.

"We have much to talk about," he said, and his voice was low, as if he was trying to keep it for her ears alone. She nodded, and he turned.

"General Marthen, Lord Terrick," he said. Marthen bowed, and everyone turned to look for Terrick. The older lord stepped forward and nodded. He was disheveled, his armor bloodied, his colors torn and soiled. Lord Tharp bowed in return. "I do not intend to lose this war, nor do I intend to pursue it with less fervor than I have been doing, just because my lady wife is returned to me. But I will accede to a truce for now to gather our wounded, send these wanderers home, and close the portal. It is more pressing at the moment."

As if to add urgency to his statement, the earth rumbled again. At sharp orders from officers, men laid down their weapons and began to help the wounded. Lynn looked around, taking it all in. Her gaze stopped on Joe. He pushed through the crowd and took her hands, then pulled her into his arms.

His kiss was real and rough and urgent, and she started crying again. It felt so good to be held by him, his arms around her and his cheek pressed against the top of her head. He was warm and strong, and she felt so right in his arms, and it was all mixed in with the sadness and loss she felt for Crae.

"How did you get here?" she said, half crying, half laughing.

"This thing called a gordath. It's been causing a hell of a mess back home."

"I know. Here, too."

He kissed her again, then held her tight. "I thought you were dead."

"I know. I tried so hard to come home." She had so much to tell him and not enough words to say it. She thought longingly of her small apartment and the chance to have all the time in the world to tell him everything. *Not the apartment. The main house. I own Hunter's Chase.*

Sudden shouting made them both look up. The ground trembled, but it took on a different note now. Arrim stood in front of the portal, his arms outstretched as if to encompass it—or draw its edges together. For an instant Lynn could see two houses, and Daw Road leading away from them.

"Time to go," Joe said. "I didn't want to rush you, but we better get Kate and get out of here."

She looked at him, puzzled. "Kate?"

He stared at her. "Yeah, Kate. Mossland. Isn't she with you?"

"Kate Mossland's *here*?"

"She came after you the next day. You've never seen her?"

She shook her head, her bewilderment turning to dread.

The fighting had stopped. Kate got up from her hidey-hole and climbed the short steps to the cellar door, pushing it up and over with a jarring thud. Her back screamed, and her arms quivered with effort. She looked around. Everyone was picking up the dead and the wounded. She wondered how long it would be before Talios was inundated with casualties. *I should get back,* she thought. *I need to help him.*

She hoisted herself out of the cellar and suddenly stopped.

On the ground in front of her lay one of Tharp's men under a second-story window. His neck was bent at a bad angle, but it was the hole in his chest that had killed him.

His rifle lay a few feet away from him.

Kate picked it up. She looked around for Marthen and saw him where he stood with Lord Terrick and Lord Saraval near the front of the house.

Perhaps he knew he was being watched. Perhaps his natural caution made him scan for enemies. Whatever the reason, Marthen turned around and saw her, and his words faltered and went still. At his sudden silence, the lords turned, too.

"Remember, Kate, justice, not vengeance," her mother always said. Kate's finger pressed lightly on the trigger. She wondered what her mother would say about this case.

Her mother would want to kill him with her bare hands. Kate knew that for a certainty. But she would always know it was vengeance, and she would take it upon herself, not leave it to Kate.

If she pulled the trigger, she stood to lose more than he did. It was terrible to think about, that she could do worse to herself than he had done, but she knew it was true.

Still.

He would be very sure that it was her choice, and not her weakness, that saved his life. She held up the rifle and aimed, finding his heart in the simple sight. And then she lowered the rifle and set it down in the snow.

Her vision no longer narrowed to the pinpoint of concentration, Kate looked around. Everyone was looking at her. There was Lynn. And Joe. And Mrs. Hunt. And Dungiven.

"Kate!" Lynn called out. The barn manager ran over to her, enveloping Kate in a hug. Kate cried out and pushed her away. Lynn stumbled back. "Are you all right? What happened? Why—?" Lynn stopped. Then she said, "We're going home. They're going to send us through and then close the gordath."

I can't go home. I'm going to med school in Brythern. Wait. No. Kate frowned, trying to make sense of things. Finally she said, "Mojo's dead."

Tears sprang to Lynn's eyes. "Oh, Katie." She took Kate's arm. "Come on. We're almost home." Kate let herself be led away. As they passed Marthen and the Council, she turned to look at him. Marthen was soaked with blood, a long scrape bleeding from his shoulder to his wrist. His dark hair was wet with sweat, and his face was feverish. He looked straight at her, and his lips parted as if he were about to say something. Kate shook her head. She didn't want to hear it. Lynn tugged at her. "Come on, Kate," she whispered. "Let's go."

"Lord Terrick!" Skayler shouted, catching their attention. He and two of the other scouts carried out another between them from the house. Terrick turned and gasped.

"Colar!"

They laid him in the snow in front of the house, and his blood melted it where he lay. Kate pushed herself between Terrick and the scouts and knelt beside him. Frantically she held her half cloak tight against the bullet hole in his abdomen.

"No," she said. "No, Colar. Don't." He breathed shallow breaths that took in almost no air. Under his sparse beard his face was very pale. His hair, wet from the snow, seemed almost as black as the boles of the trees surrounding them. "Oh God no," Kate cried. "He'll die here. He needs a hospital."

Lord Terrick wept. He knelt beside his son, dwarfing the young man, his dark blue cloak spreading out to cover the snow. "Colar—" he said, his voice hoarse. He spread his hands out but dared not touch his son. He looked at them. "Can your world save him?"

"Maybe. He's hurt pretty badly," Lynn said. "We'll have to

hurry." She looked behind her at the struggling guardian. "I don't think he'll be able to come back."

Terrick's eyes were dark with the enormity of his loss. He turned to Kate. "I place my son in your parents' care," he said. "He will be a good foster son to them. Never—" his voice broke. "Never let him forget he is Terrick."

Kate nodded. "I won't," she whispered. "We'll take good care of him. I promise."

Terrick bowed his head and then placed his hand on Colar's forehead. The boy did not move, and his father stood, his cloak crusted in snow, and stepped back.

"Let's get him up," Joe said, and together he, Lynn, and Terrick took hold of Colar and picked him up out of the snow. The boy gasped and cried out. Kate hurried ahead of them and swept out the backseat of the Jeep, making a place for him. They set him in as gently as they could.

"All right, everybody in," Lynn said. Kate turned around. Terrick stood with his hands over his face. Lord Saraval stood by his side, his plain old face grieving with his friend.

Kate slipped into the driver's seat and turned the key. The Jeep started right up. Lynn got in the passenger side. "Let's go. Joe, come on."

The portal widened even farther, and the guardian stepped back. "You must cross *now*!" Arrim cried. "I cannot hold it open much longer!"

It was funny, Joe thought, how he knew exactly what to do. He could stand with Arrim, right *there*, and *push* just so, and the portal would stay open long enough to let the Jeep slip through. *I can do that,* he thought.

He turned to Lynn. She was so good to see. He figured he could hold that memory of her with him for a long time.

"I'm gonna miss you," he said, and he leaned forward and kissed her.

Confusion and then understanding flooded her face. "You're not coming," she said.

He shook his head and put his hand over hers on the door handle. "No. I'm going to help Arrim take care of the gordath. Don't know if we can keep it closed after you're gone, but we'll sure try." He reached into his jeans pocket and pulled out his wallet. Lynn took it in a daze. "Colar might need this. The driver's license picture don't look much like him, but my social security card's in there, and he can get another one made. Not much money, but what there is he's welcome to."

"Joe, no," Lynn said.

He leaned in close.

"I know. I thought maybe we'd get a chance, just the two of us. Thing is, all my life I've been running, and this is the first time I ever felt like I stopped. I think I'm meant to be here." He reached out and tilted her chin, giving her a light kiss. "Best go now. That boy needs a doctor."

Arrim nodded at him when Joe joined him. He didn't even really need to be told what to do, just a glance and follow his lead. The portal locked steady with a click he could feel in his bones.

Oh yeah, thought Joe.

Kate shifted and gunned the motor, steering the Jeep into the gordath flickering between Joe and Arrim. She and Lynn both took a deep breath as they passed through the portal, and the Jeep slipped on an icy patch of ground and they bumped out from the forest into an overgrown driveway. The tall stone house had disappeared; now there was only the run-down house on Daw Road.

The Jeep dropped, as if the road fell out from under them, and they all cried out, Lynn reaching back to steady Colar. *We're through,* Kate thought. She looked up at the rearview mirror, but all she could see was the retreating house and power lines. There was one more bump and shift, and she knew. The portal had been closed.

Kate looked at Lynn. "We're running out of time. Which way?"

Lynn scanned the road, then pointed. "Take a left up there. We can get to town the back way."

Kate slewed the Jeep through the turn where the dirt road met asphalt. She accelerated again, and they plunged forward. When she passed a car going the other way, she gasped. It looked so out of place.

They began passing more cars, registering shock on the

faces of the other drivers. Kate stamped on the gas, the needle edging up toward sixty. In the open Jeep, their loose cloaks fluttered behind them. *We're showing our colors,* she thought.

"Slow down," Lynn said, her voice edged in an effort to stay calm. She reached up for the roll bar, holding on tight. She threw a look back at Colar, and Kate followed with a glance in the rearview mirror. The boy was white, almost gray, blood cascading down his armor.

"Is he dead?" Kate cried. She could hear the panic in her own voice. She tightened her grip on the wheel, swerving around an oncoming car. The other driver blared his horn.

"No, he'll be fine. Take it easy. He'll be fine." Up ahead they could see the hospital towers. "We're almost there," Lynn shouted, and then they were there, Kate pulling up in the drive in front of the emergency room.

Lynn jumped out of the Jeep almost before Kate stopped and bolted for the sliding doors. Kate set the brake and looked back. Colar's eyes were open, but his gaze was blank. *Soldier's god, protect him,* she prayed and hoped the god could hear her in this foreign place.

Emergency room personnel streamed out with a stretcher, Lynn following close behind. They lifted Colar onto the gurney, and he disappeared into the hospital in a swirl of medical activity. Kate watched them go, numb. She looked up, squinting at the metal and glass towers looming over her and stomped her stained and broken boots on the pavement for warmth.

A nurse wearing a pink cardigan over her scrubs came up. "Are you all right?" she said. She looked at Kate quizzically. "What's your name?"

Kate said nothing. *I want Talios,* she thought. The nurse bit her lip, then took Kate by the arm. "Come along. Let's take a look at you."

Kate went with her through the sliding doors, wincing at the fluorescent lights and the blast of heated air that met her. Her half cloak and trousers, faded and tattered, were dark and foreign under the bright light. She squinted at the strange lettering everywhere. *I can't read,* she thought.

The nurse flung a curtain around a hospital bed, making a

room. She helped Kate ease off her half cloak and gasped. From the wet feel of the shirt on her back, Kate figured that her back was soaked with blood.

Kate moved slowly, getting back into her dirty clothes, wincing at the feel of them against her skin after the crisp cleanliness of the hospital gown. The doctor had rebandaged her back and given her a dose of antibiotics. She heard the hospital personnel talking in low voices. Periodically someone would come in and ask her name, which she refused to give, until they left her alone. She peeked out the door of the examining room, wondering if she could leave without being spotted. In the waiting area, Lynn leaped up when she saw her. She gripped Kate's hand.

"All right?" she said, her thin face filled with worry.

Kate nodded. "How's—Joe?" she asked. Lynn's expression acknowledged her choice of names.

"He's in surgery. But reading between the lines, I think the doctors think he will make it."

A nurse came over to them.

"Miss Romano? The police are here. They want to talk to you."

Lynn took a breath. "It begins," she muttered. "I'll be right there." She looked at Kate. "You'll be all right?"

"Yes. I'll be fine." Kate watched Lynn go meet the police, where a salt-and-pepper man in a gray suit waited, his notebook out and ready. Kate looked at the nurse and took a deep breath. She was as ready as she would ever be.

"I want to call my parents."

The nurse nodded at the phone on the counter at the nurse's station. "You can use that one."

Kate stared down at the phone, and after a long moment she lifted the handset. She fumbled with the numbers; she had forgotten what each one symbolized, and had to stare at them for a long time to find the right sequence.

The phone started to ring. Kate stared at the speckled institutional counter, and her courage began to fail. She almost hung up when the phone connected.

"David Mossland." Her father's voice was deep and strong, the way she remembered it. She remembered how safe it could make her feel, but at the same time a little afraid, as if he could withdraw his protection at any time. "Hello?" he said, and Kate willed herself to speak, to push the words past her swollen throat. She could hear him waiting, impatient with the connection, and she could hear him breathe out in disgust, and she knew he was going to put the phone down.

Daddy, she tried, and then, with a croak, she managed to say it out loud. "Daddy."

There was silence at the other end of the line. Then, "Kate?"

"Daddy," she said and began to cry.

The Aftermath

A cold blue sky looked down on the Temian encampment. Despite a warming sun, an icy wind gusted, snapping canvas and blowing remnant trash across the expanse. Rows and rows of damp squares marked where men had pulled up their stakes and marched off. Only Marthen's tent remained, mostly packed, a wagon and horses waiting patiently out front.

Marthen looked around. The tent was cold, the fire long burned out. It smelled musty, wet. *We fit the Aeritan Council in here.* The whimsy made him uncomfortable. He began gathering up the things he would pack in his saddlebags. He would ride his saddle horse south, let the wagon go on ahead with Grayne and his orderly, his warhorse tied to the tailgate.

He picked up the small bottle, the clear sack, now torn and fragile, and the helmet and tossed them on the pile on his table. Her saddle was already loaded onto the wagon. He didn't know why he kept it—as spoils of war, it was a ridiculous thing, too small to be useful as a war saddle or even a riding saddle, and really just a reminder of his failure.

Not at war—the council had won, after all. Peace talks had consumed the winter months at Red Gold Bridge, with all the lords present. Lord Terrick looked as if he were eighty years old. Lord Tharp had not softened, though Lady Sarita had returned to him. Marthen wondered if perhaps her homecoming had more of the bitter than the sweet. He sat by and watched as they disposed of one fate after another. Only once did Terrick look at him, when a captain had been granted a lordship, and Marthen knew then that the man would be true to his word. He would never be given Council rights.

Because of the girl. The girl he had foolishly pinned his

hopes—his future—on. She had disappeared through the cut between the two worlds, and even that option was closed to him.

They called him mad; he knew it and let his reputation work for him. He hadn't known, till then, when she disappeared from sight, that he had been in love as well. No. Time for the truth, he told himself. He had known; it was why he had her strung up and flogged.

Grayne ducked in and saluted. "We're ready to begin loading your things, sir."

"All right. I'll let you know when I am ready."

Grayne nodded and ducked out.

Marthen gathered up his gloves and the small wrapped package lying on his stripped camp bed.

It was a gift, the Brytherner had said. He had cornered Marthen in the halls of Red Gold Bridge.

"What could you do with this, General?" he had said, handing him over the gun. It felt heavy in his hand.

"I thought all the weapons were accounted for," Marthen said. His head started pounding.

"They are," said the Brytherner. "Though not to the Council's satisfaction, perhaps." He nodded at Lord Tharp, being questioned by the Council. "Would you like to finish what you started?"

Marthen laughed, taking the Brytherner by surprise. "I have no quarrel with Lord Tharp," he said. "Why do you?"

The Brytherner regarded him. "You're right." He nodded at the gun. "It's a gift, nothing more."

He left not long after that, Marthen found out, and he took the stranger man with him, Tharp's stranger, who had brought all the weapons to Aeritan and set the war in motion.

The wind gusted hard, tossing his tent around as if it were made of no more than paper. Marthen slipped the gun out of its wrappings. Its grip was pebbled and rough against his palm, the barrel smooth and shining. The chamber where the shells were loaded rotated smoothly.

This weapon was so strange, and yet so commonplace in her world, according to her tales. It felt like a talisman, made him feel safe.

A man who walked in her world with one of these weapons would not be out of place.

He put it back in its wrappings. A door swung both ways, he thought. If he could get through, find her, perhaps not all would be lost.

"Kate Mossland," he said. "I will find you."

In the high school student parking lot Kate waited for Colar by their candy-apple-red Jeep Wrangler, jangling the keys absently. Students streamed out of the high school into the bright spring sunlight, jackets and backpacks flung over their shoulders. People shouted to each other or gathered in knots, heads together in intense conversation. A few of her friends waved. She sighted Colar walking with Josh Bradford. When Colar had gotten out of the hospital and started at her high school, he and Josh had bonded. Mathematics, physics, engineering—Colar was catching up by leaps and bounds. It helped that the school bought his cover story—homeschooling and dyslexia—to explain the strange gaps in his education.

Colar saw her waiting and said something to Josh. They hurried, Colar still moving stiffly. Kate herself had mostly healed, but she still had a few rounds of plastic surgery and skin grafts to go. When her parents saw her back, she thought that Marthen was lucky the gordath was closed.

"Sorry about that," Colar said and grinned, showing off his new braces. He tossed his books into the back of the Jeep.

"No problem," Kate said and smiled at Josh. "Hi." They had known each other since the fifth grade. He was still the smartest kid in school like he was back then, but the strange, scrawny boy who talked endlessly about building robots had grown up and filled out, and wasn't half-bad-looking.

"Hi," he said, his ears turning pink.

"See you at the house," Colar told him. He turned to Kate. "We think we have the operating system figured out." She nodded. *Robots.*

"You should come," Josh offered. "You want to? It'll be fun."

It sounded fun. She wanted to go and forget everything. Just be a normal kid, with two friends, hanging out together. Except nothing would ever be normal again. "Thanks, but—I have to see a girl about a horse."

That much was true. Lynn had her working with Allegra,

of all horses. After the events of Gordath Wood, Carolyn had abandoned the weedy, hysterical mare and fled to the city, where presumably her bony behind would not touch a saddle again. Lynn had wanted Kate to try to rehabilitate the mare.

Kate knew she was hoping Allegra would return the favor.

Once I used to be a girl who liked horses, she thought. She wondered when it changed. When Mojo fell in battle?

Or when Marthen had her tied to the crossbar in the center of the camp?

It was hard enough having to tell her parents everything that had happened to her. She didn't think she had the heart to tell them that she was no longer the same horse crazy girl she had been last summer. So she dutifully rode Allegra each afternoon with all the heart and spirit of a sack of potatoes.

Josh jogged over to catch his bus, and Colar threw himself into the passenger seat, buckling the seat belt. Kate got in and started the engine. When her dad and mom said they could have a car ("Used, now, you kids are spoiled enough as it is"), they had pored over the want ads, Kate explaining the abbreviations. As soon as she came to the Jeep ad, they looked at one another, and that was it. Kate's mom looked like she was going to object, but at a look from her husband that did not escape Kate's notice, she subsided.

They didn't talk as they pulled out of the parking lot and headed down the twisting road toward the stables. The outskirts of Gordath Wood sailed along beside them, freshly picked out in pale green on black branches. They could see rushing streams in the woods, spring runoff trailing over rocks and swirling with last year's leaves. Ice still hung along the stream beds, and in the sandy places on the edge of the road, coltsfoots and bloodroot poked out of the litter.

Ahead of them the Wood proper hove into view, the central spars looming into the sky. She cast a quick glance at Colar. He seemed absorbed in the view. He looked like a regular high school student in jeans and T-shirt, his shoulders filling out his jacket, his hair cut short. She had never noticed his acne before, when he was Colar Terrick, and not Cole Mossland, her adopted brother.

To remind herself that he was someone different, she said, "Do you miss home?"

"Yes. And no. I miss my mother and my little brother and

sisters, and I worry—" he stopped but plunged on almost immediately. "I see your mother, and I think, you came back, but my mother is left behind, and I did not. And she was worried, when I went to war with my father, that that would happen. I was the eldest son and would have brought her a wife to keep her company when I went away to war as the Lord of Terrick, so now she has neither me nor a daughter."

Kate kept her attention on the road, but she could see him out of the corner of her eye. His face was sad, his voice tired.

"And my father was harsh and serious, but I miss him, too. He taught me many things, and I think he would have liked to have seen the world on this side of Gordath Wood. I miss being able to go back and tell him what I've learned." She felt him glance at her. "But I'm glad I'm here and have this chance. Someday I'm going to try to get back and bring back what I learned."

"What!" she exclaimed. The Jeep swerved, and she brought it back under control. She threw him a glance. "Colar, you know you can't."

He made an impatient face. "Shouldn't or can't? Maybe Lord Tharp had the right idea but the wrong method. Maybe the more knowledge people have of the gordath, the more that can be used to open and close it at will."

They pulled up into the driveway of Hunter's Chase, and she put the car in neutral and set the brake.

"Promise me you won't go without telling me," she said. He hesitated, then nodded. She knew a promise meant more to him than it did to anyone else.

"But you have to promise me something," he said, and surprised, she paused in the act of getting out and letting him slide into the driver's side.

"Become happy again." He looked uncomfortable. "You should come to Josh's," he added. "He likes you."

"But you don't." She said it flatly.

"I—I—" He looked away. "Kate, it's not that."

She got out and began gathering her riding gear from the rear seat.

"It's not that!" he said again. His voice was urgent, desperate. "Kate, you don't understand. You're my sister now. That's what fostering means to us."

She stopped, her arms full of her boots, chaps, and helmet. Her throat was swollen with unshed tears. "I know. I know. It's just—it's like we never liked each other at all. Like it never happened."

She started bawling and buried her face in the suede chaps. Colar turned off the engine and got out to stand beside her.

"Kate—" he said, and she heard the helplessness in his voice.

That made her feel like an idiot, and she wiped her face. "Look, you should get going. Josh is waiting."

"Will you be all right?"

She nodded and smiled through her tears.

"I'll be fine. Don't worry. I'll come to Josh's the next time, okay?"

"Okay." He said it reluctantly but got behind the wheel and started the car.

After he drove off, Kate walked up the drive, hoping she didn't look too tearstained and swollen. She saw Allegra in the field along the drive look up from grazing. After a moment, the mare ambled over, her eyes soft and her ears forward. It was a far cry from her usual half-crazed expression. She wasn't really a bad horse, Kate had to admit. Carolyn had her in a heavy bit and wore spurs when she rode her. Kate soon discovered that Allegra hated even the slightest pressure on her mouth, and she goosed easily. She responded well to Kate's lack of personal interest, as if she had had too much emotion under her previous owner and was fine with Kate's neutrality. Kate stopped and leaned over the fence.

"Oh, so you decide to be good now," she told the horse. Allegra snorted at her but didn't come any closer. "Well, I just promised to be happy, so I guess you can be good, right? I mean, miracles can happen."

Allegra opened her mouth and reached out her long neck. Kate shifted her armload to scratch the horse's mane. Something was breaking loose inside her, and she wondered if the crying had something to do with it. "Just don't expect me to get all mushy over you, okay? Because it's not my way anymore."

Lynn watched from the kitchen at Hunter's Chase as Kate made her way up the drive, Allegra following her along the fence line. *Those two have made peace,* she thought. She finished pouring two cups of coffee and went into the living room where her guest waited.

Lieutenant Spencer turned at her approach. He was looking at the photos and silver cups on the mantelpiece, and now he turned his same quizzical gaze on Lynn. He took the coffee she offered him.

"Nice room," he said. "All this yours?"

Lynn sipped her coffee to give herself a chance to restore her composure. It wasn't hers. None of it was. It seemed easier just to let things be for now, but it still felt like living in a hotel. She had only been to her barn apartment once, to gather a few of her things. There were more ghosts there, to tell the truth, and she didn't fit in anywhere.

"Yes," she said coolly. "That's the way it worked."

She knew she shouldn't be too belligerent; this man was dangerous. He knew there was more to the story than he had been told.

Spencer set the coffee down without even making a pretense of drinking.

"Our investigation stated there was no foul play. She signed over the farm to you, via her lawyer—and disappeared." He looked at Lynn, his eyes penetrating.

She held his gaze.

"She went home," Lynn said.

"To her husband." It was not a question. Lynn nodded anyway.

"Was she happy?"

That was unexpected, and she found herself answering cautiously.

"I think—relieved. I think she felt she made the right decision."

He raised an eyebrow. "You were there?"

Not in the official version of the story, no.

"No. I'm just guessing from what little I knew of her."

"Lucky you, then, that she made that decision."

"Lucky me." *You have no idea, Lieutenant.*

He nodded. "Let me give you some advice, Ms. Romano. Don't get too comfortable here. You might not be staying long."

She watched him go from the front door, his car as nondescript as himself, and then went back into the kitchen to rinse out the mugs. Her arm twinged. It still did that, even though she had had it reset and diligently practiced the physical therapy exercises she had been assigned. Lynn dried her hands on the dish towel, watching from the window as Kate warmed up Allegra in the ring. The girl had lost so much weight—not only from dysentery from the camp, but also pneumonia, not to mention her poor back—she looked frail and unwell. She seemed to be coping, but coping wasn't thriving, and Lynn knew that it would have repercussions for a long time to come.

From the window she could see the apartment, the white curtains just a blur in the distance. The apartment was musty and lifeless. A few of Joe's things were scattered around, but he didn't have much; he was used to traveling light. She hadn't been back inside since.

She set the mugs to dry in the sink and rested her forehead against her hands. *So many lives rearranged,* she thought. She wished she could peer through the gordath and catch a glimpse of them, if just for a moment. She remembered the last time she had seen Crae, holding Dungiven's rein so he could kiss her good-bye. And Joe, holding the gordath open.

Be well, she sent silently. *Be well, take care, don't get lost in the woods. Be safe. I love*—She stopped abruptly. Some things were too big for words to contain.

A light spring rain misted down on the ter-races of Trieve. A faint blush of green tinged the grasses and the trees, bringing a dusting of green to the gardens as the first shoots poked out of the dark brown soil. Crae looked through the blurred windows, trying to see out past the rain and the wavy glass. Behind him a fire crackled in the fireplace, taking the chill out of the air. He was warmly clothed: a thick brocaded brown vest over a rich cream shirt, the material soft as lamb's wool. His trousers bloused over fine shoes, so different from the boots he had worn for so long. A chain hung around his neck, and his hair was trimmed.

He heard a knock on the door, low down toward the floor, and smiled and turned around. "Come in, Tevani," he called. The door handle rattled and turned.

"Captain Crae!" She ran toward him, and he scooped her

up. She put her head against his shoulder and her thumb in her mouth.

"Calyne said you are going to stay with us always now," she mumbled around her thumb.

He nodded, wondering how much she understood. "Yes, I am. Do you know what today's ceremony is?"

The little divot appeared between her eyebrows. He had seen it a lot, whenever they—he and Jessamy—had tried to explain to her. Her father's death. Crae's place at Jessamy's side. Today's ceremony, in which he was to marry Jessamy.

"You and my mother are to wed," she said.

"That's right."

"But what about my father?"

He died in a war he didn't want, in a fight that wasn't his. His last act was to give his chain of lordship to Crae and make him promise.

Take care of them, Crae.

Crae sat Tevani down on the chair in front of the fireplace. He knelt before her and coughed to control his voice.

"Your father had to go away to battle for Lord Tharp," he said. "And he died in the fight. But before he did, he told me to take care of you and your mother. And I promised him I would."

The confusion in her face deepened. Crae thought he knew how she felt. Stavin had not meant this, he was sure.

Trust the Council to take their revenge where they could. The lords had been furious with Jessamy for turning Kenery, and they expressed it in their sanctions against Trieve. Tevani was to be fostered out to another lord's family, and the unborn child Jessamy carried would, once weaned, be sent to yet a different country. The line of Trieve would have been broken, were it not for Crae.

For after they were through venting their bile on her, they gifted Crae with Council rights for his role in helping close the portal. His first act was to petition to wed Jessamy and thus void the sanctions against her. He almost thought she would have turned him down, but her back was to the wall, after all.

There came another knock on the door, and Jessamy came in, her kerchief askew. Her belly was huge. She tsked. "There you are," she said. "Tevani, what are you doing, bothering Cap—Lord Crae?"

"I'm not!"

"She's not," he said.

"Here. You need to go to Calyne," Jessamy said and held out her hands. The little girl squirmed out of the chair. Jessamy looked at Crae, her gaze half-appraising, half-guilty. "You look—very well."

He nodded. "Thank you. You look—disheveled."

She sighed. "I am so busy, trying to get everything ready in time, and the baby wants to kick his way out today." All of a sudden, she caught herself. "I will be much more presentable for our vows."

"I know."

She hesitated and then looked at Tevani. "Please go find Calyne, there's a good girl. Then you can help me get into my pretty gown."

"Okay!" Tevani left them at a run, calling for her nurse.

"I don't know what is going to come of this," Jessamy said, toying with her kerchief. "I know this isn't what either of us wants." She held up a hand, forestalling his protest. "No. There is no love here, where there had come to be love between Stavin and me. I don't know if I can do that again, Crae. I don't know. I am so *angry* at him for doing that to Tevani. To me."

As if Stavin had gone and gotten himself killed on purpose. Crae bit back his anger. "I am not asking for your love or your gratitude, Jessamy. I made a promise that I intend to keep. That's all." *No matter how much you wish to drive me away.*

Her lips went white.

"Then we know where we stand," she said, and she followed her little daughter out the door, leaving him alone.

Crae sighed. He had hoped Jessamy would accept him as a companion, a friend if not a beloved, but her heart had hardened to him. She blamed him for Stavin's death, after all. He turned to look out the window again, letting his gaze focus on the terraces and the woods beyond. The mist shrouded the land beyond, but he knew it by heart, when it had been covered by a blanket of snow, under the cold light of the winter stars.

Be safe. Be well. I love you.

Joe tapped Arrim on the shoulder and nodded at a half-buried object in the woods up ahead, next to a flashing stream. The forest was coming back to life. The burned wood was birthing new shoots, pale and golden green, though snow and ice still clung to the hollows and the north side of swales and banks. Joe had learned to take the cold. He learned to accept the closeness of the woods that only allowed the barest slivers of sky to cut between the trees. He learned not to think about the wide-open roads in Texas, in case homesickness made him lose his way.

The object was white and black, soiled from the weather and smudged with moss. Joe knelt and fished it out of the leaves and mud in which it lay, knocking dirt off. A riding helmet.

"It was Lynn's," he said. "That day she crossed over."

Arrim knelt beside him. "She gave me water in it." He looked around. "The portal was not far from here."

Joe held his breath, but no nausea hit him. It had been happening less and less as the gordath closed in on itself. The guardians walked softly this past winter, avoiding the gordath to keep from reopening it. Arrim said it was still sensitive, like someone after a fever. Joe couldn't blame it.

Soon, the guardians would be able to walk from one length of Gordath Wood to another, and the only signs of the portal would be cracks in the ground. Even they would close and become covered up with brush and leaves, the cracks in buildings and in rocks just simple oddities with nothing to account for them. Then everyone would forget the stories about the strange Wood, and they would be back to vague warnings and folk tales, with only the guardians to know the truth.

Joe put the helmet back in its bed of dirt and composted leaves, packing it into place. This helmet would become just another part of the folk stories that clung to the Wood until finally its materials deteriorated. He didn't plan to come back until it did. Mrs. Hunt's tale of yearning to be lost stayed with him. He knew if he returned to the helmet often enough, he would begin searching for the portal just as she had. Joe got up, brushed off his hands, and took one last look at the helmet in its grave before following Arrim through the Wood.